S.J. MARTIN

The Papal Assassin's Curse

Desire. Despair. Damnation

First published by Moonstorm Books 2023

First edition

This book was professionally typeset on Reedsy.
Find out more at reedsy.com

Contents

1 The Papal Assassin Series 1
2 Chapter One 2
3 Chapter Two 9
4 Chapter Three 18
5 Chapter Four 27
6 Chapter Five 41
7 Chapter Six 51
8 Chapter Seven 64
9 Chapter Eight 72
10 Chapter Nine 79
11 Chapter Ten 91
12 Chapter Eleven 105
13 Chapter Twelve 119
14 Chapter Thirteen 129
15 Chapter Fourteen 137
16 Chapter Fifteen 150
17 Chapter Sixteen 164
18 Chapter Seventeen 173
19 Chapter Eighteen 184
20 Chapter Nineteen 195
21 Chapter Twenty 209
22 Chapter Twenty-one 227
23 Chapter Twenty-two 234
24 Chapter Twenty-three 245

25 Chapter Twenty-four 251
26 Chapter Twenty-five 259
27 Chapter Twenty-six 272
28 Chapter Twenty-seven 287
29 Chapter Twenty-eight 296
30 Chapter Twenty-nine 311
31 Chapter Thirty 325
32 Maps 329
33 Glossary 333
34 Character list 337
35 Read More 341
36 The Papal Assassin's Wrath 343
37 Author note 351
About the Author 354
Also by S.J. Martin 356

1

The Papal Assassin Series

The Papal Assassin
The Papal Assassin's Wife
The Papal Assassin's Curse

Published by Moonstorm Books

2

Chapter One

November 1095 – France

Finian winced as the whip-thin branches lashed across his face and arms as they rode through the close-packed birch trees, down towards a fast-flowing stream and long rocky gully. The undergrowth was thicker here and relentless as their horses forced their way through, but they had no other option as two groups of dark-clad men were pursuing them.

It had already been a long day, and the first fingers of the dusk mists were falling on the forested hills to the south of Paris as they rode towards home. Their destination was over five leagues away, but it had been a worthwhile journey, for they had viewed and bought a young Flemish Blue stallion. He was four years old, well over seventeen hands and solid, just what Finian had been searching for this year.

Finian Ui Neill, an Irish lord and famous warrior with a troubled background of warfare and heartache, was now enjoying a less traumatic life, breeding warhorses on the estate of his friend, Chatillon. He watched his comrade ahead who turned and gave him a defiant grin. Finian laughed aloud. Piers seemed to revel in danger even when they were so closely pursued, but he had so much to be grateful for from this man.

Piers De Chatillon; Finian wondered how anyone would begin to describe this enigmatic, dangerous man or even explain their friendship. A French lord, a Papal Envoy, an accomplished courtier, a consummate diplomat. It was true that others in Europe had these attributes, but Chatillon was also a master swordsman and lethal assassin who ran Europe's biggest spy and informer network. Together they were two of the most feared swordsmen in Europe, yet here they were, riding for their lives to escape at least ten pursuers. No wonder Piers was grinning at the absurdity of it all.

Unusually, they had been caught somewhat unawares by these men. They were tired after a long journey and were talking about other things when they finally spotted the first group following behind them in the distance. Fortunately, they were not far from home, only half a league or so, as they had already entered the paths in the dense woodland bordering the Chatillon estate. They knew this area's terrain well, as they regularly hunted boar in these woods. Then Finian, who had the eyesight of a hawk, spotted another group high in the trees on their left flank. The strangers were obviously carrying out a pincer movement hoping to cut them off. They had quickly pushed on for home, speaking little since they realised their pursuers were now in double figures.

'Could it be the Sheikh's men?' rasped Finian through clenched teeth as he manoeuvred his horse down a particularly steep rocky slope towards the water below.

'I'm not sure from this distance, but they seem relentless. Edvard did mention that there was a rumour of deserters and mercenaries in the woods last week; it might be them hoping for easy pickings.'

'Whoever they are, they're good. We've tried to shake them off twice, and they're still behind us,' added Finian.

Reaching the rock-strewn stream bed, they stopped and listened. Their pursuers were now careless, making enough noise while crashing through the thick undergrowth and shouting to each other.

'We are forcing both groups into the gully, and we should be able to even the odds at the end of the narrower ravine. They will not be able to emerge at speed, and we will be waiting for them,' threw Piers over his shoulder. Finian nodded in agreement, and they pushed on along the narrow, steep banks.

When the stream emerged from the trees into the meadow, Finian dropped his reins, dismounted and, running back, climbed the steep bank behind them, hiding in the undergrowth above the following riders. Chatillon, remaining mounted, knotted and dropped his reins; a sword in one hand and a dagger in the other, he placed himself slightly behind the bushes and trees on the left.

As the first men appeared in the mouth of the dark, dappled ravine, with its overhanging branches and rock-strewn water, they suddenly found their quarry waiting for them. Chatillon charged forward at the first grizzled older man, hitting his horse in the side; he whirled his blade and took the man's head clean from his shoulders. The body toppled into the water, and the scared horse panicked and backed into the horse behind, which reared and scrabbled sideways onto the slippery leaf-strewn bank, but the hooves could not get any purchase, and the animal slid down into the horse behind. It righted itself and panicked, racing for the light and the meadow ahead, the rider clinging on as it ran straight at Chatillon, who quickly ran the second man through.

Finian dropped from above, landing behind the rider on the third horse, who had just managed to get his plunging animal under control. Finian cut his throat and pushed the man's body sideways, which landed half in and half out of the stream. Blood ran down the steep bank to colour the water below, and the smell of it unsettled the following horses. Finian could hear the cries and splashes from behind, so he pushed his new mount forward, praying that in the now dim light of dusk, Chatillon would realise it was him.

As he emerged into the meadow, Chatillon surged forward, sword raised; Finian pulled the horse into a rear while shouting it was he. Chatillon laughed and lowered his blade.

'I think, Finian, we should make a dash for home while they're occupied.'

Finian leapt to the ground and mounted his own horse before turning and galloping after Chatillon across the meadow ahead. They had not gone far when a loud cry of rage and anguish rented the air. An unmounted rider stood with his hands to his head. As they slowed and watched, he dropped to his knees beside a fallen comrade.

Other men were now emerging from the gully, and one stood in his stirrups shouting orders. Piers and Finian stared as he turned to watch them, and then kicked his horse into a gallop after them.

Is the man mad? thought Finian as he watched the lone warrior approach, before kicking his own horse forward.

'We don't need this, Piers; let us get back to our families before his friends join him.'

Chatillon nodded, and they raced across the grazing lands

towards the walls of the large fortified chateau in the far distance. The man followed them, now shouting and waving an arm. They slowed to a canter in front of the large gates while several of Chatillon's men emerged, mounted, armed and warily watching the approaching rider.

The man was now close enough to hear and see. He was dark-skinned but with a mane of hair bleached by the sun.

'Finian Ui Neill is this any way to greet family?' he yelled, pulling his horse to an abrupt stop several horse lengths away.

Finian narrowed his eyes; he did not recognise this man claiming kinship. Chatillon, glancing at Finian's face, could see the bewildered expression, so he waved the man forward.

'We do not take kindly to being pursued like dogs through the forest by large groups of men. Did you expect us not to defend ourselves? I am sure you would react in the same way. You claim kinship with Finian Ui Neill, so tell us who you are!'

However, before the man could answer, another half dozen men galloped up and, pulling their horses to a halt, stared belligerently at Chatillon and Finian.

Attracted by the shouting, Edvard, staff in hand, emerged from the gates accompanied by another ten men.

The two groups confronted each other.

'I know not who you are! I do not recognise you as family,' shouted Finian, drawing his sword. Chatillon leaned over in his saddle and put a hand on his arm.

'No, Finian, let him have his say.' Chatillon smiled, for if this man was an impostor, he and his men might well pay with their lives, as Finian was fiercely proud of his family name and legacy. Finian reluctantly re-sheathed his sword, but the anger on his face said it all.

'Just tell us who you are, and let us end this charade,'

shouted Chatillon.

The man rode further forward, and now Finian could see the weathered and scarred face, but although there was a small spark of recognition, he still could not place him.

'I am Padraig MacDomnall, the cousin of Finian Ui Neill on his mother's side, and we've not seen each other for over twenty years.'

Finian went cold. 'Padraig,' he whispered and turned in shock and dismay to Chatillon, who shook his head in amazement. Piers had heard the story of Padraig's death a few times, usually when Finian was drunk, and pouring out his guilt for his cousin's death. For Finian had managed, with help, to escape from the sinking galley in the rough seas and storms of the Mediterranean while his cousin Padraig was still in chains and too far away from him. Finian had clung to a barrel, watching in horror as the galley sank, leaving a mass of debris in the turbulent wake of the sinking ship.

Now the two cousins faced each other in the deepening gloom.

It was Edvard, their friend and comrade, who broke the silence. 'If that is so, then why were you pursuing them?' he asked Padraig with suspicion.

'At first, we didn't realise it was them, but our guide recognised Chatillon. We tried to catch up, but they were always too far ahead of us.'

Edvard was not convinced, and shrugging, he turned to Piers. 'It is your decision,' he murmured.

Chatillon stared at this man who had appeared suddenly in their midst, back from the dead. 'Let us go inside and discuss this further. If you can prove you're whom you say, then you and your men may join us in our hall tonight. However, they must disarm now if they want food and palliasses for the night.'

They turned and entered the chateau with Edvard following and shaking his head, for he was not convinced. He watched as the men disarmed inside the gate—most did so willingly, and he escorted them to a long old outbuilding where they could wait while the problem was resolved. Braziers were lit in the old building, and food and ale were forthcoming, so most of the men were content. As they unbuckled their swords, a younger man caught Edvard's attention. The man's face was contorted with emotion, but when he saw he was being observed, he had dashed away the tears and turned away.

His name was Pierre. He refused the food on offer but accepted a sack of wine and was morosely drunk before long. He wrapped himself in a blanket and curled up on the thin straw-stuffed mattress with his back to the rest of them. The other men knew better than to comment or disturb him. He was a volatile character at the best of times, unpredictable in his response and could be brutally violent in his reaction. Several men glanced in his direction, worried that today's events would unleash a torrent of abuse and violence. For Pierre's older brother had been Chatillon's first victim today as he emerged from the gully, and Pierre had found his brother's dismembered body in the meadow. It had been his cry that had rent the air, and all he wanted was vengeance.

3

Chapter Two

Padraig MacDomnall was escorted to the Great Hall, where the families of the two men were gathered. However, after just a quick nod to their wives, Chatillon led the way up the stairs to his large solar-come-business room, which overlooked the physic garden Isabella had planted. It was left up to Edvard to explain what had happened to Finian's wife, Dion and Pier's wife, Isabella. Isabella accepted this, trusting Chatillon's judgement as always, but Dion was more concerned at the impact of this cousin's sudden reappearance. She had seen her husband's guilt and sadness when relating the story of the death of his young cousin many years before, and now, Lazarus-like, he was suddenly here amongst them.

Chatillon waved the others to chairs by the fire, adding several smaller logs to the large open fireplace and positioning them firmly with his boot. He waved to the manservant to fill the goblets with wine before dismissing him. Settling himself in a large wooden armchair, he regarded this cousin of Finian with interest. His gaze took in the warrior garb; he had already noticed his sword's worn hilt and well-used blade as he disarmed. He found himself eager to hear this newcomer's story if he was who he claimed to be.

Finian, however, stared openly at his cousin's face, trying to find any trace of the young man he thought had drowned. His cousin Padraig had always had an unruly mop of light auburn hair, a pale complexion and the light blue eyes that often went with such colouring. It had been rumoured in the family, that Padraig's grandmother had fallen in love with one of the many Viking traders in Dublin just before she met and married his grandfather. Now, however, Padraig's hair was bleached almost white, and his skin was dark and marked by overexposure and burning from the sun's harsh rays. The pale blue eyes with the light lashes were still there, but a deep old scar, puckered at the edges, ran from the side of his mouth down to his jaw.

Chatillon, deciding that the silence had gone on for too long, took a mouthful of wine and placed the goblet down firmly on the table.

'So, Padraig MacDomnall, tell us of one incident from your youth that only yourself and Finian would know. I believe you spent much time together as boys, following your older cousin like his shadow.'

Padraig nodded and smiled, stretching his legs out in front of the fire. At that moment, Finian knew it was indeed Padraig, and his stomach clenched. He remembered how Padraig's face lit up so clearly with that wide smile.

'I must have been eight or nine years when the new cross-bows arrived, and we were all excited, but of course, we were not allowed near them. It was the light nights of summer, and we stole down from our beds to the chest in the armoury where the crossbows were kept. We took two to the forest to try them out. It didn't end well, for the castle dogs followed us, and Finian missed the target we had marked on the tree and killed the King's dog. We buried it, but then they began to search as it was a famous hunting hound, and they found it with the bolt still in its side. Finian persuaded me to say that I had shot it by accident. He swore that because I was truly born and not a bastard like him, I would get away with it. However, they would beat and banish Finian if they found it was him. Therefore, at the tender age of nine, I took the blame for the cousin I hero-worshipped. I was beaten almost senseless by my father, who now had to pay for the King's dog. I couldn't walk for a week.'

Chatillon glanced at Finian, who nodded with tears in his eyes; this was indeed his cousin Padraig, as no other man could know that story.

Edvard arrived moments later to say that dinner was on the table. He raised a questioning eyebrow to Finian.

'Edvard, let me introduce you to my cousin whom I long presumed dead.' Edvard, seeing the pleasure on Finian's face, grasped arms with Padraig and welcomed him to the Chatillon estate.

The family were intrigued by the new arrival but welcomed him. The twins, Gironde and Gabriel, immediately began firing questions at Padraig, but Chatillon held up a hand for quiet.

'We can all wait until midday tomorrow to hear the story of Padraig's miraculous escape. Tonight will be about the food, the drink, and the wonderful Flemish Blue stallion we have just bought, which will be arriving in a week.'

Everyone laughed. The twins were disappointed, but no one dared to cross their father. Instead, Gironde bombarded

Finian with questions.

'How tall is he? Will his offspring be as big as him?'

Finian, recovering from the shock of Padraig's arrival, now went into full Irish storytelling mode. By the time he had finished, the like of this stallion had never been seen before.

Listening to this, Padraig felt suddenly nostalgic. The singsong lilt of Finian's voice took him back to the halls and campfires of his childhood. The cousins had indeed been inseparable, and he felt sadness for the life he had lost and would probably never experience again. He was snapped out of his reverie by Finian.

'Padraig's family were also famous for their horse breeding and racing. It made the MacDomnall family very wealthy. They would travel ten leagues or more to race or sell a horse. I tell you that Padraig here could ride any horse. No matter how wild, he would calm them; he was a true horse whisperer.'

Chatillon looked at Padraig with interest—perhaps he may prove useful to Finian, but they had yet to learn his plans. All would become clear tomorrow.

The next morning, Chatillon, Finian, Edvard, and a group of their men were in the pell yard as usual. They would practice at least three or four times a week to keep their skills sharp and train the men who needed improving. Edvard had constructed the yard from what had been a large walled cattle pen, bringing in sand from the riverbanks. Meanwhile, Padraig walked over to see his men, who were in good spirits apart from their thick heads. Pierre's attitude and demeanour, however, had not improved.

Glancing around to check they were not observed, Padraig led Pierre to the side of the large bailey. 'You need to calm down, Pierre. Yes, you are grieving, as is only right, but there is much to be gained here, and we cannot put that at risk by letting our emotions run away with us. I have reason enough to mourn your brother, Roget, for he saved my life.'

Not a flicker or change of expression showed Padraig that Pierre had even heard his words. His mouth was still a hard, thin line, and his eyes narrowed as he stared into the distance. The sound of clashing blades from beyond the gatehouse could clearly be heard in the bailey, so Padraig slapped Pierre on the shoulder.

'Come, let us go and see what's afoot out there.' Pierre turned and gripped his leader's arm.

'I'll play your game Padraig MacDomnall, but I swear I'll avenge my brother's death by slitting the throat of his killer when we are done here.'

There was little Padraig could say, so shaking the grip on his arm loose, he gave a curt nod and walked away from him. Pierre stood for a few moments and reluctantly followed.

Sword practice and mock fights in pell yards were common all over Europe, although Padraig had not seen it since he was in Ireland as a teenager. However, nothing prepared him for what he saw here on the Chatillon estate, for they took it up to another level with little quarter being given to the men for mistakes or careless moves.

There must have been twenty men in the walled yard. One group at the front with Edvard were fighting with heavy wooden staffs. Padraig found himself wincing at the crack of some of the vicious blows, which were only just parried by some of Edvard's opponents. The two men watched, fascinated by the speed and ferocity of the blows. There was nothing about this that resembled mock battles. Every blow, if not met correctly, as they had been trained to do, could have wounded or seriously hurt a man. Padraig had never seen such skill with a staff—a weapon he often dismissed as far inferior to a sword.

They made their way along the wall to the far end, where Finian and Chatillon were talking to half a dozen men. They leaned against the wall to watch as the men spread out. Finian was stripped to the waist, his broad shoulders and chest covered with a sheen of sweat from the workout. Chatillon, however, wore a sleeveless leather doublet that, from the cuts and marks, had obviously seen years of service. Piers leant on his sword, looking cool and composed, unlike the sweating men whom Finian was giving their instructions. Finian moved to one side with two men before raising a hand in greeting as he saw his cousin.

Meanwhile, the four men in the middle, swords drawn, warily approached Chatillon, who had not moved but stood with a slight smile as they approached.

'Is he fighting all four of them?' hissed Pierre.

'It looks that way. He has quite a reputation, as I seem to remember—this man whose throat you want to cut,' he said sardonically.

Pierre grunted and sneered in contempt. 'He cannot be that good. He must be in his forties now, from what you said. He'll be slower and not have the stamina for a longer fight. A younger, fitter man like me, in my thirties, could take him easily.'

Padraig eyed the tall, lithely muscled swordsman still leaning on his sword. Physically the man looked as if he was also in his thirties, not his forties. Just as he wondered which of the four men Chatillon would attack first, Piers erupted. It happened so quickly it was almost a blur, sword in one hand, dagger in the other, Chatillon burst into a run at the middle two men. Leaping high in the air, he brought the hilts of his sword and dagger down onto the two men simultaneously. The man on the left dropped like a stone as the bone handle connected with his skull. The second man dropped his weapon as the heavy hilt of Chatillon's sword slammed into the top of his right shoulder, numbing his arm and hand. Chatillon then whirled at speed and brought his weapon round in an arc to slice straight through the throat of the man on the far left. Everyone gasped as they realised how it would play out, but Chatillon stopped the momentum just as the blade touched the man's throat, leaving nothing but a red indentation and a few drops of blood. The man dropped his weapon and backed away, holding his hands up to admit defeat.

However, the fourth man seeing an opportunity with Chatillon facing away, raced towards him and swung his sword... into thin air as Chatillon turned just in time, dropped into a low crouch and quickly brought his blade up under the man's chin, as he slammed his dagger into the thick leather of the man's doublet.

The young man stepped away, breathing heavily. He laughed. 'For the first time ever, I really thought I had you there, Chatillon.'

'You almost did, but instead of thrusting or swinging for my legs as you should have done, you gave away your move that you were sweeping for my head!'

The young man shook his head at his mistake, then sheathing his sword, he went to help carry their comrade who was still on the ground. Finian would berate the first two men roundly for not seeing those blows coming and stepping aside from them.

Padraig, leaning against the wall, had watched all of this grim-faced. The level of expertise here was well above that of any of his men, most of whom he intended to send ahead into Paris tomorrow. He turned to Pierre, who had watched open-mouthed.

'The speed of him, I couldn't believe my eyes,' he whispered.

Padraig gave a sardonic smile, 'Oh yes, you and I could take this slow older man easily,' he spat at him. Pierre glared at him, but Padraig just laughed at his expression.

'I was told by the Steward this morning that Piers De Chatillon killed his first knight in a duel in the French court when he was only sixteen, and he has never stopped killing since.'

Pierre, gritting his teeth, hissed at him, 'Yes, including my brother, Roget!'

'You need to put that—' Padraig never finished the sentence as Pierre strode off towards Chatillon, drawing his sword. Padraig launched himself off the wall to run after him. Pierre was unpredictable, and he could ruin all of their plans with his actions.

Edvard saw them coming and quietly placed his considerable bulk in front of Pierre before he got any closer.

'The practice is over for today, but I would be happy to accommodate you and any of your men tomorrow,' he said with a smile. Padraig gripped Pierre's shoulder tightly.

'Yes, Pierre, we will join them tomorrow.' With some reluctance, Pierre sheathed his sword and turned away.

Edvard watched with narrowed eyes before he turned back to Finian and Chatillon. Undoubtedly, the younger man had a grievance; Edvard could see his tension and aggression. He decided to make it his business to find out what he could about

Pierre and keep a close eye on him.

4

Chapter Three

With some anticipation, the family gathered at midday for a nuncheon of cheese, bread, and cold meats washed down with ale. Edvard and Chatillon had planned to ride out to visit tenants that afternoon, but they all wanted to hear the story of Padraig's survival of the shipwreck and eventual escape from North Africa.

Tearing a large chunk of warm bread, Chatillon waved Padraig to leave his men down in the hall and join them at the L-shaped table on the dais.

'So Padraig, we are all keen, none more so than Finian, to hear of your exploits of the last twenty years, and we would be interested to know what your plans are for the future.'

Padraig wiped the ale from his lips and nodded. 'I'm not surprised that my cousin thought me dead. My case seemed hopeless as my feet were manacled and chained to the heavy foot block, and the ship was sinking fast. However, at the last moment, Roget, Pierre's older brother, used his oar to hit the overseer, who was about to jump ship. The keys to the manacles were at his belt, but he fell half into the water; the waves nearly washed him away, and we thought all was lost. However, I stretched as far as possible and managed to grab his foot. I clung on for grim death to his ankle as I tried to push away the panic and find the strength to pull his body towards us. Fortunately, we were at the front of the bow, for the stern was underwater by then. The ship plunged further in, and the waves began to wash over us, but this helped as I finally pulled the big unconscious man between us, and Roget unhooked the key from his belt. He unlocked his shackles and mine, but before we could swim away, the ship went down, and a maelstrom of waves and debris hit us. I am sure that Finian will remember the scene. It was hellish—the screams of the men who were still chained and the cries of men in the water who could not swim.

'Then I was hit by a heavy chest, which tumbled from the bow, and I knew no more. It gave me this scar. Roget saw this happen and dragged me almost lifeless onto the snapped mast and rigging. The currents pulled us away from the distant shore, and we floated all day as he stemmed the bleeding, and I raved in a delirium. Finally, we were picked up by a fishing dhow which took us into Tunis.'

There was silence in the room. Even the men at the long trestle tables had quietened as Padraig's voice echoed around the hall.

'Tunis, the worst possible place to land!' added Edvard, shaking his head at their misfortune.

'Yes, indeed, for they took us straight to the large slave market and sold us. We were a sorry sight, bleeding and bedraggled, so they put us in pens for a week to recover while some butcher stitched up my wound. A week later, with food and rest, the hakim oiled our muscles and put us on the block.

We spent another torturous year in the galleys until one day, a man arrived at our ship. He was a captain for the notorious pirate Sheikh Ishmael, and everyone cowered and shrank into their oars at the name. No man wanted to end up on his galleys. They say a man only lasts months with the beatings and poor food.' He paused to take another draught of ale for his dry throat.

'We have all had an experience with Sheikh Ismael in the past. He attacked our ship off Marseille, and Chatillon killed his son when they tried to snatch Isabella,' said Finian.

Padraig shook his head in horror, 'I don't know how you survived that, for we've heard he now slaughters all of the crews and passengers.'

'On that day, our God was with us, for he chose the wrong ship to attack. But we interrupted you. Please continue,' said Edvard.

'Fortunately, this captain was not looking for galley slaves. He was looking for craftsmen. The next thing we knew, Roget shouted the man over, announcing that he was a master stonemason and we were his two apprentices, myself and his very young brother Pierre. He came and questioned Roget, and to my astonishment, he was truly a stonemason who had worked on several great buildings in Paris. Our shackles were removed, money was exchanged, and we were taken into a large walled compound, which housed the slaves for the building site. We soon learnt we were building a palace complex for a powerful and wealthy Berber family.

'We spent the next ten years of our life working in the scorching sun in that palace. Roget taught us everything he knew, and we became competent stonemasons. At night, he also taught us the mathematics behind the buildings. We now knew how the arches and towers stayed up, and we became fluent in spoken and written Arabic. Before long, Roget and I were drawing and labelling the plans ourselves.'

'Did you not try to escape?' asked Finian.

'Repeatedly, and I have the scars to prove it. We worked every day, and we were locked in every night. It was impossible, as there were guards everywhere. We may have lost our shackles, but we gained a heavy riveted slave collar around our necks and a brand on our shoulders.' He shrugged out of his sleeve to show a large deep brand burnt into his upper arm.

'What's that?' asked Gironde leaving his seat to peer at the image on Padraig's shoulder. Chatillon smiled at his eldest son's curiosity, but Isabella frowned at Gironde and told him to sit down. Padraig laughed and ruffled his hair.

'It is a peacock, and there were dozens of them in the grounds and gardens of the palace—noisy horrible birds. It was the emblem the family adopted, a type of crest that marked us as their slaves. They fed us well as we were valuable to them because of the work we were doing, but the punishments were brutal.' Gironde ran his fingers over the shape before returning to his seat.

'So how did you finally escape?' asked Isabella, intrigued by his story.

'We were moved to Tripoli to work on the next project; for several years, we built stone wharves and quays along the harbour. The discipline was laxer there, with fewer guards. Less of the lash and more threats. The compound walls were lower and were not as secure as Tunis. We had more freedom to move around at night. We bade our time, for it was not just escaping the compound—it was escaping from Tripoli. It had to be by water as the lands around the town and citadel were desolate deserts.

'Fortunately, I found an opportunity to carry on an affair with a local fisherman's daughter, and she helped us to escape. Her father removed our collars for us and took us out in his boat one moonless night. He would only take us as far as Sicily, but we hoped to find a boat from there to take us to Marseilles.

'We sailed to Sicily, but luck was with us, for we enlisted in the mercenary forces of the Norman Lord Roger Bosso for several years. It was a good life as we were well paid, well fed and supplied with women for the asking.'

'Did you not marry and have a family?' asked Finian.

'I did, but they both died in childbirth. Then, I decided I wanted to go home, and Roget and Pierre wanted to see their family in Paris. When we reached Genoa, we began hearing about the fabled Chatillon and his Irish warrior Finian Ui Neill, so I knew I had to come and find you to show you that I had survived.'

A silence descended after these revelations as they absorbed the fascinating and dangerous tale. The twins stared at him open-mouthed. This man had been through adventures they could only dream about. Padraig's men also sat silent and watched, knowing their future depended on what happened next.

'So what are your plans now, Padraig? For you're welcome to stay here with your cousin for a while,' he said, glancing at Finian and Isabella for affirmation. They both smiled and nodded.

'Most of my men will leave for Paris today with Pierre for a month or two, and then some will return to their homes and what remains of their families. As you can imagine, there is reluctance; wives may have remarried, and parents died since they left so long ago. Like me, they'll have been presumed dead.

'I'll take your offer Sire; I'll be happy to stay here for a while, then I'll probably head back to Ireland, back to my home and what is left of my family.'

Chatillon nodded. 'Of course.'

They all stood to leave and began to make their way across the hall when a thought occurred to Finian, 'Which one of you is Roget?' he asked, looking around for an older man.

Not one of Padraig's men answered. They stared at the floor, and Dion noticed several looked at Pierre with worried expressions. She noticed the younger man's hands gripped the table, his knuckles white as he began to stand.

Padraig, seeing this, quickly replied, 'Unfortunately, Roget is dead, and we all feel his loss. He was a great man. It is still raw to some, especially his brother,' said Padraig staring wistfully at him. Dion watched as Pierre, glaring at Padraig, stood and turning without a word, he left the hall.

Edvard and Dion had watched this with concern. She glanced across at Edvard and met his eyes; he nodded and followed Padraig into the winter sunshine. Finian and Chatillon, seemingly unconcerned, went to the stables, ready to ride out across the estate.

Edvard found Padraig gazing at the old ruins. 'Tell me, Padraig, was Roget one of the men killed at the gully?'

Padraig turned a sharp gaze on Edvard; this man was far too astute, so he chose his words carefully.

'Unfortunately, yes, he was in the lead, but we are putting that incident behind us. It was a misunderstanding. These things happen, and his brother will soon get over his grief,' he said, shrugging it off.

Edvard looked at him for several moments and then turned away. He knew it was in his nature to be naturally suspicious, but something about all of this did not feel right. He was unsettled by the total lack of emotion in Padraig's voice or face. This man Roget, had saved Padraig's life twice, yet he seemed unaffected by his brutal death.

However, Padraig was well satisfied with how his story had been accepted as he made his way to see to the departure of the men to Paris. He had decided to keep two men with him. The rest could enjoy their time in the alehouses and stews of the city, awaiting their next orders from him. He knew it would certainly be weeks, if not months before he contacted them, but they had money in their pockets and the promise of much more if his plan came to fruition.

When he reached the large, partly dilapidated building, all was bustle and activity as saddlebags were packed and blankets rolled up. However, Pierre sat apart on his palliasse with nothing packed. His eyes were closed, and he repeatedly banged the back of his head against the crumbling wall behind him.

'Pierre, you must ready yourself. You're leading the men to Paris!' said Padraig watching him in concern.

'No, I am not. Bertrand can lead them as well as me, for I am going nowhere. My brother's body lies in pieces on a cart behind the stable with two other of our men. They were thrown there like so much offal. They tell me they're burying them this afternoon, and I'm not leaving here until I avenge his death.'

For a few seconds, Padraig watched him, and then he felt anger growing inside him; Pierre could ruin everything. He gripped the younger man by the neck of his tunic, tightening it around his throat, as he pulled him to his feet before slamming him into the old wall behind, a dagger now at his throat. Pierre's eyes were wide as he realised he had gone too far, for the calm demeanour that Padraig was showing here on the Chatillon estate was rare. Usually, he was full of bitterness and anger. He was also one of the most ruthless men Pierre knew, and he did not doubt that Padraig would cut his throat without a thought.

'You may stay because of Roget, but one word or gesture that jeopardises our future here, Pierre, and I swear that your corpse will be floating in that river yonder moments afterwards.' Pierre swallowed and nodded, and Padraig released him to slide back onto the floor.

'Bertrand, take the men to Paris. You know the name of the inn you're staying at in the north; the rooms are booked for you. Enjoy yourselves but stay out of trouble, and do not get yourselves thrown out, or you're on your own. I'll be in touch in a few weeks. By then, we will have more information to work with.'

He dismissed them and suddenly caught a movement from the corner of his eye. He whirled around and ran to the doorway to silence a curious servant, but he breathed a sigh of relief as he saw that it was only Chatillon's small daughter; she was running across the yard. She must be six or seven years old and no threat, so he dismissed her from his thoughts.

Annecy ran around the corner of the stables straight into Edvard's legs as he was returning to the Hall. He laughed and picked her up, throwing her playfully into the air. However, he didn't get the usual giggles, which was odd as she was usually a very happy child.

'What is it, Annecy?' he asked, smiling at her reassuringly.

She glanced over her shoulder, 'Those men, I don't like them. I want them all to leave.'

'Most of them are leaving now, but Padraig is family. He is Finian's cousin and will stay a little longer,' he explained.

Annecy scowled and whispered, 'He is a cruel and nasty man; he cut one of them with a dagger to his throat and said he would kill him in the river.'

Just then, Padraig's men rode out through the bailey to the gatehouse. They raised a hand in farewell, but seeing them, Annecy buried her head in his shoulder. Edvard immediately noticed that Pierre was not leading them, which meant he was staying here at Chatillon. A decision that Edvard was not comfortable with at all.

5

Chapter Four

Early December 1095, London

The last rays of winter sun shone through the yellowed glass panels of the window in Ranulf Flambard's business room. A log fire blazed in the large stone fireplace. It was a comfortable room with rich furnishings and a large oak table with carved legs. The room's walls were lined on one side with wide shelves loaded with dozens of vellum sheets and scrolls. All perfectly indexed, they were invaluable documents recording the tax affairs of England over the last ten years or so.

Flambard had indeed come far from his days as a clerk to Bishop Odo of Bayeux. His efficiency and grasp of economic matters soon brought him to the attention of King William Rufus. He thanked the King by working to increase the Crown's income. Some of his methods were highly dubious, but William Rufus turned a blind eye, gradually promoting him until Flambard was awarded the prestigious post of Lord Keeper of the Seal.

Now, Flambard was not only the confidant and friend of

the new king but also his chief minister and advisor. Like his father before him, William Rufus was happy to leave the country's finances in Flambard's very capable hands, for he seemed to be able to raise vast sums of money. That much of this was by taxing the nobility, the abbots, and churches he knew did not worry the King unduly, for he needed the money to pursue his ongoing war against his older brother Robert Curthose in Normandy.

Three years ago, the war had been going well. A truce and treaty had been signed that awarded William Rufus all the lands in Normandy above the Seine. However, his nobles had recently condemned the King for breaking the treaty, and the war again swallowed any money Flambard raised.

At that moment, the door opened, and a squire ushered in the King, who dropped into the carved armchair with a sigh.

'I presume it is something of import that has persuaded you to climb all those stairs,' said Flambard. He smiled at his friend as he poured a rich red wine into two beautifully etched Venetian glasses.

'As usual, it is the Pope,' muttered William, sipping the deep red liquid.

Flambard raised an eyebrow and came round the table to sit in the other chair by the fire. 'We've kept him off our backs for some time. In fact, since we finally agreed to appoint Anselm as Archbishop of Canterbury last year. We lost the revenues we were collecting from the vacant See, but we received the Pope's favour and blessing. So what exactly is Pope Urban demanding now?'

'As you know, Urban hosted the Council of Clermont last month. It lasted for ten days. Archbishop Anselm tells me it was the usual church issues of discipline and corruption.

Although there was some criticism of kings and princes failing to fill empty posts and raking in the revenue money instead.'

Flambard laughed, for he had been doing exactly that in England for years.

'However, Anselm said that things became more serious at the end. The Pope has excommunicated King Philip of France because of his adulterous marriage to Bertrade of Montfort, who is, as you know, still married to Count Fulk of Anjou.' They both absorbed that shocking news for several moments. Excommunication for a prince, a king or an emperor was not to be taken lightly, for it affected all of the people of their domain. Churches were often closed across the country, with no funerals or marriages allowed.

'Is the King of France mad? Why in God's name did he not just keep her as his mistress?' asked Flambard.

'They say that King Philip is besotted with her. She has given him two sons over the last few years, but Bertrade is still legally married to Fulk, hence the anger of the Holy See. As you know, Philip had put his previous wife, Berthe of Holland, aside three years ago. Fortunately, Berthe conveniently died last year, although she was only thirty-nine years old, and I believe it was not in childbirth,' answered William Rufus.

Flambard shook his head in disbelief.

'There is more!' said William, taking another mouthful of wine.

'Pope Urban received envoys from the Byzantine Emperor Alexius asking for assistance to fight the ever-encroaching Seljuk Turks sweeping down into his lands. As you know, he had already garnered support for an army of knights undertaking a holy crusade, possibly next year. Well, this relit the Pope's passion for the idea. He gave a rousing speech on the final day at Clermont, calling for a just war, a holy war, to free the Christian people in the Holy City of Christ, Jerusalem. He has even promised the remission of sins to all those who decide to go on the crusade and reach Jerusalem. It was a clever speech as he appealed to their knightly honour and chivalry.'

Flambard raised an eyebrow and met the King's eyes to see how serious he was about this. 'Does this appeal to you, Sire? Do you also wish to take part in this to wash away your sins?'

William Rufus burst out laughing. 'As you know full well, Ranulf, it would take far more than a pilgrimage to Jerusalem to wash away my many sins.'

The King turned away and stared into the fire at that point, his face reflective, his mouth a thin line. Flambard left him to his thoughts while he refilled their glasses.

As Flambard seated himself again, William looked up earnestly. 'I have no wish to become a soldier of Christ and toil for a year, or more, through the deserts of the Levant, Ranulf. My real fear is that many of my knights may wish to answer his call to arms at a time when I need them here to help me seize the rest of Normandy.'

Flambard nodded in agreement. 'Yes, I am relieved you're not considering it, for I would be the first to admit that we like the comforts and pleasures of our lives too much. Sire, I suggest you refuse permission for the knights you need but let other lesser warriors take up arms freely for the Pope. For this crusade could prove advantageous,' he said, twirling the wine in the glass and holding it to the light.

'How so?' asked the King, intrigued.

'A crusade such as this will prove to be an expensive undertaking for any knight. After all, they must equip themselves, their servants, and retainers. For a journey such as this, a knight must have at least four good horses, plus many pack animals. Then they'll have to feed and often arm their men. They will also have to provide and carry fodder for their animals for at least a year. I can see many knights struggling to raise a sum that will be three or four times their annual income. It occurs to me that they'll need loans for all of this. Usually, they would go to Jews, the Church or the local abbot, but what if they came to us? We would take some of their lands as surety for any loan they raised.'

The King interrupted in surprise, 'What? So you would have us become no more than usurers?'

'We already are in some ways with the bribes we pay your knights in Normandy. This would be no different, but it will work well for us, Sire. The Levant is a notoriously unhealthy place, and even fit pilgrims drop like flies of disease and sun-stroke in the searing heat. Then there is the constant warfare and attacks from the local raiders. I would imagine that many knights might not make it back to England. This would leave us in possession of their land, as their impoverished families will not be able to raise the money to pay back the loan and will therefore be forced to forfeit it to the Crown.

'A toast, Sire, to this first crusade of Pope Urban. May it prove to be a lucrative but successful enterprise for us.' They smiled at each other and raised their glasses.

It was early morning at the Chatillon Chateau, and Padraig

stood at the well. He turned the handle to raise the bucket and poured the icy cold water over his head and shoulders using the large dipper. This habit was instilled in North Africa, where they were covered in sweat and dust daily, but the water was scarce, and they were allowed to wash only every three or four days. He rubbed his body vigorously with a rough cloth.

Finian, who had been coming to find him, stood at the top of the steps and watched. His cousin appeared in good shape, but his back was a latticework of deep scars from the beatings and punishments he had suffered. Finian still had the lash marks on his own back, but they had faded and were only a fraction of what he was looking at here. He was also surprised to see how red and prominent the shackle marks still were on his cousin's ankles and wrists. He was sure Padraig had said they were not shackled while building.

Padraig pulled his long-sleeved tunic back over his head and turned to see Finian on the steps. 'Well met Cousin, this is a very impressive home you seem to have found for yourself and a very comfortable life you've established with your wife, child and friends.'

Dion came out to join Finian on the step and heard the end of this sentence. She didn't like the bitter tone that Padraig was using, so different to how he was in the hall the previous day.

'It has not always been thus, Padraig. Get Finian to tell you of his slaughtered wife and children in Ireland when you get some time alone,' she snapped and turned on her heel back into the house.

'Fiery little thing, isn't she?' he laughed and then raised a questioning eyebrow. 'So what happened?'

Finian shrugged it off. 'Some other time, Padraig, when

I've had enough drink to be able to visit it again in my mind.' Padraig saw the pain in his face and left it there.

'Yes, this is now my home. Piers is my friend; he has saved my life on several occasions, and I've saved his. We now hope to live in peace and harmony with our families and horses for a while. This will not be easy as Piers De Chatillon seems to attract and revel in both danger and death.'

Padraig smiled. 'Yes, I've heard of his reputation many times and watching him yesterday, I would certainly never cross him.' He opened his arms to encompass all the buildings around him, 'This is a huge chateau and estate, certainly much bigger than I expected when I heard you were living in a manor house in a French village called Chatillon. It is a veritable castle, it's so well fortified.'

Finian stared around at the walls and buildings he now took for granted. 'Chatillon's father, Gironde, extended it considerably, almost doubling its size. You can see the ruins of the old fortifications in the far corner. The building your men slept in was part of the old hall, part of the manor attached to the castle.'

Padraig stood and stared at the ruins for some time.

'There is a great deal of good stone in those ruins for the taking.' He turned and looked at a wattle and daub building at the base of the high wall. 'How many men sleep in those small barracks?' he asked.

'We keep twenty to twenty-five men here and another hundred or so spread around his other houses and estates.'

Padraig whistled. 'These are armed men, not servants?' Finian nodded. 'I knew he was French nobility and wealthy, but that is a small army and all trained to the highest standard by you three. They are some of the best fighters I've ever seen.

I may have a proposition for him, and I'll tell you about it when I think it through.'

Finian was not used to this confident, assertive cousin. The young man he had left chained in the boat had been a quiet but carefree soul, always following him into trouble but never leading.

'Come and see the horses, Padraig. I would value your opinion on an Arab mare we bought.'

The two men walked out of the gatehouse and down to the paddocks near the small river. They leant on the fence and watched the dozen or so mares, some with foals of about four months, cavorting around their dams or racing across the grass.

Finian had thought about this moment and judged the time was right. 'I shall only say this once, Padraig. I'm sorry that I could not save you that day, but you were too high up in the bow, and the boat was also listing to one side. It was impossible to reach you. I assure you that I have suffered sadness and guilt every time I thought of it. I also had to go back and tell your parents and brothers what had happened to you. They blamed me for taking you out on the trading cog that day. Unfortunately, they're both dead and can never know that you lived, but your younger brothers are still alive and running the family trade.'

Padraig's brows came down in a frown, and Finian saw the tears in his eyes for a second before Padraig pulled him into a clasp. 'Finian, I tell you true that I cursed you at times for abandoning me, especially during that first year back on the galley. At other times, I thought of the laughter and good times, wild times we had together. So let us put the past behind us, for it is over and gone. Instead, let us look to the future.'

They turned back to the horses as Finian found his own eyes were wet. Padraig pointed out a very light bay mare with a black mane and tail. 'That's the mare, I believe. She has the smaller, neat, intelligent head of an Arab; just look at those large black eyes watching us. She isn't too short in the back and has plenty of bone in those forelegs. She will have the endurance and speed you want, and I presume you're considering putting her to the Flemish Blue when he arrives.'

Finian nodded. 'I rode for several years with the Breton Horse Warriors. Their leader Luc De Malvais and his family breed the most formidable warhorses I've ever seen. Huge animals with a fiery temperament, trained to fight and strike out with teeth and hooves. I tell you, Padraig, a long line of those coming at you is terrifying. So I hope to do the same here; it will take time, but I am hoping that Chatillon's boys and my son, Cormac, will carry it on.'

'You are leaving them a legacy; by God, you're a lucky man Finian, and I envy you!'

'I assure you, Padraig, it has not always been this way. Come, we must go back; I have to begin the training.'

When Finian left him, Padraig looked at the quickly constructed barracks. They were certainly small and cramped for that number of men. At dinner that evening, he approached the subject with Chatillon.

'I wondered if I might make myself useful to you if I am to stay for a few months,' he said, smiling.

Engrossed in slicing a choice piece of venison, Chatillon looked up fleetingly. 'In what way?'

'I thought I might give you a larger, less cramped barrack block for your men. You have ample stone in the ruins and an old hall that needs repairing and almost rebuilding at one end.

Pierre and I could begin tomorrow to start shaping the stone, and it would pay you back for your welcome and hospitality.'

Dion heard the slam of a dagger on the table, and she fleetingly caught the hatred on Pierre's face as he glared at Chatillon. She blinked and looked at him again, but he had dropped his eyes. She glanced around the table to see if others had seen it, but they were all engrossed with Padraig as he explained how he would enlarge and finish it in a month or so. Chatillon was impressed and nodded his permission while Finian smiled at his cousin.

Dion stared down at her plate. For years before she met and married Finian, she had been the leader of a band of archers famous for their accuracy, and she always had an unerring eye for danger. This trait had served her well in the past, and now something about these men made her uncomfortable. Was it only her who sensed this about them?

After dinner, Padraig spotted the citole hanging on the wall and with Chatillon's permission, he took it down and began to tune it. Before long, he produced lilting Irish airs and haunting tunes that brought tears to Finian's eyes. Then he began to play lively tunes, and Finian, grabbing a laughing Dion by the hand, pulled her up into a dance. Before long, several men were out of their seats, jigging around the Great Hall with the serving girls. The children were delighted; young Cormac clapped his hands, and even Annecy smiled. However, the person most affected by the music was Gabriel, the more sensitive of the twin brothers. Gironde was the elder, brash and bold, a risk taker, while Gabriel was a reader who enjoyed the lessons with his tutor. He was an artistic boy and spent hours copying the illuminated letters from his father's large bible. Now he was entranced by what he was hearing and watching. He had strummed the strings several times but never managed a tune. He watched Padraig, whose fingers flew on the strings, while his right hand strummed with the long ivory pick. While his brother Gironde ran, leapt and twirled around the hall, pursued by barking dogs, Gabriel stood and watched, entranced.

Watching him, Isabella smiled; she loved both of her boys dearly, but Gabriel held a special place in her heart.

Finally, Padraig stopped playing, rubbing his sore fingers. 'It must be twenty years since I played this,' he said, holding the citole by the neck, but my fingers seem to have a memory of their own.'

Gabriel came closer and, reaching over, touched the strings. 'You made it sing!' he announced to much laughter. Putting his head on one side, he said wistfully, 'Can you teach me how to do that, please?'

Padraig nodded. 'We will find some time tomorrow before dinner.'

At that moment, the children were ordered to bed, and as Dion stood to go with Cormac, she noticed that Pierre was making for a group of servants by the trestle table. He was grinning and laughing for the first time, and he seemed a different person. Maybe she was wrong after all, but as she glanced back, she saw he had his arm firmly around the waist of one of the young serving girls.

The black-haired, dark-eyed girl was in awe of this handsome young man. The group gasped at the tales he told of pirates and fish bigger than houses. Gradually the hall emptied, and he pulled her to his side. 'Come, let us go outside where I can steal a kiss from those sweet lips.' Once outside, holding her face in his hands, he kissed her. 'What is your name?' he asked, running his hands down her arms and then pulling her hard against his body.

'Cecily, after Saint Cecilia,' she whispered. It was so cold out there that they could see their breath. He took her hand and pulled her towards the old hall.

'Come, Cecily, for I want to hear about your life, but let us not do it in the cold.'

At first, she held back, protesting she had work to do and was unsure of his intentions. He brushed off her protests and pulled her inside, closing the old wooden door and sliding the wooden bolt.

'I cannot be long,' she whispered, dismayed by the expression on his face as he came towards her. He pulled her down onto the nearest palliasse and put his hand over her mouth to still her protests.

'Be quiet, Cecily or I might have to hurt you,' he said as his hand lifted her gown and slid up her thighs. Pierre was not stupid; he knew he could not cause a scandal with this girl, so he removed his hand and smiled at her as he unfastened his braies. 'I've been watching you since we arrived, Cecily. You know you're the prettiest girl here, all that long black hair and those flashing dark eyes, and I want you to be mine. When we leave, I want you to come with us, for I tell you we will be rich. As my woman, you will want for nothing. Now open your legs and smile at me, for I'm sure you want this as much as I do.'

Wide-eyed, she did as she was told, for although she believed him and wanted the life he was promising, she also felt afraid of him. She cried out as he entered her, and suddenly there was a loud banging on the door. She put her hands on his chest in panic, fearful it was the mistress, but he ignored her and kept going until he had finished. By now, the thumping was furious, and he re-tied his braies and went to open the door while she pulled down her gown and got to her knees.

Padraig stormed in, 'Why was it locked, Pierre?' Then he saw the dark, pretty young girl. 'Was she willing?' he hissed.

'Of course, Padraig. What do you think I am?' He laughed and waved Cecily to his side, kissed her on the top of her head, and sent her on her way.

'Remember, I know what you are, Pierre, and I have seen what you've done to some women.'

'They were whores Padraig; they deserved it, and this dalliance is different. She is very pretty, and I may take her with me for a while. It will save me from paying for money-grubbing whores.'

Padraig shook his head and, glancing at the palliasse, he suddenly saw the stains. 'She was a virgin! A young, innocent maidservant in the house. God help you if this blows up in your face, Pierre, for I swear I will not aid you.'

'Do not fear, Padraig. She will stay quiet and be here on her back waiting for me tomorrow night. God's blood, it is only a bit of swiving with a servant girl.'

Padraig turned around and left, heading for his bed in the hall. He had seen Pierre leave with this girl and was hoping to intervene, for he had noticed that old Jean the Steward and his wife, Madame Chambord, looked after this young girl, and he wondered if it was a relative of theirs. If so, he knew they wouldn't be happy with what had just happened.

Pierre was proving to be a liability; his brother Roget had always kept him in check, but he was no longer here. Padraig sighed and stopped in the bailey to look up at the stars, thinking things through. Despite Pierre, everything was going to plan, and he was carving a niche with these families. He was building trust, and he would not let Pierre jeopardise that. He would slit his throat first.

6

Chapter Five

Yuletide was always special on the Chatillon estate and more so this year. Not only were all of the family, their friend Ahmed and Finian's cousin Padraig going to be there, but Chatillon's uncle, Pope Urban, had sent a message to say he would be arriving. Isabella, who loved a house full of guests, was delighted. The children positively bounced with excitement as they rode out with the men to choose the huge Yule logs that had been felled the previous year. It was a jovial party in the woods. Servants had brought spiced mulled wine. Logs were examined and chosen, ropes were attached, and they were pulled back to the Great Hall. The men and servants sang traditional yuletide songs, and young Annecy thought she would burst with joy, when her father sat her on one of the logs and told her to hold tight as it was dragged along.

For a while, Padraig felt conflicted as he watched his family and friends laughing and singing, their breath clear to see in the cold winter air. Part of him had yearned to have a life like this again for so long. Now here it was at his fingertips, for the taking if he wished. Then he shook those thoughts away, for debts were to be paid, promises to be kept, and revenge to be taken.

They arrived, laughing and breathless, back at the house just as Chatillon's uncle arrived. Pope Urban had never travelled lightly and had a considerable cavalcade of servants, guards, two Papal Secretaries, his chaplain and three priests, who would accompany him back to Rome early in the new year.

Isabella and Dion were immediately occupied with finding beds for the additional guests while Padraig took the twins out for sword practice with Pierre. He had stressed to the young man the importance of forging a relationship with the boys to gain their trust. He had already done so with Gabriel and the citole. Now he needed Pierre to do the same with Gironde, the more martial of the two boys.

Chatillon was always pleased to see his uncle, who had been like a father to him since he was a young boy. He had enabled Chatillon to rise through the ranks in the Holy See, creating opportunities that Piers had exploited. He loved his uncle, and usually, their thoughts were aligned on policy and the politics of Europe. However, for the first time, Piers had doubts about his uncle's insistence on a holy crusade to the Levant. Through his informers, he knew the gist of the inspiring speech that his uncle, the Pope, had delivered on the closing day at Clermont. The ripples the speech had caused were now turning into waves across Europe. His uncle had created a cause appealing to the chivalry of the nobles, and it offered the danger and excitement that many of them lacked in their lives.

Chatillon had to admit he had been surprised by the overwhelmingly positive response from the nobility of Europe. Ever practical, he now had grave concerns about the practicality and logistics of such a journey with the numbers being mentioned. With Finian and Edvard, he joined his uncle in the solar, where he had seated himself beside a blazing fire.

'I'm finding, Piers, that my older bones are really feeling the cold this year,' Odo said, rubbing his hands together.

Chatillon smiled and regarded his uncle with a raised eyebrow. He looked fit and well; the thick dark hair swept back from his brow was streaked with more grey, but his uncle's eyes were just as piercing as ever and shone with intelligence. He looked nowhere near his sixty-five years and seemed full of energy.

'You've spent the last year visiting almost every European court, pushing your holy crusade. I'm surprised you've not dropped with exhaustion,' said Piers, throwing another log on the fire before settling in the chair opposite his uncle.

'It was worth every weary mile, for you would not believe the enthusiasm I have seen, the clear desire to be part of this army which will reclaim Jerusalem.'

'You know my thoughts on that, Uncle. If the numbers you claim are anything near the truth, I don't know how you expect to manage it.'

'Do not fear, Piers, I have it all worked out, and several senior nobles will help me by leading their cohorts. Many who are to take part will assemble at Le Puy, which has always been a pilgrim city, and from there, they'll travel to Lucca, where I'll meet with them. I will give them my blessing, and we will travel in procession to Rome. On the way, we will show the northern cities of Italy the type of support I can garner and the great names I can summon for this War of the Cross.'

Chatillon still looked dubious, as did Finian.

'I presume you're gathering them in Le Puy in the summer months so that the roads over the Alps will still be passable,' ventured Finian.

'Of course, and from Rome, they will travel south to cross to Constantinople and then Anatolia, where Emperor Alexius will be waiting for them. He'll send them south to defeat the Seljuk Turks, and they will then make their way to Jerusalem.'

Finian was not convinced. 'You make it sound very easy, your eminence, but I have experience of moving with an army. If, as you say, so many wish to participate, there will be huge numbers to feed. Then there are the dangers of disease which seem to spread quickly in large numbers and can decimate any army.'

For a while, there was silence. Few people ever questioned or challenged the Pope's decisions. His uncle was no longer used to this; however, he was fair, and he listened.

'You may be right, Finian Ui Neill, so any advice you can give me while I am here will be gratefully received.'

The peace was shattered by the two boys bursting in to show their father the cut Gabriel had sustained in sword practice. Isabella appeared in pursuit of her sons.

'Ahmed has just arrived,' she announced.

'Just in the nick of time, as we have a badly wounded warrior,' said Finian pointing at the bleeding but slight cut on Gabriel's hand.

'Who better to attend to it than the King's physician,' laughed Odo.

Ahmed was a much-loved family friend who had known Chatillon since he was sixteen serving as a squire in the French court. Ahmed's skill was not only as a physician and bone-setter. It was what Chatillon called his *backroom activities* which brought him considerable fame and money. He made potions and poisons of every type and severity. Chatillon had happily sent Isabella to Ahmed to learn everything she could. She was now an accomplished apothecary and poisoner in her own right.

Ahmed had spent every Yuletide with them since he had delivered the twins eight years before. The twins loved him, as did their sister, Annecy, and they treated him like a grandparent. He always brought them a box of honeyed sweets from Paris and several delicious large rounds of cheese. More importantly to them, he was a storyteller of great skill, and Padraig suddenly found that they saw far less of the boys now he had arrived. Pierre actively avoided the Arab as he found his direct gaze disconcerting.

When Finian told the tale of his cousin's escape at the table that night, Padraig and Pierre saw the narrow-eyed puzzled glance Ahmed gave them as the story unfolded.

Dion had also noticed Ahmed's expression, so the next day, she tracked him down to the long building at the end of the kitchen garden, where Isabella brewed her potions and kept her snakes. Dion was not overly fond of the snakes, which Isabella handled several times a week. She was particularly wary of Octavian, the large male asp who was now as long as Finian was tall.

She entered the low door and greeted them. Their heads were close together, discussing a swirling liquid Isabella held up to the light. She asked if she could have a few moments of Ahmed's time. It was a cold bright day with frost on the ground, and to his surprise, she asked if they could walk in the garden.

'I could not help but notice your reaction to the tale of Padraig's escape. Is there something about it that does not ring true?' she asked, raising a concerned face to his. He indicated a bench against the wall in the rose arbour, and they sat in the winter sunshine while he gathered his thoughts and wondered how much to tell her, for she was a fiery impulsive young woman. Dion waited patiently, for Ahmed was an exceptionally clever and astute man. She knew he would tell her if there was a problem, particularly if he thought Finian was in danger.

'You obviously have concerns, or you wouldn't be here asking me,' he said. Dion nodded.

'Yes, but I cannot put my finger on what it is, Ahmed. Part of me is delighted for Finian's sake that his cousin is alive and has come looking for him, for they were like brothers when they were younger. But there is something afoot between Padraig and Pierre—the looks, the glances, the words muttered under their breath and the anger in the younger man, which Padraig tries to keep a lid on.'

Ahmed turned and looked her full in the face. 'You're right, for their story does not ring true in a few places. I know that Roger Bosso was not in Sicily then; he was ill in Apulia, on the eastern coast of Italy. Yet they talk as if he recruited them and as if they spoke to him. I'll leave it for a few days to allay their suspicions and get them to lower their guard. Only then will I probe further. Have you shared any of these concerns with Finian yet?'

'No, he is pleased and relieved that Padraig is alive and that he has come here. I do not want to ruin that.'

Ahmed placed his hand over hers in understanding. 'We will be vigilant without appearing to be so. Make sure you laugh and smile when in their company.'

She smiled, thanked him and went on her way, relieved to have voiced her doubts and concerns and shared them.

Ahmed sat for a while, thinking about what she had said. Certain parts of their story were difficult to believe and made him question exactly what they were doing there on the Chatillon estate. He headed for the staircase to the tower and the pigeon coop, where he wrote several messages to Marseilles, Tunis and Tripoli. He had several friends and informers there. It would be well known if any men escaped from there as it was an unusual occurrence. Meanwhile, he would watch them, listen and bide his time.

The Yuletide celebrations were noisy and raucous, with much laughter, dancing and singing. The Steward's eldest son became the Lord of Misrule and ordered outrageous games and kissing dances, which Chatillon's men enjoyed as much as the serving maids they pulled up to dance. One of them even had the temerity to pull Isabella from her seat and give her a smacking kiss. For Chatillon, the highlight of the evening was when Gabriel played and sang a well-known yuletide song on the citole. He sang the first verse on his own, his pure, clear voice echoing up to the rafters. To his delight, everyone joined in the second verse and applauded rapturously when he finished. Chatillon could not believe how quickly his son had learnt to play, and to Gabriel's joy, his father came and slapped him on the shoulder to congratulate him. Padraig told them he was a natural and had a good ear for music.

Eventually, the children's heads were nodding, and the celebrations drew to a close. Padraig and Pierre went to their beds, and a small group gathered in the solar, Chatillon, Isabella, Urban, Finian and Ahmed. As usual, the talk turned to politics.

'I believe you excommunicated King Philip of France at Clermont,' said Finian.

Pope Urban inclined his head, 'Not even kings of the blood can defy the Holy See and God's law. Marriage is a holy sacrament and cannot be abused openly by the nobles of Europe, or even the lower orders will think that adultery is acceptable.'

'So, if he had secretly carried on his affair with the woman he loves—set her up in a house of her own, as several bishops do—then a blind eye would have been turned to it all,' said Isabella mischievously.

Chatillon and Finian cringed at her statement; for even though she was right, she almost called the Pope a hypocrite.

It went deadly quiet for a while, and Ahmed had to raise a hand to cover his smile. Then the Pope laughed. 'Touché, Isabella. You are, of course, right. Our society tends to have double standards that have been around for centuries and will probably endure long after I have gone. However, King Philip slapped the Holy See in the face by marrying Bertrade and making her Queen of France.'

'Even though his wife Berthe was dead?' asked Finian.

'Yes, Finian, for Bertrade may be estranged from her husband, Count Fulk of Anjou, but she is still married to him.'

'The man is a monster, and she fled from Fulk in fear. You do know both of his previous wives died in suspicious circumstances?' she asked.

Pope Urban sighed, 'She should have come to the Church, Isabella. The marriage could have been annulled, but instead, she ran into the arms of her lover, King Philip, whose wife then conveniently died.'

Chatillon raised a hand. 'Wait, you think that the Queen of France was deliberately killed to remove her as an obstacle? I know Philip well, and it is true that he no longer loved Berthe, but he wouldn't murder her!'

The Pope met his nephew's stare. 'No, I agree, but someone else may have smoothed the way for him.'

'How did she die?' asked Finian.

'They said she died of gluttony for she was exceptionally plump. This was supposedly the reason for the King putting her aside. However, her chaplain and physician have their doubts.'

Isabella looked up at that moment and met Ahmed's eyes. Had he been doing the bidding of the King? she wondered. However, he met her gaze and gave an almost imperceptible shake of his head.

'Who found her?' asked Isabella, praying it was not her children.

'I believe it was Gervais, the Seneschal of France. Rumour had it that she had been his mistress for several years,' explained Pope Urban.

Isabella went stone cold as she remembered a conversation from a year ago. Gervais had come to her for a poison that he could deliver in a small dose to a troublesome husband, just enough to incapacitate him. However, in a larger dose, that poison could trigger heart failure. Meeting Ahmed's eyes, she put her hand to her mouth and stood up. He indicated that she should leave, so she bade goodnight and headed to the door. Outside, she leant her forehead against the cold stone wall. Ahmed came out to join her.

'I knew Queen Berthe well, Ahmed. I spent time with her, as did you. Now I find that I have enabled someone to kill her. If this is true, how can I meet Gervais de la Ferte with any equanimity ever again? It could be the poison I made that killed the Queen of France.'

'It is not your fault, Isabella. Stop this soul-searching. We are assassins in our own right, and we live with that. We give our potions, poisons and remedies to people in good faith. It is out of our hands if they use them for more nefarious purposes.'

She looked into his eyes. The flickering light of the flaming torch in the wall sconce cast shadows over both of their faces, and after a few moments, she sighed.

'As always, you're right, Ahmed, but it is different when it is someone you know well. I must have killed or enabled the killing of over a dozen people, but this one resonates for some reason,' she whispered.

He placed a hand on her shoulder. 'Go to bed, Isabella. Tomorrow is another day; put this behind you.' She placed her hand on his, for she had a huge affection for Ahmed, and then turned and left him there. Ahmed watched her go and found he was pleased that this news had affected her. He believed one should not always be able to kill without compunction as her husband Chatillon always could.

7

Chapter Six

January 1096

Henry Beauclerc, the youngest son of King William I, had left his leman naked in his bed and now stood bare-chested in the bracing air on the high walls of the newly fortified keep at Domfront. The castle had been built on an outcrop of the Armorican stone plateau and was a strong defensive site he was developing further. Henry had spent his brother William's money rebuilding and refortifying the castle, and he was determined that neither of his brothers would ever take it from him.

His relationship with his brothers, Duke Robert and King William Rufus, were precarious at the best of times. They had tricked, deceived and defeated him in the last few years, so he was determined that they would not do so again. His fingers gripped the top of the wide sandstone wall as he considered what he had lost because of them.

He had lent his brother, Robert, five thousand gold coins in good faith. In return, he had received land in the west of Normandy, becoming the Count of the Cotentin and Avranches. In early 1091, William Rufus and Robert had signed a treaty at a meeting in Rouen, to which he was not invited. Once there, they had agreed to cut him out of the succession by becoming each other's heir. Duke Robert gave all of Henry's recently acquired land in the Cotentin to William Rufus, but with no thought of reparation to him for the money he had paid as if he was of no account and not a prince of the blood.

Just the thought of that betrayal made his bile rise, for they had assembled their troops and jointly moved against him to drive him out of his lands. He had retreated to Mont St Michel, where they had laid siege to him. The disadvantage of Mont St Michel was that it was an outcrop surrounded by the sea and had no fresh water supply; Henry soon found that he was forced to flee. They had exiled him from Normandy, so he had gone south to Brittany and then even further to the court of King Alphonse of Leon, a distant cousin. He had stayed there for some time, licking his wounds and planning his next move against his brothers.

He did not have long to wait, for, at the end of 1092, the people of Domfront had revolted against their notorious overlord Robert de Belleme, who was now the Earl of Shrewsbury. They had willingly transferred their allegiance from the Earl to Henry Beauclerc and sent messages to Spain pleading with him to return. He returned, made his home there and spent every coin he had left on improving the fortress. In 1094, he made peace with King William Rufus and took his money to attack Robert's lands in Normandy. However, most of the money went instead into building a new fortified keep, strengthening his fortress at Domfront.

Henry was brought out of this reflective reverie by the

spatter of rain on his bare skin. He stood there several moments longer, staring at the forests and lands to the east. Messengers had arrived last night telling him that the Archbishop of Rouen had called a Synod, a religious council, to discuss the future crusade that Pope Urban had called. His informers told him that the Pope had asked his brother, Duke Robert, to lead this enterprise. If it were true, then this would leave Normandy without its Duke, and knowing the conditions in the Levant, it was highly likely that Robert would not return. Henry had made his peace with William Rufus, and now it was imperative that he, Henry, should become the King's heir. He knew that William would never marry or have children, as the King's inclinations did not lead in that direction.

He decided to contact Piers De Chatillon; if anyone could help him, the Papal Envoy could. Chatillon had access to information that no one else would be privy to on this issue, and with Chatillon's help, the Pope may be willing to support his ambitions to become William's heir.

He shivered and rubbed his arms before turning away to return to his bed and the warm arms of his mistress. However, his thoughts were all of Chatillon; he needed to convince the arch manipulator that, as the heir to King William Rufus, he would support the Pope in rebuilding the relationship with the Holy See in England and Normandy that William Rufus had ignored.

He was restless and flung the covers off the bed, pulling on his clothes. He would go to Rouen himself to see what was afoot. He could not be seen inside the city, or word would soon get to his brother Robert, but he was sure that Chatillon would be there for the Pope's proclamations to be ratified. He would send a message and arrange a meeting on the outskirts.

His uncle was readying to leave to return to Rome when the message from Henry Beauclerc arrived. Chatillon laughed when he read it and walked over to the deep window embrasure in the solar where his uncle stood in a pensive mood.

'Is anything amiss?' he asked his uncle.

He smiled. 'No, Piers. Instead of being a Pope weighed down with the worries of the world, in my mind, I was a boy again running with your father through the woods yonder. I also remember the day he brought your beautiful mother, Annecy, home to this house; now they're both gone. They would have been very proud of what you've achieved, Piers, as am I,' he said, placing a hand on his nephew's shoulder.

'Perhaps there are parts of my life and calling that my mother might not have been as pleased with,' Piers said with a wry smile.

His uncle laughed. 'Needs must, Piers, needs must, for the good of the Holy See and the policies of Europe. Remember that you often remove people who are so evil or malicious they should never have been allowed to draw breath, although some were just inconvenient obstacles to the change and progress our church needs to make. Now, what's the message that made you laugh aloud?' his uncle asked with a twinkle in his dark eyes.

'Henry Beauclerc has just discovered that his brother, Robert, is committing to lead your crusade. He sees this as an opportunity and hopes I'll be at the Synod in Rouen, where he believes we can offer each other mutual assistance.'

His uncle turned back to the window while he mulled over this information.

'It could play nicely into our hands, Piers, for Henry to become Duke of Normandy. It suits our policy of divide and rule. We do not want King William Rufus to become too powerful. He has little regard for the Church as it is, him and his creature Flambard. Go to Rouen and meet with Henry. Let's see what he has to offer. Now I must go as I have a long and tiresome journey ahead to Rome over the snow-covered passes in the Alps.'

Isabella usually took Chatillon's constant absences in her stride, for he was often called away at short notice. However, the news that he was suddenly leaving for a few weeks unsettled her.

'What's amiss, my love?' he asked, raising her chin to look down into those large amber eyes. She shrugged because she was not really sure herself. 'I know the news about Queen Berthe unsettled you, but in our profession, one cannot become sentimental about these things.'

She nodded in agreement. 'It isn't that, Piers. I don't like Pierre, nor do Dion or Ahmed. There is constant anger in him that he struggles to keep under control. It worries me.' Chatillon raised an eyebrow as he saw the genuine concern on her face.

'I have also noticed that, and so I've spoken to Finian and Padraig, who have given me assurances about Pierre's behaviour. I promise we will return home once we've shown the Papal presence at the Synod and seen Henry Beauclerc in Rouen. It will be two weeks at the most.'

She slid her hands around his waist. 'As you know, Dion is with child again, and I'm disappointed that we have not had another child.'

He smiled at her. 'It's not for the lack of trying, my love, but as my uncle would say, it is as God wills. Come, let us go and steal an hour together, for this may well be the time.' She smiled and, taking his hand, they ran like young lovers laughing up the stairs.

Pierre had not had a good morning...

He had been humiliated again in the pell yard by that oaf, Lazzo. The big man had repeatedly knocked him on his back with his staff, which was not Pierre's preferred weapon. Now Pierre was determined to practice with it every morning with Edvard, whom he tolerated and respected. Also, Lazzo was Finian's captain and had been put in charge of Pierre and Rollo, which Pierre resented. After the session, Pierre, nursing his bruised ribs and further bruised ego, made his way to the stables. He decided to ride out into the winter sunshine and shake the dust of this place off his shoulders for a few hours. Padraig and the rebuilding project could wait.

As he walked through the stable door, one of the many stable kittens strayed into his path, chasing a wisp of straw. Without a second thought, he swung his foot and kicked it viciously against the far wall. It dropped into the straw lifeless. There was a gasp beside him, and he turned to see Annecy, Chatillon's daughter, sitting in the straw surrounded by the rest of the litter. Her face was a mask of shock at what she had just seen. Pierre quickly dropped down into a crouch beside her.

'I'm sorry, but I have tripped over one of the stable cats,' he said in a sad voice.

Tears fell from Annecy's eyes as she shook her head. She

was a bright, obedient girl who knew right from wrong.

'No! You killed it. You've broken its neck,' she whispered.

He stared at the little girl for a moment, and then his hand shot out, grabbing her small neck. She gasped at first, but as his grip tightened, she found that she could not breathe.

'If you say a word about this, I swear I'll snap your neck as well. I know where you sleep, and I'll come in the night for you. Do you understand?'

Annecy was only six years old and terrified, so she said nothing, but she nodded as his grip tightened again. He let her go and walked over to lead his horse into the yard to tack up. Annecy stayed cowering against the wall until she heard him ride off across the yard. She stood on shaking legs and made her way to pick up the warm body of the kitten. Its head lolled to one side as she carried it across the stable yard towards the hall. Padraig and Gabriel were crossing the bailey, and they stopped.

'What do you have there?' asked Padraig, smiling at the child.

Seeing his sister's tear-stained face, Gabriel answered, 'It's one of Midnight's kittens. Is it dead?' he asked with a boyish interest, lifting its small head and watching it flop.

Annecy nodded. 'He killed it! He said he tripped, but he lied. It was my favourite, and your friend killed it!' she cried in shaking sobs.

Padraig straightened up, his lips a thin line as he took her by the shoulder. 'It must have been an accident, do you understand? It was an accident.' he repeated. Finally, Annecy, still afraid, looked away and nodded.

'Gabriel, take your sister and bury her pet in the garden.'

Gabriel rolled his eyes but put an arm around his sister and guided her to the kitchen garden. Padraig strode to the stable; immediately noticing the empty stall, he realised Pierre was gone, and spat in annoyance.

The next morning they all gathered to see Chatillon and Edvard as they set off for Rouen. Padraig breathed a sigh of relief as their absence took the pressure off him slightly. However, Ahmed was still assessing him with his dark, narrowed eyes. He seemed to be everywhere they went, watching them.

Ahmed was suspicious, as his Tripoli informer had heard nothing about an escape but promised to investigate further. Meanwhile, Ahmed wanted them to know he was onto them. He wanted to trigger a reaction, to stir the pot and see their true side. At dinner, he began the interrogation.

'How did you find life following and serving Bosso? They say he is a hard man to work for.'

Padraig glanced fleetingly at the Arab. 'We followed orders and did as we were told, so we had no problems,' he said, ladling a rich venison stew onto his trencher.

'Does he still limp as badly?' asked Ahmed. 'He lost nearly all the toes on one foot fighting the Lombards.'

Before he answered, Padraig, tore a chunk of bread to dip in the rich gravy. 'We didn't see very much of him. We were under one of his captains, Veneto, but yes, I noticed the limp.'

Ahmed smiled, for Bosso did not limp. He was a huge fearsome warrior in the prime of his life.

Isabella, meanwhile, was worried about Annecy. Usually a happy, laughing, carefree child, she had begun to cling to her mother's skirts, and she slept fitfully, often ending up in Isabella's bed. At first, Isabella put it down to Chatillon being away, for she adored her father, but eventually, she asked Gabriel if something was amiss, as he was closer to his sister.

'It is since the kitten died. I helped her bury it in the rose garden.' Isabella was perplexed, as animals died around here all the time, it was part of the cycle of life, and Annecy was used to that.

In the solar whilst stitching that evening before dinner, she broached the subject with her daughter. 'I hear you buried one of the kittens,' said Isabella, looking up from her embroidery while Annecy sorted the fine, coloured silk threads for her.

'It was killed in the stables,' the girl replied, not looking up.

'Did one of the horses stand on it? That often happens,' said Isabella in a level voice, but there was silence, so Isabella tucked her needle in the tapestry and laid it aside.

'I'm not allowed to say!' answered Annecy finally, her eyes downcast.

Annecy was blonde like her mother, with the same unusually large amber-coloured eyes. Isabella swept the hair from Annecy's eyes. There was no doubt that she would be a beautiful young woman growing up.

'Who told you that?' asked Isabella kneeling before her daughter.

'The man who killed the kitten said it was an accident, but it wasn't; he broke its neck on purpose.'

Isabella was puzzled, but she nodded in sympathy. 'That must have been frightening and sad to see, for I know you spend a lot of time in the stables with the kittens.'

Annecy raised her eyes to her mothers. 'Will he kill me now for telling you?' she said plaintively.

Isabella laughed. 'Of course not. Your father would cut off his head and put it on a spike if he thought this man had threatened you. Was this Pierre?' Isabella asked, realising that it could only be him. The girl nodded.

'Well, do not worry about it anymore. It is your anniversaire in two weeks; you will be seven years old, and I believe your father has found you the most beautiful pony. But you cannot tell him that you know, or it will spoil the surprise.' Annecy clapped her hands in delight as Isabella held a finger to her lips. At that moment, Dion came in with Cormac, and Isabella left her daughter in their care and headed for the garden.

Entering her candle-lit workshop, she nodded to Ahmed, who was measuring ingredients into a bowl, and she went straight to the large covered tanks at the end. Edvard had carefully constructed these so that her snakes had far more room and even sunshine at certain times of the day. Isabella put down her candle, removed the heavy wicker lid, and, using a hooked stick, lifted Octavian, her favourite, out of the enclosure. She did not wear gloves as his poison sacs had been emptied that morning. She carried him out into the bright moonlight and stroked his head.

Ahmed strolled after her. 'If I had not seen it repeatedly with my own eyes, I would not have believed the attachment that snake has for you.' Eyes closed, the snake's head was swaying as she stroked it. 'Are you taking him for a walk in the dark?' he asked amusedly.

'No, this is far more important. Come along if you wish,' she said with a thin smile that he recognised. It usually boded no good for someone. The tall thin Arab followed behind, and they headed for the old hall where the men had finished work for the day and would soon be assembling in the Great Hall for dinner. Opening the door, she entered. A bright fire roared in the original large fireplace, and Padraig and Rollo were sat dicing on an old barrel top while Pierre lay on his palliasse, his eyes closed and his hands behind his head. She walked swiftly over and, uncoiling the large, heavy snake from her arm, looped Octavian down to gently drop onto Pierre's chest.

She heard the gasp from the men behind her, and so did Pierre as he suddenly felt the weight. He unlaced his fingers.

'Oh, I wouldn't move a muscle if I were you. Octavian is an asp, one of the fastest-striking snakes in the world, so Ahmed tells me. Look at how he is raising himself to a height. Look at the hood that has spread out behind his head. He is poised to strike.'

Pierre was terrified. His face was white, and his eyes were wide. Ignoring her advice, he used his hands to attempt to throw the snake off him. Octavian immediately struck, burying his long fangs in the soft area at the base of the man's throat. Pierre screamed, and Padraig and Rollo leapt to their feet. Ahmed raised a hand to stop them as Isabella calmly bent and unhooked Octavian's fangs none too gently.

Pierre, sitting up, was gasping for air. 'Padraig, help me. Do something. These snakes kill in hours.'

Isabella laughed. 'That is true, for you would be dead if his poison sacs were full, but this time you were lucky.'

Pierre leapt to his feet and went for his dagger, his eyes blazing. Padraig ran forward and grasped his wrist.

'No!' he shouted at him.

Isabella had not moved; the half-smile was still on her face. 'You want to kill me, Pierre? I thought it was only two-month-old kittens you liked killing, something soft and helpless that could not fight back. I am neither soft nor helpless. If I tell Piers of this, of what you've done, he'll probably kill you far too quickly for my liking, for I would like to see you suffer.

'If you go anywhere near my daughter again or threaten her in any way, I promise I'll slip Octavian into your bed one night.'

Nodding sternly at Padraig and holding Octavian close, she left.

Ahmed, a smile on his face, followed her. They walked around the side of the garden and placed Octavian back into his enclosure.

'I tell you, Isabella, whenever I visit you and Chatillon, I am never bored. I should visit you more often.'

She laughed while feeding Octavian a large rat. Ahmed, watching her, knew that she had meant every word she said to Pierre. Chatillon may be away, but God help them if those men ever crossed her, for she had become just as lethal.

Back in the old hall, Pierre was downing copious amounts of wine and dabbing the blood from the wounds in his throat.

'God's blood, Pierre. I thought you were a dead man as well,' said Rollo. Padraig, however, said little; he just stared at Pierre, his lips white with anger.

'I swear, Padraig, when I have my revenge for my brother, and I slit his throat, I'll enjoy slitting hers as well. Who is she to treat me like this?' he yelled whilst standing and swaying.

Padraig pushed Pierre so hard that he hit the wall behind him with a thump and slid down it to the floor.

'I tell you who she is, Pierre, the wife of a French noble with the ear of the Pope and all of the nobility of Europe. It is a good thing that Chatillon and Edvard are away because they would have flayed you alive. I've heard the stories of what that defrocked monk can do. You would have given everything up under his knife, Pierre, our plans, the gold, and you would have destroyed everything. You threatened a small, helpless child, for God's sake. What were you thinking? You've wasted your last chance here; you're coming to Paris with me in a few weeks. I cannot risk having you here anymore, for you don't think, and you're a liability.'

At that, he stormed out, and Pierre pulled himself to his feet, fists clenched. 'As God is my witness, Rollo, despite our plans, I will take my revenge on them before we leave here,' he growled.

8

Chapter Seven

It was still a cold and misty winter's morning as Chatillon and Edvard rode through the packed streets of Rouen with five of their men. Fortunately, they had a room at the castle, for there was no accommodation to be had in any inn within the city. Even the richer burghers were offering rooms to knights, many of whom had travelled some distance to hear the proclamations of the Archbishop. They stopped at the gates of the considerable fortress, and Chatillon could not prevent his eyes from raising to the tall tower above them. It was the first time he had been back to the city since the leader of the rebellion had been thrown to his death from the top of that tower by Henry Beauclerc.

'They call it Conan's Leap now,' the grinning guard at the gate said, noticing Chatillon's stare. The Papal Envoy did not deign to reply as they rode through into the bailey, which was full of tents and banners. As they dismounted and handed their horses to their men, Chatillon noticed Edvard's perplexed expression.

'My uncle's call to arms seems to have resonated across

Normandy, and many knights with their entourages are now flocking to Robert's banner as they have heard he will lead this crusade.'

However, on entering the Great Hall, even Chatillon was surprised to see the number of senior Norman nobles gathered around the Duke. Count Stephen de Blois, Duke Alan Fergant of Brittany, young Robert II of Flanders and even Robert's old enemy, Helias de Fleche, Count of Maine.

Robert was delighted to see Chatillon, others not so much. Alan Fergant had not seen the Papal Envoy since Chatillon had questioned the sudden death of his young wife, Constance—a heated exchange, as Piers was convinced that she had been conveniently poisoned on her husband's orders.

Robert clasped arms with Piers. 'Well met Chatillon, you're no doubt here to see the Pope's decrees at Clermont ratified. This means we will carry the Papal banner to liberate the church of God, the Holy Sepulchre of Jerusalem, presently being trampled underfoot by savages.'

There were cheers at this rousing speech, with much banging on tables and clashing of swords on shields by retainers who lined the hall's walls.

Chatillon smiled, for try as he must, he could not summon any enthusiasm for this madness, a holy war that the Pope was advocating. However, this was certainly not the forum to air his views.

'I'm sure Archbishop William will do what is right, Sire, in ratifying the Pope's wishes. Urban has sent me to see how the nobility and lesser people have responded to his call. Looking at the faces gathered here, I think he'll be pleased. There has never been such a gathering of people for a Synod.' Various nobles bowed at the compliment paid them.

Duke Robert was so engaged with knights coming and going that Chatillon could not get any time alone with him until much later. He found him in his business room with his very harassed and frustrated Steward, who was trying to find beds for another dozen knights and their retinues.

Chatillon laughed as the man left. 'I'm so pleased I sent ahead, or Edvard and I could be in a stable loft with my men.'

Robert snorted with laughter at the thought. He looked so young, almost boyish, when enthusiastic about an idea or project. Chatillon sat opposite him and regarded him with amusement. 'The logistics of this crusade must be a nightmare for you. If you have only a fraction of those committed to going in the summer, tens of thousands will be on the road to Jerusalem.'

Robert nodded. 'My uncle, Odo of Bayeux, and Stephen de Blois, are working on that. We will leave towards the end of summer when we can take advantage of the harvests for fodder and grain.'

Chatillon's eyes never left Robert's face. 'Then there is the cost to undertake or equip for a journey such as this; it is expensive. How many men are you taking, Robert?'

'I will take at least a hundred, as will the others. We are making lists and costing everything we need.'

'A hundred men,' said Chatillon in a bemused voice. 'Then, there will be the knights, squires, servants and grooms to go with them. Spare mounts, pack-horses and carts full of food, ale, wine and fodder.'

Robert nodded enthusiastically. 'We have thought of all of this, Chatillon, and we are planning for it.'

There was silence in the room except for the sound of a falling log and the fire crackling. Chatillon crossed one elegantly booted leg over the other and pursed his lips. 'Can I ask how on earth you're paying for all of this, Robert? Years of war with your brothers, and Helias of Maine, have left your coffers sadly depleted.'

Robert did not answer at first, looking away as if he could not meet Chatillon's questioning gaze.

To give him time, Chatillon threw another question. 'What of Normandy? You fought long and hard for your Dukedom, Robert, and have been fighting for the last eight years to keep it. Who will defend and keep it while you're gone? You will no doubt be gone for several years; do not underestimate the conditions you will be travelling under or the challenges you will face.'

Finally, Robert looked back at the Papal Envoy. 'I have come to an arrangement with my brother, William Rufus. I am signing a Vifgage with him next month. In return, he'll send me five thousand marks and make promises to keep Normandy safe until my return.'

It was with some difficulty that Chatillon managed to control his face and keep it immobile; otherwise, the shock and disbelief would have shown. He forced himself to look at the floor for a few moments to control his voice.

'A Vifgage, that is a living pledge, I believe, for when someone gives an estate in return for a loan, is it not?' Robert nodded.

'However, you would never expect such an arrangement to be applied to a whole country. Also, you're trusting the word of your brother—the man whose own nobles openly criticised him for tearing up the recent truce with you and breaking his word.' Chatillon shook his head and resisted the temptation to shout, *Are you mad? Have you lost your mind?* at Robert.

It would have been to no avail as he could see the stubborn, mulish expression around the Duke's mouth.

'Tell me, Robert, do you expect him just to hand Normandy back when you return? That is if you return at all. It is a win-win situation for your brother while you're shouldering a mountain of debt that will take your whole life to pay back!' said Chatillon, failing this time to hide the exasperation in his voice.

'My brother has changed, Chatillon, and he wants to protect Normandy, for we wouldn't put it past King Philip to invade while I'm away. Only King William Rufus can prevent that from happening.'

At that moment, a knock came on the door and Edvard appeared. 'Sire, a message has arrived for you from Pope Urban.'

Chatillon nodded but stood unmoving for several moments, looking down at Robert. 'I can only pray that you know what you're about and don't live to regret your actions, Sire.'

Robert did not reply; he merely held out his hands as if to say, what is done is done.

Chatillon felt a sense of helplessness for the first time in this situation. The Holy See had spent years and a fortune in gold, backing and moulding Robert Curthose to become Duke of Normandy. By some twist of irony, the Pope's vision of a holy crusade was taking Robert away and allowing William Rufus to rule England and Normandy, as his father had done before him. Ranulf Flambard must be rubbing his hands together in glee at the thought of what would be almost a bloodless coup.

Edvard was surprised at the speed with which Chatillon strode off and across the Great Hall, but he now caught up with him.

'The message, Sire,' he said, holding out a small roll of vellum that had not come from a pigeon's leg or from Rome. Chatillon took it without a word and moved to a window. It was from Henry Beauclerc. He was staying at Fecamp Abbey as relations with his brother Robert were strained. He arranged to meet them on the morrow at an inn on the city's outskirts. Chatillon nodded and handed the thin strip back to Edvard, but he did not move; he stood in the window embrasure for some time, weighing up everything he had just heard.

It was madness, pure madness.

As Papal Envoy, Chatillon had a privileged position, so he was allocated one of the few chairs in the cathedral, at the side of the altar, with Duke Robert. This was a Synod, a gathering of the senior clergy, so they had precedence and were standing at the front. Behind them came the nobles, the lords and knights to hear the Archbishop's speech. Then, in precedence, came the rich merchants and burghers of the town. The general populace took up any space left, some even sitting on the shoulders of others to see and hear what was said. The grand Cathedral of Notre Dame was packed.

Archbishop William Bonne-Ame was a Breton, a fiery individual who had made quite a name for himself, in the past, with his forceful rhetoric. Today he was not to disappoint them. At first, he preached on the usual reinforcement of church law, with a brief discourse on corruption and the sin of simony. Then he raised the volume and began a rant against beards and long hair. Christian men must be clean-shaven, their hair must be short, and monks must be tonsured. Chatillon regarded Robert beside him; the Duke's hair was not overlong, but he did sport a short blonde beard. Seeing his gaze, Robert gave a quiet laugh and pointed at Chatillon's thick, black hair, which almost reached his shoulders. He also had a neat black beard.

'These rules don't apply to lay people, so you're safe,' he said to Robert in a stage whisper.

'And from this time forth, all crusading knights will be expected to conform to these rules. They must not look like the heathens and savages they'll defeat,' boomed the Archbishop.

Chatillon could not hold back a snort of laughter and received a glare from William Bonne-Ame as he asked the Synod to ratify the Pope's decrees at Clermont. He received a resounding aye from the clergy and most of the assembled congregation. Chatillon expected a blessing to be bestowed, and then they would leave, but unfortunately, the Archbishop was getting into his stride—he had a huge prestigious audience in front of him, and he did not intend to halt there.

The Archbishop drew himself up to his full height, arms raised. William Bonne-Ame was an impressive figure as he began a tirade that was obviously close to his heart. 'There is one group living in our midst responsible for the imprisonment and killing of our saviour,' he announced as silence settled on the crowd in anticipation of what he would say next.

'These people are no less responsible than the Muslim heathens that hold the Holy Sepulchre in Jerusalem. These Jews should pay for their sins; indeed, they should be the very people that should be funding this holy war. They have no respect for the cross, and they deny the crucifixion took place. They refuse to believe that our saviour Jesus Christ was the Messiah.'

By now, the Archbishop was shouting and spitting his words in a fury, his arms flailing as he talked of the Muslim atrocities committed in Jerusalem. Chatillon watched him in dismay, and glancing around the cathedral, the fervour and belief on the faces of the congregation were even more alarming.

Chatillon knew that Rouen had a large, vibrant, prosperous Jewish community. They had their own quarter with several synagogues, their own school, and a cemetery. Like most Jewish communities, they had economic power but no political power. They were hard-working families of merchants, and he had friends and informers amongst them. They had been in the city for hundreds of years and had been tolerated and left in peace until the last few years when attacks on their property had suddenly increased since the talk of a crusade.

Archbishop William now reached a crescendo. 'We will go to the east to attack the enemies of God in the Holy Land, but here in Rouen, under our very eyes are the Jews. Of all races, they are God's greatest enemy.'

Chatillon reached over and gripped Robert's wrist. 'This will not end well, do something, Robert!'

The Duke shrugged helplessly.

'God's blood, Robert. They will slaughter the Jews; get your men on the streets to stop them.'

However, it was too late, for the Archbishop had ended his speech with a cry to go forth, and the multitude was surging out of the large double doors onto the streets of Rouen, swords and daggers drawn, ready to obey the Archbishop.

9

Chapter Eight

Chatillon dropped Robert's wrist in annoyance and stood searching for Edvard, whose tall figure he could see making his way against the crowd towards him. At first, they tried to fight their way through the hundreds pushing towards the doors, but it was pointless, so he shouted at Edvard to follow him and went back towards the altar. They reached the Archbishop, who still stood transfixed by the huge crowd forcing their way out. Chatillon grabbed him by the front of his chasuble, pulling his face close to his.

'The blood of these people will be on your hands, William Bonne-Ame, and I swear I will make sure Pope Urban knows exactly what happened here today—the slaughter of innocents you have just instigated.'

The man stared back at him, almost in a trance, then muttered, 'It is God's will. You cannot fight against God's will.'

Chatillon let go and pushed him away in disgust as they made for the sacristy, where he knew there was a side door onto the street. It was locked, but Edvard found the key on a hook on the wall, and they tumbled out onto the teeming streets. They set off at a run through the crowds heading towards the Jewish quarter.

'We head for Jacob's house. I just pray we are not too late,' gasped Chatillon over his shoulder, wishing he had brought his men with him. When they reached the Rue des Juifs, it was impassable, the screams and shouts telling them that the slaughter had begun.

'They're herding them into the synagogue,' shouted Edvard over the screams and sound of clashing blades. Chatillon turned back and headed down several side streets to get to Jacob's large merchant house. He saw at once that Jacob had had the sense to close and bar the large wooden gates, and his guards were outside fighting an encroaching crowd. Edvard began to lay about the angry crowd with his staff while Chatillon used the flat of his sword to deliver some brutal blows. Still, they found they were fighting against armed fervour-crazed fanatics who seemed to know no fear as they repeatedly flung themselves against the defenders.

Seeing they were seriously outnumbered, Chatillon backed up and hammered on the gates until the small wicket gate opened a crack. 'Let us in before we are overcome,' he shouted. They gratefully tumbled through, followed by the guards, but the last man did not make it and was pulled backwards to be torn apart by the crowd. With some relief, Chatillon heard the wicket gate being slammed and bolted behind him.

His friend Jacob stood in the centre of the large walled courtyard, his fists clenched in anguish. He pulled Chatillon into a bear hug and held him at arm's length. 'I heard you were in the city, and I prayed you wouldn't let them kill my family!' he exclaimed, still holding his friend's arms.

'The Duke's men will soon be out on the streets trying to control the mob, but they are also sorely outnumbered, so I'm afraid it is just a waiting game, Jacob.'

He waved them inside the house, but Edvard decided to stay and direct the men on the gate. He had heard shouts to set fire to the gates, and he ordered buckets of water to be brought from the well and a ladder.

Meanwhile, Chatillon followed Jacob inside, where his two sons and his wife, Miriam, waited. The fear was clear on their faces as they listened to the shouts and continuous banging on the gates. Chatillon reassured them as best he could; his calm demeanour helped as he accepted the offer of refreshments to keep Miriam occupied. Then he sent Jacob's two sons out to Edvard, telling them he desperately needed their help.

Jacob smiled and thanked him. 'All sense and practicality seem to disappear when your family is in danger. You lose all perspective.'

Chatillon inclined his head in agreement, thinking of how he froze when he saw Ishmael's son, Malik, taking Isabella. He had seemed rooted to the spot with fear for several moments.

'This has been coming for a while, Piers. Considerable discontent directed at our community and far more so since your uncle's speech in Clermont. It almost seemed inevitable as the city filled with crusading knights and their entourages over the past weeks. I hired extra guards and closed the gates early rather than risk my family being in danger. Now I wonder if that was wise, for if they set my house and yards on fire, we will all perish.'

Chatillon put a hand on top of his to reassure his friend. 'We will not leave you until this madness stops; they'll tire as it darkens. Now, more importantly, do you still have the tunnel?'

'Yes, we have the tunnel; few people know of its existence.' The older man's eyes twinkled with amusement as he said it. 'You never forget anything, do you, Piers? It must be twenty years since I mentioned that to you one night, in some seedy establishment, in Rome.'

Chatillon laughed. 'Good, as I have five men with me at the castle, and I need them here, as two of them are very useful English archers. Do you have a clever servant to go back through the mayhem on the streets?'

'Even better, Piers, the tunnel comes out near the river. He can take a boat around the castle's far side and avoid the Jewish quarter.' The servant was summoned and sent on his way down through the cellars and into a long damp tunnel that had not been used for over a decade. The two friends sat silent for a while as fresh fruit, cheese and silver cups of warm spiced milk were served.

'I hear you're to meet with Henry Beauclerc. Is that true?' asked Jacob as Chatillon chose a ripe fig and halved it with his dagger. He looked at his friend in amazement and then laughed.

'This is why you're one of my most invaluable informers Jacob. How on earth could you know that?'

It was the merchant's turn to smile. 'It was easy. I'm aware that Henry has arrived and is staying at Fecamp. He is still very much at odds with Robert, and the most influential guest in Rouen is Pope Urban's Papal Envoy! It was a guess, I just had to ask you the right question, and your response gave it away. You're getting careless, my friend,' he said while chortling with laughter.

Chatillon thanked them for the refreshments, and they went

back outside to see how Edvard was faring. The gates had been soaked inside and out. Jacob's men were still up a ladder, pouring water down onto the bundles of kindling stacked against the outside gates while dodging well-aimed missiles from the angry crowd. Some had dispersed to find easier prey, but it was still sizeable and volatile. 'We need a distraction, or help, from someone. We can't keep the mob at bay forever,' said Chatillon, concerned by the threats and abuse from the other side of the gates.

'I have an idea,' said Edvard, descending the ladder and handing the bucket to Simeon, Jacob's eldest boy. 'Where is the cesspit?' he asked the boy.

'This way, Sir,' he said, leading Edvard to the rear of the house. Edvard stood and looked at the stinking pit, 'Find me some really old clothes, almost rags. Then show me where this tunnel is,' he shouted, grinning.

A short time later, Chatillon could hear the cries of alarm from the other side of the gate and then shouts for someone to clear off if he wanted to keep his life. Suddenly there was the sound of a new, broken, rasping voice. 'Death to the murdering Jews,' it cried.

Chatillon risked climbing the ladder and tentatively looking over the gates. He felt no fear or apprehension, only anticipation and curiosity. There were at least three scores of the mob still there. The crowd who had been pushing and thumping were backing away slightly from the gates. 'Make them pay!' the broken voice cried; Chatillon heard the sound of a bell and risked another look. He was vigilant as he dodged the missiles; a rock had knocked a guard clean out cold moments before.

'Get out of here, you stinking leper, before we decide to burn you with them,' shouted the fat vociferous merchant who had led the crowd for hours. He had huge debts with Jacob, and it would suit him if the Jews were killed or driven out.

'God and the Church protect me. I'm a monk who has been afflicted. You cannot kill me,' the leper grunted, wiping his hands along the front of the gates. A woman screamed, 'Look, he is alive, but his skin is rotting, look at the gate!' The crowd moved further back in alarm.

Chatillon could not see, but he presumed the leper was in the last stages and had left a trail of blood and pus on the gates. He heard the leper groan with a thump as he dropped to the ground in front of the gates, and it brought a smile to his face, for he realised who it was.

Suddenly, he heard the sound of running steps behind him and felt some relief as he turned and saw that his men had arrived and, more importantly, two of Dion's archers. Within moments, they had stacked crates and barrels and were up on the walls on either side of the gates, bows drawn. They let several arrows fly over the heads of the crowd, as Chatillon suggested. The arrows hit the wooden doors and shutters behind the mob with a satisfying thwack that made many run in alarm. In no time at all, the crowd were dispersing. Most were unprepared to risk their lives when easier prey could be found elsewhere. The fat merchant was one of the last, shaking his fist at the gates as he left.

Chatillon descended the ladder and found Jacob and his family. 'They have gone for now. Edvard has just given the performance of a lifetime out there as a leper. I imagine he'll stay out there until the Duke's men arrive, but I think several buckets of water will be needed to clean him up,' laughed Chatillon.

They remained in Jacob's house for the night, leaving at

dawn to return to the castle for their horses, as they were to meet Henry at an inn on the northern outskirts of the city. The consequences of the Archbishop's speech could be seen everywhere in the Jewish quarter. Bodies of men, women and children lay slaughtered in the streets. Houses had been looted and destroyed. They were told that over a hundred had been driven into the synagogue. The children were snatched for conversion to Christianity, and the rest were slaughtered in a frenzy of killing.

Chatillon had never seen Edvard so shocked. He was as white as a shroud by the time they reached the castle, and even his men, hardened warriors, were silent and grim-faced.

'There is nothing Christian or holy about this so-called crusade, this War of the Cross if they can murder as many unarmed innocents as this,' Edvard muttered, as they turned away from the horror on the streets behind them to head to the stables in the castle.

10

Chapter Nine

Finian watched the big Flemish Blue stallion run along the fences of the paddock. For a large, heavy horse, he was light on his feet, his mane flying, his tail raised in the air as he assessed his surroundings and gave loud whinnies to the mares he could smell in the distance.

'You may need a bigger, stronger fence,' laughed Padraig, watching as the young stallion stopped and gazed at the horses in the distance while stamping his foot. 'How old is he?'

'We were told he was four, and we have no reason to doubt that, looking at his build and teeth,' answered Finian.

'Has he been backed?'

'They tell me so, but apparently, he is still a very lively ride.' Finian grinned at the prospect.

'You will need to start his training now and keep it up every day, or he will become dominant and develop those habits you don't want in a warhorse.'

'Are you going to help me with that, Padraig, or is it that you're leaving for Ireland soon?'

'I have had news that my parents are dead, and my younger

brother is running the family lands and business. He now knows I am alive and may return. I cannot imagine that he would have been pleased with the news. The prodigal older brother returns from the dead to steal the inheritance that he thought was his!'

Finian laughed. 'Ah, families, sometimes they can be the first to stab you in the back.'

'Speaking from experience?' asked Padraig. Finian did not answer for some time. He then decided to tell Padraig what had happened with his cousin and the murder of his family in Ireland.

'So you see, Padraig, I have no desire to go back over there, and I'll repeat what I said just after you arrived. You're welcome here for as long as you wish.'

Padraig stared into his cousin's sad eyes and thought of what he had just heard. Finian's generosity of spirit almost overwhelmed him, and for the first time, he felt regret for his chosen path. However, he was committed and could not pull out without losing so much. He shifted his gaze back to the stallion, which was showing interest in them for the first time.

'Thank you, Finian, but I'll only stay for a year until next spring when I will return home to Ireland. And, of course, I will finish the building.'

Finian smiled, pleased by the decision. 'However, that invitation does not extend to Pierre. I'm afraid we cannot have him here for much longer. He terrified little Annecy, and I dread what Chatillon would have done had he been here!'

Padraig shook his head, expressing his exasperation with the young man. 'I have warned him again and again, Finian. He is young, foolish and still raging at the death of his brother, Roget. I have decided that he will come to Paris with me at the end of the week. He has family there, and he will not return.'

Finian paused and turned his eyes to his young stallion, pawing the ground in impatience. 'Alright, I agree, Padraig, but he must be gone by Saturday at the latest.' Padraig thanked him for his forbearance and strode off to threaten and warn Pierre again.

Finian made his way up to the Great Hall, where Isabella was busy, but he could also see she was buoyant. He mentioned that Pierre was to leave by the weekend, but she impatiently brushed it aside as a message had arrived.

'Chatillon and Edvard will be home on Thursday; his business will be concluded today, and they will set off immediately.' Her smile was infectious, and quite honestly, he was also looking forward to their return. There was no doubt that the chateau changed, and spirits were lifted when Chatillon was at home.

After hearing the news, Ahmed took a few moments in the garden to sit in the sunshine. He was also looking forward to their return, for he had news that he wished to share with Chatillon. Things were not at all as they seemed with Padraig and his friends.

The Steward headed into the kitchens to warn the cook that the master was returning. He knew that his wife, who now held the grand title of Madam Chambord, had been at the chateau since she was a young girl and had a soft spot for Lord Chatillon since those early days when he used to flirt with all the female staff. She would begin to make his favourite dishes for his return.

However, she was nowhere in sight. One of the maids said there was trouble with young Cecily, and she was talking to her in the bakehouse. He made his way outside and could hear the raised voices, and sobbing, as his wife scolded the girl. Opening the door, he was surprised to see Cecily on her knees in tears while Madame Lacy had her hand raised to slap her again.

'What's amiss?' he asked, for it was rare for her to chastise the maids, especially this one, given who she was.

'This foolish girl has been making the beast with two backs with that villain, Pierre, almost every night. She says he loves her and will marry her, and she is stupid enough to believe him. However, she is now four months gone; I found her being sick in the herb garden. He has had at least three of the other girls as well. Even the milking maid was in tears the other day after he forced her into the stable and took her on the hay.' At this, Cecily sobbed even louder and wrung her hands in despair.

'I will have to tell the mistress; she is in a good mood and may listen to reason, but you will likely be called into the hall to confront him.'

Cecily blanched at that, for when she was dismissed, and her father found out, he would be angry and ashamed of her.

Madame Chambord felt a twinge of sympathy at that point, for as a maid here herself, she remembered Cecily's grandmother, Rosie, falling in love in the same way with a handsome young man, which had not ended well. She had also been dismissed but had died in childbirth. Fortunately, Cecily's mother, Maria, had survived. She reached down and took the girl by the arm to pull her up, but Cecily flinched and cried out in pain.

'Have you beaten her?' asked her husband in concern. His wife shook her head while he bent and put his hands under her armpits to raise her to her feet. It was cold outside, so Cecily wore a heavy overgown with long sleeves. The cook raised her arm and let the sleeve fall back, and the girl's arm was badly bruised with what looked like rope burns around her wrists. She told her husband to leave and lifted the gown over the young girl's head. Her thin body was black and blue with bite marks in several places.

'Is he an animal that he does this to you?' she asked softly in concern. Cecily could not meet her eyes.

'He is so passionate that he gets carried away, but Pierre loves me. I know he loves me,' she whispered, her voice breaking in embarrassment and shame.

'No one who loves you could do this to you,' she said, pulling the girl's gown down over her head.

'Come, we will ask him what he is about!' she snapped, taking the girl's hand and pulling her along behind her.

They found Pierre shaping stones for Padraig. He regarded the big figure of the housekeeper bearing down on him with a wary eye as he could see Cecily being pulled along in her wake. Pierre straightened up. Padraig was on the ladder above, putting the finishing touches on a collapsed wall, almost rebuilt.

'Do you know that young Cecily here is carrying your child?' she demanded of him.

Pierre rubbed his hands together to brush off the stone dust while he regarded this angry woman with a raised eyebrow.

He gave a half smile and shrugged. 'How do you know it is mine? I know she has been taken by several men here,' he said casually.

The cook narrowed her eyes. 'Cecily is a good girl; she would never do that. You've taken advantage of her innocence; she was a virgin, and now you shall marry her.' Pierre laughed, which was too much for the housekeeper who rained abuse down on him. Hearing the uproar below, Padraig sighed and, reluctantly placing his trowel on the top stone, descended the ladder.

'What's all this?' he asked, but seeing a tear-stained young Cecily, he could guess.

'The little whore is carrying someone's bastard, and they're trying to pin it on me! We all know she has been with half of the stable hands. Ask her!' said Pierre to Madame Chambord and Padraig while stepping back and folding his arms.

Padraig held his hands wide open to the cook, in supplication to her, to ask the question of Cecily. After all, she was in charge of the servants in the kitchen.

She turned to the girl, 'Have you lain with other men, Cecily?' she whispered, never for a second believing it was true.

Cecily stared at the ground, but she nodded. Madame Lacey felt the wind go out of her sails. If the girl had lain with other men, no one would marry her, and the mistress would immediately dismiss her. She raised her eyes to Pierre, for she was not finished with him yet. 'That may be true, but none of them has beaten and marked her as you have, you cruel bastard.' With that, she turned on her heel and, waving Cecily ahead of her, headed back to her kitchens.

Just outside the door, she stopped and faced the dark-eyed young Cecily. 'I'm shocked to the core. I never expected this of you, and I don't know how you will face the mistress or your parents when she sends you back. Why did you do this, girl? The other men as well? You had a good position here. You are bright and willing and could have gone far.'

The tears ran unchecked down the girl's cheeks as she

stumbled over her words. 'Only one man and Pierre forced me to do it. He paid one of the other men because he liked to sit drinking and watch him take me. I told the man no, and that excited Pierre more. Pierre said he would leave me if I did not do as he said, and I can't help myself because I love him. But I know the child was Pierre's because I was already with child when he made me do this. I told him that,' she said in an almost apologetic whisper.

Madame Chambord found that she was so angry she could hardly speak. She would take this to Mistress Dion tomorrow, and she would know what to do. He had taken advantage of a naïve and innocent girl and used her abominably.

'Go to your bed and stay there. I will talk to the Steward, but he will have to tell the mistress either tonight or tomorrow morning, so expect to be summoned.'

Madame Chambord stood there outside the kitchen door for some time. Of all the girls in the house, Pierre had to pick this one. If her parentage came out, she knew that Lord Chatillon would slit his throat; knowing the master, he might do so anyway for impregnating one of his staff.

Cecily wearily climbed the old staircase to the room she shared with the other maids. No one came near her until late that night, when the other girls dropped exhausted into their beds. In the early hours, she heard a spatter of stones on the shutter and, barefoot, tiptoed across the rough boards. She knew who it would be, for this was how he had called her out on several nights.

'Come, we are leaving tonight. We are going to my home in Paris. I told you I would keep my promise, Cecily,' he said in a loud whisper.

Joy filled her heart, and she quickly and quietly bundled

her few belongings into a cloth bag and ran silently down the stairs and into his arms. Pierre kissed her and then put his finger to his lips, as they did not want to alarm the dogs or the guards at the main gate. He led her softly along the high stone walls to a small bolted postern gate, which was never guarded, and, pulling it closed behind him, he led her north into the woods and towards the city. He smiled as he pulled her into the deeper brushwood and onto the path to the river. Padraig had told him to sort it out before Chatillon returned, which is what he was about to do.

When Edvard and Chatillon arrived at the inn on the outskirts of Rouen, Henry Beauclerc was already there. It was a bright spring morning, but the mist still lay in the fields close to the river, and a chill breeze blew from the east. Henry had ordered warm mulled breakfast ale for them, and they joined him at a table near the recently lit fire. The innkeeper was apologetic, as he had been unprepared for such notable guests this early in the morning. He bustled around, cleaning tables and adding logs to the fire until Edvard shooed him out of the room.

'Tell me, Henry. You've spent many of your formative years here in this city. Why are the citizens of Rouen so keen on slaughtering their neighbours?' asked Chatillon, peeling off his gloves and throwing them down onto the empty stool beside him.

Henry sighed. 'I have thought long and hard on this, Chatillon, while studying other civilisations such as the Greeks, their city-states and the people of Rome who would turn on each other at the drop of a hat. It comes down to our basic instincts when we obliterate our Christian values or chivalry. We may appear to be God-fearing on the surface, but greed, envy, jealousy and avarice often produce a stronger destructive and vengeful drive.'

'And this time, it was the Jewish quarter; innocent people, women, and their children bore the brunt of it,' said Edvard, shaking his head.

'Are you surprised, Edvard, after our friend the Archbishop's speech? I know William Bonne-Ame had his own agenda when he incited the congregation to riot and kill the heathens and unbelievers. My source tells me he is hoping for a Cardinal's red robe,' said Henry watching for a reaction from Chatillon.

Not a muscle moved in the Papal Envoy's face as he raised the tankard to his lips and drank. He placed it carefully back on the table before raising his eyes to Henry. 'I think perhaps you may be right about his ambition, but encouraging the slaughter of over five hundred innocents in the name of a Holy War isn't the way to achieve that. In fact, I intend to ensure that it never happens.'

'You know, this is all about money, Chatillon. We now have thousands of knights across Europe trying to raise funds for this crusade. As you both know, it is against the laws of church and land for any Christian to become a usurer or money lender. Therefore, this role has traditionally fallen to the Jewish merchants. They are visibly prosperous people in our cities and towns. Many of these knights are already in hock to these people, so we get the vices and inequities, such as envy and greed. After all, a dead Jewish merchant with a slaughtered family cannot call in a loan. As for the common tradespeople of the town, we have the usual ignorance, intolerance, fear, and of course, opportunism for plunder in the houses of these rich Jewish families.'

Chatillon was impressed by the young man's discourse. It appeared that he was a thinker and philosopher, again placing him apart from his brothers, Robert and William Rufus.

'So Henry, you have called on us. You must have a reason, and so we came.'

Henry inclined his head in thanks. 'Last time we spoke, you mentioned possible support from the Holy See. As you know, my foolish brother, Robert, is about to ride off on this crusade while my more cunning brother, William, stays at home. He is also refusing to let his senior lords take part. He is keeping them close, like hunting dogs to heel. Robert will hand Normandy to William, on a platter, in return for a very large loan. William is planning to travel to Normandy with the gold as we speak. Neither of my brothers is married, so we have no legitimate heirs to either seat of power, and there is no doubt that Robert is riding into danger.' He paused and took a long draft of ale before wiping his mouth with the back of his hand, and then he continued....

'I have consolidated my position with William Rufus, but once he has Normandy, he has no further use for me. I intend to retire to my fortress at Domfront and stay there until Robert returns—that is, *if* he returns. However, in the meantime, I am asking for the support of the Holy See, the support that the Pope once offered me. I want Pope Urban to accept me as the legitimate heir to these lands.'

Chatillon blinked. This was not exactly what he had expected from Henry Beauclerc. He had expected a request for funds to hold Domfront and the lands in the Cotentin, but this plan was far more ambitious. He banged on the table to summon the landlord for more drinks to give him time to think.

'Henry, I have pointed out to Duke Robert the dangers of handing Normandy to William Rufus, but he truly wants to believe that his brother will keep his word. All of Robert's thoughts and focus are now on this crusade and the successful seizure of Jerusalem. He is gathering thousands here before they ride for the rendezvous in Le Puy in June. He has closed his mind as to what may happen here in Normandy. However, I will put your plea to the Pope. He sees a lot in you that he likes and respects, Henry, which will be in your favour, but none of us knows what fate has in store for these crusades. Therefore, it will be a waiting game.'

Henry smiled, inclining his head in acceptance; he was pleased with how the conversation had gone. No matter what happened, he intended to have both Normandy and England one way or another. He would be the picture of patience for the next year or so while he built up his resources and gathered allies.

Chatillon bade adieu and rode east towards their estate outside of Paris. They were heading home. They had ridden in near silence for the first few hours as Chatillon mulled over the events, and conversations, of the last eventful few days. The ratification of Pope Urban's decrees, the disturbing slaughter in Rouen and finally, the ambitious plans of Henry Beauclerc. Chatillon had not been deceived in the slightest by Henry's concern for Robert. He could only imagine the anger, the fury that Henry had felt when he heard his brother was signing Normandy over to William Rufus.

He pulled up at a stream for a while, as he needed to piss

while Edvard watered the horses. He watched the fast-flowing water for a while and then looked across at Edvard, who was leaning against a tree.

'Those two older brothers may not realise it, but they now have a very dangerous and determined adversary, and enemy, in their younger brother.'

Edvard nodded. 'I was thinking the same—especially if Duke Robert does not return from Jerusalem, for then we might be embroiled in another fraternal war. That will not please Finian as he came close to losing his life in the last one.'

Both men laughed, and it lightened the mood slightly.

'Come, Edvard, let us push the pace. I'm suddenly impatient to hold my wife in my arms,' added Chatillon as he turned and galloped towards home.

11

Chapter Ten

Isabella cried out with delight and relief when Chatillon, Edvard and their men clattered into the cobbled yard half a day before they were expected. She realised that they must have ridden out before dawn that morning. Chatillon had hardly dismounted from his horse before Isabella was in his arms, her head nestled under his chin. He held her tight and then raised her face to kiss her. He was surprised to see tears in her eyes, as Isabella was so strong.

'What is it, my love?' he murmured, kissing her eyelids.

'It is nothing, Piers. I've just missed you so much this time. Each night I have stretched my hand out in the bed and wished you were there.' She tucked her head back under his chin and still clung to him. Looking across at Finian, who stood waiting with Dion on the steps, Chatillon raised a questioning eyebrow, but Finian just shrugged. Dion beside him was not as complacent. Her pregnancy was now clearly showing, but Piers could see from her eyes that she was also unsettled.

He took Isabella's hand and walked towards the steps, as a flying bundle of energy hit him and wrapped her arms around his thighs.

'Papa, Papa, I'm so pleased you're home,' said Annecy, in a plaintive voice he had never heard from her before. He picked her up and carried her into the Great Hall.

'I must go away more often if everyone misses me this much and is so demonstrative on my return. And what of you, Finian? Have you missed me as well?' he asked with a smile.

Isabella laughed aloud at the joke; part of it was a relief to have him back to rest her fears. He was always calm and measured in his approach to problems, but lethal in his response to threats. She could not explain why but Isabella felt a threat still hung over them. Chatillon kissed the top of Annecy's head, and putting her down, he promised to find her later, but now he needed to talk to Finian. The child went with some reluctance with her mother, who arranged food for the men, whom she knew would be closeted in the business room for at least an hour.

The one thing that Chatillon had learnt from his previous lover, Bianca, was that you should never deny yourself comfort, and so his business room was designed for both. A large table was placed under the south-facing window, which overlooked the kitchen garden. Solid oak shelves completely covered one wall laden with scrolls and documents. Chests of various sizes were stacked on either side of the door, many with locks. However, on the other wall and around the fireplace were several colourful tapestries, some of them made by his mother. In front of the fire were two comfortable chairs with carved arms.

Edvard closed the door as Piers and Finian settled into the chairs; he pulled up a stool and joined them. Piers quickly brought Finian up to speed on the happenings in Rouen. Finian was shocked to the core by the slaughter they described.

'Neighbour against neighbour, just like last time. Did they learn nothing from that?' he asked in exasperation.

Chatillon shrugged. 'To give the people their due, although some of the burghers and merchants were out to settle scores, three-quarters of the attackers were from outside the city. Crusading knights and their uncontrolled retainers were whipped into a frenzy by the Archbishop's speech. However, that was not the only shock. Duke Robert intends to sign Normandy over to his brother, William Rufus, while he is away on the crusades.'

Finian blinked twice, and his mouth dropped slightly open in disbelief. 'So all your hard work and all of our efforts to protect Normandy, all that death and destruction were in vain,' he said bitterly.

Chatillon shrugged. 'This is the way of kings and princes, Finian; they're fickle. We do our best to move them in the right direction, but sometimes a strong wind can blow everything astray. The irony is that my uncle, Pope Urban, has whipped up this wind of change that is handing William Rufus the Dukedom of Normandy.'

'So half of Europe seems to be signing up for this crusade. How will that affect the balance of power, Piers?'

'Well, Finian, the clever ones, and the opportunists are resisting the call. King William Rufus refuses to go, as does King Philip of France, who we know has designs on absorbing Normandy into France. The Holy Roman Emperor, Henry VI, will not leave Frankfurt, although many of his knights and nobles are to go. I have been summoned to ride as Papal Envoy with Duke Robert's crusade from Le Puy to Lucca in northern

Italy, where the Pope will meet the crusaders and travel with them to Rome. I have not broken this to Isabella yet, as I could be away for nearly six months. She seems unnaturally unsettled by my absence of only a few weeks, so what has happened here, Finian?'

At that moment, Jean, the Steward and several servants arrived with platters of fresh bread, roast meats and cheese, which they laid on the table. This interruption gave Finian the time he needed to find the right words.

'On the whole, everything is well on the estate. The new stallion has arrived and is every bit as good as we hoped,' he said, grinning as they helped themselves to food. However, Chatillon was not one to be sidetracked.

'So what has unsettled both my wife and yours?' he asked, pinning Finian with that dark stare that made many men quail.

'We've had several problems with Pierre, the young man whose brother you beheaded, Piers. He began a flirtation with a serving girl who then claimed she was carrying his child; he said it could be one of a dozen men and denied it was his. The black-haired young girl, Cecily—you may remember her—was distraught and fled; no one has seen her since. Her father appeared this morning and said she had not arrived home; apparently, the cook had sent a message saying she was being dismissed. There was also an incident in the stables. Pierre says he tripped over one of the kittens. Annecy, who was there, says he kicked it across the stables and broke its neck. She was very upset, but Isabella dealt with that very well. She terrified him. She frightened me just telling me what she did to him.'

Chatillon smiled at the thought of an angry Isabella exacting revenge, but the smile did not last as Finian continued. 'I have talked to Padraig, who says Pierre is still consumed with an angry grief, so he is leaving for Paris in a few days, taking Pierre with him, and the young man will not return.'

To Finian's surprise, Chatillon said nothing as he lifted another slice of ham onto his plate. In fact, he was mulling over Finian's words, but he decided he did not want to undermine or be seen to question Finian's authority on this as the Irish warrior was often left here in charge when he was away. Also, the man Pierre was leaving in a few days.

The young man in question was still working with Padraig on rebuilding the south end of the old hall. Rollo was helping them as a labourer, cleaning, shaping and taking stones up to the two men above. The following day, the roof would be repaired, and it would be finished. They had turned a semi-ruin into a large waterproof serviceable building. The original fireplace was still intact, so it would be ideal when equipped as the new barrack block.

At the top of the ladder, Padraig watched Chatillon's arrival with apprehension. He knew that Pierre had gone too far, and he expected Chatillon to come and throw Pierre off the estate immediately. However, several hours passed as they continued their work, and nothing happened. Padraig could only think that he had Finian to thank for that.

In fact, Chatillon's mind was occupied with a far more exciting train of thought. Leaving Edvard and Finian to talk, he headed up to the solar, where he found Isabella and Dion repairing linen. He bowed his head to Dion; she was such a pretty little thing, he thought, as she smiled and he kissed her hand. Her skin positively glowed with her pregnancy. She had made Finian very happy, which was important to him. He straightened and strode over to Isabella, lifting the mending from her lap; he dumped it unceremoniously on the floor and pulled her up into his arms.

'Come, you've far more important things to do,' he said, taking her hand and pulling her out of the room and towards their bedchamber.

'Piers, the children!' she murmured as he pulled her through the door and whirled her around to face him. He shook his head at her words, peeled off his tunic, and unlaced his chausses before moving behind her to bar the door.

'Now forget everyone else. I want all of your attention. You tell me you've missed me, so show me how much!' he said, his thin linen braies hanging low on his hips. The soft winter light from the window and the flickering firelight behind him back-lit his muscled torso. She knew he was fitter than men that were half his age. Her eyes swept down from his broad shoulders across his chest, following the almost black hair down to his groin, and she realised it had been too long since they had stood and admired each other's naked bodies.

Isabella giggled, for this reminded her of those first years when they had both been insatiable, unable to keep their hands off each other. However, he did not smile back at her; instead, he placed his hands on his hips.

'Are you going to take that overgown off, or do I rip it off you?' he said in a deadly serious voice.

She met his gaze with amusement and a small laugh as she stepped forward to place her hands on his chest.

'Too long, I'm not minded to wait, Isabella; I intend to have you now, and I expect obedience from my wife, not laughter at my requests.'

Isabella's large brown eyes widened. Her mouth dropped open, for his black eyes stared at her with an exciting and unnerving intensity. With Chatillon, even after so many years, she never knew if he was serious or playful. Suddenly he took hold of the neck of the soft linen gown and ripped it apart.

'Now take it off and get onto my bed,' he said, his expression never changing. Naked, she clambered quickly onto the fur coverlet and watched him as he untied his braies and, fully aroused, he kicked them away and strode purposefully towards the bed. He pushed her shoulders firmly back and, pulling her legs apart, guided himself in and plunged deep inside her. By now, her anticipation had heightened her excitement. Piers could be frightening and dominant like this, but God's blood, he was exciting, she thought as she arched her hips to meet his deep thrusts. His lips and teeth descended onto her breasts, and she gave in to a wave of pleasure as she climaxed. He followed shortly afterwards, and they lay entwined—neither of them wanting to move, enjoying the warmth, the closeness and intimacy.

Finally, he pushed himself up on one elbow and looked down at her. Still unsmiling, he kissed her.

'You may be pulled in many ways by your responsibilities as a mother and as Chatelaine of my houses, Isabella, but always remember that, first and foremost, you're mine. When I want you, then you will be here, ready and waiting, will you not, Isabella?' he said, grinning wickedly before he kissed her deeply.

She ran her hands through his dark shoulder-length hair as he dropped his head onto her shoulder. She loved this man so much that she would always be there for him. In minutes, he was asleep, but she stayed still beside him, as she knew he would be tired after two days of hard riding to get home. As their bodies cooled, she gently pulled the fur covers over them, ignoring several light knocks on the door.

It was dusk when Piers stirred and found Isabella sleeping beside him. He stroked her cheek, thinking she was just as beautiful now as she was nine years ago when he first laid eyes on her. He kissed her eyes, and she woke and stretched, then realised how late it was.

'Come, Piers, we must get dressed, for the boys will be impatient to tell you what they have been doing,' she said, swinging her legs out of bed. She reached for her gown and laughed as she remembered what he had done. He came behind her, pressing his body against hers. Cupping her large breasts, he kissed and bit her gently on the nape of her neck.

'I will buy you a dozen more dresses, Isabella, and I promise I'll rip a few off you again when the desire for you takes me.' She could feel him hardening against her again, so laughing, she quickly moved away as she knew he would take her again and they would never get downstairs.

A short time later, they entered the solar to the grins of their friends. The children raced to Piers, all talking at once and clamouring for his attention. Isabella made them stand quietly and wait until their father was seated. Gabriel told his father he could now play half a dozen new tunes on the citole and immediately began to play. They all applauded. Gironde told his father that Finian had taught him to jump fences higher than himself on his new horse, and he had only fallen off twice.

Meanwhile, Annecy came and sat on his knee and babbled happily about the animals on the estate. An early set of lambs had been born, and she wanted him to come and see them tomorrow. He determined to ask Edvard to get her a puppy more her size than the big dyerhounds and wolf hounds that graced the floor, in front of the fire, in the Great Hall each night. He was sure that one of his tenant knights had spaniels.

They moved down into the Great Hall, which was far busier tonight with the return of Chatillon's retainers. Although he was Finian's cousin, Padraig, who had never been into the solar, joined them on the dais at a side table. Pierre and Rollo sat with the men at one of the long trestle tables.

Pierre was drinking heavily and still dicing and laughing loudly when the children and women went to bed. Padraig watched him. They only had two days to go before they left for Paris. He looked away to answer a question, and when he looked back, Pierre was gone. He had either gone for a piss or headed off to bed; hoping it was the latter, Padraig relaxed. There was far too much at stake here to let him off a short leash; he even thought about leaving a day early to get him out of the way now that Chatillon was back.

Pierre had gone to piss, but he walked on the path outside the hall to come in by the kitchen door. If he were lucky, only the young serving girls would be there, and he was determined to swive one of them tonight. However, his luck was not in as Jean, the Steward, and his wife, sat at the huge wooden table having their meal. He nodded at them, but he was met with stony glares, so he made his way along the long stone corridor back to the hall. A woman approached him as he turned to come out in a second corridor behind the large solid wooden screen that hid the servant's doors. Her hands were full of empty platters. He laughed playfully and cornered her, as she tried to get past him, shepherding her back along the corridor towards the steps that led down to the buttery. This was where the butts of ale and wine were kept in a long stone cellar, and he intended to pull her in there and take her. It was only lit by one torch in the corridor behind the large wooden screen, and he was unsure who the woman was, slightly older with braided hair, but she was buxom enough.

The young woman teetered on the top step, trying to keep her balance and escape around him as his hands roughly squeezed her breasts. Then she fell backwards, dropping the platters, and he was on her within seconds, ignoring her cries that she had grazed her back and arms on the stone steps. He pushed the heavy door open, clamped one hand over her mouth, and dragged her inside the buttery. He moved on top of her forcing his knee between her legs while she thrashed beneath him. The more she struggled, the more it excited him.

Suddenly he was lifted by the back of his neck and flung unceremoniously across the floor into the wooden barrels. From the light cast by the wall sconce at the entrance, he saw it was Lazzo, Finian's captain. Pierre believed that this man had set out to humiliate him since he first arrived at Chatillon. 'What are you doing with my wife?' Lazzo yelled.

Hearing this, Pierre smiled. He knew she was older than the young serving girls were, but she was very attractive. It was a bonus if she was this oaf's wife.

'I was told that she is anyone's woman as soon as you turn your back or go away, so I was planning to plough a well-worn furrow,' said Pierre, baiting Lazzo while using the barrels to pull himself to his feet. Within seconds, the two men exchanged blows until the Steward arrived with Finian just as Pierre hit the barrels again.

'God's blood, Lazzo, I expected better of you!' spat Finian.

'He tried to rape my wife, Finian, and you would have done the same.'

Maria had managed to get up, but the marks and grazes on her arms were clear in the light from the Steward's torch.

Finian turned and glared at Pierre, who shouted at him aggressively, 'She is a whore! She goes with anyone, why not me? I am half the age of this old man she married, if they married at all,' he said, sneering at Lazzo, who lunged forward again until Finian stepped between them.

'I demand satisfaction, Finian; he needs to be punished. If you had not interrupted us, I would have killed him for what he has done and said,' shouted Lazzo, his face red with anger.

'I must speak to Chatillon, Lazzo. His house—his rules. He will decide if you can fight. You've made a serious mistake Pierre. We all know Marie, she is the Steward's daughter, and she loves Lazzo; she would never look at another man. Now get out of here before I decide to lay into you.'

Pierre realised that he had made a serious mistake and made for the outside doors. Lazzo pulled his sobbing wife into his arms to comfort her.

'I tell you, Finian, something is wrong with that man. He has a really nasty streak that is more than his recent grief. He will harm someone.'

The Steward agreed. He was furious that Pierre had attacked his daughter. 'He has forced himself on several of the maids who were too frightened of him to say no. We now know that young Cecily never made it home. I sent a few men with her father to search the woods, but they never found her.'

'He will be gone from here in a day or so. I will go and speak to Chatillon. Send the men out tomorrow to search for Cecily. Try the river. I remember seeing her walking down there sometimes,' said Finian heading back to the hall where he told them what had happened.

Padraig swore long and loudly. 'God's blood, that young man attracts trouble,' he muttered.

'Yes, but by his own actions,' snapped Finian, annoyed at the situation.

Chatillon said nothing at first, but he narrowed his eyes as he quickly scanned the remaining groups in the hall. 'Where is he now?'

'I sent him to bed,' said Finian.

Chatillon pushed his chair back, stood and strode down the hall. Padraig stood to follow him, fearing what Pierre would do or say if he was drunk. However, Finian put a hand on his arm and stayed him.

'Leave it; you will only make it worse. Chatillon will deal with him.'

Pierre and Rollo sat on an old bench placed beside the brazier. Glancing around the old building Chatillon was pleased with what they had achieved with the ruined building. The roof was nearly repaired, the crumbling end wall rebuilt, and a new door and wooden shutters were in place.

Pierre's face registered alarm when Chatillon entered, but the usual sneering truculence replaced it.

'You come to no doubt chastise me, I imagine,' he muttered.

'That isn't my job, Pierre. You're a grown man, and you make your own decisions, although your friend and mentor, Padraig, is very disappointed in you and the choices you make. You seem to throw our hospitality back in our faces repeatedly. They call you young, and you're in their group, but you're in your thirties now. That is not young, which means that you're naive and stupid to take risks which will end in your death.'

Pierre was thrown by this calm, measured reply from Chatillon, who pulled forward a stool to join them and then complimented them on the transformation of the old hall. Rollo, an easygoing man who enjoyed living and working on the

Chatillon estate, was pleased and thanked him. Silence descended for a few moments, the only sound being the burning logs settling in the brazier.

'I've decided to let you fight Lazzo tomorrow. He is in the right of this and demands satisfaction. However, this fight will not be to the death. It will purely be to when the first man yields. I hear that you now have far more skill now with a staff. Is that so?'

Pierre nodded but looked surprised.

'Well, then you will need it with Lazzo. No blades, just a staff apiece,' he said, standing to leave.

Pierre seemed to nod in acceptance, but Rollo saw his fists were tightly clenched, his knuckles white as he stood and glared at Chatillon.

'You killed my brother. You slaughtered Roget like a pig!' he spat.

'Yes, I did, and I feel no remorse for that. You had tracked and followed us for days, and we were seriously outnumbered. Your group came out of the woods after us, swords in hand, ready to attack. What did you expect us to do?'

Pierre did not meet his eyes, as he did not want to accept the truth, so he stared at the brazier.

'You didn't give him a chance. He was no swordsman, really.'

Chatillon snorted in disdain at the young man's naivete. 'What? A chance to kill us? No, I didn't. It was unfortunate, but it's now in the past. You let your emotions rule you, Pierre, like a spoilt child. You should be controlling them, or you're putting yourself and others in danger.' Without another word, he turned and left.

Rollo watched his young friend.

'You may not like it, but he is right, Pierre, and you know it, but you are happier believing that the world is against you.' So saying, he crawled into his blanket and curled up to sleep facing the wall.

Pierre sat for a while, letting the Papal Envoy's words rankle and circle in his mind. As far as he was concerned, nothing had changed. He still intended to cut Chatillon's throat, even though it was against Padraig's plan that no one would die here. He would just wait for the right moment and have his revenge.

12

Chapter Eleven

Almost everyone gathered in the pell yard the next morning to watch the fight. Benches had been placed against the far wall so the women and children could watch from a distance. One of Finian's men was making a brisk trade in bets, and to Chatillon's amusement, Gironde went to help him and count the coins. Chatillon felt a tug at his waist, and Annecy was there holding her arms up. He shook his head and, picking her up, explained that she could not stay there as it was too dangerous. He waved Gabriel over to take her away to her mother.

Pierre had stripped to the waist. The branded mark on his arm was clear to see, as were the scars on his back from his short time in the galleys. 'Look, Papa, he has one of those marks as well!' shouted Gabriel.

'He is a beast. I hope Lazzo kills him,' shouted Annecy, to Chatillon's surprise. The crowd had stilled just then, so her shout was heard by most. Pierre turned and stared sullenly at the small girl. Chatillon made a joke of it.

'You're turning out to be as bloodthirsty as your mother!

Now go with Gabriel.' He could see that Isabella and Dion had laughed at Annecy's outburst, but her words unsettled Chatillon. It was so out of character.

Moments later, both men stripped to the waist and faced each other, staff in hands, in the large pell yard. Lazzo was an older man in his late forties but was in good physical fighting condition. He had to be in his position as Finian's captain. He was also very tall with a long reach, which would give him an advantage over the younger, more agile man. Lazzo had also learned his lesson from a fight with Edvard long ago. Since then, he had trained with Edvard regularly and learnt every trick possible.

Chatillon strode over and placed himself between the two men. 'This is a fight about honour and satisfaction. Pierre has both attacked and impugned the honour of Lazzo's wife. This isn't a fight to the death, nor do I want either of you maimed if possible, so there will be no tearing with teeth or gouging of eyes. Rein in any of your wilder or more dangerous impulses if the red mist descends, or I'll stop the fight immediately. Do you both understand me?' He looked pointedly at Pierre. Both men nodded and began to circle each other warily.

Suddenly Lazzo lunged forward, and he swept Pierre's long legs from beneath him, ready to slam the staff into his opponent's midriff. Lazzo was surprised when Pierre rolled and sprang to his feet in a back flip that took him out of range. The twins applauded, they both wanted Lazzo to win, but that was an impressive move.

'He is very supple and fast. Will Lazzo be able to match that?' Isabella asked Dion in concern.

'Watching them, I've noticed that Lazzo is calmer; he has more patience and skill. He needs to wind Pierre up, so he becomes angry, for when the emotions take over, the skill often dissipates.'

Isabella blinked; Dion had been such a happy domestic wife, Isabella often forgot that she had led a band of famous archers, fighting in several skirmishes.

The men fought long and hard, matching stroke for stroke and delivering punishing blows to their opponent's torso. The thwack of the heavy wooden staff on flesh and bone made Ahmed flinch. He could just imagine the damage he may have to repair if this fight continued for much longer. He had shared some of his concerns about Padraig and the story of the escape, with Chatillon and Finian yesterday, but as he had no real evidence yet, they agreed that they had found Padraig's answers and explanations plausible. So Ahmed had sent a bird again to Tunis and Sicily for more information, but he knew it could take a month or more to get a reply.

Both men were slowing, even Pierre, who had danced away from Lazzo initially.

Lazzo was a big, broad-shouldered man with a lot of upper body muscle and strength, and the constant punishing blows he delivered were taking their toll on Pierre who blocked many of the blows, but his shoulders, arms and wrists were aching. He knew he had to do something soon. He would not suffer the ignominy of having this ageing mercenary defeat him.

Lazzo gave a grin. He saw that he was wearing Pierre down, so he began taunting him. 'I hear forcing women is the only way you can get them. You did that to Cecily, and even she ran away from you.' Pierre gritted his teeth in anger and rained a flurry of blows on Lazzo, who deflected them with ease.

'I am told that your brother was not a fighter, which is why he died so quickly—or was he a coward? Some say he dropped his sword in fear!'

Both Padraig and Finian flinched at those words, for they knew how on edge Pierre was about his brother's death. It was too much for Pierre, who suddenly launched himself feet first at Lazzo's knees to topple him. Finian had seen Chatillon take men out in a sword fight using a similar risky tactic. Lazzo fell heavily and awkwardly whilst his staff jarred on the ground and flew from his hand. Pierre was on him within seconds, his staff held against his throat. 'I have you now, Lazzo. Shall I stand on the staff and break your neck? That would look almost accidental,' he whispered.

Everyone was surprised at the delay, for the crowd expected him to yell at Lazzo to yield. Instead, Pierre reached back and pulled a long dagger from the concealed sheath in his knee boot.

Finian shouted a warning to Lazzo, who, with the pressure of the staff removed from his throat, managed to move slightly to the left as Pierre plunged the dagger downwards towards Lazzo's heart. It was plunged with such force that it went through Lazzo's shoulder and into the ground below, the hilt buried into Lazzo's flesh. The big mercenary let out a strangled scream as Pierre struggled to pull it out. Finally, he succeeded and raised the dagger again.

Everyone had initially stood shocked and frozen at the violent scene unfolding in front of them until Annecy gave a high-pitched scream, and Chatillon raced forward. Pierre found his wrist held in a deadly grip, and heard the snap of it breaking as Chatillon flung the young man up and slammed him on the ground. Chatillon placed his booted foot on Pierre's throat and drew his dagger as the young man choked and squirmed.

'You've used up your last chance Pierre,' he growled. Pierre closed his eyes. He knew Chatillon's reputation and fully expected to die, but instead, Chatillon slashed his face open from his eye down to his jaw.

'I could easily kill you, Pierre, and if Lazzo dies, then I still might, a slow, painful death one night in a dark alleyway in Paris. But for now, I have marked you with the well-known traitor's mark to show the world that you're a treacherous, cheating dog who does not deserve an easy death.'

He removed his boot and, picking up Pierre's dagger, stepped away to where Ahmed was staunching the bleeding on Lazzo. His wife Marie knelt beside him, sobbing.

Padraig and Finian walked over to Pierre, who was still coughing and gasping but had struggled to his knees. His left hand was held to the huge gash on his face, and the blood ran between his fingers; his right hand dangled, useless.

'Get him out of here, Padraig, now, this morning! You can have time to dress the wound and set his wrist but then go, and he never sets foot here again,' said Finian through clenched teeth. Padraig nodded and pulled the stumbling, shaken young man away. Once in the old hall, he padded and bound the wound, as best he could, with strips from an old tunic while Rollo packed Pierre's saddlebags for him. He then used old thin wooden lats to hold the wrist in place and bound them tightly with frayed rope.

Padraig was white with anger. 'That was not only a stupid thing to do, which could have got us all killed, but a dishonourable one, Pierre. Now let us go before Chatillon changes his mind and comes looking for you. That man has no soul; he will kill you without a backward glance. God help you if Lazzo dies. Let us hope that Ahmed can treat that wound and that the rot does not set in.'

Shortly afterwards, they rode across the bailey and out of the gates.

On the road, Pierre slowed, his eyes tear-filled with pain could make out the tower of the fortified chateau.

'Oh, I'll be back, and I *will* have my revenge,' he said softly, before turning and galloping after Padraig, his reins clutched in his left hand.

A week later, at noon, Padraig made his way through the narrow stinking streets of Paris to a small inn, which was tucked away in one of the less salubrious areas on the north bank of the river. This was one of the more dangerous areas of the city, but upon seeing the well-armed man with the dark-tanned, lived-in face striding purposefully down the street, the chancers let him be.

He reached the inn; the dark stained, faded sign swinging in the cold biting breeze off the river showed the words *Le Coq d'Or*—a highly dubious establishment but perfect for this rendezvous.

He stood for a while outside, glancing up and down the street. He had changed direction several times to ensure that he wasn't followed, for he knew Chatillon had a dozen informers in the city. Pierre's erratic and violent behaviour had made him even warier, and he knew that the damned Arab was still suspicious and asking questions.

Satisfied with what he saw, he entered the inn. The ceilings were low, resulting in a fug of smoke from the fire and the cheap tallow candles. The innkeeper approached him; the man was exceptionally thin, with an almost cadaverous pock-marked face. He bowed and waved him to follow him to the back, wending their way through tables and stools. It was also a bawdy house, and men pulled girls onto their knees and openly fondled them.

The innkeeper led him through a low door into what was once a long narrow storeroom but was now used as a private room. Padraig's lip curled in disgust at the smell, and he noticed several stained palliasses against the far wall. However, a fire had been lit, and a long table set against a dirty window. Several of his men sat around it, waiting for him.

'Bring me some decent wine—one that I wouldn't pour down the privy,' he demanded of the innkeeper. The man was being paid enough; it was the least he could do. Padraig clasped arms with his men, ignoring Pierre, who looked slightly better as his sister had neatly stitched and dressed the wound on his face, and an apothecary had reset his wrist bone.

Padraig realised they were missing one. 'Where is Bertrand?' he asked.

Some of the men shrugged.

'He has gone! He was restless at the end of the first week and then disappeared. We think he has gone north to look for his wife and children on the farm he owned near the coast.'

Padraig shook his head. 'That may not end well if she has married again. Sixteen years is a long time to be without a man when you've had no message to say that your husband is alive.'

Padraig sighed. He needed Bertrand. He was a large, reliable, and trustworthy man with a sensible calming influence on the group, and now, he had to find a replacement.

Pierre sat forward. 'So when do we go? The men here are ready, as they have had their fill of the backstreets of Paris. We all want to earn the gold we were promised and be on our way to get our lives back.'

'Oh, so you're their spokesman now that Bertrand is no longer here? Is that right, Pierre? At the moment, I would rather trust that cockroach,' he said, pointing to the insect that scurried under the candle bowl.

'We just need to know what's happening,' muttered Pierre with a wary glance, for Padraig, when angry, could be unpredictable.

'We will wait for our guest to arrive,' said Padraig, in a tone that brooked no disagreement. He folded his arms and sat silently while his men glanced nervously at Pierre, who was obviously out of favour.

Opposite the inn, a small, thin, birdlike man was dressed in beggar clothes. He had successfully trailed Padraig to this establishment, and now he sat in his stinking rags, calling for alms from passers-by. Suddenly a shadow was cast over him, and a small coin dropped into his cup. He looked up to see a tall, hawk-nosed man with deep-set, assessing eyes. His hood was up, and his mouth was covered, but there was no doubt of his ethnicity. Abdo, the beggar, thanked him in Arabic for his generosity, and the man nodded, before crossing to duck his head and enter the inn. He had two bodyguards with him, and one remained outside the inn. Abdo kept up his performance for some time before struggling to his feet and using the battered Y-shaped crutch to help him hobble and limp down the street.

Two streets later, he abandoned the crutch and trotted briskly to his premises, a tall narrow house in a small close, with a sign above the door that said Abdo was an apothecary.

Ahmed had trained Abdo, and he still often made potions for Ahmed and his clients. However, he was also one of their main informers on the streets of Paris. He wrote a quick note in code to Ahmed, telling him what had occurred at the inn. He had recognised the tall, dark Arab. The sharp nose and the deep-set eyes struck a chord, but he could not remember his name or where he was from. It would come to him. He handed it to the promising young man, his apprentice.

'Send it to Ahmed immediately. He is still at Chatillon, I believe.' The boy smiled, climbed the narrow steps to the next floor, and then took the ladder to the flat roof, where he tied the message to a pigeon's leg and sent it on its way.

Suddenly, there came a pounding on the door, just as the apprentice reappeared. 'Go, quickly, go across the rooves and hide,' whispered Abdo, as the frightened boy took no second telling.

Abdo went towards the door with foreboding as the loud banging continued. His fears were realised as he opened the door, and the large bodyguard, from outside the inn towered over him. Unfortunately, he had not rid himself of the beggar's rags but tried to bluff it out. 'Are you ill? Can I help you? Do you need a potion?' he enquired, his head on one side, a half smile on his face. The large, stocky Arab pushed his way past Abdo into the narrow corridor which led to the workshop.

'Tell me why a man who lives in a house like this, making expensive love philtres and potions, would dress as a beggar on the streets?' he asked, backing Abdo into a corner. The apothecary was usually quick-witted, but a knot of cold fear in his stomach seemed to stop all thought, and he found that his mouth was opening and closing. The bodyguard glanced around.

'Tell me, is there anyone else here?' he growled, walking to the narrow, steep staircase and looking upwards. Abdo shook his head, and the man smiled. He walked back towards Abdo, who knew what was coming and closed his eyes. In seconds, the man's hands reached out and snapped his neck. The small thin body of the apothecary dropped to the floor.

It was sometime later when the apprentice dared to come down. He had heard the crashing and bangs, and from a neighbour's roof, he had watched the large Arab leave and stride off down the narrow close. When he warily descended the steps, he found that the workroom had been destroyed. Smashed pots and glass vials of all shapes and sizes were strewn over the floor in liquid pools. Abdo's lifeless body lay under the broken table. The apprentice held his knuckles to his mouth in dismay. He had genuinely liked and cared for his employer, who had taught him so much over the last five years. He dropped onto a surviving stool and surveyed the damage. Looking down, he saw a thin blank strip of vellum lying at his feet. He knew what to do; he would send a message to Ahmed. He knew he would come. He did not know the code, so he wrote in Latin...

Please help me! They have murdered Abdo. I think they were Arabs.

Meanwhile, Padraig welcomed their guest at the inn, bowing deeply to him.

'Al Cazar, we are honoured that you've come to meet us in

Paris.'

Al Cazar removed his cloak, took the seat, looked around at the eager faces, and smiled. *Ah, the power of gold. Anyone could be bought*, he thought. His eyes lighted on Pierre.

'I see someone has gone to war already,' he said with a thin smile.

'The handiwork of our friend Piers de Chatillon,' said Padraig bitterly. He had told his men not to say a word unless they were questioned directly.

'I'll have my revenge on him. I swear I'll cut his throat while he sleeps,' spat Pierre, receiving a glare from Padraig.

Al Cazar raised an eyebrow and stared at Padraig. 'I thought you understood our agreement!' he snapped.

Padraig nodded. 'Take no account of Pierre. He's just an angry, thoughtless young man.'

Al Cazar leant forward and placed his hands flat on the table. 'Let me be clear—if a hair is harmed on Chatillon's head, there will be no gold, and I'll personally hunt each one of you down and gut you. Do you understand?'

The faces of the men around the table blanched, and they nodded, even Pierre, who nervously glanced at the large armed bodyguard with his back to the door.

'So, bring me up to date on our plans and what you've discovered,' he said, folding his arms and sitting back.

'I have ingratiated myself into the family, and I believe they have accepted and welcomed me. Others less so,' he said, indicating a morose Pierre. 'The only fly in the ointment is the Arab physician Ahmed, who seems highly suspicious of our story and asks countless questions.'

'Yes, I encountered one of his men outside who had followed you here, but he is being dealt with.'

Padraig raised an eyebrow in surprise, for he had not seen the tail, but he continued.

'What became apparent very quickly was that we could not carry out the plan while Chatillon was there; we would never succeed, and most of the men would be killed. However, he travels regularly on the Pope's business, and Finian has told me that he intends to join the Pope's crusade at Le Puy in June, to travel to Lucca, where they'll receive the Pope's blessing. This role will take him away for many months, quite a distance away in Italy. He will leave either Finian Ui Neill or Edvard behind, and we can easily deal with either of them.'

Al Cazar considered his words for some time. He took a mouthful of the wine offered and then spat it on the floor in disgust. Pierre laughed.

'Foul stuff isn't it.'

Al Cazar ignored him and sneered. 'So another holy war against Muslim peoples, this time against the Seljuk Turks, while we've spent years fighting King Alphonse and El Cid in Spain. However, this will be a good window of opportunity. You have done well, Padraig MacDomnall; just make sure the rest of the plan goes smoothly. I will arrange everything you need. A tenth of your gold will be delivered to your inn on the city's northern outskirts. The rest will be delivered when you succeed. I was certainly not risking bringing any of it to this hell hole,' he said, looking around in distaste.

At that moment, the second bodyguard appeared and inclined his head to show that his task had been accomplished. Al Cazar stood and put his thick hooded cloak back on, 'The Sheikh will be pleased, Padraig, and you will all be well rewarded.' With a swirl of his cloak, he and his bodyguards were gone.

A babble of excited conversation broke out at the table. Padraig raised his hand for silence, they quietened, but their grins remained.

'Rollo and I will return to the Chatillon village and estate today. I will be back to meet with Pierre for the final plans in June when Chatillon has left for Le Puy. I anticipate we will begin our plan in early September when he is far enough away. You will all remain on the outskirts of Paris. Yes, it is a waiting game, so be patient, keep your heads down, and find yourselves a nice clean woman to spend time with instead of throwing it away on whores and dying of the pox before you have time to enjoy the gold. I'm leaving another bag of coins with Pierre for your expenses.' This brought more laughter and grins.

Padraig stood and left, followed by Rollo, who tugged on his arm as they walked swiftly away from the inn and the dark, stinking streets of the city. They emerged by the bustling wharves and walked down towards the bridge, but Rollo was persistent and tugged on his sleeve again.

'Padraig, we're not going to kill the children, are we? I don't think I could do that. I like the family, I like working at Chatillon, and I'm seeing a woman in the village,' he said in a loud whisper.

Padraig stopped and, turning in frustration, took him by the shoulders. Rollo was a nice, gentle giant who found pleasure in simple things.

'Of course not, Rollo. What do you think we are, savages or animals? No, the boys will be taken, kidnapped and held for ransom. We hand them over to Al Cazar, and then our job is done, and we are on our way. We escape to a life of comfort with pockets full of gold.'

Rollo nodded in acceptance, but he was thinking when they walked out into one of the open squares where a bustling market was taking place.

'Will he kill them, Padraig? He seemed a ruthless and violent man.' Padraig pulled Rollo to one side, sighing in exasperation.

'No! those boys are far too valuable. If they get the ransom, they will go free. If not, they will no doubt go to the slave markets in Istanbul. Now be quiet. We must wait for the gold, pack and be gone before dusk.'

Rollo was quiet, but he was not happy. He was not naïve and had been enslaved for over twenty years. If the ransom were not paid, the lives of those children in the east would become a living hell. He could also imagine Chatillon's rage and revenge when he discovered they had been taken. They would need to use that gold to disappear, for he would hunt them down relentlessly, and no hole or cave would be deep enough to hide them.

Rollo shivered at the thought, but there was no escape for him; he was too deeply embroiled in the plan.

13

Chapter Twelve

May 1096 – London

Flambard smiled with satisfaction as he watched the last bags of gold being packed into the sixty-seven barrels. It had taken him almost six months of cajoling and threats to gather that much gold to be paid to Duke Robert for the Vifgage. Most of it had been extorted out of the abbeys and the nobles. He had to admit he initially had doubts about this undertaking, but King William Rufus had talked him around. They were literally buying Normandy in a bloodless move, with no more fighting and expensive battles. The King had successfully occupied Normandy, north of the River Seine. Now, he would get the rest of it without a sword being unsheathed. He was given the legal right to occupy the land until the huge loan was repaid.

The King walked into the long cellar as they were hammering the lid into place on the last barrel. 'Is it done?' he asked, looking at the barrels stacked high.

'Yes, Sire, we are only waiting for the weather to improve. We are sending it spread over five seaworthy vessels in case of a mishap. You realise that if Robert dies on this crusade, it is highly likely that you will never see a penny of it again. However, you will have the right to take full possession as the Duke of Normandy on his death.'

The King seated himself at the table. 'Any pilgrimage is a dangerous undertaking, Flambard. We know many who have set out for Jerusalem in the past and never returned, including my grandfather, Duke Robert I.'

'We will, of course, have prayers and devotions said in the churches and Abbeys of Normandy for your brother's safe return,' said Flambard with a sardonic smile.

William laughed and turned away before quipping back over his shoulder, 'Yes, of course, but not too many, I hope.' As he reached the door, a thought occurred to him, 'I've just heard that my treasonous uncle Odo, Bishop of Bayeux, is now going with them on this crusade.'

Flambard nodded. 'Yes, that was surprising news. He must be over sixty years by now, and again, it is doubtful that he will survive the journey.'

'He has long been a thorn in our side, Flambard. Even now, banished from England and serving Duke Robert, he rails against us, plotting and manipulating. He did everything he could to prevent Robert from signing the Vifgage. It would be very fortuitous for us if he didn't reach Jerusalem, for as a successful crusader who had stood in the Holy City, he would have even more influence if he returned!'

Flambard met the King's eyes and understood exactly what the King was saying. He nodded. William smiled and placed a hand on his shoulder.

'What would I do without you, Ranulf,' he said before turning and leaving while the men heaved the barrels of gold into place in the vast cellar behind them.

Flambard stood for some time, his mind turning over the possibilities of whom he would send to Rouen or Le Puy to arrange this assassination. When it came down to it, there was only one assassin he wanted, one man who would be discrete and professional, but it would take a deal of persuasion and a lot of gold for him to take it on, to make sure that Bishop Odo never returned to Normandy.

It was a warm June evening when the family gathered in the Great Hall for dinner. A commotion from the dozen or so dogs—including Annecy's new spaniel pup, who thought he was a wolfhound—heralded the arrival of a visitor. Moments later, Ahmed strolled in. He had been in Paris for a month or so, sorting out various affairs and visiting his own home to check all was well.

'Well met, Ahmed. Have you arrived to see me off to-morrow?' asked Chatillon with a grin, knowing Ahmed's disapproval of the crusade.

'Of course, my Lord, and I'm here for Lady Dion, whose child is due in a fortnight. Second children can be fickle and force their way out early, so I thought I would return.' He beamed around the table as he took his seat.

Everyone responded except for Padraig, who did not lift his head from his trencher. The last thing he needed was the meddlesome Arab back in their midst.

It was Friday and a fast day, so there was an assortment

of fish and cheese dishes. Madame Chambray had produced Chatillon's favourite dish of spiced sardines, but the tables were laden with everything from lamprey to trout from the river.

'You were called away very suddenly. Did you resolve your business in the city?' asked Isabella.

'Yes. Unfortunately, a friend of mine, Abdo—some of you knew him, a gentle soul I trained many years ago as an apothecary—has been murdered.'

Edvard shook his head, for he had met Abdo several times. 'The streets of Paris can be dangerous, and he was such a small, thin man, was he not?' he asked.

'Yes, he was, but he was not murdered on the streets. His apprentice tells me that it was Arabs who smashed their way into his workshop and killed him.'

Chatillon's ears pricked up, for he had noticed the tone of Ahmed's voice and the mention of Arabs. He would get Finian to dig further into this, for it was suspicious, and he had to leave at dawn.

Meanwhile, Ahmed, in a friendly voice, began to question Padraig on his time in Tunis, questions that only someone who had lived there could answer. At first, Padraig smiled and took it in good stead. However, Dion sat opposite and could see his fist clenching. Chatillon, Finian and Edvard were deep in conversation at the other end of the table and were not following. Padraig glanced at them and suddenly replied to Ahmed in Arabic.

'What is it, old man? Are you trying to catch me out? My name in Tunis was Al Dhakii, so when you send a bird to your spies, make sure you use that, for no one there knew me as Padraig.'

Dion could see that Ahmed was visibly taken aback until Padraig burst out laughing. 'I spent nearly five years learning to speak, write and read Arabic. It often shocks people but can prove very useful, and it also helped us to escape.'

Ahmed managed a weak smile while thinking his concerns about Padraig were probably justified. It had been a good answer, for he was indeed *The Clever One*, but Ahmed knew that he could still not act, as he had no evidence or justification yet. He needed more information from Tunis and Sicily. He was also aware that the questioning had put the man very much on his guard. He vowed to watch him like a hawk.

It was almost the longest day of the year and a beautiful warm, light summer evening. Ahmed was on the roof, standing beside the chicken coop, tying a message to the leg of an unusual white and pink dappled pigeon. It would wing its way to Marseille, and from there, another message would be sent on to Tunis to find out more about the man the Arabs called Al Dhakii, for Ahmed had seen the hard glitter of hate in the man's eyes before he hid it. Ahmed carried the bird to the tower's edge, gently stroking its head before launching it south. He rested his hands on the stone edging and gazed out over the fields and forests in the lovely June dusk light. The bird had barely gone a field's length when a large hawk took it down with a flurry of feathers.

Ahmed gripped the stone turret in alarm. He strained his eyes to try to see the hawk on the ground with its prey, but dusk was falling. He did not believe for a second that this was a coincidence—he had never seen a hawk here of that size before and he was convinced that Padraig was behind it. He determined to send another bird at dawn, and walk out to find the remains of the downed pigeon.

In the garden below, Isabella and Chatillon walked arm in arm along the paths she had created. Most of the large walled garden was given over to herbs and kitchen plants, but a few years before, rose arbours and flowers had become fashionable, and Isabella had planted several, which scrambled up over an arbour and climbed up the walls. His arm around Isabella's waist, Chatillon pulled her down onto a bench against the wall. The stones behind them were warm with the summer heat, and the heady perfume of the roses surrounded them. Isabella dropped her head onto his shoulder with a sigh.

Chatillon put a finger under her chin to raise her face to his and kissed her. 'Do not be sad, my love. The time will fly; before you know it, I'll be back for our Yuletide celebrations.'

'You will be away for so long, so many months, Piers. I will miss you, both by my side and in our bed. I'm hoping for another child, but you will be gone.'

Chatillon held her face in his hands. 'I have to go, my love, you know that. I am the Pope's official representative on this crusade until he meets us at Lucca.'

'Promise me that you will go no further than Lucca Do not go on to Rome with them, Piers. I cannot be without you for that long,' she implored him.

'I promise, Isabella. 'Let's go upstairs so I can bury myself deep inside you, for I, too, will miss your warm, soft body entwined with mine.'

She smiled up at him as he pulled her into his arms and led her upstairs, but her heart was heavy at the thought of so long without him, and she still had that feeling of foreboding she could not shake.

Ahmed spent some time searching the meadow in the early dawn light for the remains of the pigeon. He had sent another as soon as dawn broke, and it seemed to fly south without being intercepted. Maybe he was wrong, he thought, as he methodically made his way back and forth through the long flower-strewn grass. Ahmed noticed tracks in the dew-covered grass when he approached the meadow's far end. He followed them, and lo and behold, there was the partly eaten pigeon. As expected, the hawk had torn most of the breast and entrails out, but the carcass, wings and legs were intact. It was fortunate that a fox had not found it and carried it away for its cubs, for he saw at once that the message in its tiny metal tube was gone. He searched the ground around, should it have been dislodged, but there was no sign. Someone had removed it, hence the tracks. So it was as he suspected—his pigeon was brought down on purpose.

He headed back to the chateau in a thoughtful mood. He knew he could not just announce it, which would give it away too soon. He needed to think this through, and he needed Dion's and, more particularly, her men's skills.

When he reached the courtyard, he found Edvard and Chatillon mounted and ready to leave. Only Finian, Isabella and the twins were there to wave them off.

'May your God grant you both a safe journey and return you back to us,' said Ahmed bowing deeply.

Chatillon regarded the mangled body of the pigeon dangling from his hand and raised an eyebrow. 'Problems?'

'Nothing Dion and I cannot deal with,' laughed Ahmed whilst mimicking a bow and arrow.

Chatillon blew a kiss to his family, raised a fist in salute, and rode out of the large fortified gatehouse with Edvard and five of his men.

The family turned and went back inside, but Dion waited on the steps for Ahmed, who held up the bird's remains.

'Dion, we seem to have an unusually large hawk that has moved into the woods on the meadow's edge. Can your men deal with it?'

Dion laughed. 'Of course. They need the practice, and this pregnancy, will not prevent me from joining them, for I'm dying of boredom and waddling like a duck. It will relieve the tedium of waiting for this baby to arrive.'

Ahmed placed an affectionate hand on her arm and laughed before walking off to put the bird on the midden heap.

Watching him, Dion did not doubt for a second that there was more to this. A hawk of that size was not native to these woods. She knew he would tell her in his own time. Meanwhile, she would see to the children and collect her men.

Padraig watched Dion and her men walking towards the woods that afternoon and swore quietly under his breath. He had paid good money for a falconer to bring a large gerfalcon into the area. The man was billeted in the eastern woodland, and he prayed he had the sense to take his small terrier, his bird, and his belongings and run if he saw them coming.

Ahmed was sitting in the garden chatting with Isabella when Dion returned. Cormac and Annecy were racing up and down the many paths through the large walled kitchen garden. The twins were with Padraig, Finian and the horses, as usual. Isabella was surprised to see Dion arrayed in her archery attire this close to the birth but was curious when Dion dropped two pieces of leather into Ahmed's lap.

'Did you kill it?' the physician asked in a hopeful voice while fingering the soft leather.

'No, but we found evidence of a quick flight if you forgive the pun. Someone certainly left in a hurry, as the scattered campfire was still warm, and the grass was flattened where he had slept. On a branch, we found a leather tethering strap recently cut, and these were on the ground below.'

Ahmed nodded. He was not surprised.

'Would someone care to explain?' asked an exasperated Isabella.

Ahmed quietly sighed; he had not yet wished to alarm the two women.

'There has been a large hawk taking down the birds I have sent out. Having a naturally suspicious nature, I wondered if someone was purposefully trying to stop my messages from getting out. However, I had hoped it was just a coincidence and that a large hawk had suddenly moved into our territory.' He held up the small broken leather jess. 'Unfortunately, these prove that I was right. These are the accoutrements of a falconer camping out in our woods.'

Dion smirked with satisfaction. 'I've said all along that I did not trust him. He is the only one in Chatillon who would want to stop you from sending messages to Tunis.'

It took Isabella a few moments to realise what they meant. 'Padraig? Do you think he has done this? But why?'

'That is what we need to ask him,' said Dion, holding her hand out for the leather pieces.

'No! I do not think that is wise. I fear that he has a bigger purpose, and if we show our hand too soon, we will not find out what he is planning.'

Isabella agreed, although her mind was in a whirl. Did he mean any of them harm, or was he just protecting his position here?

'So we just wait?' spat Dion in disgust.

Ahmed nodded, although he could see her building up to a tirade against waiting, when suddenly she gasped in pain, and her hands dropped to her lower back.

Isabella jumped to her feet. 'Ahmed, help me to get her upstairs and then run and tell Finian that his son or daughter is eager to be born two weeks early.'

'It's a boy. You can tell by how it is lying and where the first birth pains are,' he said confidently.

Padraig, hawks and jesses were forgotten for the rest of that day as Fergus Ui Neill was born an hour later.

14

Chapter Thirteen

Chatillon had arrived in Rouen just in time to witness the handing over of the barrels of gold to Duke Robert and his senior nobles. He smiled as he thought of the queues of tradesmen, merchants and farmers stretching out of the gates. Many were there to sell Duke Robert goods, and many were there with promissory notes in their hands for goods already supplied. Word had spread that the gold had arrived.

Crossing the bailey had been chaotic to say the least. They were overwhelmed by the noise, the smells, and hundreds of animals, horses, mules, and oxen. Carts and foul-mouthed carters were everywhere, haggling over spare wheels and axles. At the same time, pigs and sheep were being slaughtered and placed in barrels of salted brine to go with them. Supplies such as sacks of grain, fodder and various victuals were piled high. Everything and anything that could possibly be needed on the crusade was being offered inside and outside the castle walls.

They rode towards the stables where at least four black-smiths were at work; the hissing of red-hot shoes and metal being cooled in cold water was deafening, as were the shouts of the clothiers and leather workers. They had all seen the barrels of gold delivered and were determined to earn some of it.

The next morning, Chatillon stood on the dais and watched the Vifgage being signed by King William Rufus and Duke Robert of Normandy. The senior nobles from both sides watched with interest, but Bishop Odo of Bayeux took an inordinately long time to check the document twice to ensure it was fair and legal. This infuriated the King. He felt it was a purposeful insult reminding him of the previous agreement he had reneged upon and implying a lack of trust. Ranulf Flambard rolled his eyes while assuring Odo, when he queried several points, that it was all above board.

Finally, it was signed, and the two brothers clasped arms while the nobles and their retainers in the hall cheered, banged on the tables and clashed swords against shields in approbation. It was done, and they would shortly be leaving on the long road to Jerusalem.

Two weeks later, the cavalcade left Rouen for the rendezvous in Le Puy. It took hours for the procession to leave the city, with over a thousand more waiting to join in the fields outside. Chatillon and Edvard were relieved that they had a place at the front. They were directly behind the senior leaders as the dust raised by nearly ten thousand pilgrims covered and choked those behind in the hot July weather and dusty roads. Experienced knights had not only already covered their own faces but also had covers placed on the noses and mouths of their horses, for the dust could fill their lungs far too quickly—they'd all witnessed a coughing horse collapse.

Chatillon found it difficult to imagine the numbers converging on Constantinople. Did Emperor Alexius realise what would be arriving at his capital? Piers knew from his uncle that there were four main streams of crusaders heading east. Duke Robert, Stephen De Blois, and Duke Alan of Brittany were classed as the northern French contingent. To the south, Raymond of Toulouse was leading another multitude, but they intended to cling to the coast and take the overland route. In the north, Godfrey of Bouillon would lead another huge contingent of Germans and Lothargarians, including his old arch-enemy Duke Welf of Bavaria, and they would take the far northern route coming down through Hungary. Finally, the southern Italian Normans would join them, led by the impressive figure of Bohemond of Taranto, who would strike fear into the heart of any Seljuk Turk.

The last horse was hardly out of the gates of Rouen before King William Rufus summoned Ranulf Flambard to the solar.

'I want proclamations in every city, town and large village. I want every knight, every abbot, every bishop to know that I am now ruling all of Normandy,' he declared. He looked down at the mess and debris left behind in the bailey below. 'I intend to stay here in Rouen until autumn, and we will ride to Caen, Bayeux and even to my father's home in Falaise. The people will see their king, Flambard, and make sure you arrange for largesse to be given or scattered to the crowds wherever we go. I will be a generous king—firm but fair. I intend to ensure they do not want their Duke to return.'

'What of your brother Henry, Sire? He is holed up in his fortress at Domfront and still styling himself as the Count of the Cotentin.'

William was silent for several moments before he turned and regarded his friend.

'Let us leave him be. We have an understanding with him at present. It is pointless stirring up a wasp's nest by poking at it. We have other matters to attend to, as I mean to strengthen the borders of the Vexin in the north. I wish to let King Philip of France see that I'm not just an absentee caretaker of Normandy. I intend to spend six months each year here. Summon my senior knights to the Great Hall—they may not be going on a crusade, but they can ride out and be seen to be protecting the borders with France and with Anjou.'

Flambard bowed and reached the door when William called him back. 'And Ranulf, I want you to find my father's royal regalia. I know it is here somewhere in Rouen or even in Caen. It might even be buried with him, but I want that crown. I seem to remember it being very recognisable. Let the nobles and people see that I am my father's son, and I am here by right.'

Flambard smiled as he descended the stairs. It seemed as if the acquisition of Normandy might be the making of the hedonistic William Rufus.

There was a point when Chatillon began to wonder if they would ever reach Le Puy. The journey would normally take four days at the most on horseback. Instead, it had taken them almost four and a half weeks. The problem lay in the fact that the crusade procession could only move as fast as the people could walk on foot, and there must be at least four thousand from all walks of life. When this was planned, no one had accounted for these numbers. A fever had gripped the population and inspired rich and poor alike to take the road to Jerusalem.

Reaching Jerusalem under the protection of Duke Robert and his knights was a draw, for even the lower orders understood that pilgrimage to Jerusalem was risky. The nobles around Duke Robert urged him to push ahead and let the people on foot make their own way, but he argued that *these were his people*—Christians, pilgrims from Normandy. Therefore, he was their shepherd, their protector, and he could not abandon them.

Then there were the hundreds of carts and wagons. These carts were important because they carried the crusade essentials of food, equipment, extra weapons, and hundreds of butts of ale and wine. The dry, rock-hard, rutted roads inflicted serious damage on wheels and axles. When a cart collapsed and broke, it often blocked the way for everyone else on tree-lined or rocky tracks, with no way to get around the obstacle. Repeatedly, Edvard told the knights to invest in packhorses, or mules, to carry their supplies, or it would take them well over a year to reach the Holy City. Some listened; many did not, so they limped on across the central massif, where the winding roads climbing to Le Puy became even narrower.

Chatillon decided he had suffered enough, and with Edvard and his men, they cantered ahead along the valley towards the famous pilgrim town. They paused to let the horses drink at a mountain stream and sat for a while regarding the town which climbed the hillside above them, while the men scooped water into their mouths and filled water bottles. Looking back, they could see in the distance the huge dust cloud that enveloped the thousands of following crusaders.

'We've been here before, have we not?' asked Edvard, who had dismounted and was wiping the thick dust from his face and neck with a cloth dampened in the stream.

'Yes, many years ago, returning from Avignon up the Rhone Valley. It has certainly grown in importance and size since then. It is an important Bishopric under Adhemar and is now the main gateway for the pilgrimage to Santiago De Compostella. This little town has always been an important meeting place for pilgrims; hence Pope Urban chose it as a meeting point for several strands heading south.'

Edvard, looking at the small town which surrounded and clung to a large pinnacle of rock, wondered where all these people would go.

'If the other crusading groups are as large as ours, surely it will be impossible for them to all meet here.'

Chatillon laughed. 'They will spread out down and across the valley. Bishop Adhemar will only call the leading nobles and bishops in for the blessing in the cathedral, while the senior clerics will spread out and deliver the blessing to the crowds. I believe the Bishop has at least forty priests here.'

'What is the building on top of the rock?' asked Edvard gazing upwards.

'Originally, it was the chapel of Saint Michel d'Aguilhe, but as you can see, Adhemar is building and extending his cathedral around the sides of the rock and up towards it. The chapel always had a steep stone staircase and some splendid frescos. Go and look while I'm engaged in tedious meetings.'

They remounted and rode through the town's narrow streets, which were already bustling with pilgrims, and stalls had been set up to sell them everything imaginable. As usual, Edvard had sent ahead and booked two rooms at the inn.

The innkeeper was overwhelmed at having the Papal Envoy at his inn again and said he remembered his last visit ten years before. Chatillon smiled in disbelief but ordered food, and they settled themselves to wait for the chaos that would ensue when the rest of the procession arrived.

Duke Robert, Ralph De Gael, Stephen de Blois, and several other senior nobles had brought their huge pavilions, hence the massive wagons. Soon they were erected in the meadows close to the town, creating a sea of colour and activity. Edvard wanted to stretch his legs and went to watch the circus below, while Chatillon decided a short nap was in order before they were summoned to the residence of Bishop Adhemar for dinner that evening.

However, his head barely touched the bolster before unwelcome thoughts intruded. This was the first time he had been alone for weeks, but sleep would not come. Instead, he could see Isabella's concerned face and found that flashes of images from the last few months filled his mind. Annecy's unusually aggressive outburst at the fight with Lazzo, Ahmed's doubts and suspicions about Padraig's story. Then Ahmed's face as he held a mangled messenger pigeon by its legs.

'Someone brought the bird down!' he announced to the room whilst swinging his legs out of bed. He made his way to the stables, where the innkeeper had built several rooms for servants above the stalls. There he found some of his men laid out on their palliasses. He greeted them and made his way to the wicker saddle baskets in the corner. Knowing he would be in the territory with no established informers or pigeon coops, he had brought three birds. He coded a message to Ahmed...

At Le Puy. All is well. Give Isabella my love. Notify me

immediately of any concerns. **C**

He rolled the message up, inserted it into the soft metal tube and tied it to the bird's leg before launching it. He stood in the courtyard and watched as it circled the town several times to get its bearings before it set off north. Having done that and knowing that sleep would not come, he returned to the taproom.

Although he felt slightly more settled, his gut instinct told him something was wrong. He felt as if he had missed something.

15

Chapter Fourteen

It had been a long and tiresome day of planning with Duke Robert, Stephen de Blois and Bishop Adhemar. They had all listened to Chatillon, as they knew he often had a wider view, travelling as much as he did. His often cynical but practical advice proved invaluable, especially after Robert of Flanders arrived in the early afternoon with over twenty thousand followers in his wake. The Count informed them that similar numbers travelled from France and Germany but were behind by several weeks.

Chatillon shook his head in exasperation and wondered if Pope Urban had any idea of these numbers and what he had initiated with this crusade. He resolved to send birds out immediately to recommend that they take different routes as the countryside was already decimated and food and supplies were running low.

Edvard's advice was now being followed regarding pack animals over carts, and there was no decent horse or mule to be had for miles around. Even the most spavined, knock-kneed beasts seemed to be going for a fortune.

The Pope had appointed Bishop Adhemar as the spiritual leader of the crusade, with Duke Robert as their military leader. Both men were disappointed to learn that Chatillon would leave them at Lucca. However, he mollified them by spending many hours planning for a staggered departure of the thousands below in the valley.

Bishop Adhemar was a charismatic man who had been a close friend of Pope Gregory and was with Piers' uncle, Pope Urban. He was a warlike bishop who had been to Jerusalem in 1087 but never with anything like these numbers. The logistics of moving and feeding such a multitude were a nightmare. Chatillon insisted that Adhemar send out his priests to identify the sick, the lame and the crippled. They were encouraged to stay behind until they were well enough to continue. Adhemar made a point of personally going down to the infirmary and refectory to bless them, and he gave them hope by promising that he would see them in Jerusalem.

Chatillon also suggested sending ahead and buying all the spare harvests, grain and fodder on the way, as well as spare cattle and sheep to be slaughtered and salted. The assembled nobles listened and acted on his advice. Edvard proved to be invaluable helping to put their plans into action.

They were late back to the inn, and both men were tired as they mounted the stairs. However, the obsequious innkeeper emerged from the large taproom and halted them.

'Sire, two gentlemen have waited several hours for your return; they're in the small taproom at the back.' Chatillon raised an eyebrow. Knowing Sheikh Ishmael's desire for revenge, they were both ever watchful.

Edvard entered the small snug-like room first. As the two men stood to greet them, he positioned himself against the wall with narrowed eyes and one hand on his dagger. Looking them up and down, Edvard did not believe for a second that they were linked to the Sheikh, but Piers had at least a dozen other enemies who would like nothing better than to see the Papal Envoy dead.

Chatillon followed him into the room and waved the two men back to their seats. He settled himself in a chair opposite and regarded his two visitors. Both men glanced nervously at the imposing bodyguard behind Chatillon before greeting him.

'Your eminence, we have travelled far to find you and to place a proposition in front of you—a proposition that will greatly benefit others and be highly lucrative to you personally.'

Chatillon gave a small amused smile at their courtly language. They were obviously from the English court, and their highly fashionable, good-quality clothing indicated this.

The innkeeper hurried in with refreshments for the group, which was silent until he left.

'So you were about to make me a proposition that I could not possibly refuse. Please do elaborate,' he said, crossing one elegantly booted leg over the other.

Both men glanced again at a stern-faced Edvard before the younger one spoke again; the older man, probably in his mid-thirties, sat further into the shadows and remained silent.

'I suggest you send your servant out of the room as what I am about to say is for your ears only,' the young courtier suggested.

Chatillon glanced behind at Edvard, and a half smile played on his lips. 'Edvard is no servant, he is a friend, a confidant and one of the most dangerous men you will ever meet. With that dagger, he could pin you to that panelling behind you before your arse left the seat.'

The younger man blinked and swallowed while the older man leaned forward and spoke directly to Edvard. 'We meant no disrespect. It is purely the sensitive nature of our request that makes us cautious.' Edvard inclined his head in recognition of their apology.

'A person of senior significance has sent us to ask if you will undertake an assassination.'

Chatillon regarded them with interest. He vaguely recognised the older of the two men now, he was sitting forward in the light. He imagined the young, more impatient and arrogant man was a younger cadet son trying to make his mark in the court.

'First, what are your names? You know who we are, and I like to know exactly with whom we deal in matters such as this.'

The older man stood and bowed his head. 'I am Sir Walter Tirel, and this is my brother-in-law, John Fitz Gilbert.'

Ah, one of the many De Clare bastards, thought Chatillon before sitting forward slightly.

'Presumably, the intended victim is a person of some importance for you to have made such a journey to approach me personally. I also presume it is someone I know who is on this crusade with me already. Am I correct so far?' Both men nodded.

'So a guess suggests that your master is Ranulf Flambard, who wants to make sure that Duke Robert does not return from Jerusalem, leaving King William Rufus to rule both countries as his father did before him.'

Both men looked shocked at the suggestion. Chatillon was

pleased, as he would not have relished killing Robert, although he would have admired Flambard's logical ambition behind it.

Walter gasped. 'God's Blood, no! We are not asking for the murder of the King's brother.'

Chatillon smiled at the response. Tirel was an earnest young man who had married well and was now linked to the royal family he seemed to remember.

'So exactly whose throat are you expecting me to slit?' he asked in a dry tone.

Tirel paled at the words, but Fitz Gilbert jumped in. 'Odo of Bayeux. We want you to use poison to ensure that he never reaches Jerusalem and never returns. He has meddled for far too long in the affairs of the King.'

It was rare that Chatillon was surprised, but this was one of those occasions he felt his eyes widen. He turned and met Edvard's calm gaze, just to give himself a few moments. He then looked back at the two Englishmen, having regained his composure.

'That is indeed a high-profile execution. A senior bishop and paragon of the Catholic Church. You quailed at killing the King's brother, but now expect me to kill the uncle of both Robert and William; is that correct?' They both nodded, although he noticed that Tirel could not meet his eyes.

'You will be richly rewarded. You will have one thousand marks on the table if you succeed.' said Fitz Gilbert with a grin that irritated Chatillon. Edvard, however, gave a low whistle, for that was indeed a fortune.

'Flambard must indeed be a desperate man if he is willing to pay that much to remove a troublesome bishop.' Neither man replied to this quip.

'Give me an hour to think it over, and then you will have

your answer,' he said softly.

'No! We need to know now,' demanded Fitz Gilbert. Tirel put out a hand and gripped his arm.

'This is a serious undertaking. Any man would need time to think of the implications, especially as we are talking about a senior man of the Church,' he said in a reasoned voice, but the younger man still had a mulish expression. *Ah, the impatience of youth,* thought Chatillon.

'Come back in an hour. We will deliberate and may have an answer for you then.'

With some reluctance, the men left, and Edvard dropped into the chair opposite, pouring himself a glass of wine.

'Not an easy decision, Piers,' he suggested.

'As you know, Edvard, I always kill without remorse or regret. I've rarely ever given a passing thought to my victims, but this request has given me pause.'

Edvard stayed silent and regarded his friend with interest but then added an afterthought. 'They are offering a huge amount of money. They will find someone else if it isn't you, and you will give him a quick and painless death.'

Chatillon met his friend's eyes and nodded, as he had also thought of that. 'I am, as you know, an exceptionally wealthy man. I don't need their money, or anyone's for that matter. I take my commissions for other reasons—the challenge, the adrenaline, and often the removal of a particularly unpleasant individual. So as for this, I am far more interested in the politics and reasoning behind this decision. Is the ageing Bishop of Bayeux still such a force to be reckoned with, still such a threat to them?'

'He is certainly powerful and influential, and if William Rufus decides to try and keep Normandy when Duke Robert returns, then Odo will, without doubt, lead the chorus of voices who will shout treachery and betrayal,' offered Edvard.

Chatillon took another draught of wine.

'That is true, Edvard, but I find that over the years, I have developed an unwilling affection for the hapless and impulsive Robert Curthose. We must remember that Bishop Odo is the staunch rock at Duke Robert's side, trying, like me, to steer that ship through troubled waters. I also respect our warlike Bishop of Bayeux, whose spirit is rarely dimmed, no matter what befalls him.'

'We should also not forget that Odo was instrumental in saving Finian's life at the siege of Rochester,' added Edvard.

They sat for some time mulling over the pros and cons of such a proposition until Chatillon reached a decision. 'Well, for the first time in over twenty-five years, I am about to turn down a commission to kill someone,' he said, placing his goblet firmly on the table just as a knock came on the door.

The two Englishmen returned. Tirel looked apprehensive to Edvard's keen eyes.

'Well, do you have an answer for us?' demanded Fitz Gilbert before he had even sat down. Chatillon steepled his fingers and regarded the young man with a growing antipathy.

'I'm afraid I have to decline your generous offer. In all conscience, I cannot assassinate Bishop Odo of Bayeux.'

There was a deathly silence for some time, and Edvard noticed that young Fitz Gilbert's face was suffused with anger as he jumped to his feet.

'How dare you turn down a request from the King,' he began before Tirel pulled him far from gently back into his seat.

'Shut up, you fool!' he growled.

'From the King? So not just from Flambard, but also from

William Rufus himself. That is interesting, but he is not *my* king, Fitz Gilbert. I am French nobility, and l owe not a modicum of allegiance to him. Also, why would I, as I am the Papal Envoy to Pope Urban, who is a far higher power in the Christian world than a mere king?'

Walter Tirel jumped in quickly. 'No, he has it wrong. It is indeed Ranulf Flambard who has sent us. He said that you might initially refuse to take the assignment. So I am authorised to offer you Pevensey Castle and a hundred acres of prime land around it if you will accept.'

Edvard's mouth almost dropped open, and he had to school his features to hide his amazement. His eyes veered to Chatillon, who he saw was equally taken aback for a few seconds.

'God's Blood! Flambard must really believe that Odo is a significant thorn in their side. But oh, the irony of it. Did Flambard intend this as a joke, something he thought would appeal to my cynical sense of humour?'

The two men looked puzzled.

'Tirel, you hail from Tonbridge. You must see why this is ironic, for he is offering me Bishop Odo's lands that were confiscated after the rebellion. Therefore, I kill the Bishop and take his castle and a chunk of his land. How would that look in the eyes of the world? I might as well announce on the street corners that I had killed him!' he said, shaking his head and laughing.

This was too much for Fitz Gilbert, who shot to his feet yet again. Edvard stepped forward, but Chatillon also stood and raised a hand.

'Gentleman, thank you for your offer and your patience, but the answer is still no, and now I believe that our business is concluded so I bid you goodnight.'

However, Fitz Gilbert had not finished. 'You had better not breathe a word of this Piers de Chatillon, you or your so-called servant, or I swear that I'll be waiting for you both, with my men, one dark night,' he sneered.

Edvard snorted with laughter, while Chatillon said not a word nor moved a muscle in his face, as his almost black eyes narrowed. The young man pushed past them to the doorway while Tirel stood up with an anxious expression.

'He is impetuous, and I fear that the importance of this mission has gone to his head.'

Chatillon did not reply but stared at the empty doorway. Seeing the tight, thin lips of his master and the hand that had gone to his dagger, Edvard gently pushed Tirel back into the chair. Chatillon gave him a quick glance of thanks and followed Fitz Gilbert out.

The young courtier had not waited for Tirel; instead, he had set off down the hill towards their basic billet in a local tradesman's house. Chatillon followed softly twenty or so paces behind. It was now in the early hours, and no one was stirring in the town. Fitz Gilbert stopped and rested his hands on the wooden bridge at the base of the hill. Suddenly a low cold voice came from behind him.

'Well, Fitz Gilbert, here we have a dark night with no witnesses, so please do your worst!'

The Englishman went cold, and his stomach clenched in what he realised was fear. The anger and bravado he had felt at the inn had evaporated, but he still had the bluster as if it was his only protection. He drew his sword while Chatillon, a dark shape against the bushes, stood and watched him.

'I meant every word, Chatillon. I have decided that I will kill

Odo of Bayeux, and I know that Ranulf Flambard will reward me greatly if I kill you as well, so there are no loose ends!' he shouted.

This time Chatillon laughed aloud and stepped forward into the faint moonlight from the half moon. Fitz Gilbert noticed that he had not yet drawn his sword, so he rushed at him, but Chatillon easily sidestepped, turned and waited. The young man grinned and, sweeping forward, took a few wild swipes at Chatillon's head, but again, the Papal Envoy easily avoided them.

'Are you so afraid to fight me that you dance away like a girl,' he sneered.

Again, Piers just stood and waited for the young man to take the lead. Fitz Gilbert heard footsteps and saw Tirel and Edvard standing on the track above them, watching with concern.

'Stand down! This is madness!' shouted Tirel, but his comrade took no notice. Encouraged by having an audience, he raised his sword above his head and jumped to bring it crashing down on Chatillon. Piers had now drawn the long dagger that was his trademark. Given to him as a reward by Pope Gregory many years before, it was distinctive for its walrus ivory handle and the legend that went with it, for this was the dagger that had slain King Wenceslas many years before.

Now Piers swiftly ducked under the raised sword arm of Fitz Gilbert, raking the dagger down the underside of his arm in a deep cut.

Tirel, watching them, felt helpless. He knew the reputation of Piers De Chatillon, and few swordsmen in Europe would take him on in a fight. He did not doubt that he would easily kill the impetuous Fitz Gilbert, who seemed to think he was invincible.

In fact, Chatillon did not want to kill him. He had something else in mind for the arrogant youth, and he intended to teach him a lesson he would never be able to forget. For Chatillon never forgave or forgot threats made against him or his friends. The young man stood, blood dripping from his fingers, but Piers could see the anger on his face as he charged forward again. Fitz Gilbert screamed in frustration as Chatillon whirled aside, but then the young man gave a strangled cry, for Piers had brought his dagger hard across the back of the courtier's thigh. The razor-sharp blade cut through muscle and tendon, and Fitz Gilbert dropped to the ground in agony. Hamstrung and bleeding, his right leg was now useless.

Without a backward glance or a word, Chatillon wiped his blade and, turning, walked briskly back up the steep hill towards the inn. Edvard stood with Tirel looking down on the groaning young man.

'I suggest you bind those wounds quickly and find a physician, for it will bleed profusely if the artery has been nicked. What was he thinking? He must have been beyond madness to threaten the most dangerous assassin in Europe,' he said, shaking his head and leaving them.

He slowly followed his master up the hill. After all these years, Chatillon still could surprise him with his cold and callous actions. Fitz Gilbert would now be crippled for life, and any ideas of knighthood were gone. It would have been better if he had died than that, as from being a rising star in the English court, he would now be the object of people's pity.

The next morning before they set off for Lucca, Chatillon sought out Bishop Odo. He found him with Bishop Adhemar at the Residence. Piers thought that Odo looked well. He was over sixty now and, next to Earl Ralph De Gael, was one of the oldest pilgrims on the crusade, but his skin and eyes were clear and bright, and he looked much younger. He bowed and asked for a private speech with Odo, who led him into a small cloistered area.

They sat in the morning sunshine.

'What is it, Piers? A message from the Pope?'

Chatillon chose his words carefully. 'Your eminence, I fear your life may be in danger, and I suggest you take more precautions than usual.'

The Bishop raised an eyebrow and then snorted with laughter. 'So my nephew is trying to kill me. Is it him, or is it that creature beside him that wants me gone?'

Piers appreciated the quick wit and intelligence of Odo. He had a blunt manner about him, never beating about the bush, which he liked. It did not surprise him that he had deduced who it was immediately.

'It is probably Flambard, but William Rufus is condoning it. I am sure you will be flattered to know that the amount offered was eye-wateringly prodigious, with the further enticement of your land in Kent.'

Odo chuckled. 'To think that at my age and with no position at the English court, I am still a hindrance to Flambard's nefarious plans. You wouldn't think I recognised and nurtured his talents and then promoted him until he came to the Conqueror's notice. He is an ungrateful devious man, now full of his own self-importance.'

Piers nodded in agreement. 'However, forewarned is forearmed. Be vigilant—poison was mentioned. If you want my advice, I would step aside from the crusade somewhere, possibly in Italy, for a month or two. You can re-join them later, but it may flush out your assassin. I'll arrange for Robert to assign some of his knights to your side for the duration, probably the Grandesmil brothers. Now we must make ready, my Lord Bishop, to take up our position behind Bishop Adhemar in the procession to Lucca.'

Odo thanked him, and they gripped arms. Odo stood and watched his tall, dark figure make his way through the stone arches. Say what they will, Odo had seen several different sides to Piers de Chatillon over the many years he had known him. He was undoubtedly deadly, ruthless and had no conscience, but occasionally, something else glimmered—call it a sense of justice, of what was right. Odo was fortunate that this was one of those times. He had realised immediately that Chatillon had been offered the assignment, but had turned it down. He was more flattered by Chatillon's decision to do so than by the ridiculous amount they offered. It showed that Chatillon respected and even perhaps valued him. That thought pleased him, and he would take the Papal Envoy's advice on increasing protection. With that in mind, he went to see Duke Robert to quietly share this news.

16

Chapter Fifteen

As had become normal, it was late when they left Le Puy. It took so long to pack up, and then for the straggling columns to get moving, that many did not leave the town until midday on the next day, the sixteenth of August. And so they embarked on the long journey which would take them to the foothills of the Alps and over, towards the holy town of Lucca, where Pope Urban was to meet them and give them his blessing.

The northern French contingent was just one of the four groups heading for Constantinople, and in the other groups, there was jostling and competition for the role of leader. However, Chatillon was pleased to see that it was not the case here. Stephen de Blois had married Duke Robert's sister, Adela, and was, therefore, family. Count Robert of Flanders was his cousin. Both men deferred to the martial expertise and experience of Duke Robert, who had fought in several pitched battles and sieges, defeating both his father and the warlike troublesome King Malcolm of Scotland.

Before they left Le Puy, Bishop Adhemar had given a rousing speech. Not one to incite the crowd to violence in the way of Bishop William in Rouen, this speech was about praising their actions in answering the call to liberate the Christian churches of the East. Chatillon smiled as he listened, for he knew his uncle's words when he heard them. Pope Urban was keen to reconnect with the eastern Byzantine Church in Constantinople since the schism in 1054. By responding to the call of Emperor Alexius for help and by presenting the Byzantines as fellow persecuted Christians, he hoped to achieve this, and Bishop Adhemar was his willing mouthpiece.

Again, progress was painfully slow, and by the end of the first week, Chatillon had persuaded most of the senior nobles to abandon their huge pavilions in favour of accommodation organised ahead, or smaller tents. Some did so with great reluctance, for the pavilions and flags declared their importance and status. However, Chatillon was persuasive as the time needed to pack up, or set up each night, took hours from their travelling time. Not to mention the dozens of ox-drawn wagons needed to transport them with all their household effects, and even considerable items of furniture they had brought.

'It was a wise move Sire, for it was madness to bring so much. Also, as the season advances, the days are becoming shorter,' proclaimed Edvard.

'Yes, less daylight, less travelling time, and the passes are becoming narrower and rockier as we climb higher in the Alps. I promised Isabella I would be back for Yuletide, but now I wonder if we will even reach Lucca by Yuletide!' exclaimed Chatillon.

Duke Robert, however, was in high spirits. He talked enthusiastically of the journey ahead, the sights they would see, of revisiting Rome. His enthusiasm was infectious, and morale was good amongst the pilgrims. The weather also favoured them as the autumn rains held off, and they basked in the late September sunshine.

After many nights in the open, it was with some relief that Chatillon rode ahead and gazed down on the foothills and plain of Turin with the glistening waters of the River Po wending its way across it. He had visited Turin many times. It was a natural stop on the way back or to Rome. The city had become a prosperous crossroads in Europe, sitting on the western bank of the River Po, the longest river in Italy flowing into the Adriatic Sea.

'At long last, decent food and accommodation,' he muttered to Edvard, who laughed.

'Do I see several rest days here, Sire?' he asked with a grin.

'Count Humbert is a good friend and keeps an excellent table. I will recommend to our erstwhile leaders that now is the time to stay here and find replacement horses, mules and fodder. There are wide, luscious meadows along the riverbanks where the grazing is very good. After the passes of the Alps, we deserve a rest.'

Edvard agreed. 'The shoes on many horses will need replacing, and the blacksmiths can set up their forges down near a good water supply. Is the Count not called Humbert the Fat due to his love of good food?'

Chatillon nodded and laughed. 'Yes, he is, and he is an easy-going, pleasant man who will be delighted to see us. Now, Edvard, ride ahead, present yourself to the Count and warn him of the numbers arriving over the next few days. Also, kindly ask him for accommodation for the senior nobles and ourselves. Bishops Odo and Adhemar will no doubt stay with the Bishop.'

Edvard galloped off, leaving Chatillon to stare down at the wide, rich farmlands below, the homelands of the Counts of Saxony. He returned to Robert to advise a three-day rest here, but his mind was back at Chatillon Sous Bagneux. Would a message be waiting for him here telling him that all was well at home? Again, he experienced that faint prickle of unease.

In fact, it was over a week before they left Turin due to various illnesses and delays, including a badly swollen fetlock on Duke Robert's favourite gelding, which needed poulticing each day. Chatillon sighed with frustration at the further delays while Humbert, who had greeted their arrival with such enthusiasm, became more eager for them to leave. The pilgrims and crusaders, now numbering nearly twenty thousand, were like a plague of locusts that had descended on the rich countryside and his villages, stripping them bare.

Once they left Turin, the roads were much better. Many were originally Roman, and even though more pilgrims flocked to join them, they still made better time on their way to Genoa. For their last few days travelling south, however, conditions were dire, with torrential rain sweeping down from the north. At first, there was some shelter in the forest that covered the hills to the north, but as they entered the Polcevera River valley, it became bleak indeed. There was hardly a shred of dry clothing amongst the pilgrims as they trudged along the rocky valley floor.

Finally, after several exhausting cold days, the rain stopped, and the sun emerged. And a strung-out bedraggled multitude made their way down the steep valley to the city and the Maritime Republic of Genoa.

Chatillon pulled in with Edvard to watch them go past, their soaking clothes steaming. A few dozen, at least, were lost—those who had dropped out, shivering and shaking, sinking to the ground—but there was no capacity or time to tend to them.

He had sent several messages to his father-in-law, the Signori Embriaco of Genoa, to forewarn him of the numbers who would be arriving and to arrange for wagonloads of provisions to be waiting, to feed the poorer pilgrims. Mounds of dry firewood had been provided, and groups gathered to light these on the shore in the shelter of the cliffs. Chatillon knew that the senior nobles would stay with Isabella's father at his sumptuous palace, so he and Edvard made their way, gratefully, to their own Castello, their home built into the cliffs overlooking the busy port.

There had been no messages waiting for him in Turin, which was a concern, but now his Steward came forward with several. He handed two to Edvard and two to Chatillon. Piers opened the first one with fingers thawing from the harsh ride. He saw the distinctive vellum from his home and smiled. It was from Isabella, sending her love and telling him the children were well, with Fergus, Finian's new son, thriving. He smiled, for Finian had a second son.

The second one, far more worrying, was from Ahmed.

I want to be more reassuring, but my concerns are still valid. I found no evidence of any slave escapes in Tunis or Tripoli. Our birds were deliberately brought down at the chateau by a hired falconer. Abdo was murdered because he was following Padraig, who met with an Arab merchant. Do not go to Rome. Return after Lucca, as I am uneasy.

Chatillon walked to the shuttered doors and opened them

onto the wide stone balcony overlooking the harbour. He had not been here for nearly four years, the last time being when Isabella insisted on bringing the boys, and Annecy, to meet their grandparents and his ward Marietta. He had forgotten how beautiful the house was with its marble columns and floors.

Edvard watched as Chatillon leant his hands on the stone balustrade and watched the dozens of boats and ships, most with their sails close-wrapped for the winter.

'Is he out there, do you think? Ishmael?' asked Chatillon gazing at the horizon.

Edvard came to stand beside him and shrugged. 'Possibly, waiting to attack the last of the autumn trading cogs, risking one more journey. The Sheikh's domain is out there, and he is the master of it, attacking when and where he wishes.'

Chatillon nodded. 'I may have a conversation with Embriaco. Suppose the Maritime Republics, such as Genoa and Venice, banded together in a concerted effort. In that case, they could sweep the Mediterranean almost clear of these Barbary raiders, who destroy so much of their trade.'

'It is a thought, but relations are not good between the Republics. Too much greed, jealousy and competition. Is there troubling news from home?' Edvard asked, wondering where this was coming from suddenly.

'Isabella says they're all well, and Finian has another son.'

Edvard sighed with relief, for this was *his* adopted family as well.

'Tell me, Edvard, what did you make of Padraig's tale of escape from the slave quarters in Tripoli?'

Edvard considered the question for a few moments.

'I thought they were very lucky. So many things fell into

place for them. The lax guards, the help of the fisherman and his daughter.'

'What about the lack of pursuit or retribution on the other slaves or guards? Such an escape would surely result in floggings and executions to punish and discourage others. Yet Ahmed can find no trace of this. Do you not find that strange?'

Realising that this had something to do with the message from Ahmed, Edvard looked for conciliatory words. 'I suppose we were so taken aback when Padraig appeared and had survived that we enjoyed Finian's relief and joy and just accepted the story. Why would we question it when it sounded plausible?'

'Yet Ahmed constantly questioned it as he thought it was implausible, but I didn't pay much attention. Why were we so gullible? Now I find that I am putting together the pieces of an interlocking wooden puzzle, and Padraig MacDomnall sits in the middle of it. In fact, he is the piece that locks it all together.'

Edvard's face showed alarm. 'You think he would harm Finian, is that it?'

'Like Ahmed, we don't have enough pieces yet to work out what's afoot, but I feel certain that Padraig is the key.'

'Do you want me to go back, Piers?'

'No. Finian, my armiger and a master swordsman, is in charge; he may be blinkered by guilt and relief, but Ahmed will share his concerns with him. I will answer Ahmed and tell him to be vigilant, and assure him that we are returning as soon as the blessing is given at Lucca. If the heavy snow does not arrive early, we can be back in nine or ten days at the most. Even if we think Finian is the target, ten of our well-trained men protect the chateau and would give their lives for the family.'

Edvard agreed, but he was uneasy and spent an hour or two reflecting on clues he may have missed, thinking of questions he should have asked. Now Padraig was accepted and sitting in the heart of the family, poised to launch whatever he might be planning. Thinking back to the odd glance he had intercepted between Padraig and Pierre, Edvard had no doubt it would come in some form of revenge against Finian. Not for a second did he consider that Isabella might be the target. Edvard did not see Ahmed's message, as Chatillon absentmindedly rolled it and threw it on the fire, for Edvard would have been seriously worried about the mention of an Arab merchant, for he still vividly remembered the poison attempt by such a merchant.

Later that day, they strolled up the steep, narrow street towards the Embriaco Palace. Chatillon knew that Guglielmo would be delighted to host such senior nobles from Normandy, Brittany and France. In the gathering dusk, a figure was coming down the hill. Edvard rested his hand on the hilt of his dagger. However, the man stopped in some alarm when he saw them and stepped to one side with his back against the wall.

'Master Tirel, I didn't expect to see you here. With the mission's failure, I thought you might return to England with your friend,' said Chatillon, in a welcoming voice that surprised the nervous Englishman.

Tirel bowed. 'I arranged for Fitz Gilbert to be escorted back, but I wanted to continue the journey and the mission given to me. I had heard so much about the Holy Face of Lucca that I wanted to see it. I may also travel as far as Rome as I have never seen the fabled city.'

'Rome is like a fickle woman that can suck you in. The ruins are magnificent, but they can also be unhealthy and dangerous. I would advise you not to walk the darkened streets on your own, or you will not live to tell your wife of the sights you've seen.'

The young knight inclined his head in thanks, made to carry on and then stopped. 'May I say I am sorry that Fitz Gilbert insulted and threatened you? He let his emotions rule his head, and he got what he deserved. I know Bishop Odo has been warned, and the Grandesmil brothers shadow him everywhere. However, I do not blame you, for I have long admired you, Sire, since watching you from afar, in the former king's court at Caen, as a young man. If I can ever be of any use in the future, I am at your service.' He smiled, but it did not reach his eyes, as he doffed his velvet chapeau and walked on, leaving the two thoughtful men staring after him.

'Well, that was an informative encounter. There is no doubt that Tirel will kill the Bishop himself or find another assassin,' suggested Edvard.

'Indeed, and as we know, many in Rome will jump to do his bidding for the money being offered. He could recruit half a dozen. I believe the Grandesmil brothers will have their work cut out to protect Odo. However, we have done our utmost, and it is now in the hands of fate and God.'

The fair autumn weather continued as they travelled south to Lucca. Despite the aches, pains, blisters, and chills they caught from their cold, wet clothes, the mood amongst the multitude was buoyant as they set off. The excitement was almost tangible as Chatillon rode down the long straggling procession, for they were about to view one of the wonders of the Christian world, the Holy Face of Lucca. The hundreds of priests and monks in the crowd fed the buzz of excitement with the stories of miracles that had happened in front of it. However, it still took another five long days to reach the city that sat on the River Serchio. Lucca had been an important Roman town, a fortress city, and many buildings and ruins remained. It had also become the capital of Tuscany.

As they rode through the city's outskirts, Edvard could not help but notice the huge workshops and storage sheds that now ran down to the river banks.

'The silk trade is booming here because Lucca's silk cloth, interwoven with gold and silver threads, is a luxury item much in demand. They say it can rival silks from the east.'

Count Robert of Flanders rode up beside them to hear the end of this. 'There are many merchants in Ghent who import the silk cloth from Lucca. My mother is particularly fond of it, as is Bertha, the Empress of the Holy Roman Empire.'

Chatillon closed his eyes. He could still never hear Bertha's name without a warm feeling flooding him. He had loved her, and she had borne him a daughter who, unfortunately, had died at the age of seven. Chatillon and Bertha had been convinced the child had been murdered because she was not the Emperor's child. He pushed the memories away and smiled at the earnest young man beside him, who was building quite a reputation as a warrior without the cruelty and brutality of his father, Robert I. He smiled again when he thought of how much Isabella had enjoyed bedding the count's younger brother, Viscount Philip Van Loo.

'Have you seen the Holy Face, Sire?' asked Edvard of the count, breaking into Chatillon's reverie.

'No, but I have heard much over the last few days, so I am full of anticipation.' Chatillon's natural cynicism resulted in him raising an eyebrow at this, and Edvard smiled.

'They say it is a huge carving, almost twice the size of a man,' added the Count.

'A small man,' muttered Chatillon with a smile.

Robert was not put off. 'They believe that it was carved by Nicodemus himself, from the cedar wood of Lebanon. They say he helped to carry the body of Our Lord into the tomb, so the face is a true likeness.'

Chatillon decided to humour him. 'The original legend says that Nicodemus had indeed carved the whole life-like figure of Christ's crucified figure on the cross. However, he fell asleep, leaving the face to be carved the next day. When he awoke, he found an angel had carved the face while he slept.' Robert's eyes widened, and his mouth fell slightly open.

'Come, let us push ahead, and I suggest you go straight to the Cathedral of San Martino, Sire, before the thousands of pilgrims line up to see it.'

They parted company with the exuberant Count and headed to the Bishop's Residence, where they knew the Pope had been for several days. Piers knew Lucca well, for his first master, Pope Alexander, had been Bishop of Lucca and had overseen the completion of the cathedral he designed.

Pope Urban was delighted to see him.'Well met, Piers. How was the journey?'

'Unnecessarily long and tiresome would sum it up. We finally left Rouen in mid-July, and it is now late November. No one could have foreseen the numbers that answered your call, and I predict that thousands will die along the way. We have lost hundreds already, leaving a trail of bodies in our wake. The old, the infirm, the very young, the stupid and the unlucky who fell and were trampled by oxen or crushed by falling wagons. God help them when they reach the inhospitable deserts of the Levant where they'll die from sunstroke and thirst or the blade of a heathen.'

Pope Urban gave a thin smile as several bishops and clergy sat behind him and listened in dismay to Piers.

'You're right, of course, Piers, but we had no alternative. As you know, the Seljuk Turks have overrun most of the Byzantine Empire's eastern provinces and are now within striking distance of Constantinople itself. They must be stopped, as we can no longer stand by and watch brother Christians being slaughtered. As you know, the Reconquista, the crusade in Spain, has been going well, with El Cid seizing and holding Valencia. I await news from King Peter of Aragon, who has taken his father's place and is fighting the long battle and siege of Alcoraz.'

'Your reasoning and motives are honourable in the east and west, Uncle, but only fifteen per cent of the huge host you've brought to Lucca are knights or soldiers. Most of the rest have never wielded a sword or staff in anger, yet you send them into battle and danger.'

Pope Urban turned, opening his arms to the rest of the men in the room.

'Every pilgrim has protection from the Church. They have the right to hospitality at any religious house. Also, they're exempt from any tolls, taxes or even arrest!'

Chatillon was tired, and he could not help giving a bark of laughter. 'I am sure that will be a great consolation to them, Uncle, when a huge Seljuk Turk is sweeping his vicious curved blade towards their neck. As it was when Peter the Hermit and his unarmed band of thousands of pilgrims were wiped out in the summer. He escaped, of course, leaving his faithful followers to die or be enslaved.'

The Pope frowned. Chatillon was one of the few people to argue with him, and in his heart, he knew that much of what his nephew said was true, for no one had expected numbers such as this.

'Come and sit with some refreshments and tell me about things at home. How are my nephews and niece?' he asked, waving the clergy out of the room. As he turned, he just caught a shadow passing over Piers' face, and he glanced up at Edvard, who grimaced.

'What is it? What's amiss? Are they ill?' he asked in concern.

'To be truthful, Uncle, I am not sure, but something is wrong, and I believe it is linked to Finian's cousin, Padraig.'

'Tell me all,' he said, waving Edvard to a chair and ringing a bell for refreshments.

There was silence for some time as Pier's uncle mulled over what he had heard. Piers had been like a son to him since the unexpected death of his parents at a young age. He had trained and developed the young man, creating opportunities for him in the Holy See.

'I have known Ahmed longer than you, Piers, from my early days as the Prior and then Bishop of Cluny and Ostia. Ahmed was the King's physician who seemed almost able to work magic. I liked him when I met him, and he was highly respected. As you know, he does not reach conclusions lightly, and he is an astute man. Before sharing his thoughts and suspicions, he will have weighed up and checked the evidence and probability carefully. If Ahmed says that their story does not ring true, then I would believe him, which begs the question, why is Padraig lying, and what's he hiding?'

'There is more,' added Edvard, and he told the Pope about the murder of Abdo and the downing of the pigeons.

'That rings more alarm bells, and if Padraig knows of Ahmed's suspicions, as it seems, then I am surprised that he has let him live.'

Chatillon felt the ice-cold fingers of fear grip him for the first time in decades. 'I know you wanted me to go as far as Rome with Duke Robert, but he has Bishop Adhemar, as your Papal Legate, by his side to guide him and Bishop Odo. I think we need to return home as soon as possible.'

His uncle sat forward and put a hand over his. 'Stay for the next ten days until the blessing is finished. I need you by my side in Lucca. Your influence and grasp of politics are significant with these leaders. They listen to you, Piers. Some of them may fear you, but they all respect you, and I was hoping you could help them plan the rest of their journey. I don't think your family is in danger, but I fear Finian may be, so send a bird immediately.'

Chatillon reluctantly agreed and nodded just as a messenger burst in, one of the Papal secretaries.

'Your holiness, news from Spain. A great victory for King Peter of Aragon. He defeated the Muslim armies and retook the city of Huesca, but more importantly, St George appeared in the sky before them. He was in armour with a lance from which flew a long white gonfalon with a red cross. It is a true sign, your Holiness, a sign from God. Hundreds of warriors saw it.'

The priest dropped to his knees in front of the Pope, overcome with emotion.

17

Chapter Sixteen

Aragon 1096

Meanwhile, in Aragon, it was cold on the walls of Montear-agon Castle in the early dawn. The castle was a formidable structure, a fortress-monastery that had been reinforced and the walls built and strengthened by King Sanchez Ramirez of Aragon, with the express intention of laying siege to Huesca. Unfortunately, the King had been killed by a stray arrow in the summer of 1094 while inspecting his new walls. His son, Peter of Aragon, succeeded him, who raised the siege after his father's death to mourn but then returned in force to lay siege again to Huesca the following year.

Georgio glanced up at his friend, who towered over him and whose face was inscrutable as usual. 'So Huesca has finally fallen. The Muslim forces of the Almoravids are defeated, and it will become the Christian city of Aragon once again. No wonder Peter and his knights celebrated into the early hours. Some still are,' he said, watching a drunken knight with a wine sack clutched to his chest making for his bed.

His friend still did not speak. He stood still, one hand resting on the stonework, the other on the hilt of his sword where it habitually rested. Georgio had been at his friend's side since they were young boys, and usually, he knew not to interrupt his reverie. But he could not resist one last thrust.

'Does this mean we can go home for a while now, even just for a few months?'

This time he had his friend's attention. The bright blue eyes narrowed and stared down at him. 'Home? This is but the beginning, Georgio. We have won back part of Aragon from the despised Berber Moors, but we must swiftly continue our advance. King Peter knighted us for a purpose, to be at his right hand and to raise the Papal banner of Pope Urban in Spain once again. We must take advantage of this victory while they're on the back foot, for Aragon is the Christian frontier in the east against the Muslims in Spain.'

Georgio sighed. His friend was right in some ways, for they had gained much wealth and prestige from their time in Spain, but Georgio was not as independent or self-contained as the tall, dark young warrior beside him. Georgio missed his family, even though they were his adoptive parents. They had cared for him, nurtured his broken body and spirit, and helped him to love life again. When the call came from King Sanchez in 1094 for the knights of France and Brittany to help him fight the forces of the Almoravids, they enthusiastically joined hundreds of others to ride south and answer the call. They were only sixteen years of age, and it was with great reluctance that their family let them go, but they looked much older, as if they had already seen too much in their short lives. They were also the most fearsome fighters and riders the Aragonese knights had ever seen. As much as he would love to go home, he knew he would stay, for his place would always be at the side of his friend, Conn Fitz Malvais, as long as he wanted him there.

Conn was an enigma to many of the other knights. They admired and respected him, and some feared him, but he seemed to live behind a barrier few could break through. He spent time with them, eating, drinking, and occasionally swiving the local women, but they knew little about what he was thinking. He rarely spoke of his life before he came to Spain, so what little they knew came from Georgio, whom they all liked. Georgio was of Italian descent—open, handsome, pleasant and funny. From him, they learnt that Conn came from Brittany. From other French knights, they learned that he was the bastard son of the legendary Luc De Malvais, leader of the feared Breton Horse Warriors.

Conn neither confirmed nor denied these facts, for he knew he had to keep his parentage secret. In reality, he was the grandson of William the Conqueror, the illegitimate child of Princess Constance and Morvan De Malvais. Even now, Conn could become a pawn in the hands of the unscrupulous to lay a claim to the thrones of England and Normandy.

Therefore, he lived a lie; it was easier to let them believe that the Breton horse warrior Lord Luc De Malvais was his father, and it certainly helped that at eighteen years, he looked like his uncle. Tall, dark with a warrior's build and the piercing blue eyes of his mother, Princess Constance, no one would think to question his parentage, for he and Luc's son, Lusian, were frighteningly alike, confirming the false story.

The dawn truly broke, and the sun hit the distant eastern walls of Huesca. They had emptied most of the city of the enemy, leaving a holding force there. Now there would be the clearing up to do in the aftermath of a battle and siege. There would be hundreds of bodies to burn, Christian burial plots to dig and a thorough search of the city for any enemy that may still be hiding. Not that many would be alive inside, as King Peter's infantry had stormed the city and taken their revenge on the inhabitants. Men had been slaughtered, women raped, and children put to the sword or herded and roped to be sold as slaves.

'Come let us go and find Diego and get some food,' said Conn, suddenly heading for the narrow stone staircase. They found Diego Rodriguez looking the worse for wear in the large refectory. He was three years older than they were and considered himself a veteran, and a font of knowledge regarding Moors and the Reconquista. In some ways, he had the right to boast, for he was the only son of Rodrigo Diaz de Vivar, better known as El Cid, and had fought at his side since he was a teenager. Georgio and Conn had fought for El Cid the previous year and greatly admired him. Fighting alongside Diego, he became their friend and one of the few people Conn felt he could trust. They also had a shared grievance, in that while each revelled in their father's fierce reputation, they also lived in the shadow of it. They both felt they had to do more to prove themselves and establish their own identity and reputation.

King Peter of Aragon had been dubious at first when his father took on two young boys, but then he saw them fight, defeating warriors twice their size and breadth. They also rode the largest trained warhorses he had ever seen; they called them Destriers, and they were terrifying. Since then, they have proven themselves over and over. Turning down financial rewards at first, they asked to be allowed to earn their knighthood. To an illegitimate child and an orphan, such an honour as knighthood was worth a chest full of gold.

Having cleared a platter of fresh bread, meat and cheese, Conn roused Diego with a harsh push on his shoulder that nearly dislodged him from the bench.

'Let us go, Diego. We have work to do, and we must ride to Huesca as an escort to the new Governor.

With some reluctance, the young Spaniard pulled himself reluctantly and shakily to his feet.

'Why are you always my conscience, Conn Fitz Malvais? Why can't you leave me to wallow in my hangover?' he laughed.

'There is a chill in the air out there and a stiff breeze coming from the mountains of the north that will wake you up. Let us ride.' Diego groaned and followed them out.

They spent the next week in the city of Huesca. The smell of burning corpses shrouded the city for several days, and dozens of graves were dug outside the city walls for the fallen Christian soldiers. There were fortifications to be repaired and wells to be cleaned, as several had been poisoned with dead bodies on purpose, as the Almoravids gave up the city. Several Muslim and Jewish merchants who had locked themselves, and their families, behind heavy cellar doors, now emerged and begged an audience with the Governor. They were, of course, willing to pay a yearly tribute to be allowed to trade and keep their houses and warehouses, and Conn adopted a cynical twist to his mouth as he saw the bag of gold being quietly passed to the Governor as a bribe.

By the end of the week, life in the city was resuming, and market stalls were open, selling all kinds of produce. Churches which had been defiled, or turned into mosques, were cleaned and reopened by the multitude of clergy that appeared.

Conn stood on the steps and surveyed the busy scene below when the sound of horns and trumpets rang clear, accompanied by the reverberation and sound of many hooves. Conn raced for the staircase to get a vantage point while shouting for his squad of men to stand to defend the gates. Surely, it could not be the Almoravid Berbers attacking again. Their scouts and patrols would have warned them. He reached the top and shaded his eyes.

A large column approached Huesca at speed, at least over a hundred strong. As they galloped towards the city, they unfurled their banners, and the flags of Aragon and Valencia were held aloft.

'It is my father!' gasped a panting Diego who had run from the stables.

'And King Peter, by the look of it,' added Conn, as they ran lightly down the stone steps to greet the new arrivals.

The name El Cid went around the city like wildfire, and by the time the new arrivals reached the square, a huge crowd had gathered. Having fought alongside Rodrigo Diaz de Vivar, Conn knew just how charismatic he was and smiled as he saw him stand in the stirrups and punch the air to the victorious crowd, who cheered wildly.

'Another victory for Christendom!' he shouted to more cheers.

They dismounted, and Conn sent Georgio to ensure that the column had access to water for their horses, ale, and food for the men. Conn followed Diego up the steps into the Receiving Hall of the palace. Once inside, Diego received a bear hug from his father, who thought the world of his son. Conn was not left out with a welcome slap on the shoulder.

'So have you come to see the retaken city, Father, or have you come to join us?' asked Diego.

King Peter laughed. 'The impatience of youth. Let your father sit down; he has ridden long and hard from Valencia.'

For several hours as food and wine were served, King Peter's commanders talked about how they had taken the city, the frustrating length of the siege and the tenacity of the Almoravids to hold on to it, no matter what their losses.

'We have driven them south, and now we need to subdue the surrounding Taifa states and drive deeper and further south than we have before, where they'll not expect us,' said the King.

'What of an alliance with Leon and Castile? Surely King Alphonse must want the same thing?' asked El Cid.

'You found out, Rodrigo, that King Alphonse can blow and change direction in the wind like a barley stalk. I am using him, and his forces in our overlap areas, but do I trust him? That is another question.'

El Cid nodded, for he had fallen out with King Alphonse, refusing to fight for him for many years. The King of Leon had even exiled El Cid from his home town of Burgos. Finally, Alphonse had realised his mistake, for he needed the famous warrior, and he had pleaded with El Cid to return to fight with his forces at Toledo.

The servants brought refreshments and huge platters of food, and then the group walked the city walls. 'It is a good, strong defensive position. You did well to take it, Sire, your father would be proud of you,' said El Cid gazing out over the scorched plains and foothills that were only now beginning to return to their winter greenery.

'We did have help,' said the King.

'Yes, I heard, but did you see this vision?' El Cid turned his piercing gaze on the assembled knights, including Conn, Georgio and his son, who had rejoined his friends.

Diego shook his head. 'We were behind with the cavalry on the right flank, but we saw what happened. The Moors were forcing us back when suddenly, a great cry went up from our front ranks, and dozens of men pointed at the sky. Then the cries and cheers grew as it spread. Afterwards, hundreds said they saw the vision of St George in shining mail, on his steed, galloping towards the enemy. Every man describes the same thing: the saint had a lance with a long wide gonfalon at its tip and a large red cross, the cross of Christ on it. They say Pope Urban described the same cross at the Council of Clermont last year. The Moors reeled back, staring at the sky. I do not know if they could see it as well. Our forces surged forward, and the enemy ran; it was breathtaking to watch. We galloped around to cut off their retreat and attacked their western flank. We killed hundreds, and when we returned, the city had surrendered, and the gates were opened after two years. However, hundreds of our men returned to drop to their knees and pray at the spot where they had first seen the vision of St George.'

There were thirty knights around them, and they had hung on every word, but there was silence as Diego finished. El Cid stood back and shook his head in wonder.

'I wish I had seen it. If one man sees it, you can dismiss it as a dream, a fantasy, but for St George to appear to hundreds, it shows us that this is real, that we have a just cause and that God is truly on our side. The Pope must be told at once,' he said emphatically.

'I believe you've met Pope Urban?' he suddenly asked Conn,

who was surprised that he knew, but Georgio jumped in and answered.

'We were captured and stolen by warrior monks when we were boys, and the Papal Envoy, Piers De Chatillon, a swordmaster, found and helped save us.'

El Cid looked confused, and Conn shook his head at his friend, who often delivered half a tale, before explaining.

'I am sure you will have heard of Chatillon; he is a godfather to me. He is also a Papal Envoy and the nephew of Pope Urban. So yes, Sire, we met the Pope on two occasions. A very clever and committed man with great plans for the church and the crusades. My father Luc De Malvais regards him highly.'

They returned to the castle of Montearagon that night for a celebratory feast, and three days later, El Cid rode back to Valencia. He had taken the city from the Moors, but it took constant vigilance and defence to hold it and the surrounding area. Conn, Diego and Georgio stood in the castle courtyard to bid him farewell and wish him Godspeed. They would meet him again in the summer when they took the war to the Almoravids and drove them out of Spain.

18

Chapter Seventeen

Ahmed had been busy; he knew he needed evidence, but it had proved elusive until now. Padraig had returned to Paris for a few days, and Ahmed had ensured that the Irishman was followed by half a dozen of his contacts in the city. Two of the serving girls in the Coq d'Or were his, as were several market traders selling chickens or fruit outside in the busy streets, one of the Paris watchmen, and a Jewish money lender doing business at a table in the inn; all of them were Ahmed's informers and were planted in place hours before Padraig arrived. They waited and watched, but there was no way they could be privy to the conversation and planning in the small dismal room. As soon as the serving girls entered conversation stopped.

Al Cazar was clever and easily lost the tails set upon them as they left the inn. However, Ahmed was a step ahead, for he had placed a clever young street hawker ahead of them. The man was one of his best, and he moved swiftly ahead of the Arabs while shouting his wares, selling ribbons and gee gaws from his baskets. He also knew the backstreets of Paris like the back of his hand and could cut through and stay ahead of them. In this way, he followed them to a livery stable near the river and waited while they retrieved their horses. They trotted along the river bank towards the bridge. It was noon, and the bridge was crowded as the young man pulled out a larger, different-coloured chapeau, pulling it low over his features. He followed them through the wagons, hawkers and people flooding into the city, as there were executions to watch that afternoon which always drew large crowds. This meant that the Arabs' horses were at walking pace, and he followed, now selling small bottles of elixir that could cure aches, pains and gout. Soon they emerged onto the still-busy road heading south.

They broke into a trot, and the resourceful young man jumped onto an empty cart heading the same way. He offered the carter coin to whip his horses on and keep the riders in sight at a distance. After a league, the riders pulled into a busy hostelry set back from the side of the road. He told the carter to keep going some distance up the road and set him down out of sight. He doubled back through the trees and across a field. He came out behind the large stable block, near the muck heaps, and bided his time by sitting on an old water trough, whittling a hollow piece of wood to make a whistle. He had not long to wait as a young stable boy appeared with two leather buckets; he stopped in surprise, startled at seeing someone there. The man began to play the partly made whistle, and the boy laughed.

'I do reckon you got some of those holes in the wrong places,' he suggested.

The young man nodded his head in resignation. 'I do reckon you be right,' he said, and they both laughed.

'Now, how do you fancy making some coin?' he said, flipping a silver piece in the air. The boy's eyes widened at the silver coin, and he nodded but looked over his shoulder to ensure the Head Ostler was not near.

'Those Arabs that just arrived, have they stayed here before?'

'Yes, a few times,' he said and deftly caught the coin.

'Now, can you find the leader's name for another silver coin?'

The boy grinned, filled the two water buckets and left. He seemed to be some time, and the young man was poised for flight; he knew what had happened to Abdo and did not want to suffer the same fate. However, the boy returned saying apologetically, 'Sorry, I was sent on an errand, and I had to find Maria, the maid. The man's name is Don Ferdinand, and he is a Castilian merchant.'

'You've done well. Now for a third coin, have you heard any snatches of conversation about where they're going?' The boy's eyes opened wide again as he already had more money than he had earned in a year, and his mother would be overwhelmed.

'As they dismounted, they mentioned ships at Rouen and what they could and could not take with them when they leave.'

'Thank you and hide the coins. We don't want any questions asked.' So saying, he slipped into the trees before running as fast as he could towards the city. He needed to get a message to Ahmed, and he smiled, for he knew he would be richly rewarded for this information.

Preparations were in full swing for the Yuletide festivities at the chateau. It was a joyous celebration, full of Christian and pagan stories, and often went on for ten days. The Great Hall and rooms would be cleaned, fresh rushes laid down, and greenery gathered to make the winter garlands that would decorate the hall. The men and boys were going to get the two huge Yule logs that were felled last year. They would be brought into the hall to dry out before they were lit in two weeks.

The kitchens were very busy, as Isabella hired extra girls and women from the village to help over the Yuletide season. She also recruited men who would come and help with the several days of hunting expeditions that Chatillon would host, if the weather was clear and bright. The villagers welcomed it, providing extra income at a difficult time of the year.

'My knees are aching from the time I have spent at my Prie Dieu praying that Piers will be back for Yule,' Isabella whispered to Dion, who, babe on her hip, was looking at the long list of tasks that Isabella had in front of them. Young Fergus was now nearly six months and teething. He watched the activities with interest while sucking and mouthing on a large bone clutched in his fist.

'Do not fear, Isabella—I know they will be here. Rarely does Chatillon not keep his promises. Now, can I cross venison haunches and fat geese off this list?' she asked.

Isabella nodded and walked over to the Steward's wife, Madame Chambord, who ruled the kitchens and house servants with an iron rod. She was busy supervising the boiling and salting of the umbles in huge pans. These would be preserved, pressed and served in thick slices to the peasants and workers on the estate on the payment day. Almost all of the village came to the chateau to enjoy the ales, the ciders, and the food on offer. There would be music and dancing, and the servants would receive their annual wages. Dion had never seen the innards of animals cooked this way before she came here, for they were cooked in garlic and herbs and served with fresh bread, and were very tasty.

Isabella thanked Madame Chambord for her hard work and then asked if they could use part of the kitchen that afternoon for an hour. Madame Chambord raised an eyebrow and looked at her as if she were mad.

Isabella laughed. ' Do not fear—we will not disturb anyone or make a mess. Ahmed wishes to treat the children by making an eastern treat. I think he called it baklava. He will steal some of your flour, precious dried fruit, and nuts, but I am sure all of us will be keen to taste it.'

Madame Chambord had a soft spot for Ahmed since he had made her a linctus for a troubling cough, so she agreed while muttering about disruption and the busiest time of the year.

Isabella came back late that afternoon to much laughter in the kitchen, most of it from Madame Chambord, as she helped Ahmed and the children. Gironde, Gabriel and Cormac seemed to have honey up their arms and in their hair, while Annecy still looked pristine at the end of the table, helping Madame sprinkle fruit and nuts on the trays of layered, honeyed pastry. Isabella took the boys outside to wash just as a servant arrived for Ahmed, who followed him up to the pigeon coop.

He stood and unfolded the message from Paris. As he read,

his chest suddenly felt tight, and he found he was holding his breath. It was a long coded message on both sides of the vellum. Young Jean Baptiste had done very well in getting this information. Ahmed dropped his hands to his sides, walked to the tower's edge, and took a deep breath while holding the message up and reading it again. He felt a triumph that his suspicions were confirmed. Padraig was working for Al Cazar, the Sheikh's right-hand man, the Arab disguised as a merchant who had tried to poison Isabella. Now Ahmed felt real fear, for he knew what the Sheikh and his men could do. He also realised that Finian might not be the only target. But why the ship from Rouen?'

He knew he had to send a message to Lucca, for Chatillon had to come home before it was too late. He wrote a message, tied it to the bird and carried it to the edge; launching it south with both hands, he glanced down and saw Padraig staring up at him with undisguised loathing and malice before he turned away.

Gironde insisted on taking Padraig to the kitchen to show him the trays of Baklava cooking in the large open-fronted stone bread ovens. The housekeeper gave them cups of buttermilk while they waited, and then, removing the trays, she placed them to cool. Padraig smacked his lips and congratulated Madame Chambord, who smiled, being very susceptible to his Irish charm.

Ahmed went to find Finian, his mind racing as he struggled to find a way to tell him that his cousin was a traitor and was planning to harm the family somehow. He walked to the stables and down to the paddocks, but he was too late, for Finian had taken the stallion out for a good gallop. Instead, he walked along the river banks to think things through. What was Padraig planning, and how was it linked to the ships in Rouen? He realised it was getting late, and the days were short, so he cut across the fields to the chateau. When he entered his room, he found that a cup of buttermilk and a piece of baklava had been placed on the small table by the window, and he smiled—one of the boys or Madame Chambord, no doubt.

He sat and ate it while his mind raced over the possibilities. Padraig could not do this on his own; he had Rollo, but he was an amiable big man, a carpenter, not a warrior or swordsman. He did not have an ounce of aggression in his body. There were ten men here, and Padraig would not risk taking on Finian. Who would? The obvious strategy was to open the gates to Al Cazar's men, but then he remembered Pierre and the other men in Paris. They could be there waiting for a summons. They should have gone to their own homes months ago, which should have raised his suspicions. All of them, still here in Paris, still in a group. As he stood, it suddenly occurred to him that Al Cazar's target was Isabella. The Sheikh's blood feud was with Piers, not Finian; the Irish warrior was purely a sideshow. It was Isabella they planned to kill. His wife was the target, at the heart of Chatillon's family.

He stood, for Finian should be back by now. Suddenly, he felt a little dizzy and put his hands on the table to steady himself as he made for the door. He walked along the stone corridor and found he was bouncing from wall to wall as if his balance had completely gone. He reached the balcony of the Great Hall and put his hands on the balustrade; it was busy down there, and Isabella was directing servants to scrub the long trestle tables. He went slowly down the open stone staircase at the side, feeling his way with his hands and looking like a lizard clinging to a wall. His feet felt as if they had been encased in lead boots. Each one was so heavy to lift and place on the next step. He stopped, and swaying, suddenly felt the desire to laugh as he realised how clever Padraig had been. He had poisoned a master poisoner, and Ahmed realised exactly what had been hidden in the sweetness of the baklava.

At that moment, he toppled forward and fell down the remaining stone steps. A serving girl screamed, and Isabella whirled around to see Ahmed hit the floor. She rushed to his side; he was pale, sweating and gasping for breath. He struggled to get the words out, 'Poison, fungi, Rouen, ship!' They were delivered in a staccato manner with an outward pant for each one.

Isabella understood the first part immediately. She shouted at their Steward, Jean, who seemed frozen to the spot.

'Pick him up and bring him to the kitchen immediately.' She raced ahead, and Jean followed, Ahmed's head lolling in his arms. Madame Chambord squealed in alarm as they came rushing in, while Isabella pushed a young serving girl out of the way and shouted at a surprised Dion, 'Bring the basket of bayberries quickly. We must grind them into a paste,' she shouted, grabbing the large pestle and mortar off the shelf. Dion acted quickly while adding a small amount of wine to make it fluid, and Isabella spooned the thin paste into Ahmed, massaging his throat to make him swallow. Within minutes some of it came back up, but they persevered until they had managed to get a large cupful down.

While they were doing this, Ahmed seemed to be slipping in and out of consciousness, but he kept repeating the words 'Rouen' and 'Ship.' Suddenly the emetic seemed to work, and he began to vomit violently, bringing up the baklava and buttermilk he had consumed a short time before. However,

Isabella had jugs of milk ready, and once he began to dry retch, she poured cup after cup of milk down his throat. She was terrified that they were too late, that his swallowing reflex would go before she could swamp his stomach with milk. He sat back, shaking and exhausted, conscious but not lucid.

Padraig and Finian came when called and stood watching what was happening with concern. 'What's amiss? Is he ill?' asked Finian.

'He has been poisoned!' said Dion glaring past him at his cousin.

Finian moved her to one side. 'It must be an accident. Who would poison Ahmed?'

'Open your blinkered eyes, Finian, the same person who brought a falconer here to take down Ahmed's birds. Someone who does not want the truth to get out.' she hissed and leaned around him to glare at Padraig again, but he was gone.

Finian had been out since very early, so he had not read the message from Lucca. Jean, the Steward, handed it to him as he entered the chateau business room.

'A bad business, Sire. I hope the old gentleman pulls through; he is like one of the family. We carried Ahmed to his room, but Lady Isabella said it would be touch and go. He seems to have lapsed into unconsciousness again.'

Finian thanked him, unrolled the strip of vellum, read the contents, and frowned as he read it twice.

I have information from Ahmed that proves that your cousin Padraig is not what he says, and he means you harm. Be vigilant, challenge him, and, if necessary, act immediately by doubling the guard, Finian. We will be back before Yuletide.

Finian went cold. *What information?* He knew Dion had serious reservations about his cousin, but he thought she was overreacting. Now he wondered if she was right. If, as it seemed, Ahmed had indeed been poisoned, was it Padraig or Rollo who had done this? If so, how did they prove it? He had just got his cousin back. If the accusations were false, he would lose him all over again. He sat in Chatillon's chair, put his head in his hands and thought about how to approach this.

Dion was already on the trail. She had seen the cup and tin plate in Ahmed's room, so she headed to the kitchen, but after a few questions, she hit a dead end. A trusted maidservant had taken it up and left it there for him. Dion knew it had to be Padraig who poisoned Ahmed, as he had reason to do so, and she would prove it.

Padraig strolled over to the barracks maintaining a calm exterior while his stomach was clenched; the last thing he wanted was for Ahmed to recover. He had heard Dion's vitriolic accusations and realised they were running out of time. Why couldn't the damned Arab have stayed in his room and died as he was supposed to? The plan had been so simple. He opened the barrack door and called Rollo outside.

'Ride to Paris; things are coming to a head. We cannot delay any more. I want the men here in the forest on Saturday night, waiting for the signal from the tower.'

'That is only four days away, Padraig; surely we are not ready to carry out the plan yet!'

Rollo clenched his fists and looked away. Padraig could feel his reluctance which was the last thing he needed.

'I saved your life, Rollo. I saved you from the worst punishments. I got you out of there, and I have looked after you since I negotiated our release with Al Cazar. Don't let me down now, for I would never forgive you,' he said, fingering the hilt of his dagger and pinning Rollo with an intense stare.

The big man sighed as he mounted his horse and rode out of the gate. It began to rain, and Padraig had told him to be back early tomorrow, so it would be a long sleepless night. If things had been different, he would have stayed here at Chatillon sous Bagneux; he was valued as a carpenter, and the bailiff had already told him as much. Now he would have to run and expect to be hunted like an animal.

Isabella sat beside Ahmed, holding his hand, and she prayed that he would live. He had always joked that he had a strong stomach and constitution, but although he didn't look it, he was in his late sixties. His breathing was still rapid, and she knew he would die within a day if he began convulsions. Everything depended on how much poison he had ingested before he vomited the rest out, for the red, white-spotted Fly Agaric was lethal.

Isabella loved Ahmed dearly; if he died, she would find whoever had done this, and they would wish they had never been born. She felt tears on her cheeks and prayed that Chatillon was on his way. She needed him, but until he returned, she had to be strong.

19

Chapter Eighteen

It had been a long and exhausting week in Lucca at the beck and call of his uncle, Pope Urban, to discuss many matters and plans with the senior nobles. The news had recently arrived, telling of the slaughter of the earlier People's Crusade led by Peter the Hermit as they took the land route. Therefore, Duke Robert had decided that the Northern French contingent would go to Rome and then head south, where they would cross the Adriatic Sea from the region of Apulia. They would not risk travelling overland, but instead, they would charter ships from the ports of Bari or Brindisi. Again, Chatillon shook his head at the madness of it all. With the number of pilgrims that followed them, they would need a fleet of a hundred ships. He prayed that many pilgrims would decide to stay in Rome, having reached the Holy City.

The route, the logistics of transporting so many, and the supplies were discussed night after night, with Chatillon being the voice of sense, reality and caution. Chatillon could feel his patience beginning to snap as he was asked the same questions repeatedly by people of rank. Fortunately, it was the blessing tomorrow when thousands would cram themselves into the cathedral, the large forum outside, and the surrounding streets, to catch a glimpse of Pope Urban. Chatillon organised dozens of priests with dippers to go amongst the crowds with holy water, blessed by the Pope, to sprinkle over their heads.

He arrived back at the residence for an hour and collapsed face down on the bed. Fighting his way through the crowds, who had been there since dawn, had been exhausting, as they grabbed at his velvet tunic with the Papal insignia to ask him when the Pope would appear. He closed his tired eyes but was shaken awake almost immediately by Edvard.

'Is it time to dress for dinner already?' he muttered into the bolster, reluctant to move.

'No, but this has arrived, and I thought you should see it immediately.'

Chatillon put out a hand without opening his eyes and clasped the vellum in his fist. Finally, he rolled onto his back and, blinking, held it up to read. In seconds he was upright, carrying it to the window's light to read again.

Come home now! Isabella is the target, and I will do what I can to keep her safe, but I fear Al Cazar's men will attack us soon. They are gathering in Paris.

'Pack the saddle bags immediately, get the grooms to take the horses the long way around to the meadow just north of the city. In these crowds, we would never get through. This way, we will be at the front to hear my uncle's blessing but can leave by the side door. Send one of the men ahead at speed now to have fresh horses at every stop. Bruno will know which inns and livery, as he has been here before with us, so send him.

We ride for home now, and if we travel through most of the night, we might make it by Saturday or Sunday.'

Chatillon covered his long Papal ceremonial robe with his heavy hooded riding cloak. His uncle was emerging from his room in the full splendour of his Papal regalia. It was too late to have a conversation as they were all moving into place in the procession. The huge cross, images of the saints and Papal banners were at the front, while a dozen young alter boys swung their thuribles back and forth so that the air was heavy with incense. The cathedral choir was beside them, singing as it headed for the great doors of the cathedral. Hundreds of guards and armed soldiers parted the crowds and held them back as they all progressed, stepping and swaying in unison to the voices in the slow traditional, swaying step—hundreds of clergy and senior nobles all moving to the same rhythm. It was a splendid and inspiring sight.

When they reached the steps of the cathedral of San Martino, the Pope indicated that a further huge banner be unfurled and raised. The crowd gasped and then cheered with many shouts of *Hallelujah* and *God be praised*, for it was St George, riding to victory with a red cross on his white shield.

Even though he was impatient and anxious, Piers allowed himself a small smile. His uncle, the Pope, had learnt the impact of the dramatic, theatrical gesture, and he now used it to good effect.

For Chatillon, the rest of the ceremony was interminable, but at long last, he and Edvard were out and running north through the streets of Lucca. His mind in a whirl, Chatillon prayed that Finian had taken notice of his message and put the men on alert, both inside and outside the house. They reached the meadow where the rest of the men were waiting, and he explained why they were racing back. Most had been with him for many years and they loved Isabella and the boys. He could see the anger in their faces as he shortened his reins and kicked his horse into a gallop; for now, they needed to ride like the wind.

'You should have listened to me!' hissed Dion at Finian, who stood just inside the door of Ahmed's room, arms folded. She was sitting beside the bed holding Ahmed's thin, cold hand and mopping his brow when the fever returned.

'Dion, we have no evidence that Padraig was responsible for this. He seems happy here, as you've seen; the boys like him and seek out his company. It is madness that he would throw all of that away by using a poisoning as obvious and clumsy as this. Padraig is far too clever for that, and he also knows that Isabella is almost as expert as Ahmed and would detect it immediately. It makes no sense. It is far more likely that the Sheikh's men have infiltrated the chateau somehow.'

Dion put a hand over her eyes and sighed. She loved Finian dearly, her handsome, strong Irish warrior, but there were times when he was just plain stubborn, and now he was refusing to see what was in front of him.

'I hope you will not live to regret that conclusion, Finian, because I know you're wrong. Ahmed found out the truth. I've just learnt that he sent an urgent message to Chatillon shortly before he was poisoned. He has paid for it. Now go away and leave us in peace.'

Summarily dismissed, Finian shrugged and left. He stood outside the room for a while, mulling over her words before making his way along the gallery that overlooked the Great Hall. The family gathered below for dinner, and his men filed in to fill the trestle tables. Rollo was with them, laughing at some sally from one of the men. Watching him, Finian found it hard to believe they meant any harm to them. As usual, Padraig sat apart with Gironde and Gabriel, who was plucking at the citole's strings and showing Comac how to hold the strings down. Finian knew that the meal would be another subdued affair, with Ahmed hovering between life and death above them.

Suddenly, there was a disturbance at the door. Every one of the dogs at the hearth leapt to their feet barking, including Annecy's little spaniel, who thought he was as big as them. A wet and dishevelled figure appeared; he swayed on his feet as the dogs sniffed at him and dismissed him as a threat. Finian ran down the stairs and found his hand had gone automatically to the hilt of the sword he now wore all the time. Glancing up at the dais, he saw that Isabella had immediately pulled Annecy into her arms as a protective gesture. There seemed to be so much tension and fear. The Steward, Jean, greeted affectionately the man whose clothes dripped onto the floor. Jean knew him well, and now Finian recognised him as he threw his hood back. His name was Alain, a good man, a tenant whose family had farmed the Chatillon land for generations, and he relaxed as he went to find out what was wrong.

As Finian approached, the man's eyes alighted on him.

'We found her, Sire; we found our beautiful Cecily,' he said, his voice breaking on his daughter's name. Finian led the man to a chair by the fire as he had come quite a distance in this foul wet, and windy weather. The Steward brought a tankard of warm mulled ale and closed the man's cold hands around it.

'Tell us when you get your breath,' said Finian, pulling a chair up alongside.

'We think it was the flooding, as the river, she be in spate now. The priest thinks the body has been stuck in the river half under a branch, and the flooding has released it. The lower part of her body isn't in a good way, but the cold weather has kept it, and you can see it is her, my Cecily, her long black hair was flowing in the river as if she was still with us.'

'So poor Cecily, she drowned,' whispered Isabella, who had come to stand beside them. The father turned his gaze on her and stood up.

'If that were the case, I would not have come all this way, my Lady, but Cecily didn't drown. Her neck had been snapped, and the black bruising where she had been throttled was clear to see. Also, there was a stab wound in her back. She had been running away from whoever did this to her.'

The silence in the Great Hall, which was filled with thirty people, was deafening. They had all heard his last sentence. Padraig stood further back, out of the light. As he heard this, he closed his eyes and ran a hand down his face. He knew that Pierre had done this to the girl, thinking the body would be taken down the river and never found. He looked up to see Finian's narrowed eyes on him, and he found he could not meet that gaze, so he looked away. That told Finian everything he needed to know.

'I will do my utmost to find out who did this to her, Alain and I swear I will bring them to justice. Cecily was a lovely girl, well-loved by the family and other servants here. Now that we know she did not take her own life, she can be brought here to lie in the chapel and be buried in the family graveyard. The Steward will deal with it and arrange a Sunday service in the chapel. Now he will provide you with hot food and a bed for the night, so go and rest.'

The man grasped Finian's hands in gratitude. 'That is only just and right, Lord Finian, because of who she is—her parentage. We have kept the secret in the family for too long, although Jean knew and has always given us money through the hard times.'

Finian did not grasp what Alain was saying as he walked over and quietly confronted Padraig. He leaned forward and, gripping his shoulder, asked, 'Was it Pierre? Did he commit this heinous crime to remove her and the child she was carrying? Two lives lost, Padraig!'

Padraig controlled every muscle in his face as he shook his head and answered quietly and calmly. 'Yes, Pierre is a hothead consumed with grief, but he liked Cecily. He does not have it in him to cold-bloodedly kill a young girl in that way. I've known him since he was a young cabin boy captured on his first journey. He went through hell at their hands, but he could not have done this.'

Again, he could not meet Finian's eyes, and the Irish warrior suddenly knew that his cousin was lying to him. However, to appear to give him the benefit of the doubt and due to Ahmed's poisoning, he told him that he had decided to take his men and scour the woodlands and farmlands around to look for any evidence of men hiding in the forests. He asked Padraig to join him, and his cousin looked pleased and nodded.

'I want answers to all this, Padraig, and I am determined to get them before Chatillon arrives home. We have just received a message from him to say they're at Lyon overnight and are on their way.'

Padraig experienced a moment of panic and what he recognised as a tight frisson of fear in his gut. It was Saturday tomorrow, and Pierre and his men would be waiting for the signal in the woods tomorrow night.

'It will be good to see them back, for I have missed Edvard's training and his dry wit. If they're at Lyon tonight, how long will it take them to get here?' he asked innocently, while showing more interest in the chicken he was tearing apart.

'My father rides like the very Devil,' answered Gironde proudly and received an admonishment from his mother for such language at the table. But Padraig just laughed and agreed.

'I had heard that. He certainly terrifies me,' he said in a stage whisper to the boys.

Watching them, Isabella found it difficult to believe the suspicions of Ahmed and Dion, as Padraig was more like a favourite uncle to the boys. Yes, he had hidden his past, but now he seemed to be a different person, and she wondered if Finian could be right—if they were doing him an injustice with their suspicions. However, Finian had kept the full contents of Piers' message from her as he was still uncertain.

'From Lyon, riding at a good pace, two days. However, it is a bad time of year to travel. We've had rain for days, and roads and fields will be waterlogged or even washed away in the foothills,' answered Finian.

'So boys, in only a few days, you could be showing your father the progress you've made in your riding and swordsmanship,' said Padraig.

Annecy, watching from beside her mother, said little. She

did not like this man, and when his eyes lit on her, she could see that he knew it.

'I wish Papa were home now. I miss him,' she whispered to her mother.

'So do I, Annecy, so do I, every day,' Isabella whispered back.

Chatillon and Edvard had a hard time on the roads north of Lyon. They had left before dawn but hit problems at La Charite Sur Loire, where the River Loire, after a week of incessant heavy rain, had broken its banks and eclipsed the roads. The area was so badly flooded it was like gazing across a large lake in the grey winter dawn. They could go no further, so they had no choice but to turn back and go southwest across to Bourges, hoping to rejoin the road north to Paris.

They had not intended to stop again that night, but they and their horses were tired and soaked through, and the warm, inviting windows of the inn at Vierzon proved too much for them, to the relief of Chatillon's men. They sat, their clothes steaming in front of the fire, partaking of a hearty warm venison stew, as this was a thickly forested area with large herds of deer. They took rooms and slept soundly for a few hours before climbing wearily back into the saddle.

'What day is it?' asked a disorientated and aching Edvard, who moaned that he had been given the boniest, oldest nag in the stable at Lyon. It had a peculiar disjointed gait that jarred a rider uncomfortably.

'It is Saturday, I believe, only a week to Yule night itself. Be your usual stoic self on that nag, Edvard. Soon, we will change horses again at Orleans, and we both know the animals there are of good quality.'

Edvard gave a sardonic half grin as he gathered his reins. 'Only because it is a route much used by the nobility!'

Chatillon laughed, and they trotted out of the yard, followed by their men. However, the bony nag proved a more troublesome animal when it developed a limp halfway to Orleans. Edvard offered to drop out and catch them up later, but Chatillon, although impatient to get home, would not hear of it. So, they ended up stopping at a large village and spending a fortune on what was no better than a plough horse, to get Edvard further. It was dusk by the time they rode into Orleans.

'Well, it seems, boys, that we may not make it back for dinner tonight,' lamented Edvard as he climbed off the broad back of his new acquisition.

Chatillon said nothing; the feeling of unease that had settled on him in Lucca had grown over the last few leagues. He sighed, as he knew these delays were frustrating but unavoidable, so he waved the men into the large hostelry to find some food. At the same time, Edvard negotiated a change of horses and then settled his considerable bulk into a chair near the fire. He glanced at Chatillon's closed, pale face.

'Do not fear, Sire, we will be home by the early hours, and hopefully, our fears will be unjustified as we've heard nothing from Ahmed, or Finian, at any of our main stops.'

Chatillon gave a curt nod. In truth, he was bone weary. The months-long journey to Lucca at a snail's pace, followed by this flight back home at a punishing pace, was taking its toll. He glanced at his men, and he could see the drawn lines on their weary faces, even though most of them were ten or fifteen years younger than he or Edvard. He ignored the food, wrapped his cloak around him and closed his eyes for an hour.

Edvard shook him awake with a concerned face, and seeing this, Chatillon gave himself a physical and mental shake; he was never usually this maudlin. In no time at all, he would be shouting at old Louis, the gatekeeper, to open the gates, and they would be clattering into the large cobbled yard. The dogs would be barking, the torches would be lit, and Isabella would run into his arms. He kept that thought in his mind as they all wearily climbed back into the saddle.

'You can come back tomorrow with the grooms and pick up your large friend, Edvard, for you seemed to have developed a rapport with him, and we could do with a new plough horse,' Piers shouted over the clatter of hooves on the cobbles.

His men all laughed, and Edvard grinned, lightening the mood as they trotted out of Orleans for the last stage on the road home.

20

Chapter Nineteen

As Chatillon and his men rode north, Pierre and his men gathered in the dense woods to the northwest of the chateau, waiting for their signal torch, which was to be waved from the tower, so they could see it above the trees. It would tell them the postern gate was unlocked for them.

It was Isabella's turn to sit with Ahmed, who had shown encouraging signs today. His colour was better, and he was restless, occasionally mumbling instead of lying prone and pale like a corpse.

'Has he said anything at all?' she asked Madame Chambord as they exchanged places. 'Just the same two words about Rouen and a ship. Sometimes you can make them out, sometimes not.' She shrugged, smiled and left as Isabella sat and stroked Ahmed's forehead.

She told him about her day and how they were all looking forward to Piers returning tomorrow or the next day. Outside the door, Padraig stood and listened, as he needed to know where everyone was in the chateau before he sent the signal.

It had been a long and disturbing day as Finian had gone

with Cecily's father to bring his daughter's shrouded body back to the chapel. They had then ridden out to search the woods north and northwest of the chateau. Tired and weary, they arrived home at dusk, so after the evening meal, the Great Hall emptied quickly as the men sought their beds; soon, they would be wrapped up in their blankets in the new barrack block. Padraig had been surprised when no one had questioned the large bolt he had put on the new solid oak door of the barracks. He now gently opened that door and waved Rollo out. The big man came reluctantly for every part of his being revolted against what they would do tonight to the family they had been part of for nearly a year.

Padraig had oiled the bolt, and he slid it closed, locking all the rest of Finian's men in the barracks. Now they only had the family, the few guards and the servants to deal with.

'Go and open the postern gate and wait there for Pierre and his men, then bring them straight into the stables,' whispered Padraig, as he went to saddle both his and Rollo's horse for a quick exit. He climbed the stairs to the top of the tower, lit the torch and waved it back and forth before throwing it into the pigeon coop. There would be no birds for Chatillon to send anywhere when he finally arrived.

Seeing the signal, Pierre and his men rode to the walls and left the horses with one man to keep them quiet. He opened the postern gate and greeted Rollo with a grin and a grip of his arm. He sent two men to run along the inside of the walls to the huge stone gatehouse, where the two guards and old Louis, the gatekeeper, had rooms, with an order to cut their throats before the men began a late circuit of the walls. He followed Rollo along the north wall of the main house, but as they reached the door of the small chapel, he stopped.

'Who is in there? The torches are lit,' he hissed at Rollo.

Rollo turned so the light of the small stained glass window lit his face in garish colours. 'The body of Cecily, the young girl you murdered, is in there as they're burying her tomorrow. She was carrying your child! Have you no conscience, Pierre?'

Pierre just looked away and shrugged. 'She was an encumbrance and risk that we didn't need. Let's go; Padraig will be waiting.'

As they crossed to the stables and reached the doorway, Pierre saw something out of the corner of his eye and stepped back into the shadows pulling Rollo with him for a moment. However, it was only a small figure who ran into the chapel. He smiled as he entered the stable to join the others. The two men who went to the gatehouse returned, the task completed, wiping their blades as Padraig pulled them into a huddle.

'Well met, everyone. The plan remains the same as we discussed, but be brisk with your tasks as we now know that Chatillon is on his way home as we speak,' he whispered. This announcement produced some nervous glances and mumbling, but he continued regardless.

'Rollo, Jean and I will go and deal with Finian and that English bitch he married. Pierre, you will take the other group and grab the two boys; bind, gag them and take them down and through the postern gate to the horses. Once there, mount up and be ready to ride. If I am delayed, don't wait for me; instead, ride west as you've been instructed. Finian's children are not to be touched or harmed, do you all understand?' They nodded.

'Good. We will go for Chatillon's wife. With Finian out of the way, there will be no one to stand against us. I cannot imagine she will come quietly, so we must immobilise her quickly. We will all meet outside the postern gate. Rollo, go and unbar the main gates and take our two horses through to the postern gate to join the others, then quickly join me. I will first go southwest and head for Rouen when we gallop down that track. Pierre and his group will gallop east and then south, heading for Marseilles. A buyer is waiting there who will take the boys further east.'

He went to his saddlebags and handed each man a small bag of gold to tuck inside their shirts. 'When we hand our cargo over in Rouen and Marseilles, you will receive the rest. Now swiftly and silently, let us be about our business, which will make us even richer.'

They split into two groups, but Pierre stopped beside Padraig. 'What about the girl, the blonde brat, Chatillon's daughter?' he asked.

'There has been no mention of her by Al Cazar. I am not sure the Arabs know she exists. She will be asleep with the nurse. They're in a separate room from the boys, so leave her be. Now go!'

They went down the side of the huge house towards the kitchen door, which Padraig had unbolted. There was not a sound from the house or the barracks. Padraig went in first in case anyone was there, but the large kitchens were empty, as he expected. They crept quietly along the long stone corridor that led to the Great Hall, but as he emerged, Padraig came face to face with the Steward, who was taken aback at first but relaxed when he saw who it was. The rest of the men flattened themselves against the wall in the dark corridor. Padraig bade the Steward goodnight and moved past him, but turned quickly to pull his head back and cut his throat. Unfortunately, he had been carrying a large stone jug of wine, which dropped and smashed on the stone flags. The noise reverberated around the Great Hall, and the dogs stirred and growled.

Padraig, swearing under his breath, let the man's body drop to the floor, and they all stood in tense silence, waiting to see if anyone stirred. After what seemed an age, they moved into the Great Hall and slowly climbed the stone staircase that clung to the wall up to the carved wooden gallery above. There they split; Padraig and his men turned left towards Finian and Dion's large chamber at the end of the corridor. Pierre went right and crept with his men towards the narrow wooden staircase that led to the three rooms, recently added, that housed the nurseries and nursemaids.

Isabella had heard the clatter in the hall and had jerked awake in the chair by the bed. She had been sitting doing her needlework but had dropped off. Some nurse she was, she thought, as she chastised herself and shook her head. The sound had woken and slightly disorientated her, but as she heard nothing more, she realised it was just a servant dropping something. She glanced at her patient and saw, to her surprise, that his eyes were open, and she gripped his hand and smiled.

'Welcome back,' she whispered. His eyes smiled, and his mouth moved, but no sound came out. She reached over for the cloth and, dipping it in the cool water, moistened his lips and squeezed drops into his mouth. He licked his lips and gave an almost imperceptible nod for more when two things happened.

There was a clatter of feet, furniture toppling, and voices from the boy's room directly above. She heard Cormac's voice shout, 'What's happening?' before a slap and a loud thump. At first, she wondered if it was just the boys fighting again, but she was reluctant to leave Ahmed's side to find out, and they had two nursemaids up there.

Then there came a piercing scream from the other end of the gallery. She made to stand, but Ahmed gripped her wrist. 'Stay safe, stay here,' he croaked. She realised that he seemed to know what was happening as if he had expected it. She poured a small amount of water into a cup and held it to his lips. He gulped it noisily, then lay his head back gasping, 'Rouen, ship.' He managed to get out.

'Yes, but what does it mean Ahmed?' she demanded.

He closed his eyes and assembled his thoughts. 'Ishmael, take you and the boys to Rouen,' he managed to whisper.

Isabella panicked, and her mind whirled, almost stopping coherent thought as she took in what Ahmed had said. They were taking the boys; this was their revenge on Piers. It did not register that Ahmed had included her as well. She had to try to stop them, but first, she put a hand on her friend's thin arm.

'Play dead, Ahmed. Do not show them you're alive,' she whispered, as the door was suddenly thrown open.

Finian had also opened his eyes at the clatter of the jug, but he had not recognised the sound. He was not even sure what had awakened him. He blinked a few times and listened, but all he could hear was the wind getting up outside; a loose shutter banged, and he realised that must have been it, for a storm was brewing. He put his arm around his wife and pulled her close. He loved this small feisty woman, and he knew that relations between them had been strained for the past few months. He had been disappointed today not to find any evidence of outsiders or mercenaries in the woods, but they would continue and sweep south and east tomorrow as he was sure that it was outsiders. He really could not believe that anyone within the chateau would betray them.

Dion nestled under his chin and put an arm around his waist just as the door burst open, and three men strode into the room. One was carrying a sword in one hand and a flaming torch in the other, which he wedged in the wall sconce.

'Get up and get dressed,' said Padraig in a soft voice, while Finian looked at him, at first with shock and then with a rising tide of anger and disappointment. Finian swung his legs off the bed and stood naked in the torchlight. His weapons were on the far side of the room on top of his clothes chest. He stood, feet planted apart, glaring at his cousin.

'How could you do this, Padraig? What do you want? Have we not taken you in and offered you a home here? I trusted you! Do you hear that? I refused to believe them when they said you would betray me,' he yelled.

Meanwhile, Dion pulled the fur coverlet off the bed, wrapped it around herself and climbed out of the other side of the bed. She stood with her back to the wall but gently edged to where her bow and quiver stood in the corner, only an arm's length away.

'Just like I trusted you not to let me rot in the galleys, Finian. All those years of my life enslaved, and the only thing I had which kept me going when I found out you were alive and well, was my hatred of you,' growled Padraig.

Finian suddenly sprang forward, his hands initially reaching and holding Padraig's throat, but as they crashed back into the wall and fell to the ground, Finian reached for the sword, which Padraig still held. Finian's left hand crushed Padraig's right hand around the sword's hilt while his right hand grabbed the sharp blade, and even though it cut into his hand, he straddled Padraig and forced the blade down onto Padraig's throat. The other two men had been frozen into place by the speed and ferocity of Finian's attack, and they were scared. They both knew how dangerous Finian Ui Neill could be. Now Jean, the older of the two, stepped forward and brought his staff down with a horrible thwack onto the back of Finian's head, and Dion screamed.

Padraig pushed Finian off him, and the naked warrior lay unconscious on the floor while Padraig stood over him with a sword.

'Is he dead?' asked Rollo in concern.

Jean bent down and put his fingers on Finian's neck. 'No, just out cold. Are you going to finish him?' he asked Padraig, who stood silently staring at the man he had hated for so long, the man who was now at his mercy.

Dion was in shock, but she now sobbed. 'He loved you, Padraig; you were like a brother to him. It isn't his fault that you didn't escape.'

Padraig glared at Dion, for he was in no mood to listen to reason, and he saw that she had been moving towards her weapons.

'Kill the bitch; she has been a thorn in our sides for a year, dripping poison into everyone's ears,' he shouted at Jean.

Suddenly Rollo, moving quickly for a big man, stepped in front of her.

'No! This does not seem right, Padraig. No one talked of killing the family. We take the boys and go, or we will all live to regret this.'

Padraig stared at Rollo for what seemed like a long time while Jean looked from one to the other, unsure of what was happening. Dion cowered behind the big man. Suddenly

Finian groaned and raised a knee. Padraig whirled around with the blade. He raised it two-handed above his head, pointing down directly at Finian's heart as the Irish Warrior opened his eyes and Dion screamed again.

Rollo leapt forward as the blade plunged down, and he shoved Padraig. The blade continued its descent and went clean through Finian's upper chest and deep into the boards below. Finian gave a strangled scream as Dion raced forward and dropped to her knees beside him, sobbing loudly and cursing Padraig.

'God's blood, tie the woman up tightly and gag her, Rollo, or I swear I'll cut her throat to shut her up, and then I'll cut yours for disobeying my orders. Now we must go. We are out of time,' he said, heading for the door and waving Jean to follow him.

Rollo did as he was bid and tied Dion's hands behind her to the bed behind. 'I am sorry—I have no choice—but if you promise to be quiet, I will leave off the gag. These men have been my only family for many long years, and they saved my life, and now I must leave; help will come soon.'

Dion gazed in anguish at Finian pinned to the floor by a sword buried more than half its length in his chest. A spreading pool of blood beneath him was ominous.

'You're not like them, Rollo, do not do this! If nothing else, try to prevent them from killing any more,' she pleaded, as he headed for the door where he turned.

'They're taking the boys west and then south to Marseille to the slavers,' he whispered.

Dion gasped. 'My boys as well?'

'No, just the twins,' he said and was gone leaving her there, trembling in the light of the flickering torch. She prayed that

Isabella or a servant would find them soon before Finian bled to death. He was the love of her life. She could not lose him, and she tugged and fought at the restraints, but they were too firmly tied.

Isabella was not surprised when Padraig came through the door, dagger in hand.

'Have you come to finish the job, Padraig? He is close to death and will not last the night. Or have you come to cut my throat?'

He had to admire her as she stood there, tall, calm, composed, with defiance showing in every bone of her body. He raised his head and smiled, running his left hand through his white hair. She saw the cut and trickles of blood on his neck.

'I presume you have slain Finian while he slept, for you would not be alive otherwise?' He nodded, and her heart sank; she loved Finian like a brother. He grabbed her arm and pulled her towards the door.

'I know about Rouen and the ship to meet you there!' she yelled.

Padraig stopped, taken aback, for how could she possibly know about the ship, unless one of his own men had betrayed him?

'He is nearly home, and he will find you and kill you for what you do here tonight, Padraig. There will not be a hole or cave small enough in the earth to hide you when Chatillon begins looking for you, and I promise you he will extract a slow and agonising revenge, for that is his trademark.'

Padraig had heard enough, so he swung his fist back and punched her hard in the side of her head, knocking her into the wall. She collapsed on the floor against the cold stone, dazed with the pain beginning to throb in her jaw and cheek.

Ahmed, hearing all this, fought to keep his eyes closed, but he was gritting his teeth. He knew he was too weak and could do nothing to stop them; he could just pray that Chatillon got here before they left.

Padraig pulled Isabella roughly to her feet, but she was not finished, and she spat in his face, so he hit her again. This time she hit the door, and she gasped at him, 'Kill me here, Padraig. Please don't do it where the children can see, for they truly like you.'

Padraig gritted his teeth, for he, too, liked the boys, but he would not let emotions ruin this plan and his future. There was too much gold involved.

'You're far too valuable to be killed, Isabella. You and your boys are about to bring us a fortune. A blonde beauty like you is worth at least double in the market. You will be the jewel in the crown for the Sheikh.' He pushed her ahead of him through the door, his left hand gripping her hair tightly.

They reached the Great Hall, and looking down, she gasped. Gabriel and Gironde were there with Pierre. They were gagged, their hands were tightly bound in front of them, and a rope was around each of their necks. Padraig pulled Isabella's face close to his, and she could smell his hot stinking breath.

'You will do as I say, or I swear the boys will suffer.' She nodded, and they started down the stone steps.

'It is time to go,' he announced while tying Isabella's hands tightly.

'Wait!' cried Rollo. 'It's freezing out there; we need their cloaks.' Padraig hesitated for a second, then realised he was right. They had a long journey ahead in the winter weather.

'Be quick; go and get them,' he said in an exasperated tone.

Rollo raced up the stairs and then up to the attic rooms

where the terrified nursery maids were cowering. Pierre had hit both of them as they tried to protect the boys, and blood trickled from the mouth of one. Rollo grabbed the cloaks from the pegs on the wall.

'Wait until you hear us leave in a few moments, then run to Finian's room, and untie his wife. You need to help her stop the bleeding before he dies,' he hissed.

Moments later, the huge oak doors were unbarred, and they went out into the night with their captives, heading for the postern gate and the horses. Jean raced to the stables and brought the other horses; unbarring the huge gates with difficulty, he took them to where Padraig was waiting outside the postern gate. Pierre pushed the boys roughly ahead and handed one to each of his men, who mounted and pulled them up in front of them. Gabriel's terror showed in his eyes, but Gironde glared hatred as he saw Padraig slap his mother when she refused to get on the horse. Pierre turned and went back through the gate.

'Where are you going?' yelled Padraig in frustration, constantly listening for the sound of hoof beats, his eyes straining into the dark of the road ahead that disappeared into the trees.

'Something I need to do, a few moments only,' he said and disappeared.

Padraig swore long and loudly, and then it occurred to him that Pierre might be going to fire the chateau. For a moment, he felt a twinge of guilt at the thought of the three children still up in the nursery, but then shrugged it off as he mounted his horse behind a rigid Isabella. She gripped the mane until her knuckles were white, praying that Chatillon was nearly home and that he would track and find them before they got any distance.

The flames from the burning pigeon coop still lit the sky and cast flickering shadows over the chateau, as Pierre ran across the bailey towards the chapel. As he opened the door, Pierre could hear the loud thumps and bangs from the barracks, so he knew he had to be quick as the men were using their bed frames to try and smash their way out. The candles on the altar flickered in the strong breeze from the rising wind outside. He pulled the door shut with a bang and walked towards the catafalque on which lay the body of young Cecily. He laid a hand almost affectionately on her cold body but then glanced around to find what he was looking for in the old chapel.

Annecy knelt at the front on the altar steps; her eyes were closed, and her lips were moving. Her little spaniel was beside her. It wagged its tail at Pierre, and he stroked its silky head.

'Are you praying for her? For my Cecily?' he whispered. Annecy opened her eyes in alarm to see the scar-faced Pierre, but she bravely nodded and closed her eyes again.

'Good, let us pray for her together, for I loved her once,' he said, kneeling beside her.

Outside, Padraig was growing more impatient and was circling his horse as finally, Pierre emerged from the postern gate.

'God's blood, you took your time! Now let us go,' he shouted. Kicking his horse into a gallop, they raced down the track to the road that ran through the village. Padraig went south with Jean and Rollo. Pierre, his men and the boys went west.

As he galloped into the night, Pierre smiled; he hoped that would be the last time he would ever have to lay eyes on Padraig MacDomnall, for he had come close to cutting his throat several times. Only the thought of the rewards to come had stayed his knife.

As the two groups disappeared, Chatillon's men in the barracks, using a bed as a ram, finally managed to smash the heavy oak door off its hinges. Swords in hand, they poured out into the bailey, but in the lurid light from the flames on the tower, no one was in sight. Lazzo appeared, having run from his cottage in the village. He was awake and heard the hooves; running out, he had caught a glimpse of Isabella on a horse in front of the white-haired Padraig.

He surveyed the scene at the gatehouse with shock; the body of old Louis with his throat cut lay curled at his feet, and his two guards lay dead in the guardroom. He walked into the bailey, sword at the ready and saw his men standing dazed in front of the huge doors of the chateau, which stood open.

Whoever it was, they had gone; he closed his eyes as he thought of trying to explain this mess to Chatillon. However, he suddenly realised that Finian was not there and raced towards the house, praying they had not killed him.

21

Chapter Twenty

Both groups rode as if the hounds of hell were after them. Padraig made for a farm several leagues south where they would pick up a large wagon laden with flour. Pierre, smiling at the thought of what Chatillon would find when he returned home, galloped southwest. He was heading for Auxerre and then onto Beaune, where they would turn south to Lyon and down to Marseille. There the captives would be handed over for several large bags of silver.

Padraig was worried as they galloped south, for he was on the far more dangerous route. He had stuffed a balled cloth in Isabella's mouth and gagged her, for he could not risk her calling out for help. He had also sent Rollo to ride ahead as this was a well-used road from the south, and they did not want to be seen. He knew that the road split not far ahead, and they would turn off for the large village of Ablis, where the farm was located on the outskirts. From there, they would travel west with the wagon to Chartres and then to St. Malo.

Isabella was not afraid as she was filled with all-consuming anger. She swore she would escape at the first opportunity, and then she and Chatillon would make them pay.

Suddenly Rollo came galloping back. 'Riders ahead and coming this way fast. They didn't see me as I had just reached the ridge, but they were clear in the moonlight as they crossed the valley floor at a gallop.'

Padraig's eyes frantically searched the thick undergrowth in the dark, before viciously pulling his horse to the right and riding up a bank and into the bushes, forcing a way through and leaving a myriad of cuts on the chest of the big grey. Suddenly an old dilapidated foresters hut appeared through the undergrowth ahead, and he hid the horses behind it. He dragged Isabella from the saddle and handed her to Jean.

'Pin her to the ground and keep her here until I return,' he whispered, before pushing back through the bushes. He ran forward in a crouch, lying flat under the low foliage he positioned himself to look down onto the road.

He had not long to wait, the sound of galloping hooves was loud, and he could feel the reverberation of several horses through the ground. He quickly rubbed some dark wet leaf mould over his face and hair in the gloom and sank even lower. They were travelling at full speed, cloaks flying, and he counted seven of them. In the moon's faint light, Padraig recognised the first two riders. Piers De Chatillon bent low over his horse's neck, his dark hair flying, pushing the animal on. The big bulk of Edvard galloped just behind him.

Padraig smiled. 'You're too late, Chatillon, and if we are careful, we will be clear away before you come looking for us. For I would lay money with what you find at the chateau, that you will not leave before dawn,' he whispered before rising and running back to his men.

He found Jean struggling with Isabella, who had managed to

pull her gag off and was punching and landing blows on Jean with her bound hands clenched into fists while Rollo stood back helplessly. Padraig drew his dagger and hit her hard with the hilt on the side of her head. She crumpled and dropped like a stone.

'Put the gag back on and tie her across the front of your horse. We only have another league to go, and then she will be in the wagon and out of sight,' he said, and mounting, they galloped west.

It was not long before they were trotting into the yard of an old manor house. A large older man emerged, and after greeting them, Padraig paid him the agreed sum of gold for a large wagon. He opened the doors to an old barn and rolled out the wagon, which was large, sturdy and already stacked with sacks of flour. However, with a grin, the miller took Padraig to the back to show him a secret compartment. Gripping it with his ham-sized hands, he slid the tailboard out, and there was a narrow compartment underneath the wagon bed, big enough for a man to lie on his back. It was full of old empty flour sacks, and he pulled them out onto the ground.

Meanwhile, Jean lifted the unconscious Isabella from the horse and untied her hands to retie them at the front. Padraig and Rollo picked up a large flour sack and held it wide open. The big miller came to help lift her into the sack; Rollo grimaced at how the man's hands roamed over her body, squeezing her breasts as he held her up, while Jean pulled the sack up and tied it with a leather thong at the top. They left her on the ground while Jean shaved Padraig's head to get rid of the telltale white hair.

'Are you sure you can't stay for a quick bite of hot food? I would give you one of these gold coins back for some time alone with her in the barn.' The miller grinned, flipping the coin in the air and staring at the sack on the ground.

Padraig looked as if he was considering it, and Rollo stepped forward.

'This isn't right, Padraig. She is from a noble family and shouldn't be swived by the likes of him!' he said, looking the miller up and down in disgust.

Padraig laughed. 'If she goes to the markets when the Sheikh becomes bored with her, she will no doubt be swived by a dozen like him. However, we must go. You're staying here on the farm for a while, Rollo. Your size gives you away, and there will be pursuit,' he said, handing the big man another small bag of gold.

Rollo looked completely taken aback. Padraig felt a brief stab of pity, for he liked Rollo, but the gentle giant had suddenly developed a conscience, which was dangerous to them and their plans. The gold he had given Rollo was part of the miller's payment. He had arranged for Rollo's wine to be drugged, and for him to be smothered by the miller tonight while he slept. Padraig knew he had to follow the instructions from Al Cazar and tie up loose ends.

Not long afterwards, Padraig and Jean were on the front of the wagon with a sack of food and drink. Isabella was still unconscious in the compartment beneath, and they were on the way to Chartres.

Chatillon emerged from the forest into the meadows very

close to where he had killed Roget over a year ago. He blamed himself for not seeing that things were not right at the chateau, for the more he thought of it, the more their escape from slavery had all been too convenient.

The horses were almost blown, their sides heaving, so they dropped the reins and let them walk through the meadow. As they mounted a slight rise at the far side of the meadow, the dark shapes of the buildings and church in the village of Chatillon sous Bagneux could be seen, but more alarmingly, the chateau, which was built on the rock bluff behind it, was lit up. There seemed to be torches blazing everywhere.

Chatillon gathered his reins. 'Ride!' he yelled, shooting forward and galloping towards his home.

As they neared the chateau, he saw that the huge gates stood open, which was unthinkable at night. They slowed to ride in, swords drawn, as they were uncertain of what odds they would be facing. Edvard's face became grim as he spotted the bodies of Louis, the old gatekeeper, on the ground and two of their guards lying dead. One half out of the guardroom doorway, his weapon only half drawn from its scabbard.

Chatillon leapt off his horse and raced up the steps into the Great Hall. Inside there seemed to be chaos, with women screaming and weeping. Most of his men seemed to be standing with swords drawn but frozen, watching the drama unfolding around them. Dion was shouting and screaming at Lazzo on the gallery balcony while he held her firmly at arm's length. The nursemaids and children were crying and screaming. Madame Chambord was on her knees, wailing and weeping beside her husband's body, that of his Steward, Jean.

'In God's name, what has happened?' he shouted.

The effect was instantaneous as everyone turned towards

him. Seeing him there suddenly home was too much for a highly charged Dion, and she gasped aloud, 'Thank God! Oh thank God!' and promptly fainted at Lazzo's feet.

Chatillon took the stairs two at a time, while Edvard grasping that they were too late and the attackers had fled, took control of the men milling around aimlessly. He sent some to sweep and search the walls and outbuildings, to ensure all the attackers had fled and to secure the gates in case they returned. The rest were sent to take up defensive positions inside and outside the chateau.

Chatillon, kneeling, gently slapped Dion's face to bring her around. 'Where is Finian? Is he dead?' he asked, fully expecting the answer to be yes.

Dion sat up and glared at Lazzo, who took a step back. 'No! But he soon will be if we don't act at once,' she spat.

'I wanted to pull the sword out to try and staunch the wounds, but she refused to let me. She said Finian would bleed to death,' explained Lazzo plaintively, appealing to Chatillon with arms wide and a shrug.

'Show me!' said Chatillon, following Lazzo to Finian's room. He looked around for Isabella, fully expecting her to be here with Finian, but only one of his men was with him. He blinked when he saw how deeply the sword had been thrust through Finian's upper chest. The hilt was less than a handspan from his flesh. Finian was deathly pale, eyes closed but still breathing. Chatillon turned and looked up into Edvard's eyes, who nodded in understanding, as he looked at the wide pool of blood beneath the naked Irish warrior.

'He has lost a lot of blood, but we must pull it out and pack the wounds on both sides. Where is Ahmed?' he asked.

'He has been close to death. Padraig poisoned him, but

Isabella acted quickly, and he is recovering slowly; he is still very weak,' answered Dion.

'Take two men, and if he is conscious, carry him here. He can tell us what to do, for he is one of the few people who may save Finian,' ordered Chatillon.

Ahmed was awake and on his feet in his room. Swaying and clinging to the wall, he was willing his leaden limbs to walk, as he knew from the cacophony of grief he could hear that his expertise would be needed. They carried him through, and relief flooded his face when he saw Chatillon, but that was replaced by concern when he saw Finian.

They sat him on the bed while he told Dion to go and rip linen, as they would need lots of bandages and wadding. He sent one of his servants to Isabella's workshop to get the herbs and salves he needed to smear into and around the wounds. Another was sent for a needle and catgut to stitch the wounds, and basins of water to rinse and wash them first.

He looked up at Chatillon, who could see how frail his old friend was.

'You need to be prepared, for he may not make it. When the sword is removed, we must hope a main vein has not been sliced. Fortunately, it is to the far left of his chest, and no blood bubbles are coming from his mouth or nose, so the lung is still intact. If he survives the removal of the sword—which his body might not cope with, given the blood loss, as it may shut down Piers—he will need constant care and nursing. He will certainly develop a high fever with a wound like this.'

Chatillon nodded, for the large pool of blood spoke volumes, and he prepared himself for the inevitable.

Everything Ahmed requested was brought and laid out, and Chatillon indicated that Edvard should remove the sword. The big man stood, one foot on either side of Finian and grasped the handle. Finian opened his eyes as Edvard began to pull. It became apparent that it was firmly wedged into the wood below, and Edvard had no choice but to lever it back and forth to loosen it. Finian gave a guttural cry and, fortunately, lapsed into unconsciousness.

The blade reluctantly came out of the flesh with a sucking noise that Dion thought she would never forget. It came with a rush of blood, and she was there to staunch it immediately. Ahmed watched carefully and gave a satisfied grunt that it was not the pumping blood of the big veins, as he instructed her to wash and pack the wound quickly. The pads and bandages had been smeared with a thick green salve. They quickly turned him over and did the same, before gently lifting him onto the bed. Ahmed sent a servant for a powerful sleeping draft, for they needed him immobile for several days.

Chatillon sat on the end of the bed beside Ahmed. 'Thank you, my friend. This is Padraig's work, I presume?'

Ahmed nodded. 'Working in league with Al Cazar, the Sheikh's right-hand man, who tried to poison Isabella.'

Chatillon suddenly went cold. 'Where is Isabella?'

Ahmed closed his eyes for a moment gathering his strength to answer, for he knew the effect his words would have.

'They took her Piers, and we could not do anything to stop them, for they came in the night, locking your men in the barracks and bringing Pierre and his men from Paris to attack the house.'

Chatillon found that his mouth had gone dry, and he could not speak. Eventually, the words came...

'Taken her where? Do we know?' he asked.

'A ship and the word Rouen were mentioned a few times, but

there is more,' whispered Ahmed, who was tired. Chatillon propped him up with a bolster beside Finian, whose breathing was disturbingly shallow and ragged.

Dion answered for Ahmed. 'They have taken your boys as well. They bound the boys' hands and took them away.' That monster, Pierre, was here. He did it; he took them.

Chatillon snarled in fury and strode from the room and along the gallery towards the children's rooms. He found the still tearful nursemaids with Cormac and young Fergus. The boys' beds next door were empty, and the covers lay on the floor alongside Gabriel's citole, which had been broken in the struggle. With it in his hands, he walked back to the maids.

'Did they hurt them?'

The maids shook their heads. 'They beat and threatened us as we tried to stop them, but they just pulled the boys out of the room,' one of them answered.

He thanked them for their bravery, but at the door, he turned to the maid who had spoken.

'Where is Annecy?' he demanded.

'No one has seen her since the attack; she may be hiding in the stables,' she offered.

He left them, heading out to try to find her. Meeting Edvard on the gallery balcony, he told him the news.

'The boys are gone, they have kidnapped them, and now Annecy is missing. For all we know, they have taken her as well, or she could be hiding somewhere, terrified. You know how she hated Pierre.'

Edvard turned back down the stairs to the hall, following Chatillon, who addressed the men below.

'Saddle our fastest and freshest horses. We ride out as soon as possible. Lazzo, you're in charge here; make the house secure and bury the dead.'

Lazzo nodded, and Chatillon headed for the doors to search the stables for his daughter. As he pulled them open, two of his men appeared visibly upset.

'Sire, there is something you need to see...' one said in little more than a whisper. He followed them to the chapel.

He was surprised to see candles burning and a body lying in a white shroud. He immediately thought it was his wife, that they had killed her and staged this.

'Isabella?' he whispered.

'No, Sire, that is Cecily. She was found murdered in the river and will be buried here tomorrow.'

He immediately felt relief but then guilt, for young Cecily had been under their care and protection, and they had let Pierre have his way with her and murder her. For Chatillon did not doubt that he had done this.

He made to turn away, thinking that this was all they had to show him, but Daniel, one of his men who had come with him from Genoa, put a hand on his arm.

'Sire, it is here by the font, at the front of the chapel.'

He walked forward to see Annecy lying on the steps. She looked asleep on her side, her hands folded under her face. Her spaniel pup, eyes closed, looked asleep beside her. There was hardly a mark on them, but with a horrible certainty, Chatillon knew she was dead. He gently moved the young dog, and it rolled off the step dead. He picked Annecy up in his arms, and her head flopped back. He saw the purple imprints of a man's hands as he had snapped her neck. He held his daughter close to his chest and gave such a loud cry of pure anguish that they heard it in the Great Hall and in Finian's room.

Ahmed shuddered; he knew the sound of extreme grief and dreaded hearing what Chatillon had found.

Edvard stood just inside the chapel door, tears streaming down his cheeks, for he had loved little Annecy as if she was his daughter. He could not help the loud sob that forced its way up from the depths, and Piers turned, Annecy in his arms, to walk over to Edvard, his friend, his brother in so many ways. Edvard wrapped his big arms around both of them, holding them close, and both men stood there and broke their hearts over the beautiful little girl whose life had been snatched cruelly away.

Edvard raised his head and wiped away his tears with the back of his hand.

'We need to go now, Piers. We need to catch them and bring Isabella and the boys back. They have possibly half a day's start, but that is nothing to us, and three of the horses they have taken will be double-ridden. We will catch them, Piers, and by God, we will make them pay.'

Chatillon stepped back and nodded, his handsome face almost unrecognisable, distraught and etched with pain. He carried Annecy's body out into the wild night and over to the hall. Servants and men stood around, shocked to the core. One of his men had told them what they had found. Madame Chambord, still weeping, stood and walked over to her master.

'Give her to me, Master. I'll take her to her room and make sure she is washed and ready.'

Chatillon reluctantly handed her over.

'Make sure she is buried tomorrow We may well not be here, but the priest will be here for Cecily. It is what her mother would have wanted. All of our dead will be buried in the family plot, but I want Annecy buried with her little dog in the chapel.

Daniel, will you see to it that a grave is dug? We will have a flat gravestone carved when we return. I want her close to the house, not out on the hillside,' he said, his voice trailing away with emotion.

He strode to the large fireplace and placed his hands on the large mantle stone while staring into the flames for a long time. The dozen or so people in the hall were silent. When he sighed and turned back, Edvard had never seen his face so grim. His eyes were black pools of anger and hatred, his mouth a thin white line.

'Before you bury Cecily, there is something you need to know,' said a voice from the gallery as Madame Chambord descended to the hall. 'She was a Chatillon! Cecily was family.'

Edvard looked perplexed, and Chatillon stood silent in front of the fire, fists still clenched, brows narrowed.

'We were only following instructions, Sire, Jean and I, as your Uncle Odo was an important Cardinal back then when it happened. He wanted it hushed up. He told us it had to remain a secret shared just between the three of us and the local priest. Now your uncle is the Pope,' she said and crossed herself.

'God's Blood! Was Cecily the Pope's bastard?' Edvard whispered loud enough for those close to him to hear.

Chatillon shook his head to clear it and brought Cecily's face to mind; she was a very dark-haired, exceptionally pretty girl. Was she his uncle Odo's child? He could understand his uncle's reluctance to make it known if she was his, and he could imagine the gossip. The scandal in the Lateran Palace for a rising Cardinal in the church having a bastard child, even before he became Pope. And now it seemed his uncle's child had been deflowered and murdered under their roof. Could it get any worse, he wondered, looking up at his friend Edvard's shocked face.

Madame Chambord stood before them, wringing her hands. 'No! She is not Odo De Chatillon's child, and God forbid that wonderful holy man would ever do something like that.'

Edvard, glancing at Chatillon's face, held up a hand and suggested they go up into the business room and away from the rapt audience in the hall.

Once there, Chatillon found that he was angry and confused. How could the girl possibly be a Chatillon?

'Now start at the beginning and tell us the truth, Madame Chambord,' he demanded.

The housekeeper put her hands on the back of the chair and began the story while glancing nervously at Chatillon. She found the expression on her master's face frightening, so she felt it was better if she turned and told it all to Edvard.

'When the master was very young, we had plague at the house, and as you know, his parents died, as did most of the servants. Jean, my husband, survived. He was only young, as was I, a mere slip of a serving girl who became a cook because there was none other to do it. However, Lord Chatillon's uncle needed people he could rely on and said Jean was loyal and bright, so he made him the Steward. Jean then looked after all the staff, including the servant girls, and there was a particularly pretty buxom girl called Rosie.'

Chatillon looked up suddenly, and she turned to face him.

'You may remember her as she introduced you to love, begging your pardon, Sire. Then your uncle took you away to the French court, and Rosie was gone when you returned from Paris that Yuletide. You were furious that she had been turned away because she was carrying a child. No one was sure if it was yours as she was a popular girl with the men, but you told Jean to find her despite that. He did but discovered that young Rosie had recently died in childbirth, as many do. He then went to your uncle because the child was definitely yours, a black-haired, dark-eyed little girl, and you were only seventeen years old. Your Uncle Odo decided that she would be called Maria and that he would support her and place her with a good family, but you should never know as you had a career ahead, possibly in the church, and you were returning to court.'

Chatillon ran his hands through his hair in exasperation. 'Of course, I remember Rosie. I remember her well. Surely everyone remembers their first,' he said, holding his hands out to Edvard, who nodded.

'Well, Maria grew into a dark-haired beauty with almost black eyes, and she made a good marriage to a young farmer, a freeman from a good family. That was Alain, your tenant. They were very happy, but they only had one child, a daughter called Cecily. Unfortunately, Maria suffered her mother's fate and died of childbed fever a month after Cecily was born. After a few years, her father married again. At first, things were fine, but the child didn't like her stepmother, so I brought Cecily into service in the house when she was fourteen. Cecily was quick and bright; I thought she could make something of herself. The old priest knew her parentage and taught her to read and write, on Odo's instructions. I thought she could even take my place and become the housekeeper someday. She never knew that she was a Chatillon, or that you were her grandfather, but she loved being in this house, especially with Lady Isabella and the children. Now Cecily is gone, taken in by that evil man Pierre who no doubt murdered her,' she sobbed.

No one said a word, and she glanced nervously from one

face to another.

Chatillon moved across the room and, dropping into the big chair behind the desk, put his head in his hands.

'Let me get this right—not only did I have a daughter called Maria that I never knew anything about, but my granddaughter has worked here for two years, and I was never told who she was. God's blood I must have passed her on the stairs or in corridors, watched her sweeping rushes or clearing the fireplaces. My granddaughter, a servant in my house when she should have been sat at the table on the dais with us,' he said, growling in rage and frustration while glaring at Madame Chambord.

'I am sorry, Sire, but we were under strict instructions from your uncle. However, he never knew we had brought Cecily into the house until his last visit, and he was unhappy when he saw her here. He decided then that he would tell you all about her once the crusade was over.'

Chatillon looked up at Edvard in dismay, and his friend shook his head in disbelief.

'We should have known Piers, for she was the image of you, that long black hair and those dark flashing eyes—such a beautiful girl inside and out.'

'And now she is dead because of me; I let Padraig bring that murdering animal into my house, and I let Pierre stay here too long. I am indeed cursed because, through my actions, I have lost another daughter, a granddaughter and a wife in a few weeks.' He slammed both fists down onto the table, which made them jump, and then kicking the chair back out of the way, he strode out of the room into the hall below.

Madame Chambord stood, hand to her mouth, fear and dismay writ clear upon her face. Edvard put a comforting arm around her, for she was also grieving for her husband, Jean, the Steward and for little Annecy, whom she had loved.

'Do not fear. You did the right thing to tell him. It means Cecily can be buried as she should be, in the family plot beside his parents,' he said and followed Piers down the stairs.

'We're leaving almost immediately, so saddle the horses. Lazzo, you can keep the men who rode with us from Lucca; they need to rest. Now I need information.'

So saying, he ran up the stairs to Finian's room. Finian's face was as white as the linen bolster, his breathing still ragged as Dion prepared a mixture of paste in a pestle and mortar. Ahmed, almost as pale, sat in a chair, a rug over his knees directing her.

'Will he live?' he asked Ahmed.

'With your God's grace, my God's grace, Dion's nursing and a miracle, I hope so, but it will be a long process. The body takes time to heal when you lose that much blood,' said Ahmed.

'I need to leave, so what can you tell me to help me find them? What do you know? Any detail, no matter how small.'

'We know they were heading to Rouen, and a ship is waiting for them. You must catch them before you reach the ship,' Dion said.

'Anything else? Anything at all?' said Edvard, who was now standing in the doorway.

'Rollo, the big man, the genial carpenter, was truly shocked at what was happening. Padraig had not told all of his men the details. Padraig was about to plunge the sword through Finian's heart and would have succeeded, if not for Rollo. He first saved my life when Padraig wanted to cut my throat, and Finian's life by pushing Padraig at the last minute. The way

Padraig stared at Rollo, I thought he would kill him; you may find his body outside,' said Dion.

Chatillon stood in thought. 'So they are racing to Rouen, but there was no sign of them on the road, so they must have taken another route. Come, we will go!'

Suddenly Dion held up her hands and shouted after them. 'Wait! I've just remembered. Rollo said the boys were going west. They were splitting up. They're in two groups!'

'Well, so must we be,' he said and strode out.

Edvard lingered for a few moments to break the news. 'They murdered Annecy. He broke her neck and that of her little dog. She will be buried tomorrow; please light some candles and say several prayers from me.'

Dion's hand flew to her mouth in shock, and Ahmed gasped, closing his eyes in pain.

'Pierre!' spat Dion. 'It will have been Pierre.'

'We will find him, for we've just found out that young Cecily was Piers' granddaughter, a truth kept from him by his uncle Odo,' said Edvard through clenched teeth, as he strode out after Chatillon.

Ahmed dropped his head onto his chest, overwhelmed with sadness. Maybe Chatillon was right, maybe the Papal Assassin was cursed, or maybe he was always fated to lose those he loved in his life. Ahmed remembered the story of Chatillon's first daughter with Empress Bertha, the young princess Adelheid, who Bertha had passed off as her husband's child. She had been quietly murdered at an early age as she began to resemble her black-haired father more and more.

Piers had always bitterly joked that it was some kind of divine retribution for the dozens and dozens of lives he had taken. However, this time, Ahmed prayed that Piers found the boys and Isabella, for he loved her dearly. He considered this to be his family, and Isabella was like a daughter to him.

Armed and ready, the men were all waiting in the hall when Chatillon ran down the stairs and strode towards the doors. As they went into the yard, he noticed it was getting lighter in the east, and dawn's first fingers of light hit the chateau rooves. Suddenly Edvard shouted, and held up a hand, for a mounted figure was riding towards them. Edvard raced forward and dragged the big man from the saddle to the ground, shaking him like a rag doll, despite his size.

It was Rollo, one of Padraig's men, and for some reason, he had returned to the chateau.

22

Chapter Twenty-one

Rollo had not trusted the farmer from the moment he laid eyes on the big dirty, unkempt man. He was cunning, a greedy man whose eyes swerved away when you tried to engage him in banter. He had also seen the lascivious way he had looked at Isabella, his hands all over her body. Now Padraig had driven off into the distance, and he was expected to stay here and work for this man for several weeks, hidden from sight until the outcry died. This part of the plan had never been mentioned before, and everything about it felt wrong.

Rollo had pleaded tiredness that night, so he had drunk little of the wine on offer, and once in the attic, he got into bed fully clothed, his dagger drawn and in his hand. When the miller came for him, he was ready and sprang out of bed. The miller was a fit, muscular man, and they grappled for some time before Rollo got the upper hand, but then the man picked up a stool and belayed it into the side of Rollo's head, and he dropped to his knees. The miller drew a long dagger and bent to cut Rollo's throat while he was still dazed from the blow. Rollo realising what was happening, shook the blood from his eyes and dropping flat, he rolled, pulling the man's legs from beneath him. He gripped the hand holding the dagger and, twisting it, he drove it deep into the miller's chest.

Rollo crawled to the bed, leaving a trail of blood from a head wound that bled copiously. He pulled himself up and took a breath. He knew the miller had two stocky sons who slept at the other end of the house, and he prayed they were not coming to investigate the noise. Rollo swayed with dizziness, and picking up his saddlebags, made his escape.

He led his horse through the trees, but being disorientated, it took him a while to get to the road. He mounted and realised that he had to go back to the chateau; the picture of Dion's terrified face as Padraig pinned Finian to the floor haunted him. They might kill him outright when he appeared, but he might be able to help, for he knew exactly where the boys were being taken. However, as he pulled into the cobbled yard of the chateau and saw Chatillon's face, he wondered if he had done the right thing.

'Stop, he is bleeding badly. Bring him inside and let us see what he knows,' Chatillon shouted to Edvard, who reluctantly pulled the carpenter to his feet.

'Are you mad to come back here after what you've done?' growled Edvard pushing him into the Great Hall.

In the torchlight, Chatillon saw that Rollo had a huge gash across the front of his head, causing a curtain of blood to come down over his eyes.

'Bind that up quickly, Maria, and someone bring him some brandy or wine,' Chatillon ordered Lazzo's wife.

Chatillon tried to quell the anger inside him as he questioned the man.

'Rollo, we know that you saved the lives of Dion and Finian, so I believe that you've escaped from Padraig and come back here to help us. Is that correct?'

Rollo nodded, but he found his vision was blurred when he moved his head, and he rubbed his hand across his eyes.

'He is badly concussed. They must have tried to kill him,' said Edvard.

Rollo put out a blood-soaked hand and grabbed Chatillon's sleeve tightly.

'They split up. They split up!' the big man muttered.

Edvard understood immediately. 'They have gone two different ways. The boys have gone west with Pierre. Is that right?'

Rollo nodded and regretted it as the room swam, and he gulped down the wine they brought. Chatillon was becoming impatient, for time was now of the essence to them.

'Where is he taking the boys, Rollo? For God's sake, tell us!'

Maria stepped in, wiping the big man's face. 'Give him time; it is a bad head wound, Sire,' she whispered, receiving a glare for her trouble.

'He is taking them to Marseille to a Turkish slave merchant. They are being richly paid for them. I told him and Padraig it was wrong, for they are very young, but they refused to listen.'

'Marseilles?' said Edvard in surprise.

'Two different destinations to split us up as well. Very clever,' growled Chatillon. 'Is there anything else you can tell us? We know Padraig is heading for Rouen and a ship with Isabella.'

'A wagon—they have a wagon, but he is heading west, not north,' he whispered before falling to the floor.

'He's out cold. He risked his life coming here to tell you this,' said Maria kneeling beside him.

Chatillon nodded absentmindedly, barely hearing her words as his mind whirled.

'We split into two groups as we intended, one going north-west to Rouen to try and find the wagon and the ship. The other will go south to find the boys.'

'Are you going to Rouen to find Isabella?' asked Edvard.

Chatillon shook his head. 'Oh no. I am going east to find Pierre and get my boys back. I intend to rip him limb from limb. I should have killed him when I had him under my dagger, for then he wouldn't have gone on to murder.....' He choked on the last word, and Edvard put a hand on his shoulder.

'Don't blame yourself, Piers, for none of us saw this coming. Padraig tricked us all. Now let us ride.'

They separated in the village, each group galloping in a different direction.

Lazzo stood on the tower and watched them go wishing he could have been with them, to watch what Chatillon would do when he caught Pierre.

Isabella thought she was suffocating. She could hardly breathe, her mouth was gagged, and flour dust caked her eyes and nose. She was lying on what seemed to be the bare boards of a wagon, as it bounced over the ruts and stones on the tracks and roads they followed. Every inch of her body ached, and the side of her face and head throbbed where Padraig had hit her.

She tried to concentrate on what had happened, for she

had no idea if Finian and Dion were alive, although she remembered Dion's screams, which did not auger well. She knew they had taken her boys and had gone a different way. A gamut of emotions flooded her as she thought of what her boys were going through at the hands of Pierre—fear, anger, and grief at losing them.

Annecy and Finian's children had not been there with the horses, so she reasoned they must be safe in their rooms. Isabella prayed it was so. She had worked out that Ishmael was behind this, but why had they been kidnapped? Why had he not killed them as he had tried before? Then she realised he wanted Piers to suffer, not knowing where his family was or what was happening to them.

Chatillon would find them. He was the most fearless and tenacious man she had ever met. She could imagine his fury when he reached home, and she had every faith that if he had, he would already be searching for them—and Ahmed knew about Rouen. She prayed that Ahmed was still alive to tell him that.

'He will find us. I know he will find us,' she repeatedly said to herself.

It was daylight now, and some light filtered through the gaps in the sides of the wagon and the weave of the old sacking. There was a lot of noise outside, and she realised from the noise, clatter and shouting that it must be a market town. It must be Chartres, she thought, so now they would turn north to Rouen, and she prayed that Chatillon would be waiting for them there. She was desperately thirsty and hoped they would stop, but it was dark before the wagon drew to a halt.

Padraig was not risking any curious eyes, so he had pulled off the road in a village with a small inn where they could get supplies. It also had a large barn where they could hide the wagon and horses. He went inside to see the innkeeper, while Jean unhitched the horses and got them water and fodder. Padraig returned with food and wine, so they pulled Isabella out of the narrow compartment. Padraig untied the sack and removed her gag, and she gasped for air.

'At this rate, I'll be dead by the time we reach Rouen. It's impossible to breathe in this dust-laden sack with a gag,' she croaked at him.

'Shut up and drink this,' he said, handing her a leather tankard full of ale. She held it tightly in her bound hands and gulped noisily.

'At the very least, you can untie me so that I can eat,' she said, staring at the bread, cheese and meat on a wooden trencher.

Padraig gave a laughing sneer. 'After your earlier stunt, I don't trust you, my Lady. Jean will feed you while he eats.'

A reluctant Jean pulled her over to sit on a box and proceeded to do so, when he only wanted several cups of wine and some sleep.

'I need to piss!' she said.

'Go ahead,' said Padraig with a grin, pointing at the side of the barn.

'In here?' she asked incredulously. 'There must be somewhere outside.'

Again Padraig laughed. 'You're not leaving my sight, or this barn, until you're back in that sack,' he said, crunching a small wrinkled apple. Isabella had no choice but to cross to the far side and do what she could, as the two men watched with amusement. She was angry and walked back to stand directly in front of him.

'Do you hear that, Padraig MacDomnall? That sound in your

head is the sound of hooves as he gallops towards us. He will be waiting for you in Rouen!' she spat at him.

Padraig said nothing. He picked up a rope, knotted it firmly around her neck, and then through and round the one on her wrists before tying it firmly to the wagon.

'Get some sleep, we leave again in a few hours, and Chatillon will search and wait in Rouen for a long time, for we're not going there. The plan has changed. You will already be on a ship heading south, while he is standing on the wharves in Rouen. A clever ruse, do you not agree?'

Isabella's spirits sank. She told herself that the ruse didn't matter and that Chatillon would see through it, and still find her. She kept her head high with a confident, knowing smile on her lips, which she knew unnerved Padraig. In reality, her stomach was knotted in fear, for if they got her on that ship, Piers would have no idea of its destination, and if Padraig was to be believed, she would disappear into the slave markets of the east.

23

Chapter Twenty-two

Pierre was making good time as they had ridden hard all night. They stopped briefly outside Auxerre, at the village of Perriguy, to feed and water the horses, buy some food and wine and set off again.

Pierre found two things that motivated his tired men to keep going—the bags of silver waiting in Marseille for each of them and the fear of Chatillon.

He grinned at them, keeping up a stream of banter, as they headed east across the River Yonne, turning south to make for Beaune, the capital of the Burgundy region. However, for all his confidence, his innards were churning, and he looked back over his shoulder more and more. He told himself repeatedly that there was no way that Chatillon could know which way they had gone or that they had split into two groups, as no one saw them. He smiled as he thought about Padraig on the road to Rouen, no doubt the same road that Chatillon was coming north on. These thoughts only comforted him for a short while, as he realised that Isabella knew, and if Chatillon caught up with them, they would come after him. He became edgier as dusk descended, snapping at his men for nothing.

They finally pulled in at an inn on the crossroads at Saulien St Cyr, for both horses, men and boys were flagging. He bespoke two rooms and bundled the boys upstairs while his men ordered food in the taproom. No sooner had they entered the room than Gironde, ever the feisty one, turned on Pierre.

'My father will be here shortly. I've seen the worried glances over your shoulder. He will catch you, rescue us and then I'll watch him spit you like a pig.'

The men glanced nervously at each other, as they knew Pierre was on edge. However, Pierre said nothing. He stood white-faced with tiredness staring with narrowed eyes at Gironde. This was Chatillon's eldest, his heir who would inherit the estates and half a dozen houses across Europe, the scion of a noble family who would want for nothing, and Pierre felt the bile rise in his throat. He half turned away from the boy with a sneer, but whirled back, and struck Gironde so hard with his left fist that he flew backwards into the wall and slid to the floor.

'You can go without food until you learn to hold your tongue,' he spat at the boy, who was dazedly pushing himself up on one arm. Pierre frogmarched Gabriel out and locked the room door as they went down to the taproom.

They sat close to the fire with a frightened Gabriel pushed into the corner with his tin plate.

'How far to Beaune?' asked the eldest of the two men, mopping the gravy on his plate with a piece of bread.

'No more than half a day; we will set off at dawn. Once there, we quickly change the horses and head south, and there will be no catching us then.'

The innkeeper, bringing more mulled ale, heard some of

this.

'You'll have problems further south, boys, as there's bad flooding, and roads washed away almost down to Lyon.'

Pierre glared at him at first but decided that nothing would be gained by antagonising the man, so he listened patiently and thanked him.

'That may be a problem for us, so we may have to cross to Geneva from Beaune and turn south. Our pursuers will have the same problem, but again, they'll not know where we've gone. Let us to bed, as we have an early start,' he said, pushing Gabriel ahead of him.

Gironde was sitting on his bed, and a large swollen bruise was appearing on the side of his face. He did not cower or flinch when Pierre took his jaw firmly to look at it. Instead, he glared back at him. Watching, Gabriel was proud of him but scared at the same time and prayed he would say no more. The boys curled up together on the bed under the flea-ridden cover for warmth.

'Papa is coming after us, and he will kill him slowly and painfully, I hope,' whispered Gironde; Gabriel squeezed his arm in agreement and prayed it was true.

Chatillon had sent a bird ahead to Beaune, the seat of the Dukes of Burgundy. Its present incumbent, Eudes, known as the Red Duke, was an old friend of Chatillon from their early days in Rome. Chatillon was also very friendly with the Duke's wife, whom he had bedded several times and probably would again, as she was a very useful source of information, and an extraordinarily talented lover. The house of Burgundy owed him a favour, as he had supported her brother Guy to become a powerful archbishop. More than that, Chatillon knew that Eudes would do everything he could to find the kidnappers if they were travelling through Burgundy.

Silver always talked, and Piers paid for the best horses at the stops along the way. At Perrigny, the ostler told him of a group of men with two boys. Chatillon was elated, for they were on the right road, which had never been certain. Now they just needed to catch them.

Chatillon mounted and whirled his horse around.

'We ride!' he shouted, galloping over the bridge on the road to Beaune.

'We must have halved the time between us,' he murmured into the wind, thinking that if they had harmed a hair on his sons' heads, they would pay in ways they could not imagine.

Edvard was not having as much luck as Chatillon. Even though the wagon would be slower, it still had a good half-day start on them. His men asked questions in every inn and village, but no one had seen it. They thought they had a lead at the large, prosperous village of Mantes-la-Jolie, as several wagons and carts had been seen, but as they galloped ahead, the trail went cold. Edvard knew the area around Rouen well, after dozens of trips backwards and forwards to Duke Robert's capital. He decided to search some of the lesser routes through the forests, but still, there was no sign. He dismounted in one glade and thumped his fist against a tree in frustration when they reached another dead end.

'This is like searching for a needle in a haystack, Edvard. Let us go directly to Rouen. There we can get some help from

Duke Robert's men. They know us and will help us search the ships,' suggested Daniel, a man who had served them for over fifteen years and whom Edvard would trust with his life.

'You're right,' sighed Edvard. 'We'll wait for them there, but Duke Robert is on crusade, so it will be the King or Ranulf Flambard, we would have to ask for assistance in Rouen. I am not sure how they will react, and more importantly, will Piers want them to know he has let his wife be kidnapped?' asked Edvard trying to decide on the right course of action.

'Chatillon will think it was worth it if we get the Lady Isabella back,' stated Daniel.

It was the next morning when they rode into the narrow streets of Rouen. Duke Robert had extended the wharves and warehouses significantly for his failed invasion, and the flourishing wine trade had taken over these warehouses. The wharves were bustling as they split into two weary groups and searched every inch of the port area. As Edvard's gaze scanned the port, he realised that dozens of vessels of all sizes were docked or anchored midstream as well, and she could be hidden on any one of them.

'You're right, Daniel, we need more help. Let's go to the inn, clean ourselves up, and I'll ask for an audience with whoever is in residence.'

An hour later, he sat impatiently with a dozen other petitioners in the anteroom that led to the Great Hall. He was aware that for Chatillon, the doors would have just opened. Finally, a Steward appeared and waved him through.

The Great Hall was busy, and numerous clerks sat at tables scribbling away in the light from the high windows. Seeing the wide-eyed stare, the Steward decided to explain.

'The King has decided to restore order in Normandy, as

he perceives the country to be in chaos and turmoil. He will become an active ruler bringing efficient and successful governance to his homeland. New laws are being passed and enforced, and taxes will be collected.'

Edvard inclined his head to indicate his thanks.

He was surprised to see that he was being taken to the King, William Rufus, whom he had known since he was quite young. As usual, Flambard hovered by the King's side. Edvard bowed deeply as William Rufus looked perplexed, and Flambard narrowed his eyes, as anything to do with Chatillon could be dangerous.

'Welcome, Edvard of Silesia. Are you here with a personal petition?' asked William.

'No, Sire, I've come to ask for your permission and assistance to search all the ships in the harbour. The home of the Papal Envoy, Piers De Chatillon, has been attacked, his servants slaughtered while he was away supporting your brother on his crusade. Lord Finian Ui Neill is badly injured and may die, and King Philip's physician, Ahmed, is at death's door.

'But worse than that, they have murdered Chatillon's seven-year-old daughter, Annecy, and kidnapped both his twin sons and his wife, Lady Isabella. We believe they're taking the boys to Marseille, and Chatillon is in hot pursuit with his men. He is hoping to enlist the willing help of the Duke of Burgundy to catch them. Meanwhile, I am searching for Lady Isabella, whom we believe may have been brought to a ship in the harbour, here in Rouen. We have searched the wharves to no avail. I ask that you give us a contingent of men to help in this search, and set up checkpoints to search wagons coming into the city, as we believe she may be concealed in one.'

King William pushed himself out of his chair and turned to stare at Flambard wide-eyed.

'Are they mad to think they can get away with this? Chatillon has contacts, spies and informers from one end of Europe to the other. He will surely track them down and slaughter them!'

Edvard inclined his head in agreement. 'However, Sire, if they manage to get the Lady Isabella onto a ship, we have no idea where it will be bound. We need to find her before that happens.'

'This is an attack upon French nobility. They cannot be allowed to get away with that. They must be severely punished, and made an example of in public. Do we know who is behind this?' he asked in concern.

Ranulf Flambard, who had his own informers, leaned forward and whispered a name into the King's ear.

'Ishmael, the Barbary pirate?' he exclaimed.

Edvard nodded and explained the origins of the blood feud to the King.

'Since we defeated him in the sea outside of Marseilles, he has made several attempts on Chatillon's life and one on Isabella, but all failed.'

The King nodded in understanding. 'This Ishmael has also recently attacked English traders off the coast of Portugal and Brittany. He needs to be stopped. However, for now, we must do all in our power to help our friend, the Papal Envoy, and I pray he finds his sons. Flambard here will provide you with men and a written sheet, with my seal, to board and search any ship in my waters.'

Edvard thanked the King and backed away to follow Flambard to a table for the order.

Sometime later, he rode out of the gates with an extra twenty mounted men, who helped him stop and search wagons and ships. It was dusk when they had finished, and they had nothing. Not one flour wagon or Arab sailor had been found. Edvard stood with the captain of the guard, who was equally frustrated, for he had known Edvard and Chatillon for several years.

'There is a chance that he saw the queue and the extra guards on the gates and turned away to another port,' he suggested. Edvard wracked his brain for the ports north and south of Rouen.

'Where would you go if you were him?' he asked.

'They're kidnapping a great lady, so they want to be able to bring the wagon to the quayside. That removes the smaller ports. Rouen was the only port with a deep enough berth for a Saracen galley, so they would now take her out in a smaller trading vessel to sea. They'll sail south until they find her anchored in a large cove waiting for them.'

Edvard gazed out to the west where the sun was setting. It had finally stopped raining, and the sky was clearing. 'It could be anywhere out there. If they get her to a boat, how will we ever find her?' he whispered.

'I'll take ten men and race north to Dieppe and see if there is any trace there. I suggest you cut across from Caen first and then go down the coast. You may see her once you reach the cliffs down there, and know they are in a port close by, waiting for the tide.'

'Could they have taken her as far as St Malo?' asked Edvard.

'It's a good deep inlet, and they could easily get a large galley into the bay,' he answered.

Edvard stood deep in thought, for he had to get this right.

It suddenly occurred to him that Rouen might have been a lie. It would explain why they had found no sign of them on any road. The galley would sail south. Therefore, it made sense that Padraig would travel south.

'Forget Dieppe, Captain. I just know that they went south, but can you take your men and check Caen and search there? We will ride for St Malo.'

The Captain nodded. 'I suggest we all get some food and a few hours of sleep first, as you have a long ride; it must be over twenty leagues and will take you a day and a half at least.'

Edvard grinned, mirthlessly. 'We are used to that, and we ride hard. I will be in St Malo by tomorrow night. I will get there before them!'

Seeing the determination and the clenched fists, the King's captain did not doubt that he would.

Isabella ached in every bone in her body as the wagon bounced along at speed. She was thrown repeatedly at the boards above and below her. Padraig had invested in two quality draught horses for the wagon, so they were making far better time than expected. They stopped at Le Mans for a few hours but were soon back on the road to Fougeres. The two men took it in turn to drive, or stretch out on the sacks of flour and sleep, which meant that they could keep going through the night. They were already pulling into the yard at Fougeres when Edvard said farewell to the captain in Rouen. They drove the wagon around to the back of the inn, and he pulled Isabella out. Her legs were so cramped and painful that she dropped to the ground and could not stand. He rubbed her legs and undid the ropes on her wrists for the first time.

'You have a choice here. We're only half a day from our destination, and there will be no rescue, as no one knows we are travelling down to St Malo. We are taking you to a room where you can wash, eat, and sleep in a bed. I don't want you to make a sound from the moment we enter the inn. Do you understand?'

Isabella was exhausted and could hardly think straight, but she knew she hated this man like no other, so she gathered every last bit of saliva she could muster and spat in his face. Retribution was swift, and she was knocked to the ground with a dizzying blow. He then delivered a kick to her midriff that made her double up and retch.

'Put her back in the sack; she can stay out here all night with no water or food,' he said, turning away.

Isabella knew that she had to stay alive for Piers and her children, and she gasped, 'No! I need water, or you'll have no one to hand over to your paymasters.'

Padraig stood looking down at her, then jerked her roughly to her feet. 'One word and you're back in the wagon!'

She dumbly nodded that she understood, and with her wrist firmly gripped in his hand, they followed Jean into the inn.

In Rouen, one young courtier in the Great Hall was very interested in the arrival of Edvard of Silesia and the news he brought. He had edged closer and got the gist of it enough to realise what was afoot. The next day he had ridden southwest out to Domfront, for he knew that Henry Beauclerc would pay well for information like this. Henry had several informers in his brother's court both in England and Rouen.

Henry listened to the tale and mulled over what he had heard. Anything to do with Chatillon could prove useful, and the news about this blood feud even more so, for Henry had influence in Leon and Castile; King Alphonse had alliances with some of these Berber families, and the King owed him a favour. This could possibly be used as leverage with the Papal Envoy, for Henry was determined to topple his brother William and seize the thrones of England and Normandy, and Chatillon was the one man who could help him do it.

24

Chapter Twenty-three

They left the inn at dawn, and Isabella suffered another agonising ride in the wagon until they finally bumped over cobbles and stopped. From the noises outside, she knew they were at a port, for she could hear the sounds of gulls, the cries of the hawkers selling fish and mussels, and the shouts of the workers on the wharves. It seemed to her as if she lay there for hours, and no one came near. Every inch of her body ached, and the ropes cut into her wrists, now tied uncomfortably behind her back and beneath her. She tried to stretch out as one of her legs was cramped again, but the sack prevented her from doing that, and there was not enough space to turn over.

For the first time, she found herself in tears at the hopelessness of her situation. Until now, her anger and thirst for revenge had burned brightly within her, but suddenly she realised that Sheikh Ishmael might succeed. If Chatillon was going to rescue her, now was the time, and she prayed that he would come before she was put on a ship.

She thought of her boys and what they must be enduring at Pierre's hands, and her anger returned. She shuffled down and, raising her knees, kicked as hard as possible against the bottom plank. However, it was thick and solid and did not give way; she screamed in impotent rage, but no one came near. They had obviously left the wagon in a shed or warehouse as it was darker and, exhausted, she fell asleep.

Hours later, she awoke when Padraig and Jean returned. They pulled her out and untied the sack. Isabella blinked and stared around. She was in a large warehouse full of crates, boxes and barrels. Padraig untied the gag and gave her ale to drink.

'Not a sound!' he threatened, as he told Jean to feed her. He was not risking untying her hands yet.

'We sail on the evening tide, and then I'll be rid of you forever!'

Isabella sat on a crate, her ears constantly straining for hoof beats, but there was nothing. The days were still short, and it was not long before the light began to diminish.

'It's time. Go and check the wharves, Jean. Make sure the coast is clear, as we don't want to risk losing her now,' he said, while shaking out a large cloak and pulling a velvet chapeau from his sack.

In minutes, he had bundled Isabella's long dishevelled blonde hair up into the hat, and standing her up, untied her hands and enveloped her in the cloak, pulling the large hood forward over her face. Jean returned and nodded that it was clear, and they took her out onto the wharves, which were busy with the last cargoes being loaded. They walked away from the port to the furthest end of the wharf, where a large trading cog was tied up.

The crew were waiting and ready to cast off. Looking across at the bow deck, Isabella thought the captain looked nervous, his eyes darting down the wharves. As well he might, she thought, turning quickly to follow his gaze and look behind. However, she could see no sign of rescue, just a portly dock official ticking off lists. His eyes met hers for a moment, and his eyebrows rose in surprise at such a beauty on his docks. She mouthed the words, 'Au Secour,' at him before she was jerked forward by Jean. Padraig had jumped down onto the deck, and he was holding out his arms.

'Just drop her, Jean. I will catch her!' he said impatiently.

The official began to walk forward, his interest piqued, but Jean drew his long dagger and picked at his teeth with it, and the man backed away while Isabella was bundled under the awning. Jean jumped down to join them, and they cast off, the sailors pushing the boat away from the wharves with poles. Isabella's heart was breaking as she saw the port and wharves disappearing. They would never find her now, she thought, wedging herself into an upright position against the wooden support.

Then, she noticed that Jean was agitated and pointing, while the captain suddenly shouted for the sail to be raised early. She stared at the port, and then she saw them, a large group of mounted men had appeared and were moving fast down the wharves, while people were jumping out of their way. It was too far away to see who it was at the front, but she could see the glint of the setting sun on the chain mail and weapons. Tears ran unchecked down her cheeks, and Padraig, hands on his hips, had thrown his head back and was laughing aloud, for they were too late.

Edvard and his men had ridden their horses to exhaustion to get there. They clattered onto the wharves at St Malo, and Edvard was immediately dismayed at the number of boats and ships in front of him. The estuary of the River La Rance was huge, and St Malo was a very busy port. They dismounted, and he split his men up to search the ships. He and Daniel rode further on, and tying their horses up, they began to do the same until an official approached him.

'Do you have permission or the right to do this?' he demanded. The look from Edvard made him cower back.

'King William Rufus himself has given me permission,' he spat at the man, as he jumped down onto the deck of the next boat, to search and question the crew.

'What are you looking for?' the pompous official asked Daniel in a low voice.

'The Saracens have kidnapped a noblewoman, and we need to find her.'

The man looked shocked and began to walk away, but then he remembered what he had seen and almost ran back.

'Is there a reward?' he asked.

Daniel shouted down to Edvard, asking if there was a reward.

Edvard was up the ladder in seconds and had the official by the throat, lifting him off the ground.

'The reward is your life! Now what do you know?' he shouted, shaking the man until Daniel put a hand on his arm and Edvard dropped him.

'I am sorry, but emotions are running high, and we have to find her and save her before they put to sea,' apologised Edvard, brushing the man down as he raised him back to his feet.

The man, rubbing his throat, pointed out to the mouth of the estuary. Nearly a dozen boats were spread out and leaving on the tide, but the big trading cog with the reddish brown sail was in the middle.

'I think she is on that as she was bundled out of that warehouse, but was all covered up. Only at the last minute, when she turned those pleading amber eyes on me with those striking black brows, did I realise that it was a woman, and then they were gone.'

Edvard clenched his fists and shouted in rage as he stared at the cog in the distance, 'Do we know where she was going?' he asked when he could breathe again.

'North to England, taking a large cargo of wine, I believe,' he said, checking his sheets. Edvard pointed to a large outcrop of rock to the north at the far end of the estuary.

'Can we ride to that?' he asked. The man nodded and told him how to cut across to reach it quickly.

'Daniel, call the men back!' he commanded while walking to the warehouse doors. He saw the wagon still loaded with large sacks of flour and shook his head at how close they had been.

Mounting, they galloped down to the long beach with the flat, raised rocky promontory at the end. If the cog was heading for England, it would turn north and come very close. Edvard thought of swimming out and attacking them, but he knew it was madness, so they sat on their horses and watched. He could clearly see the figures on board, but while the other boats turned north, the cog kept going west. He put his hands over his eyes.

'Look, Edvard, look!' shouted Daniel and Edward's heart fell. A huge galley had emerged from the south and was now standing off, waiting for the cog.

The other boats all scattered as fast as they could. Some even tried to battle the tide to get back into the safety of the port. They recognised a pirate ship when they saw one.

Edvard was filled with frustration and rage as he narrowed his eyes and watched the cog tie up alongside the galley. Several of the Saracen crew scrambled down the sides, and as he watched, he saw them pass a figure back up to the deck above. He saw the white robes of the Arab captain against the darkening sky as he took her from them, and they disappeared into the ship's depths. The cog then went on its way, turning north. Soon after, it passed them, and Edvard saw a shaven-headed Padraig standing on the deck. As they sailed past, he raised a fist in salute, and Edvard could hear his laughter over the water.

The galley pulled away to the south, being just a dark speck in the distance in no time.

Edvard turned to his men, many of whom stood there with forlorn expressions of despair, for they had failed, and none of them relished the thought of returning to Chatillon without her.

As for Chatillon, Edvard had no idea how he would tell him that his wife was now in the hands of the Sheikh. He took a deep breath as he realised he had to send a message to the chateau, and they would forward it to wherever Piers was.

Edvard prayed that he had found the boys, for Isabella was gone!

25

Chapter Twenty-four

Pierre was cocky and confident as they rode towards Beaune. The fortified city sat on a plain surrounded by the hills of the Cote d'Or. As there was still no sign of pursuit, Pierre thought they could probably risk spending the night here, once they had changed the horses. They would stay at the inn and leave at first light the next morning, when the city gates reopened. The boys had been unusually quiet since he had hit Gironde. He could see that the journey had also taken it out of them, with little sleep and long, exhausting hours on horseback in the wet and cold. However, for him, the quieter they were, the better.

'Cheer up, boys, tonight you will have hot food and a comfortable bed,' he announced, glancing back at the twins.

'Where are you taking us, Pierre? How much further do we have to ride?' asked Gabriel in a soft, plaintive voice. Before he could say a word, Gironde answered for him.

'He is taking us to Marseilles, Gabriel, the Devil's cauldron Edvard calls it. All the unsavoury criminals, murderers and thieves in Europe gather there, so Pierre will fit in very well,' he muttered. Pierre jerked violently at the reins and pulled his horse close to Gironde's horse, so their knees pressed hard against each other.

'Did I teach you nothing about keeping your mouth shut?' he said, raising a fist, but the older man sitting behind Gironde stopped him.

'You don't want to mark or disfigure him any more than you've done, or they may not pay full price in the market,' he grumbled.

Pierre stared at them both for a moment and then pulled his horse away as Gabriel let out the breath he had been holding He found his hands were shaking, and he hid them under his cloak. Pierre rode slightly ahead and passed through the high western gate in the walls. He rode to a street hawker to ask where the livery stable and inn was. He told Pierre that it was inside the walls close to the south gate, so they would have to ride across the main square and take the narrow street in the right corner, which would take them straight to it.

However, when they reached the square, it was crowded. On the far side, they were building a new cathedral, which was a hive of activity with dozens of stonemasons and workers. There were also market stalls down both sides of the square, with lots of people milling around buying the produce. He glanced back at the boys and told them to stay quiet as they wended their way forward. It was then that he noticed the soldiers, some mounted, most not, but they were all in a distinct blue and gold livery, which he presumed was the Duke of Burgundy's.

At first, he was not too concerned as he wove his horse through the crowds at a walking pace, but then Pierre noticed that the soldiers were moving towards the narrow street that he was riding towards, to get them to the inn. He stopped, and the other horses pulled alongside.

'What is it?' asked Philippe, the older of the two men.

'I am not sure, but something doesn't feel right—look at the soldiers,' muttered Pierre uncertainly, his eyes darting back and forth across the square, his fingers now gripping the reins. He noticed his hands were sweating and wiped them on his horse's neck.

'They're not interested in us, Pierre, and they're not even looking our way. They are probably heading back to their barracks. Look, the market traders are packing up as well, and their customers are leaving.'

Pierre narrowed his eyes as he scanned the square; Philippe was right, the soldiers were gathering at the far end, and people were beginning to stream past them to leave. It must just be a morning market that was now over. He gave a nervous half-laugh and nodded at him, as he began to move forward again. Then he noticed the nervous glances from the people hurrying past, as they were being herded out of the square by several men in leather jerkins. Also, the market traders were leaving, but their stalls still had produce on them, vegetables and eggs. Looking ahead, he realised that the stone masons and workmen were all standing, staring in their direction. The soldiers had now spread in a line across the street entrance to the south and were facing them, pikes planted forward at the ready.

'It's a trap!' he shouted and yanked the reins to race back the way they had come in. His men did the same, but a cavalry troop surged out behind them into the square when they turned to try to escape. At their head was an impressive broad-shouldered figure, sword drawn, and people scattered in every direction expecting a blood bath. He walked his huge chestnut warhorse towards Pierre, whose stomach was knotted in fear. He stopped only a horse's length away from them....

'I am Eudes, the Duke of Burgundy, and you are my prisoners. There is no chance of escape. Now let the boys go!'

In a flash, quick thinking Gironde was off Philippe's horse, and he pulled his brother Gabriel to the ground before daggers could be held to their throats. They raced towards their saviour on the chestnut horse.

'Take them!' shouted the Duke pointing his sword at the three men. The cavalry quickly surrounded them, pulling them from their saddles into the hands of the foot soldiers below. The Duke looked down at the two boys clinging to his stirrup and lower leg and smiled with relief. He had not seen them for a few years, but they had not changed, just grown, especially Gironde.

'Your father will be here soon, and he'll be so pleased to see you,' he said.

Gabriel, the slightly smaller of the two, promptly thanked him and burst into tears, but Gironde, the image of his father with his almost black hair and eyes, was burning with anger. The Duke noticed the massive swollen purple and yellow bruise that covered one side of his face.

'Sire, my Lord Duke, I demand your sword as I need to kill that man,' he said, pointing at Pierre, who was now bound and held between two of the Duke's soldiers.

'Perhaps later, Gironde, as I think your father needs to talk to him first. He may have information about your mother to help us find her.'

Gironde looked up and, meeting the Duke's eyes, sighed and reluctantly nodded.

'Yes, I understand, but then I want to stick him like a pig, over and over again,' he announced, to the amusement of the Duke and his captains; he was certainly Chatillon's son.

'Take the boys away, clean them up, and give them some food. The Duchesse Sibylla knows they're coming.'

The Duke then rode over to Pierre and studied him for a few moments. 'Did you honestly think you could steal the children of Piers De Chatillon and get away with it?' he asked, a thin smile on his lips.

Pierre did not answer. He could not meet the Duke's eyes and stared at the floor.

'Take them to the cells, strip them and chain them up, but make sure we give them a taste of our welcoming Burgundy hospitality first.'

The soldiers grinned. Philippe closed his eyes whilst praying they beat him so badly that he died before Chatillon arrived.

With that, the Duke turned and rode away, leaving all three men white-faced, and one visibly shaking, before they were dragged away.

It was dusk when Chatillon finally rode into Beaune on sweating horses that were almost blown. The Duke's Captain was waiting for him at the gates and led him and his men to the Duke's Hall. Chatillon was hardly through the double doors when he was hit by Gabriel and Gironde, who clung to him. He picked Gabriel up and kissed his forehead, while putting an arm around Gironde and pulling him close.

'I knew you would come, Papa. I knew you would find us,' cried Gabriel, his arms wrapped tightly around his father's neck. Chatillon, never usually emotional in any way, felt his eyes fill as he held his sons.

'You have to kill him, Papa, and I have to watch!' shouted

Gironde.

Chatillon put Gabriel down and looked at Gironde. His anger was white hot as he saw his son's swollen and bruised face.

'Did he do this to you?' he asked quietly, while bending down to look at him.

Gironde nodded and, standing almost to attention, announced, 'Yes, but I didn't cry out, Papa. You would have been so proud of me.'

Chatillon closed his eyes for a second to try to contain his fury. He straightened up and took a deep breath.

'Now I must go and greet the Duke and thank him for springing the trap,' he said, taking them by the hand as he led them back to their seats and food.

'Well met, Piers,' said Eudes standing to greet his friend and clasping arms.

'I have no words good enough to thank you, Sire, but I know that as a father, you will understand,' said Chatillon softly.

Eudes nodded. 'Now come and eat—for you can hardly have had any sleep to get here so soon—and enjoy some time with your boys. Everything else will wait for a while.'

Later, with the boys fed and in an exhausted sleep, Chatillon sat in the solar with his friend and related the story to the Duke as he knew it. He could see that Eudes was shaken by what he heard.

'So the Sheikh's men planned and carried out the attack, murdering your daughter, your servants and taking Isabella and the boys?' he asked incredulously. 'How could they possibly do that? You have some of the best-trained men in Europe guarding your home, led by that wild Irish warrior Finian Ui Neill.'

Chatillon grimaced. 'From within, Eudes. They did it

from within—a veritable Trojan horse, a long-lost cousin of Finian's, and we didn't see the signs until it was too late. Although Ahmed never believed the cousin's escape tale, he tried to find the truth and they poisoned him.'

Eudes shook his head in disbelief. 'Ahmed, the King's physician? Is he dead? That will be a great loss if so.'

'No, he survived, as does Finian, hopefully with God's grace. Despite being pinned to the floor with a sword through his chest, both were fighting for their lives when I left. However, although very weak, Ahmed is awake and directing the nursing, so there is hope.'

'Do you know where Isabella is now?' Eudes asked tentatively.

'Edvard is galloping after them. We think they're putting her on a ship in Rouen. I just pray he gets there ahead of them,' said Chatillon, his voice cracking with emotion.

Eudes put a hand on his friend's arm. In all the years they had known each other, he had never seen Chatillon like this, as he was always so self-assured, confident, and downright dangerous.

'Edvard is one of the best. He terrifies me at times, but he is a good man and a dear friend. If anyone can find her, then he can!'

Chatillon stared into the flames. His friend's words were comforting, but the doubt and fear remained.

'I used to joke that I was cursed, paying the price for my calling—that everyone I loved was killed or taken away from me. Now it seems to be coming true.'

'You cannot think like that, Piers, and it isn't true. Today your boys were returned to you, and Isabella will be as well. Let us raise our glasses to that.'

In the cells below them, the three captives huddled and shivered in the filthy straw. Badly beaten, stripped of their clothes and chained to the wall, they tried not to think of what would happen tomorrow.

Bravado gone, Pierre searched his brain for any information that might keep him alive. By dawn, he had not slept but had come up with nothing he could use. As the harsh grey light of day filtered through the small barred window high above him, Pierre faced the unpalatable truth. He had killed Chatillon's daughter and kidnapped his sons, and nothing he could do or say would prevent the man from taking his revenge.

He had once experienced the blackness of the Papal Envoy's eyes when he had slashed his face in the pell yard. He put a hand up to the scar, remembering the threats and thinking that the slash of that dagger would be nothing to what he might do now. They said Chatillon had no soul, conscience, or empathy, killing and torturing his victims without a qualm or regret. Pierre could well believe it, as this was not a man who would show him the mercy of a quick death, and he shuddered at the thought of what would surely come.

26

Chapter Twenty-five

When Gironde and Gabriel finally woke, their father sat in their room, head back, eyes closed. Gabriel wondered if he had watched over them all night; the thought gave him a warm feeling. As they stirred, Chatillon opened his eyes.

'At long last, you two lie-abeds,' he joked. 'Come, we need to break our fast, for I find that I am prodigiously hungry.'

They dressed quickly and fired questions at him that he could not, or would not, answer as they descended into the hall.

'Have you killed Pierre?'

'Have you found mother?'

'Is she at home now?'

'Has Ahmed died?'

Chatillon held up a hand and raised an eyebrow, and they quietened.

'We are all tired and have travelled far, so let us go and eat. You will then join Duke Eudes' sons for the day while I deal with other things. I believe hawking was mentioned. The Duke has a fine collection of gerfalcons, I remember.'

Gironde was immediately excited, but Piers found Gabriel's thoughtful eyes on him, and he mouthed the word 'later' to him. Shortly afterwards, the boys left with the falconer and the tutor of Eudes sons.

The Duke stood. 'Now I think we should question your prisoners to see if this Sheikh has any further devilment planned,' said Eudes leading the way down several flights of stone steps.

'You do not have to watch this, Eudes. It will not be for those with a weak stomach,' murmured Chatillon while glancing at his friend. Eudes laughed at the thought.

'Have you ever known me to have a weak stomach? You and I have fought out of several dicey situations in Rome, and we went back and took our brutal revenge.'

Chatillon grinned at the memories and followed his friend along a short, torch-lit tunnel to the cells. They were not extensive, only half a dozen cells and a larger room with a brazier full of hot embers. Wooden lats were fastened to the walls with chains to spread-eagle a victim, and a large leather-aproned assistant stood at the side. Chatillon walked over to a solid, long, narrow, wooden table with chains and shackles at the bottom of the legs to fasten the victim down. He ran his fingers along the surface and nodded in satisfaction.

'Bring the two accomplices in first,' the Duke ordered the two guards.

The two men were pushed into the room, shackled and naked, with terror clear on their bloodied and bruised faces. Chatillon recognised them both from their stay on his estate. The silence stretched forever as he stared at them without saying a word. Then he spoke softly.

'I invited you into my home. You partook of the hospitality

of my family and me. Finian Ui Neill trusted you and vouched for you, even though he didn't know you well. You betrayed that trust, so now I will ask you some questions, and you will answer truthfully. If you do so, I promise you a quick death. If not, I'll keep you alive for a week, and they'll hear your screams in Dijon. Do you understand?'

White-faced, they both nodded though the younger man on the right lost control of his bladder in fear, and the Duke stepped back in disgust to avoid being splashed.

'Who did you meet at the inn in Paris?'

The older man, Philippe, answered. 'It was Al Cazar, Sheikh Ishmael's captain.'

Chatillon nodded in encouragement. 'This was the man who staged your false escape from Tunis or Tripoli?'

They both nodded.

'So everything was a lie, a ruse to get Padraig MacDomnall into my family?' he asked.

Again, they both nodded.

'Therefore, you arranged to kidnap the boys, and where was Pierre taking them? Did he tell you?'

Philippe answered. 'A Turkish merchant was buying them. He was taking them to the east as slaves for a wealthy Emir, but we only found this out yesterday, when we questioned the direction we travelled. Padraig had told us that the boys wouldn't be hurt and that they would be taken to Paris, to be held for a ransom.'

'Clever,' growled the Duke.

'Do you know where they have taken my wife?' The two men looked at each other.

'We were surprised when Padraig brought her out through the postern gate. We thought we were only taking the boys.

Padraig took her west, and we heard him mention a ship at Rouen.'

Again, Chatillon nodded as if thanking them, but when he took a deep breath, a stillness settled on the room until fists clenched at his sides. He quietly asked, 'Did either of you kill my daughter, Annecy?'

Both men looked shocked and again looked at each other, shaking their heads.

'We never saw the little girl, and no one told us to kill any children. We killed the guards, and the old man at the gate, because we needed to escape that way, but that is all.'

The younger man realised his mistake almost as soon as the words were out of his mouth.

Chatillon smiled. 'That was all? Ah yes, old Louis, it was probably time for him to meet his maker. He began in the chateau for my father, as a young groom. I used to occasionally sit with him in the sunshine and hear stories of my father from that time. His wife developed arthritis and could hardly walk, so I gave him the job at the gates over twenty years ago, so he could look after her at the same time as being the gatekeeper. Who will look after her now, I wonder? Does she know his body lay outside their door all night?'

You could have heard a pin drop, and the younger man began to shake as Chatillon, in a flash, stepped forward and cut Philippe's throat, who dropped to the floor with a gurgling sound. The other man stared at his friend in horror and then looked up to meet Chatillon's pitiless eyes.

'I promised him a quick and clean death, and I delivered it,' he said, wiping his blade with a cloth on the table.

'Unfortunately, with the killing of a defenceless, unarmed old man, I don't believe you deserve the same.'

The man began to babble, to plead as tears ran down his face. Again Chatillon half turned away and then whipped back and gut-slashed the man from one side to the other. The man screamed and then dropped to his knees, clutching his gaping stomach.

'Take him back to his cell. He can die alone, holding in his innards and slowly bleeding to death. That thought gives me a great deal of pleasure,' he said, wiping the blade of the long, razor-sharp dagger again.

The guards dragged the moaning, crying man out.

Eudes, who had taken a step back, was dazed at the speed with which Chatillon had despatched the two men. He stepped over to an old wooden table and poured them some wine. He took a long mouthful while handing his friend a goblet.

'So Rouen was mentioned again. That is hopeful.' Chatillon was frowning, but he nodded.

'It sounds like the Sheikh planned this for several years. He trained these men and somehow found Finian's cousin, Padraig. That was a fortunate find for him indeed,' added Eudes, sitting down on one of the stools.

'Finian warned me,' whispered Chatillon.

'About his cousin, and you didn't listen to him?' the Duke questioned in surprise.

'No, he warned me about the blood feuds of the Saracen Berbers. He said they were far worse than Irish blood feuds, never-ending.... Sons and grandsons would carry it on until they wiped out the entire families of their enemies. However, I didn't listen to him. I have dozens of enemies, and like those, I became complacent as I thought this would peter out.'

'Maybe that is what you need to do then, wipe out him and his entire family.'

Chatillon drained his goblet in one go and signalled for it to be refilled.

'No, Eudes, that just perpetrates the blood feud. There has to be a way of stopping this. Otherwise, my sons will spend their lives looking over their shoulders, a dagger under their pillow. I cannot allow that to happen. Gabriel's eyes are already haunted by what has happened to him and Gironde.'

'You need something you can use as leverage against them, something they would fear.'

Chatillon nodded and stood. 'Now, let us have our last prisoner brought in.'

Pierre tried to look defiant as he stood there naked and filthy in his shackles, but it did not last, as his eyes scanned the room and took in the horror of what they might do to him.

'Why? Oh, why? Why did I not kill you that day in the pell yard instead of letting you live to wreak this havoc?' asked Chatillon, in a soft voice.

Pierre stayed silent, eyes cast down, as Chatillon walked around him.

'Like your friends, I'll ask you some questions, and your answers will decide what I do with you.'

Pierre looked away to the three barred small windows above him, but Chatillon had seen the brief glimmer of hope in his eyes, and he smiled as he indicated to the large apron-clad man that Pierre was to be strapped to the table. It took him and two guards to manhandle a struggling Pierre flat onto the long, narrow table. He was spread-eagled; his lower legs hanging over the sides were cruelly pulled down hard to have shackles snapped around each ankle, attached to the rings at the bottom of the legs. The same happened with his arms, stretched to their limit, to have his wrists shackled to the base of the legs. His neck was clamped tightly in an iron collar nailed to the table. He was now stretched as tight as a drum and immobile, the table's sharp edges cutting into his thighs and upper arms.

Chatillon walked over and stood looking down on his victim, who had his eyes tightly closed, as if not seeing what was about to happen would help. Instead, it accentuated the senses, so when Chatillon lightly ran the tip of his dagger across the tight flesh of his rib cage, drawing blood, the man screamed.

Chatillon laughed before turning to his friend. 'You may not want to watch this, Eudes.'

However, Eudes knew it was said to enhance the effect it would have on his victim, so Eudes smiled and shrugged. The contrast between the calm velvet-clad Duke and his surroundings was stark, as he settled back to sip his wine and watch Chatillon take his revenge.

'I know all about the fake escape from Tunis, the made-up story about Tripoli and Sicily. Your friends sang like songbirds.'

Pierre's eyes flew open. 'No! We did go to Tripoli. We worked there on the palace for six months; that was where Al Cazar found Padraig. He promised us gold and our freedom.'

Again, there was silence.

'And what of Sheikh Ishmael?'

'We never saw him in Tunis or Tripoli, although he had palaces at both places. We only saw him years before while we were on the galleys. My brother and I were from a family of stonemasons, but we only ever dealt with Al Cazar.'

Eudes could see that the calm questioning was lulling Pierre into a feeling of false security. How he gave so much information showed how eager he was to please.

'So you came to my home, and to give you your due, Pierre, you were not the friendly mealy mouthed liar that Padraig MacDomnall was. For doing that, part of me does admire you. For you showed your true character from the beginning, wrapping it in the guise of grief for your brother.'

Again, Chatillon saw a glimmer of hope in the man's face, but then Pierre made a grave mistake.

'We are alike, Chatillon, you and I, more than you realise,' he pleaded.

Piers had to turn away so that Pierre would not see the blaze of fury and white-hot anger that consumed him.

Eudes saw it and, holding out a goblet of wine, which Chatillon downed, whispered, 'Ask him about Isabella.'

It took several moments before Chatillon could turn back, his face under control, but his left fist was still clenched, as he resisted the temptation to plunge the dagger into the man's heart over and over again. He took a breath.

'So the plan was hatched and carried out. I believe my sons were going to a Turkish slaver in Marseilles to go, no doubt, to someone with a penchant for boys instead of girls?'

Pierre gave a slight nod.

'Now, this is where you can be useful to me, Pierre. Where did they take my wife, your two friends who died did not know, but you were Padraig's confidant. He shared everything with you and put you in charge of the men in Paris. He had faith in you for all your volatility. So where did they take her?'

Pierre said nothing as he tried to work out what to say to save his life.

Chatillon impatiently gestured to the big man, who put a thick leather glove on his right hand and took a long heated dagger from the brazier. The blade glowed almost white hot as he walked to stand on the other side of Pierre, who seeing what he held, strained against the shackles and mumbled, 'No, no,' as he came close.

'I know they were taking her in a flour wagon to Rouen. It had a special hidden compartment in the wagon bed, and she was in a sack. They were taking her to be put on a trading ship which would meet up with the Sheikh's galley.'

'And where was the ship going?' demanded Chatillon, fearing the worst.

'I don't know, I swear I do not know,' gasped Pierre as Chatillon nodded, and the knife was pressed on the inside of Pierre's thigh. He screamed and tried to move, but he was chained so tightly it was impossible. He sobbed and groaned as the knife was finally lifted and returned to the brazier to reheat.

'I think you do know,' snapped Chatillon.

'They were taking her to the Sheikh, to one of his seraglios. He has several, but I swear I do not know where; he has so many bases, some as far away as Greece. I remember Tunis being mentioned, or it could be Tripoli. He calls there regularly, but I swear I don't know,' he gasped.

Chatillon stood silently watching Pierre, whose body was now covered in a sheen of fear-induced sweat. Chatillon knew he could not put into words, even if he tried, the extent of his hatred and loathing for this man.

'Castrate him,' he said calmly, and the torturer lifted the blade again from the brazier. Pierre squealed and sobbed while trying to thrash a body chained down so tightly, it could hardly move an inch.

'Let him feel the blade's heat down there for a while. It might jog his memory.'

The man did so while Pierre panting in fear, yelled repeatedly, 'I don't know, I swear I don't know, but it will be in the Mediterranean!'

Chatillon sat at the table, turned to Eudes and held his hands up in mock acceptance. 'I think I believe him, Eudes. I don't think he knows,' he said, nodding at the man to continue. As the glowing blade descended, Chatillon took a mouthful of wine. The high-pitched scream from Pierre made Eudes' face blanch, and he found his hand gripping the goblet as the scream went on and on until it finally died. Chatillon was hardly conscious of the sobbing man on the table.

'They could have taken her anywhere, Eudes, if Edvard has not arrived there in time.'

'Let us just pray that he did for your sake and that of those boys upstairs.'

'They don't even know that their sister is dead yet,' said Chatillon with an expression that would terrify any man. He stood and walked back to the dribbling Pierre, whose face was contorted in pain and shock.

'You killed Cecily, a young, innocent girl. You stabbed her as she ran away from you, and you then broke her neck. Do you know, Pierre, that I have just discovered that Cecily is my granddaughter? Her father is heartbroken, and I am distraught that I never got to know her.'

Pierre began to physically shake with fear.

'Yet you think we are alike in some way? I could not kill a sweet young girl whose only fault was falling in love with me. As you did,'

Pierre was beyond answering at first, although his mouth moved while saliva and blood, where he had bitten through his lip, ran down his chin. Finally, he stuttered, 'Kill me, just kill me. Finish it, I beg you.'

Chatillon stared at him and then laughed, surprising Eudes, who sat looking on.

'Kill you? That is the last thing I want to do, Pierre. I could have castrated you myself, which would have given me pleasure, and you would have bled out in no time at all, but the advantage of a red-hot knife is that it seals the wound and limits the bleeding. I intend to keep you alive for years, Pierre, and make you suffer in ways you never thought possible.' He nodded again at the man in the apron who lifted a red-hot poker from the brazier.

'You killed my daughter....' Chatillon had to stop for a few seconds. The pain of her death was so raw. 'My daughter Annecy. She was only seven, but she saw straight through you, and I should have listened to her. I thought you were a nuisance, an annoyance. I missed the fact somehow that you were a cold-blooded killer, and I'll never forgive myself for that. You killed a granddaughter I never knew, sixteen-year-old Cecily, a total innocent. Small defenceless animals, two beautiful girls with their whole lives ahead of them—this was your legacy, the mark of a coward, and you will pay for that, Pierre.'

Pierre had gone very still, his eyes fixed on the grim face of Chatillon. There was no word he could say as Chatillon straightened up and turned away. The big man moved forward again, the poker still glowing red.

'Blind him,' said Chatillon calmly, while finishing his wine and making for the door, as the high-pitched screams started again, echoing along the stone corridors. Even the guards were white-faced as they emerged with Eudes, who was striding after his friend. The Duke found that he had to lean on the wall for a while in the bailey. Chatillon took a deep breath to get the smell of burning flesh out of his nostrils and then turned to face his friend.

'Eudes, I need to ask for your hospitality for my prisoner for a few months.'

Eudes nodded. 'Of course, if he lives.'

'Oh, he will live, I'll make sure of it. I'll send a physician tonight to see to his wounds, and then I want him chained in a cell but given good food. He will live for many years, I hope. Now let's go and find the boys, for we'll be going home tomorrow.' He set off across the bailey, a still-shaken Eudes following him.

When they sat for a final dinner that evening, the mood lightened, and Chatillon remembered why he had enjoyed Duchess Sibylla's amusing company until the Steward appeared with a message. It was from his home, forwarded by Ahmed to Beaune. He slowly unrolled it, and a feeling of foreboding came over him, fearing the worst, Finian dead, Edvard killed trying to rescue Isabella. Isabella dead.

Unfortunately, Edvard did not get there in time, Padraig had gone to St Malo, not Rouen, and the ship had sailed with Isabella.

Chatillon closed his eyes as a bleakness settled in his very soul. He passed the message to Eudes and excused himself to go up the steep circular staircase to the tower. He stood forlorn and lost as he gazed out at the southwestern sky. It was a clear star-studded night, and he wondered if she was staring at the same stars, terrified of what would happen to her.

'Stay alive, Isabella. No matter what happens or what he does to you, stay alive, and I promise I will find you,' he whispered.

27

Chapter Twenty-six

As Isabella's feet landed on the galley's deck, the pure hopelessness and horror of the situation overwhelmed her, and she found that her legs would not support her. She dropped to the deck, but she was gently lifted to her feet, and strong hands gripped her elbows. She looked up at the man in the white robes and met the dark eyes of Don Ferdinand, the so-called Castilian merchant who had tried to poison her with perfume.

'You!' she exclaimed, pulling back. The Saracen let go of her arms, took a step back and bowed.

'Welcome on board, Lady Isabella.'

'You tried to kill me. Why do you want me alive now?' she shouted at him.

He did not answer; instead, he turned and opened a door under the high bow deck. Isabella felt apprehensive as she was shepherded in front of him, but to her surprise, there was a richly appointed cabin with a long low divan, a low table and a chair instead of the usual cargo hold. He indicated to her that she should sit, which she reluctantly did. Two men had followed them in and now stood in front of Isabella. One bent to lift her gown, and she slapped his hand away.

'I am afraid this is necessary. We cannot have you jumping overboard after all the trouble and expense we have gone to,' said the Saracen, pointing to the shackle and chain held in the second man's hand. She glared at them as he attached it to her ankle and hammered a locking bolt into place. The other end was chained to a ring on the floor beside the divan.

'You did not answer me,' she accused him with a rebellious glare as she tried to kick the man away from her ankle.

'At that time, it suited the Sheikh to have you dead, but now it suits him more to have you alive. We are all servants of his whim and a word to the wise from painful experience—it is better to do as he bids. This is your cabin for the journey, and you will be here for several weeks. The chain is long and will allow you movement within these walls. Don't open the door or try to look out on the deck, as you would be a great distraction to the men who rarely see hair of that colour,' he said, lifting a long lock of Isabella's long thick, honey-blonde hair.

They left, and Isabella was left alone with her thoughts and fears. She leaned back against the wooden bulwark and closed her eyes; tears came unbidden, and she dashed them away. She was determined to stay strong and not show any weakness in front of them, but it was hard. She had no idea where her sons were, she did not know if Finian or Ahmed still lived, and Chatillon, the man she loved so deeply, where was he? Had it been him on the wharves at St Malo, or had he gone after the boys? She prayed he had.

Suddenly she thought of Chatillon's tenacity in finding young Conn, the son of Morvan De Malvais, his friend. They had searched for years, and Chatillon had found him, held by warrior monks in a remote hermitage in the bleak Italian Alps. If anyone could find the boys or even find her, it would be him. She had to believe in that, and survive for him and their children, no matter how far away they took her.

A few days later, they hit violent winter storms off the coast of Portugal, and Isabella felt real fear. She thought they would die, as the wild Atlantic waves hit the long galley. Listening to the loud cries and prayers of the galley slaves, she realised that they were just as terrified. They were chained, as she was, to the ship's deck and would all go down with it if it sank.

The Captain, Al Cazar, was one of the most experienced sailors of the wild storms of the Mediterranean, so he steered the galley into a wide sheltered bay to sit out the worst of this Atlantic one. Although the ship was still badly tossed and buffeted, and the crew bailed constantly, she remained intact.

Al Cazar checked on her regularly and lifted her off the floor at times when the violent motions of the pitching ship had thrown her across the cabin.

'We are lucky she is so well built, for she is Sheikh Ishmael's flagship. So many of these long galleys can break in half in storms like this, but she always survives. We called her 'Spirit of the Wind', an omen, I think.' She found that he was always courteous and pleasant to her, bringing servants to see to her needs. However, she was not taken in by this smiling assassin and murderer.

'You murdered Abdo, didn't you?' she said in an accusing voice the next day. He looked perplexed.

'Abdo?' he enquired with a raised eyebrow.

'The apothecary in Paris, a harmless, intelligent little man, a learned physician who often treated the poor in Paris for no recompense.'

She saw his face and eyes harden. 'An informer and spy and, as such, an enemy of Sheikh Ishmael, who insists that all of his enemies are vanquished. The sheikh shows no mercy, and Abdo took the risk. He knew what the risks are when you dare to dabble in the affairs of great men.' So saying, he got up and abruptly left.

No one came near her for the next two days. She did not starve as she had fruit, bread and wine, but the air was stale in the confined space, and the stench of the leather latrine bucket became overpowering.

On the third day, a servant appeared, and she pleaded with him to leave the door ajar for a while, but she did not see Al Cazar for the rest of the week. Finally, he appeared with the two servants and ordered her shackle removed. He handed her the thick hooded cloak and told her to cover herself, before taking her arm and leading her onto the deck. He took her to the gunwale in a sheltered corner to the side of the cabin door. She gulped mouthfuls of the sea air and raised her face to the sun, revelling in the spray thrown up by the bows, as the ship forged through the waves.

'We are approaching the Pillars of Hercules, and I thought you might like to watch us sailing through into the Sheikhs domain, the waters of the Mediterranean,' he explained.

She bit her tongue to stop herself from saying that it was also her father's domain, the Signori of Genoa—a man who had destroyed a large pirate fleet fifteen years before—but she had learned her lesson, and instead, she thanked him. She had only ever sailed from Genoa to Marseilles and back, so despite her predicament, she could stand and stare with interest as they approached the entrance to the Mediterranean.

Al Cazar stood close beside her. 'We are looking to the north, and that peak is Calpe Mons, the other pillar to the south, in Africa, is the mountain of Monte Hacho. They say that these two peaks were originally part of one huge mountain Hercules was told to climb, but instead, he decided to use his strength to smash his way through. So he created this gateway, a strait to link the Mediterranean to the Atlantic.'

She asked him if she could stay there for a while to feel the sun on her face, and he agreed as the galley began to veer north. She knew the shape of the Mediterranean from her father's precious maps and that this must mean she was not being taken south to Tunis or Tripoli. She wracked her brain to think of the other places mentioned by Edvard or Chatillon when they discussed Ishmael. She felt a small ray of hope that they were going north, closer to Spain and France.

She remembered that Ishmael had a large pirate base on an island where he docked most of his galleys in a large port. She decided to risk asking Al Cazar. At first, he did not reply, but then he shrugged as if he decided it did not matter if she knew.

'We are sailing into Medina Mayurqa. My master is an Emir in the Banu Hud dynasty, and these islands now belong to their Taifa of Zaragoza.'

'What is a Taifa?' she asked, desperate to know, as much as possible, anything that might help her to escape.

'A Taifa is an independent Muslim state ruled by a dynasty, and there are several on mainland Spain. Now you must return to your cabin,' he said, ushering her through the doorway.

Almost a week later, they sailed into the port, the heart of Sheikh Ishmael's empire. As the galley was docking at the wharves of Medina Mayurqa, a grim-faced Chatillon was riding through the gates of his home in Chatillon sous Bagneux.

The news that Isabella had gone hit Chatillon hard. The first few nights after the messenger arrived, he had stayed in Beaune and inconsolably drank himself to oblivion. In one of these drunken bouts, Eudes had to physically stop him from going to tear Pierre limb from limb. On the third day, he had emerged from his chamber white-faced and hollow-eyed, but now there was more anger and tight-lipped determination in his face.

They sat in the solar. The boys were being kept busy in the pell yard, and Eudes found that he quickly ran out of conversation with the taciturn Chatillon.

'Piers, I know you're blaming yourself, and I cannot imagine how heartbroken you must be, but you also have two sons. Take them home and plan how to find her, get her back. You're not the type of man to wallow in despair and self-pity. You're a man of action. I am here to help in any way I can. Just ask.'

For the first time, Chatillon brought his deadpan stare onto Eudes face and seeing the concern there, he sighed.

'Eudes, I thank you for your friendship and hospitality, but all I can see is Isabella. I imagine what she is going through and what they're doing to her. I can see it whenever I lie down and close my eyes.'

Eudes put a hand on his friend's arm. 'Piers, I understand, of course, I do. If it was Sibylla, I am sure I would be the same, but to run those images constantly through your mind, that way madness lies. If anyone can find and rescue her, it is you, for you have a network of hundreds if not thousands of informers and messengers. Now is the time you should be sending out those birds. He has taken her south. We know that much. She is a tall, pale-skinned woman with striking, long blonde hair, and she will be noticed. Also, from what I've seen of Isabella, she will not go quietly. She is strong-willed, independent and outspoken, and they'll find it difficult to silence or hide her. As we speak, she will be looking for avenues of escape, and you and your men must be ready to help her when she does.'

For the first time, Eudes' words seemed to resonate with Chatillon, and he sat forward. 'You're right, Eudes, we will leave today, and I'll take you up on your offer of help again if I need it. Meanwhile, keep our friend downstairs safely chained for me. After a few months, he will permanently move to my house in Avignon.'

Over a week later, Chatillon rode back through the large gatehouse of his home, a place that until recently had been a sanctuary, a place of happy memories. Now because of Ishmael, that was gone, replaced by different memories as he found his eyes automatically went to the half-open door and stool where old Louis used to sit.

The subdued boys rode in behind him. He had given them their own palfreys to ride, to give them something to focus on instead of their kidnapping. They had never ridden themselves on a journey this long before, and it had not been easy. They ached, and their thighs were chafed from long hours in the saddle. Also, their father had hardly said a word to them, sending them up to their rooms in the inns while he sat on his own in the taprooms, thinking things through. He needed more information, and he needed it as soon as possible. He prayed that Ahmed was alive, for he had never needed him more.

His question was answered as Dion, and a frail-looking Ahmed came out onto the steps to greet him. There was no sign of Finian, which worried him, but a tall, graceful young woman came out behind them. Marietta, his ward, had come from Genoa. He greeted them as the grooms ran to take the horses, and his tired men headed to the barracks. As Piers dismounted, he found his eyes went to the chapel where he had found his daughter's broken body. He hoped they had buried her in the chapel as he requested and that now she was running in a meadow somewhere with her little dog, in whatever heavens existed.

Marietta could see the distress playing across her guardian's face, and she ran lightly down the steps and put her arms around him. He closed his eyes and hugged her close.

'I had to come. Dion sent a message, and they have been so busy saving Finian's life and nursing him that I knew I would be needed to run the household and entertain the children,' she said.

'I am glad you're here, Marietta. You've always been like a daughter to us, and Isabella would be pleased to know you're here too.'

She smiled and went to greet the boys, who looked lost. The chateau was their home, but so much horror had happened here, and their mother was gone. Marietta put her arms around them as they wearily climbed from their saddles.

'Come, there is buttermilk and warm buttered bread in the kitchen, and Madame Chambord will be so pleased to see you. You two will bring a smile back to her face, for she lost someone too, her husband, Jean. Gabriel. You must ask her to make your favourite apricot tart; that will please her.'

Chatillon smiled as he listened to her chattering away to

them and then wearily mounted the steps to Ahmed and Dion. Ahmed took both of his hands and stared deeply into his eyes.

'I never doubted that you would find the boys and bring them back, and now you will do the same for Isabella,' he said as Piers hugged Dion.

'How is Finian?' he asked.

'Come and see,' said Dion taking his arm and drawing him inside the hall, which now looked more like home. There had been blood and chaos the last time he had seen it.

'Finian came down with a bad infection, and we nearly lost him. I think it might have been splinters from the wooden floor below, which were drawn deep into the wound when the sword was extracted. I probed the wound, to his dismay, but I could not find them. However, he is a fit, strong man, and Dion here nursed him through the sweat and shivers that assailed him.'

Finian was in his chamber, sitting by the fire. The blood had been scrubbed from the floor, but a stain and a hole remained to remind him what had happened. He was still heavily bandaged, and Ahmed had plastered one of his foul-smelling herbal unctions on a poultice on both sides of the wound to draw out any further infection.

'I am pleased to see that you're still in the land of the living and recovering. You lost so much blood I feared it would not be so,' said Chatillon warming his hands in front of the fire before sitting down.

Finian, who had been given much time to think about the actions of his cousin Padraig found it difficult to meet his friend's eyes.

'If it had not been for Ahmed and Dion, I believe I might not have done it,' he replied as silence descended for several moments.

'Piers, there are no words I can say to alleviate the pain you must feel, and I have this weight of guilt for bringing Padraig and his men to your door.'

Again there was silence but for the crackling of the fire. Finian risked a glance at the cold and closed face of Chatillon as he sat in the chair opposite. He did not blame him for finding it difficult to forgive him, his sons and wife had been taken, and the blame lay in his lap for ever believing Padraig.

'I do not only blame you, Finian, for I was just as guilty. I blithely opened the doors of my home to a group of men we didn't know—a group who had all miraculously escaped from slavery in the palace of Sheikh Ishmael's brother. The same Sheikh who has a vendetta against me. Yet we all seemed temporarily blinded, unable to see what was happening in front of us. The genial, helpful cousin Padraig was here in my house for over a year, yet we never saw him for what he truly was: a bitter, vengeful man who hated you. Dion and Ahmed did, and they told us, but we shrugged it off, and we made excuses for Padraig or Pierre, that cold-blooded killer. The murder of Abdo should have rang dozens of alarm bells. So no, I do not blame you alone for that, for I am also culpable.' He stopped for a while to control his anger at himself and Finian and stared into the flames. No one said a word as they waited for him to continue.

'However, when real evidence came to light here, the falconer who Ahmed found in our woods bringing down our birds, the murder of my granddaughter Cecily, the discovery that Padraig was meeting with Al Cazar, and the poisoning of Ahmed, you did nothing, Finian. I sent you a message from Lucca, telling you to act immediately and double the guards, but as far as I can see, even then, there was that reluctance in you to accuse your cousin, hesitation that cost my little Annecy her life. So because you refused to follow my orders and imprison or kill your cousin, my sons are traumatised. Gironde's cheekbone is broken because Pierre hit him so hard, and Gabriel has screaming nightmares. My beautiful daughter is dead, as is old Louis and our Steward, Jean, while my wife has gone, taken by Sheikh Ishmael and is being beaten and raped every night for all we know. So yes, I blame you for not stopping all this—for your reluctance to act while you had the chance. It may take a long time for me to forgive you for that, Finian.'

At that, he stood, turned on his heel and strode out of the door. Ahmed and Dion stood in the doorway, their faces shocked as they stepped aside to let him pass.

Dion went straight to Finian, who had dropped his head into his hands.

'He is right, Dion, he is right. I have betrayed my position and his trust and friendship because I didn't want to listen to what you said. I wanted to give my cousin the benefit of the doubt. My guilt over leaving him on that sinking ship blinded me to what was happening here in Chatillon sous Bagneux. I was in denial about what you and Ahmed had found, and I could not, or part of me didn't want to believe it was true. As I saw the hatred in his eyes as he stood over me with that sword, ready to plunge it into my heart, I recognised that you were right all along.'

Ahmed wearily sat in the chair opposite that Chatillon had vacated.

'Piers is hurting in so many ways, but what do you expect, Finian, after your failure to act? However, we both know that he is a fair man, usually totally loyal to his friends. It may take time, but he will come around.'

Finian looked up at Dion, who took his hand. 'We must leave here, Dion. Staying here would now be unbearable with this failure and betrayal hanging over me.'

Dion and Ahmed looked shocked at Finian's words. Ahmed pushed himself out of the chair and drew himself up to his full height.

'You will do no such thing, Finian Ui Neill! I never took you for a coward. You will stay here and do everything in your power to recover quickly, begging his forgiveness daily if you have to. But he needs your friendship and support more than ever now, so show him that it is still there and help him find Isabella. I'll talk to him now while Dion helps you find your backbone.'

With those damning words, he left them and went to find his friend. Piers was not in his business room or the Great Hall. However, he finally found him on top of the tower. He was gazing at the charred remains of the pigeon coop and the burnt carcasses of over a dozen birds.

Ahmed put a hand on Piers' shoulder. 'In the darkest and blackest of times, we must always look for a little light, for that will help us rebuild and keep going. We need to sit and talk to Rollo now that he is fully recovered. He is a brave man, and he may know more than he thinks about the Sheikh and his bases, for I have noticed that he is a listener, and listeners often store knowledge away.'

Chatillon nodded his thanks. 'I have said this before, Ahmed, and you've never taken me seriously, but I am honestly beginning to believe that I am truly cursed or that this is some form of divine retribution for the hundreds I have killed without a backward glance. Every woman I have loved or who comes into my life is tainted. They are either viciously murdered, they die like my mother at no age, or they're taken from me by someone else. Gabrielle, Bianca, Adelheid, Hildebrand, Isabella, Annecy and Cecily. I should send Marietta back to Genoa immediately before I lose her.'

Ahmed theatrically rolled his eyes. 'I did take you seriously before, but I am a pragmatist, a realist, as I believe you are too under this maudlin wallowing. I do not believe in curses, and I do not think you do either. You live a dangerous life in a dangerous world. I also have killed hundreds with my poisons and potions, so following your line of thought, I might have brought this curse to your door. See how ridiculous it sounds? You're a man of action, so throw off this mood and act!'

Piers nodded and gave a rueful grimace before turning to the damaged pigeon coop.

'I must get this cleared away and get them to build a new one,' he said, kicking at the charred planks. 'I have also sent messages to bring birds back here from all our usual information centres, Paris, Rome, Rouen, Ghent, Florence and London. The baskets should be arriving daily.'

'By all means, get them to clear it now, for time is of the essence. We need information. But you should build the new one as you told me you did many years ago in Monte Cassino when you first set up this network. I will help, of course, for I will sit on this bench and critically assess your efforts. Doing something physical like this will give you the thinking time you need. You will be occupied using your hands rather than sitting brooding or blaming others when we all had a part to play in this nightmare by not acting soon enough.'

Ahmed sat on the bench in the early spring sunshine and

watched Piers as he still listlessly rubbed a booted foot in the embers. To his surprise, his friend then turned and nodded.

'You're right, Ahmed; summon the servants and Rollo—he is a carpenter, I believe. Let us make a start now.'

Ahmed and Piers sat on the bench as the men cleared the debris, discussing the pigeon coop's new shape, size and site. Ahmed described a rain runoff system he had seen to fill the water troughs, first used by the Romans. Piers was immediately interested in how to construct it. For an afternoon, as wood and nails were brought by Rollo, Piers could put aside the pain and anguish tearing him apart.

Despite his friend's reluctance, Ahmed insisted that Piers come down and join his sons, friends and men for dinner in the Great Hall that evening. Ahmed pointed out that everyone would be looking to him now and that his behaviour and how he handled his grief would determine theirs. They had hardly taken their seats when Edvard and his men arrived back. Piers rose to greet him, and they clasped each other for a long moment, the pain in both of their eyes clear to see, as was the relief when he saw the boys at the high table with Marietta.

'I am sorry we could not get to her in time. They tricked us, Piers. The ship was not in Rouen. It was in St Malo, and we arrived just as it left the harbour. I could see Padraig MacDomnall standing on the deck of the cog as he sailed out to meet with one of Ishmael's large galleys that swept into the bay. It all happened so fast, so well planned, that we could do nothing. We spent days following it down the coast, hoping they might pull in, but the wind was in their sails, and they sped south. We spent more days questioning all the captains and fishermen in the Normandy ports to see if anyone knew anything about either of the ships, to no avail.

However, one man said he thought the cog was an English boat returning home. So, we can presume that going north, Padraig is returning to Ireland with his gold, as he planned.'

Chatillon put both hands on Edvard's shoulders, 'Thank you, old friend. I know you and your men will have done everything you could. Now we need to work together, all of us,' he said, sweeping his arm wide to include Finian on the top table and all the men in the hall who had hung on Edward's every word.

Chatillon stepped back to the table, filled his goblet, and filled another, which he handed to Edvard. He then turned to the full hall and raised his goblet high.

'We will find Isabella. We will bring her back to where she belongs, here with us,' he shouted. Everyone raised their goblets and tankards and drank. 'To Isabella,' they all cried, and suddenly, all his men in the hall were stamping their feet and banging on the tables, shouting her name louder and louder. Piers could not prevent his eyes from filling with tears as he stared around the hall. His friends, his family, his men, everyone was now on their feet cheering.

They would find her, he swore, even if he had to die trying.

28

Chapter Twenty-seven

It was in the early hours of the morning when Isabella was woken, wrapped in the all-enveloping cloak and hat and taken off the galley onto the quayside. All was deathly quiet, not a soul stirred and any who did scurried out of sight when they saw a twenty-strong mounted troop of Sheikh Ishmael's men.

It was so dark she could barely see her hand in front of her as she was pulled up onto the horse in front of Al Cazar. They then cantered out of the port, in Mallorca, through the town and into the countryside beyond. Isabella clung to the horse's mane as they seemed to ride northwest from the port. She had overheard Al Cazar answering one of the Mozarabic servants, and she knew they were riding to Alaro over two leagues away.

The dawn began to break behind them as they galloped over the plains towards their destination. The men clearly knew the way, and the road was in good condition and well-travelled, with groves of almond trees and meadows on either side. The first rays of the sun lit up the impressive mountain range ahead, and Isabella thought about how beautiful it looked with the mist around its base.

'The Tramuntana Mountains, but we are not going over them,' said Al Cazar as if he had read her thoughts. 'That is our destination, the village and Castell of Alaro built atop the big southern outcrop you can see. It is the occasional summer home of Sheikh Ishmael when he is not at sea.'

As they rode closer, she could see a cluster of buildings surrounding the foot of the rocky outcrop. A steep track wound upwards towards the large imposing fortress on the top. Glancing up, Isabella thought it looked formidable, and it had a view not only over the plain but over the sea surrounding the island. She could see why he had chosen this spot, as he could escape in any direction or disappear into the mountains just within reach.

They reached the first of the large, heavy wooden gates studded with metal. It was early, and they were still barred. Al Cazar shouted for the gatekeep.

Isabella turned, and throwing back her hood, looked back the way they had come to get her bearings. She could see the large port of Medina Muyarqa far in the distance and the shapes of other islands in the east.

The gates finally opened, and they rode into a large yard with stables where they dismounted. She was led through an archway into a cool, tiled courtyard full of flowers and greenery, which servants were already watering before the day's heat. The castle seemed designed to wrap itself around this courtyard with half a dozen archways and doorways, some covered in thin drapes on rings. From what she had learnt, Isabella presumed these were the women's quarters, and she wondered if that was where they would keep her.

To her surprise, she was led down half a dozen steps and through a series of heavy locked doors to a dark, stone tunnel that was so long it seemed to be heading out onto the very cliffs. Isabella's heart dropped as she dreaded being imprisoned underground in a dark dungeon, left there and forgotten.

They went past several cells, some empty. Some with groaning inmates. Finally, they reached another door with a barred window designed to let in air, and she felt the breeze on her face as Al Cazar pulled it open and then locked it behind them. A steep set of narrow steps went upwards, and he unlocked a further door into an empty round room. She glanced around; there was a pallet bed on the floor, and stone jars, some full of water, some stoppered for wine, stood against the walls. A table stood to one side with fresh unleavened bread, olives and cheese on a platter. There were no windows, and the only light came from a large hatch in the roof, which was open. Al Cazar pointed at the ladder propped against it and indicated that she should climb it.

She did so tentatively and emerged into a round room the same size as the one below. This also had a large hatch to the floor above, but no ladder and Isabella realised that she was in one of the several round towers she had seen as they had ridden up. Al Cazar and his two men followed her up as she stood and looked around. This room had half a dozen long arrow slits at head height, about a small handspan wide, and they let in light and a pleasant cool breeze. She turned and, to her surprise, noticed an older thin woman dressed in a black Moorish costume. She sat cross-legged on a mat and seemed to be working at weaving or making heavy lace. She took little notice of what was happening around her. Al Cazar took Isabella's cloak and hung it on a wooden peg near the hatch.

'This is now your home. She is an elderly relative of the

Sheikh who will be with you at all times to see to your needs. She speaks no language other than Arabic, so you will have to sign your needs for the time being. He then nodded to the larger of the two men she recognised from the ship as the leg shackle and long chain were emptied from the bag onto the floor. She stood in rising anger, arms folded as she was again shackled to a ring on the floor. She winced as the locking bolts were hammered and bent into place. Having seen to that, Al Cazar bowed.

'I cannot imagine that I'll see you again, so I wish you well and a word of advice—lose your pride and don't anger the Sheikh, for I warn you, he is pitiless.' So saying, he descended the ladder followed by his men, and the hatch was lowered into place. As they left the lower room, she heard the large wooden bar also being lowered into place.

It was indeed a fortress; at present, she could see no escape and certainly no help from any servants as she glanced down and caught a bitter glance from the older woman. She looked around the plain walls of her new home. There was a solid but old rope-strung bed with a large but thin mattress folded on top. There were several folded clean linen covers, and she busied herself unfolding the mattress and spreading them on the bed. A table with two stools stood against the wall, and a latrine bucket was on the other side of the hatch. She looked around in despair, for this was now her world until Chatillon found her.

No one came near them for four days, and Isabella veered from anger to anxiety about what would happen to her. She found a small sharp stone on the floor and began marking each day on the side of the old bed's wooden frame. Each night the woman climbed down the hatch, locking it behind her to sleep on her pallet bed below, leaving Isabella with her thoughts as she replayed the attack and the kidnapping of their boys over and over in her head.

On the fifth day, there was the sound of arrival below, and the older woman opened the hatch. Three veiled women arrived with two servants carrying two buckets of water each. The servants left, and moments later, Sheikh Ishmael climbed the ladder. He seemed much taller and bigger than she remembered from her fleeting glance at him, and his presence certainly filled the small room. He gave Isabella a thin smile of triumph and satisfaction, for he had taken and imprisoned his enemy's wife.

She noticed that two women watched him like mice watch a snake, while the third older but beautiful woman held her head high and lowered her veil. Ishmael waved them to continue, so they pulled Isabella to her feet and, lifting the hem of her gown, they tried to pull the gown and chemise below it over her head. Isabella slapped their hands away, receiving a hefty slap across the face in return and a spate of Arabic from the older woman. The Sheikh laughed.

'You're angering my chief wife, Zaynab, and I warn you that it is not wise to cross her. She rules with an iron rod over my three seraglios here, in Tunis and Zaragoza. She is the mother of my three legitimate heirs, including the one your husband murdered. So she is already not well disposed towards you, and it would probably please her to have you beaten regularly. I know of two of my troublesome women who were smothered in the night on her orders, but I do not interfere. Let them get on with what they do. They'll clean you, for you're filthy, your hair is matted, and you stink from no doubt lying in your own piss in that wagon. Zaynab will not let me lay a finger on you while you're like that.'

Isabella lowered her eyes and arms and gave in while the women stripped her and roughly scrubbed every inch of her body. Sheikh Ishmael sat back and leaned against the wall, his eyes half closed, but she knew his eyes were raking over her naked body as they turned her, bent her over and washed her long, thick heavy blonde hair in one of the buckets. All three of them dried it with cloths for what seemed an age until Zaynab poured perfumed oil onto her hands and rubbed it through the long locks to make it shine. Isabella still had her pride; she had not jettisoned it yet and stood, head held high, her skin glowing from the rough cloths they used. Her hair hung over her shoulders and down to her waist in golden waves. Even the women seemed in awe of its colour and repeatedly ran it through their fingers until Zaynab, who had stood back, eyes narrowed, snapped at them.

Sheikh Ishmael now stood and walked over to her. He looked down into the deep amber eyes that glared hatred at him. He ran a finger gently along one dark brow and down the side of her face to hold and lift her chin. Isabella thought about spitting at him for a few seconds, but that had always resulted in painful retribution, and she was more afraid of this cruel killer. He walked around her, his fingers trailing around her waist, and then, with both hands, he lifted the heavy blonde hair, and after gently biting the nape of her neck, he let it fall onto her back. Isabella felt a shiver of revulsion go through her. The Sheikh thinking it was something else, smiled as he ran her hair through his fingers.

'So beautiful and such a shame it will only be like this for a few days.'

Isabella raised a questioning eyebrow, but he ignored her

and snapped an order in Arabic to his wife, who ordered the older woman and the girls out, pulling the hatch closed behind them. Zaynab sat on one of the stools and watched her husband with a sour expression. Isabella stared up at the man she despised. He had tried to poison her, and his men had tried to kill Piers a dozen times. Then he had cleverly infiltrated her home, kidnapping her and her boys. However, she kept her self-control and stared back at him without saying a word.

'We can do this in one of two ways, Isabella. You can make it difficult for yourself, or easy and have a comfortable life here. I intend to keep you here at Alaro for several years at least, and it suits me to do so as I put in more times at this port. Please do not get your hopes up, for there will be no rescue. They'll never find you, and I already have them running in different directions. On my orders, Al Cazar bought three tall blonde northern women in the markets, and I have planted them in different bases making sure that the locals have seen them. They're wasting their resources searching in places where you cannot be found, and you will no longer be a blonde, my beautiful Isabella. In three days, you will be dyed a very dark brown to match your eyebrows,' he said, lifting the blonde tresses. 'Even here,' he said, putting his hand firmly between her legs and grabbing the blonde curls down there so tightly that she flinched and gasped, trying to step away from him, but instead, he pulled her firmly against him.

'You have a choice. Will you fight me every inch of the way so that I inflict pain on you when I take you anyway and beat you afterwards? For in truth, part of me would enjoy that very much. Or will you decide to obey me, doing everything I ask? That way, your home here will improve with more luxurious furnishings, better food and an opportunity to go to the top of the tower daily for air. I will also give you news of your family, for as you know, I hold your boys and your daughter close to the slave markets in Marseilles. There is a lot of interest in them, and men are paying just to peer through the bars of the cells. If you set out to please me, I will make their lives easier, or I can make them far more difficult and painful.'

Isabella gasped as she realised that Chatillon could not have found the twins.

'No, even you would not do that. They're so young, only children, and you would not be that cruel.' Ishmael smiled as he removed his flowing white robe and handed it to his wife. The thin linen baggy trousers did nothing to hide the large erection he had. He was excited at the thought of her, and Isabella knew that, given what she had just heard, she had no choice but to obey him.

'Al Cazar tells me that Chatillon trained you as a top European courtesan, one who has bedded King Philip and several others in the French court. They tell me that these men never forget a night with you. So now you can show me the tricks you used to please these men,' he said, pushing her back onto the bed and dropping his linen trousers to the floor. Isabella glanced alarmingly at Zaynab, who was sitting watching, but Ishmael laughed as he stood between her legs.

'Don't worry about her, for she is getting too set in her ways, and I want her here to learn your tricks as well.'

Isabella saw the flash of absolute hatred Zaynab directed at her husband, and she hid a smile. She could try to find a way to use that hatred. She then closed her mind as Piers had taught her to do when she made love to other men and tried to pretend she was somewhere else with someone else.

An hour later, Ishmael dressed without saying a word,

waving at his wife to go. As he descended the ladder, he turned.

'They were right. You're very good, and I'll be back much later tonight for you to show me more. Tomorrow morning an Arab tutor will arrive, for you will only speak Arabic after this first week. Then Zaynab will return to pierce your ears as I'll turn you into my Berber mistress, a dark-haired beauty with black kohled eyes and tribal ownership tattoos on her hands, whom I bought from the tents of the deserts. This will be the story the servants and soldiers will be told if they ever get a glimpse of you.'

He pulled the hatch closed with a bang, and as she heard the bolt being shot, she closed her eyes against the tears that threatened to overwhelm her. The women had left her a silk Arab dress with a headdress and veil that she refused to wear, so she lifted her bruised body off the bed and dressed, dreading his return with or without Zaynab later that night. No matter how she had tried to encourage it, there was nothing gentle or tender about his lovemaking. He had treated his women brutally for years, and she doubted if he knew the meaning of love anymore. However, she had decided on this pathway no matter how hard it became because she was determined to protect her children.

Isabella would not learn for a very long time that Annecy was already dead, murdered by Pierre or that her boys were safe back on the Chatillon estate.

29

Chapter Twenty-eight

Castile August 1097

While Isabella was being hidden in the fortress on the large island, across the sea in Spain, the two horse warrior friends were riding to war. They had been placed in the combined forces of King Alphonse and his allies against the Berbers.

Georgio untied the long scarf wrapped around his nose and mouth and used it to wipe the sweat from his face and neck. It was high summer, and they rode south through Castile, heading for Toledo, where El Cid and his forces would meet them. Georgio narrowed his eyes and stared with envy at Conn Fitz Malvais riding beside him on Lune Noir, one of the huge Malvais steel-grey warhorses. Conn had captured a Berber headdress which seemed to cover not only his nose and mouth from the dust clouds but also his head and shoulders.

Feeling his scrutiny, Conn turned towards him, and Georgio, seeing his friend's eyes crinkle, knew he was laughing at him.

'You may laugh, Malvais. I'm sweating like a pig while you look as if you've been out for a stroll under the trees. That thing on your head does not even look damp, while I could wring this scarf out and water the horses.'

This time Conn laughed out loud. 'I did tell you to find, steal or buy one of these. We can learn from our enemies, Georgio. They come from the great deserts of Africa and know how to deal with the heat and dust. They wear thin flowing robes while we boil in padded gambesons and chain mail.'

Georgio pulled his horse to one side. He had filled his leather water sack from a fast-flowing stream in the hills behind. It had tasted fresh and clean, but after three days in the plains, it was hot and brackish.

'I could cook chicken or rabbit in that as I ride along; it's so hot,' he yelled, spitting out a mouthful.

'Do not fear Georgio, we only have a few hours to go, according to Diaz, one of King Alphonso's captains. Then we will be inside the high cool walls of Toledo.'

Conn narrowed his eyes to look ahead at the snaking columns of the forces of King Alphonse of Leon and Castile and his allies—over 30,000 men and more when El Cid joined them in Toledo. They were taking the war to the Almoravids, the Berber tribes that had swept across and occupied three-quarters of Spain. Now they hoped to drive them south to reconquer and hopefully establish Spain as a Christian kingdom once more in this Spanish crusade under the banner of Pope Urban.

Conn had heard much of Toledo, a fortress town sitting on the north banks of the River Tagus. King Alphonse had finally retaken it and the surrounding Almoravid territory over twelve years ago. Since then, the King had improved the fortifications further and built and established a Benedictine monastery as part of the castle, which perched on the far bank of the Tagus, guarding the only other road into the city.

Toledo was still attacked regularly by Emir Yusuf Ibn Tashfin, who seemed determined to take it back as this wide peninsula of Christian occupation thrust deep into his realm. Now the King's forces were to plunge even further south.

Before long, the high walls of Toledo hove into view, to the relief of Georgio. It was almost dusk when the camps were finally set up outside the walls, but Georgio could not wait and unsaddled his warhorse and rode him into the river to cool off. Conn watered his great warhorse and was tempted to do the same, but although he had borne the huge coloured tattoo on his back for over ten years, he kept it hidden by a linen shirt all of the time. This tattoo had been inflicted on all seven captured boys by the Warrior Monks when they were only nine years old. It was a huge sword that had been turned into a cross with a crown of thorns hanging on the extended crossbar, dripping seven drops of blood. It was to mark them for life as soldiers of Christ. It stopped people in their tracks, this huge cross that ran from his neck down to the base of his spine and across his shoulders.

He never forgot it was there, for it made them a target. He and Georgio had discussed what could happen if the Berber force ever captured them, and it was discovered that they had the cross of Christ on their backs, the mark of their God. At the very least, there would be a flogging to try and destroy it. At worst, they would flay them alive, nail their skin to their walls, or use it as a banner. Georgio had made Conn promise he would kill him if they were ever taken alive.

Conn was pulled from these harrowing thoughts by the arrival of their friend Diego Rodriguez who laughed to see Georgio swimming up and down with his horse.

'Is he mad to go in fully clothed? He will drown,' he declared.

Conn laughed with him. 'No, he swims like a fish, and he did take off his mail shirt and dump his saddle and saddlebags. I am left here as a mere guard for his belongings.'

Diego grinned. 'Well, pull him out and dry him off, for we are summoned by my father, El Cid, who has been here in Toledo for several days.'

A short while later, the three young knights were given a place at a privileged side table for dinner in the great Galiana Palace built by the Berber king, Al Mamun. This king had once promised his allegiance and had indeed paid tribute to the Kings of Leon and Castile. It was a very impressive Moorish palace.

The kings and lords of northern Spain sat deep in discussion with El Cid, and the young warriors listened attentively.

'They say that Yusuf Ibn Tashfin is leading this force against us himself,' remarked King Peter of Aragon.

King Alphonso nodded. 'My informers tell me that he has been back in Spain for about six months. As you know, the Emir has now established his capital at Marrakesh in the Maghreb, but he is determined this year to take back Toledo and Valencia, the cities we've taken from him.'

'He will certainly not take Valencia while I have breath left in my body,' said El Cid.

'They say he has over twenty thousand men made up of the usual Saharan tribes and Sudanese and Christian mercenaries. Do we have sufficient forces to take on these numbers?' asked Count Garcia Ordonez, a long-time rival of El Cid.

'Is that fear I hear in your voice Ordonez? I have beaten the Emir twice in the last three years while you were hiding at home in Navarre,' said El Cid with a sneer. 'If he had twice the number, we would still defeat him, and you forget to mention the six thousand Senegalese cavalry he has assembled. He has them all wearing white flowing robes and riding white horses whilst bringing a contingent of mounted drummers with them to put the fear of their God into their enemies. When they hear those drums, will your men turn and run Ordonez?'

Count Pedro Ansurez, the King's majordomo and a friend of El Cid, held up a hand. 'Let us not fight and argue amongst ourselves, for we have a strategy to plan.'

Both men reluctantly agreed, but Conn noticed that Ordonez still glared at Diego's father, and his fists were clenched in anger.

They stayed in Toledo for another four days until messengers arrived to say that the Emir's forces were on the move, coming north. King Alphonso and El Cid pored over the maps while the lords and nobles stood around with their armigers waiting in anticipation for orders to ride. Suddenly the King turned and waved over a tall, dark-bearded warrior to join them.

'Who is that?' asked Georgio, in a whisper loud enough for almost everyone in the room to hear.

Conn smiled. 'That is the man we will fight under, Georgio. He is general Alvar Fanez, one of the great cavalry leaders of Spain. He has fought with El Cid for years. I believe he is a kinsman of your father's, Diego.'

Diego nodded. 'Yes, he is actually my father's nephew, although there are only four or five years between them. He followed my father into exile and fought beside him to take Valencia. A good and loyal man to have at your side, and a fearsome warrior.'

Moments later, King Alphonse turned and faced the crowded

hall. 'We ride at dawn for Consuegra. Make ready!' he ordered.

'At last,' said Conn striding for the door with Georgio trying to keep up. They spent the next few hours grooming and watering their mounts—oil was rubbed into hooves to keep them from splitting in the harsh dry conditions, and manes and tails were docked or trimmed for battle.

'Are you ever afraid, Conn?' asked Georgio leaning his arms on his horse's neck. Conn straightened up from checking Lune Noir's fetlocks and looked at his friend.

'I have certainly known fear in my life, as have you, Georgio, but no, I don't feel fear as I ride into battle. I believe every warrior is apprehensive. You would be a fool if you were not, for only God knows what's waiting for us in the heat of battle. But, I have faith in my skill with a sword and in my horse, who has the blood of my uncle Luc's great stallion, Espirit Noir, running in his veins and will attack with hooves and teeth. He certainly knows no fear, and I trust him to get me out of dangerous situations.'

Georgio nodded and stared off over the camp, which was a hive of bustle and activity. However, Conn looked at his friend with concern, for he had never heard him talk like this before, and he was aware that twice recently, Georgio had talked wistfully about going home to Brittany.

'Georgio, you've been trained, as I have, from a very early age, to be a warrior. There is nothing wrong with feeling fear at times, but there is hardly a man in this camp you would not defeat with a sword except maybe El Cid himself and, of course, me.' He grinned, and Georgio smiled and faced him.

'Oh, it isn't fear for me, Conn. It's for you and Diego. You're like family to me, and I would hate to lose my friends.'

Conn laughed and slapped him affectionately on the shoulder. Picking up his and Georgio's sword, he went to have the blades sharpened by the armourers, whose grindstones were constantly turning from the long queue of warriors and squires with their lords' weapons.

They were barely out of the gates of Toledo the next morning as the sun rose when a messenger on a sweating horse appeared demanding to see El Cid. The huge column had stopped, and the main leaders pulled their horses close to listen to the messenger. Diego galloped forward to join his father and find out what was afoot.

'What is it, Father?' demanded Diego, trotting up as his father jerked his horse out of line.

'The Emir has tricked us, and he has purposefully drawn our forces into central Spain to make us believe that he was again massing to attack Toledo. However, we now find that he has sent a large force under Muhammed Ibn A'isha to attack and take my city of Valencia. I have no choice but also to split my forces, so I intend to take all of the cavalry back, as we need to make haste to protect Valencia while it is vulnerable. I have told the King that you're in charge of my infantry. I am sure you will make me proud, my son.'

So saying, they clasped arms, and El Cid rode away, taking several thousand of his cavalry with him. King Alphonse watched in dismay but could do nothing but lament the fact that he had lost the one man who could always inspire his forces to defeat the Almoravids.

Two days later, they were in the fortress of Consuegra, awaiting news from the scouts who were tracking the forces of Emir Yusuf Ibn Tashfin. The next night the campfires of their enemies could be seen on the far side of the plain. Conn, Georgio and Diego stood on the wide battlements of the large square Albaranna tower in the fortress, staring at what seemed like an immense force.

'Are the scout's estimates of the enemy numbers accurate?' asked Georgio in alarm.

'They could be using the age-old trick of the Romans to light dozens more fires to stretch out the camps to make their force look much bigger. The Berbers are renowned for playing mind tricks such as that. It is all meant to intimidate us. Even my father used a trick like that when they defeated King Malcolm in Scotland. They left a dummy camp behind while the army had actually moved out to force march ahead and be waiting for the Scots.'

'Your real father, Morvan De Malvais, is a great horse warrior as well, is he not? I heard that he fought on the side of both King William and for his son, Robert Curthose, for many years,' said Diego.

Conn nodded. 'He is also a great battle strategist and helped Robert defeat his father, King William, yet we are still all eclipsed by my uncle, Luc De Malvais, whom I pretend is my father. Even now, with him in his late forties, I hesitate before taking him on in a sword fight, for he would give no quarter to a nephew, and I wouldn't even think of challenging him on horseback. He is truly terrifying to watch and has taught me much.'

Diego listened wide-eyed; he had seen Conn fight and thought him unstoppable and unbeatable.

'I can understand what it is like to live up to the reputation of such warriors, for we are still young and honing our skills. With a father like El Cid, I just pray every time I ride out that I can live up to his expectations of me.'

Conn put a hand on his friend's shoulder. 'I am sure you

will, Diego and anyone can see how proud he is of you.'

Georgio sighed. 'I envy both of you these problems. My father and uncles were weavers, the best in Milan. So I must warn you that I am lethal with a loom at ten paces.' All three of them burst out laughing at that.

'Come, let us abed, for we will almost certainly face the enemy on the morrow,' said Conn.

The forces of the King moved forward into their strategic positions the next morning. The infantry forces of Count Ansurez were on the left flank, and Conn and Georgio, under the command of Alvar Fanez, were protecting them. Diego and El Cid's troops were on the right flank, and King Alphonse ordered Count Ordonez to position his cavalry on that flank to protect them. Conn felt uneasy when he heard this, but he was not sure why, as Ordonez had proved himself in other battles.

By the time the sun rose, the two forces faced each other on the plain below the fortress at Consuegra, the sun glinting off the huge array of shields and weapons on both sides. The senior knights and nobles held the centre ground on their trained warhorses with several troops of archers and crossbowmen in front of them. When the enemy moved into range, and the horns blew, they let fly all of their arrows and bolts and then swiftly retreated through the mounted nobles, whose horses were champing at the bit. The mounted knights smashed their way through the Berber infantry and then retreated, leaving their infantry running forward with loud war cries to attack the enemy.

The fighting was fierce and brutal as Diego ran with his men giving the war cry of 'El Cid! We fight for the Cid!'

Hearing this, the infantry thought that the Great Cid had returned, giving them the heart to push ahead. However, the superior numbers of Almoravid cavalry and light horse-mounted archers began to tell, and the Christian infantry was beginning to be overwhelmed.

Conn and Georgio had cut a swathe through the enemy, but they were fighting for their lives and soon feared they would be surrounded. Count Alvar Fanez did what he could to protect the infantry on the left flank as they decimated the mounted enemy. Still, the numbers were against them as the white-clad Senegalese cavalry appeared, their drums echoing across the plain.

Watching from the tower, King Alphonse and his chief nobles had an overview of what was happening below. He gripped the stone of the battlements as he watched wave after wave of the Almoravid white-robed cavalry sweep around to attack the flanks of his forces. It was apparent that they could not succeed with the loss of El Cid's cavalry, so he ordered the horns to sound a recall.

The infantry of Count Pedro Ansurez on the left flank retreated with the cavalry of Alvar Fanez fighting the rearguard to protect the withdrawal. However, on the right flank, with the appearance of even more Berber cavalry, Count Garcia Ordonez retreated, galloping back to Consuegra and leaving Diego and his father's infantry unprotected on the plain. Thousands of Berber white-robed cavalry quickly surrounded Diego and his men.

Conn and Georgio clattered into the large bailey of the castle with the rest of the fleeing cavalry. The last of the infantry ran through them and even under the bellies of the horses to reach safety from the mounted archers behind them. Conn left a highly relieved Georgio to dismount whilst throwing his reins to a groom and racing for the staircases to the tower.

He reached the top and saw the King and his nobles in the far corner.

All eyes were on what was happening below on the plain. As Conn reached the walls and scanned the plain below, he saw that Diego and hundreds of infantry had been abandoned. They were now completely surrounded and being ruthlessly slain in front of their eyes. Conn was shocked to the core....

'Treachery and cowardice,' he shouted, which made the nobles turn.

'Ordonez ran and abandoned the men he was supposed to be protecting. We must ride out again and rescue them!' demanded Conn.

The King turned with a steely glance at Conn.

'This is the Cid's fault for taking all his cavalry. He should have left half of them here. He is as much to blame for this!'

Conn, white with fury, was about to argue that El Cid would never have run and left men on the field when King Peter of Aragon put a hand on his arm just as Georgio arrived, panting at the top of the stairs.

'Be calm, Malvais. We can do nothing. Riding out will only result in your death. Look!' he pointed to what was happening on the plain below. The forces of the Emir had advanced, and now, even more cavalry surrounded the trapped men. Conn could make out Diego in the centre in Aragon's bright blue and gold tunic. The young warrior held his sword high, and the sun glinted off it as he brought it crashing down on the heads of his enemies, but then he and his men were engulfed.

Conn put his hand over his eyes, he could not watch the slaughter, and as the enemy began beheading the Christians, he turned away.

That night he led a group over the walls of the fortress to try and rescue Diego's body. Although the enemy now completely encircled the small town and castle of Consuegra, they were still not close to the walls. Yusuf Ibn Tashfin had decided not to waste any more warriors today. He would starve them out.

There was a sliver of moon as they crept low to the ground, around the walls and onto the plain to the scene. The ground was dark, soaked with the blood of the slaughtered four hundred men. As they had done in other victories, the heads of the Christian soldiers had been piled in large pyramids. Georgio had brought a sack to put the head of Diego Rodriguez inside if they could find it, so that it could be buried with his body as his father would expect.

Later Georgio would describe walking over and through the hundreds of decapitated corpses as one of the worst moments of his life as they searched for Diego. The smell was overpowering, and the moon's dim light gave the scene a lurid and horrifying air that made all of them blanch except Conn. He was heading for the exact spot where he had last seen his friend, and to his surprise, Diego's body was untouched. They must have recognised the son of El Cid, and the Berbers tended to respect the bodies of leaders killed in battle. It lay with several of El Cid's captains, who were also intact but had died trying to protect Diego.

Conn closed Diego's eyes and picked his blood-soaked body up in his arms to carry back to the fortress. This time, he did not cower or hide from the enemy in the shadows. He strode openly across the plain to the gates, his friends, their swords drawn, following behind him.

The guards on the walls shouted he was coming, and dozens appeared on the walls to watch. As he neared the gate, they all began to bang their swords on their shields, and as the gates opened, the same sound met Conn as he walked in. Torches were lit and held high, and hundreds of men banged on their shields in tribute to Diego, the only son of El Cid, a true warrior. Conn saw that General Alvar Fanez was there, as was Count Ansurez, along with many other lords who stood on the walkways and stairs. They all bowed in salute as Diego was carried to the chapel.

As the siege continued, the Benedictine monks embalmed the young warrior's body and laid it in a stone sarcophagus until his father could be told and let his wishes be known. A mass for his soul was said, and the chapel was packed. Conn came face to face with Garcia Ordonez on the way out and stopped.

'I am leaving here when the siege is lifted, and I will make it my life's work to ensure that the whole of Europe knows of your treachery and betrayal.' He then spat on the ground at the Count's feet.

Ordonez's hand went immediately to the hilt of his sword, and Conn, towering over him, leaned close to the Count's red angry face.

'I beg you to challenge me, a fight to the death, revenge for your murder of Diego and his four hundred men.'

A noble at the Count's elbow hissed in his ear. 'Don't respond. It is Malvais. No one here could stand against him.'

The Count stepped back, and Count Alvar Fanez put himself between them.

'It is not seemly to argue or fight in the house of God. The King shall hear of this.' He indicated that Conn should leave, which he did reluctantly. Meanwhile, Alvar Fanez looked Ordonez up and down with contempt before following Conn out, and he caught up with him outside in the bailey.

'Come, we will share some wine Fitz Malvais,' he said, leading him into the Great Hall and to a table in a window embrasure.

'Did you mean what you said about leaving Spain when the siege ends?' he asked while waving a squire over.

Conn nodded. 'The betrayal and death of Diego have sickened me, but it also made me realise that I have not seen my family for over three years. I intend to go back to Brittany.'

'That is a great shame, and a loss for us—you and Georgio are great horse warriors, and I would have welcomed you by my side. If you change your mind or wish to return, there will always be a place here for you.'

Conn nodded his thanks.

'Will his father, Rodrigo Diaz de Vivar, El Cid—will he know yet?' asked Georgio, who, as usual, was inseparable from Conn.

Alvar sighed. 'I sent a message to Valencia immediately, but we don't even know if he still holds the city or if it has fallen. He will be devastated, Diego was his only son, and he adored him.'

'Will the King punish Ordonez for disobeying his orders?' asked Georgio.

'I doubt it. The King's mood changes with the wind, and as he is no strategist, he is angry with El Cid. He cannot see that the Cid had no choice but to go and save Valencia. There has always been bad blood between Ordonez and Rodrigo. The Count even tried to assassinate Rodrigo over thirty years ago when they were both young knights. Now I must leave you and check on my men on duty. I've put a guard on the wells in case they try to poison them, for they'll have men within the walls and fortress. Tomorrow we will start to ration the food.'

With those pleasant thoughts, he left them.

Five days later, the siege was lifted. Amir, a local translator, told Conn that it was because the Emir was losing too many of his men to heat exhaustion and sickness. Also, the Emir had heard that a large Christian relief force was coming to attack them. The Emir had made his point—he had defeated King Alphonse and halted the Christian push south, and now he would leave and go back to Marrakesh.

The next morning Conn and Georgio rode out of the gates with their two servants, extra mounts and their war gear on their packhorses. They were returning home to the windswept northwestern coasts of Brittany—back to their home and estates in Morlaix, back to their family. They had been strapping sixteen-year-old boys when they rode out and left home. They were returning as two fully grown, experienced warriors with gold in their pockets and eyes that had probably seen too much on the battlefields of Spain.

They would return to Spain, but it would not be in the way they expected.

30

Chapter Twenty-nine

It was nearly a month before they rode into the streets of Morlaix, a busy little port on the north coast of Brittany. They made their way wearily up the winding road to the imposing fortified home of the Malvais family on the eastern bluff. It had been added to greatly and extended over the years, and outside the eastern walls was a huge stable block and a dozen cleared fields, where over a hundred famous Malvais warhorses ran free in large meadows.

The guards on the huge stone gatehouse regarded the two dust-covered men and horses with suspicion as they approached the gates, but then the Serjeant recognised the great steel grey warhorse, Lune Noir, and he turned to the other guards.

'Ring the bell! Ring it loud, for Master Conn, and Georgio have come home!'

When the bell rang, Morvan and Luc were in the home paddock, putting three promising youngsters through their paces. It was such an unusual occurrence in these peaceful times that both men strapped on their swords as they headed for the gates. The two young warriors had already dismounted, and Merewyn and Ette were hugging them when the two Malvais men burst through the postern gate at a run. Luc stopped and laughed before standing back to let Morvan go first. The joy on Morvan's face as he clasped and embraced his son was a pleasure to see.

It was a boisterous and joyful meal that evening as they caught up on their news.

Lusian, Luc's eldest son, was still in the court of King Philip. He had been sent to serve his time as a squire there and earn his knighthood in the right way rather than having it handed to him by his father. He was now twenty-five years old and courting the daughter of a count, for as the heir to the Malvais name and estates, he had a lot to offer.

Conn and Georgio could not believe how Garrett, Luc and Merewyn's youngest son, had grown. He was a mere annoying stripling when they left, but now Georgio did not doubt that Garrett would rival Conn in height. However, Georgio only had eyes for one person, Chantelle, their beautiful silver-blonde daughter. Unfortunately, she was now betrothed to the heir of the Penthievre title and would leave them in a month. Georgio thought she was the most beautiful creature he had ever seen, and Conn teased him unmercifully.

Conn related all of their exploits in Spain. Both Luc and Morvan could see the pain on his face as he described the death of his friend Diego. 'It is a hard life lesson Conn, but I assure you that your father and I have come across such betrayal several times in our lives, and sometimes it is difficult to walk away when you want to take his head from his shoulders. But you did the right thing, and we are proud of you. With luck, one day you may get your revenge, or El Cid may take it for you,' said Luc.

Conn nodded, but his eyes still showed his pain. To deflect their attention, Georgio jumped in with a question.

'Tell us, Sire, what is happening with the huge crusade led by Duke Robert? We've heard little for several months.'

Luc waved at Morvan to let him tell it, as he was still in touch with his friend Duke Robert.

'Robert told me that the huge numbers that left Le Puy dwindled because of hardship as the Crusade progressed through the Alps and down to Rome. Many left because they were disillusioned by what they found when they reached that holy city as the troops and supporters of the antipope, Clement, had taken the Lateran Palace. However, Robert tells me the numbers were still immense as they travelled down to Bari, easily close to twenty thousand.

You may not be aware, but last winter was one of terrible storms in the Mediterranean that went on for months. Against local advice, King Philip's brother, Count Hugh of Vermandois, decided to sail. All of his fleet sank, losing hundreds of men, horses, weapons and equipment. Fortunately, he was washed ashore, saved along with some of his warriors, and taken to Constantinople. Hearing this, Duke Robert and Count Stephen de Blois decided not to risk it, so they overwintered in the south in Calabria. Many of the pilgrims now stuck in southern Italy for the winter felt abandoned by their leaders as they wandered aimlessly and so returned home. We last heard that Robert had finally sailed and reached Constantinople. He was full of praise for a beautiful woman he had met, the daughter of Count Geoffrey of Converano, before he headed south to join the siege and battle for Nicaea.'

'It is a dangerous undertaking to travel that distance. We

took on three groups of bandits just traversing the Pyrenees, yet with straggling numbers that size, you have hundreds of targets, many carrying their life savings with them,' said Georgio.

'Yes, but to reach and see Jerusalem, to take it back from the heathens, that must be something special. It makes our efforts in Spain seem trivial,' added Conn with a faraway look in his eyes.

'There is nothing trivial about what you and Georgio have been doing for the last three years. The Reconquista is an equally important crusade, for if we don't stop the Berbers in Spain and take back cities such as Valencia and Toledo, to hold a line, they'll be over the mountains and sweeping into France. King Alphonse may have suffered a setback, but he is doing the right thing, and he will succeed,' exclaimed Luc.

For the next month, Conn and Georgio worked with Morvan on the schooling of the young warhorses, and Conn found a kind of peace he had not found before. He enjoyed spending time with his father and stepmother, Ette. The rest of the family had gone as part of Chantelle's bridal party to Penteur, to Georgio's dismay, so it gave Conn some time alone with his father. The Steward and the older servants in the castle knew about Conn's parentage, but they were loyal and not loose-lipped. His half-brother Gervais, now fourteen years old, tried to follow him everywhere, while his half-sister Marie, now sixteen years old, followed Georgio everywhere with her eyes. This made Conn laugh even more as his friend coloured up.

'The eternal triangle of unrequited love, you're in love with my cousin, who has now married someone else, while my half-sister is in love with you, and you ignore her,' he teased, but his friend was not amused.

Georgio was often lost in Conn's shadow, but the young Italian man was very handsome. With dark curly hair and large brown eyes, he turned many a maiden's head. He did not have Conn's towering height but was still respectably tall with a lithe warrior physique through years of training.

As they moved into the later autumn, the family returned, and Conn and Georgio were happy to stay at home for the winter after the harsh winters in northern Spain. They had no definite plans yet, and Georgio was becoming highly excited about Yuletide, which he loved. He found it difficult to remember his family in Milan, who had all died of the plague when he was only five years old. He deliberately shut out the six spartan brutal years with the Warrior Monks at the Hermitage, as he still had nightmares about his time there. He was just ten years old when he was rescued and given a home with Conn here at Morlaix, and Georgio loved his adoptive family, especially Merewyn, whom he regarded as his mother. She had taken to the thin, bruised, sad-eyed boy as soon as she saw him, and they had become inseparable for that first year after the rescue. Even now, as a young man, he found he would gravitate to her wherever she was in the house if he had no other work to do, often just sitting and talking with her in the solar, helping her sort out tangled embroidery threads. The rest of the family accepted his love for Merewyn, apart from the odd joke asking him when he would be embroidering his own tapestry.

However, something was on its way to disturb this peace.

In early December, a messenger arrived in the driving rain to deliver a letter. Messages usually always arrived by a pigeon in these wild far-flung parts of western Brittany, a message of only four or five short but important lines. This message was in a large leather pouch brought by a priest travelling south to Nantes. It was addressed to Morvan. They welcomed the soaked man and bade him sit by the fire while extracting the sealed sheets of vellum. He noticed at once that it was the red wax seal of the Holy See. He had seen it enough before as Chatillon used it on official business. However, when Morvan's eyes travelled down to the bottom of the second thick vellum page, he saw that it was from Pope Urban himself.

He looked up and met Luc's raised eyebrow.

'It's from the Pope; give me a moment.'

A buzz went around the high table about what it could be. Ette and Merewyn both presumed that it would be a summons from the Pope for the Horse warriors to be deployed somewhere. Merewyn put her hand on Luc's thigh and reminded him that he had retired. He laughed, but his face gave away his interest in knowing what the Pope wanted. Luc had a lot of respect for the man and had known him well as Chatillon's uncle and the Cardinal of Cluny over the years before he became Pope Urban.

Having read it twice, Morvan handed it to Luc, who scanned it. Conn noticed that his father's face had paled. He was obviously shocked by what he had read, as was Luc de Malvais.

'The Pope is asking for our help in the new year. His nephew and our friend Piers De Chatillon is in trouble. He does not go into much detail, but Piers' home has been attacked, and they have murdered his daughter and kidnapped his wife, Isabella. Chatillon has been searching for her for a year, but he has not found her. He does not even know if she is alive or dead. Pope Urban is now seriously concerned for Piers' physical and mental health as Piers is convinced he is cursed. He is going to Chatillon Sous Bagneux for Yuletide and will summon his nephew to Rome in March as soon as the snow on the passes clears. He hopes to try and snap him out of this depression and lassitude, and he worries that Chatillon is giving up and thinks the search for Isabella is hopeless.'

Morvan met Luc's eyes. 'How did we not know about this? We certainly didn't give up while looking for Conn, and it was Chatillon who drove us on for several years. He found the Hermitage and helped us chase the Warrior Monks to Avignon to rescue the boys. We all owe Piers De Chatillon so much, a huge debt of gratitude, and he is a dear friend. The Pope asks for our help; he wants me to be in Rome when Chatillon arrives in March, to bring fresh ideas and strategies and pull his nephew out of this despair.'

'The answer to that will always be yes!' said Luc while Morvan nodded.

Merewyn leaned over and put her hand on top of Conn's hand. 'Piers has saved your life twice, Conn. You do not know this, but Alan, Duke of Brittany, discovered that your mother, Constance, was carrying Morvan's child. He ordered that you were to be taken out and exposed on the hillside as soon as you were born. Piers blackmailed Queen Matilda into coming and saving you. He then arranged for a stillborn child to be found and taken out on the hillside. You were handed to your nurse, Hildebrand, and Luc brought you to us, to safety. Duke Alan, fortunately, never found out the truth, he thought the child was killed, but Chatillon risked his life and reputation to do that.'

'Georgio and I will come with you, Father, for I believe I owe this man a great debt. This will become our quest to try and repay him.'

Luc and Morvan looked at the two young warriors and

smiled. They were proud of the boys.

'We will leave mid-February to travel to Rome. Luc will stay here now that I have two warriors at my side. I have no idea what we will find or how long we will be away, but I swear we will help him find Isabella. I'll send a bird to Pope Urban tomorrow,' proclaimed Morvan, and they all raised their glasses to the quest.

Later that night, Morvan and Luc sat alone by the great fireplace, reflecting on what they had read.

'I cannot imagine what he is going through. I saw young Annecy two years ago when we took the horses to King Philip. She was a beautiful little thing, the image of her mother. Who could murder a child like that?'

'Send for me, Morvan, at any point if you need me. Lusian will return with his bride in the early spring, and I can leave at once. I don't know who has done this or why yet, but if Chatillon has not found and killed them all, then I promise we will, and they'll taste the true blade of vengeance,' said Luc.

Morvan leaned forward and clasped arms with his older brother; few, if any, could ever stand against the Malvais brothers...

Chatillon was indeed in a dark place. After the rousing speech on his return, they had thrown all their resources and informers into finding Isabella but to no avail. She seemed to have disappeared off the face of the earth. There had been no sightings of her whatsoever in any of the ports, bases, or haunts of Sheikh Ishmael. Chatillon could only assume she was deeply hidden in some dungeon and never saw the light of day. He tormented himself nightly about her suffering, and what she would face daily.

At first, he had tried to remain buoyant and positive for his sons, for he could see the changes in them, the impact of their ordeal and the loss of their mother. Gironde was back to being his boisterous self, but Piers noticed a brittleness about him, a hardness that had not been there before. Gabriel had still not recovered. Piers noticed he jumped if something was dropped; also, he gave nervous glances over his shoulder if they were riding or hunting, and the nightmares still came to him several times a week. The anger and fury of what had been done to these innocent boys sometimes consumed him to the extent that he had to leave the hall and walk in the kitchen garden, no matter the weather.

Ahmed, fully recovered, watched him in concern as he retreated further into himself and spent more time alone in his study or riding the estates on his own. Yuletide was approaching again, and Ahmed, watching Gabriel staring hopelessly into the fire, sent a message to Pope Urban begging him to come this year as his nephew, Piers, needed his counsel.

The Yule logs were brought into the hall with the usual singing, and some merriment, but Finian and Edvard had organised it to give the boys some celebration. Chatillon did not appear.

However, the next day with the usual fanfare and huge entourage, Chatillon's uncle, Pope Urban, arrived at his old home. Everyone except Chatillon and the boys knew and had prepared for this arrival. Madame Chambord had been cooking for weeks, and all the servants had been forewarned, lining up outside to greet the Pope. The nonstop barking of the dogs drew Piers from his business room, and he looked, in surprise, down on the bustle and crowd of people pouring through the doors. Then his uncle looked up, saw him on the gallery, and opened his arms in welcome, and Piers found that, inexplicably, the tears were streaming down his cheeks.

The boys had finally gone off to bed exhausted, and to Ahmed's eyes, the arrival of Pope Urban had lifted all of their spirits. Even Dion, still concerned for Finian and his relationship with Piers, had found herself laughing at some of the tales he told of happenings in Rome. Before long, the five men retreated to the solar to sit around the fire, in warmer surroundings, leaving the men and priests below to enjoy themselves drinking and dicing.

'I am sorry I have left it so long to visit you, Piers, but as you know, I have had a great deal of involvement not only with the crusade but also with the actions of the anti-Pope Clement and his supporters. I was reluctant to leave the city after taking back the Lateran Palace and winning the support of Roger Bosso and his mercenaries. However, I have tried everything I can to help you find Isabella. I have called in favours across Europe to no avail. There have been no sightings anywhere. Have you managed to glean any further information since your last message to me?'

Chatillon shook his head. 'She is gone, Uncle, gone, and no matter what I do, I cannot find a trace of her. I must now presume that she is so well hidden that I will never find her; she could be veiled in a Bedouin tent in the Great Desert for all I know, or she is dead. Ishmael has murdered her as well to take his revenge on me. I have had men watching and following him, but she is never seen at his side. He is doing what he has always done; sailing the Mediterranean attacking other helpless souls, slaughtering them, stealing their cargo or ships and then returning to Tunis, Tripoli or spending time in his brother's palace in Zaragoza. We have several servants there who are informers, and there has been not a whisper of Isabella.'

Urban regarded his nephew as he sat back and closed his eyes. He had lost weight, looked unnaturally pale and, more importantly, that burning light had gone out of his eyes, that zeal that he always had and zest for life. It had been extinguished by grief.

'You can do no more than you're doing at the moment; someone somewhere will make a mistake, and you will receive a lead, but until then, you must face reality and not become the recluse you've turned into recently. It would be best if you snapped out of this Piers. When was the last time you took your sons into the pell yard? They need you, and you're allowing Gironde and Gabriel to become shadows of their former selves. Yes, they have lost their mother, but by your actions, you're ensuring that they have also lost their father. I have brought Gabriel a vielle as a Yuletide gift, a slightly different instrument from the smashed citole, but I was hoping you could encourage him to play it and let us at least try to get the light back into his eyes. I have also brought them a new tutor, a lively young man from Turin who will take their education further. They have long outgrown the limited tuition of Father Dominic, who seems to spend every afternoon asleep.'

Chatillon opened his eyes and allowed himself a small smile, for his uncle's speech reminded him of how he had swept into his life after the death of his parents, and had rescued him then as well.

He glanced at the faces of Edvard, Ahmed and Finian, who had hung on the Pope's every word and watched him like a hawk as he realised this was a conspiracy. His uncle had been brought here, summoned to shake him out of this dark mood. Ever the pragmatist, Piers realised that they were right, but the pain he felt as he thought of his beautiful wife, in the hands of Ishmael, filled him with a despair that dragged him back down. However, he nodded, agreed to listen, and spend more time with his sons.

Soon, the others left them, and Urban turned back to more worldly matters, 'I presume you received the news about Bishop Odo?' he asked.

Piers nodded. He had received the message, but in the trauma of everything that had happened, he'd barely thought of it since.

'He took your advice and left the main crusade as they ventured south. He took ship for Sicily and established himself in Palermo. Unfortunately, the Grandesmil brothers, protecting him, didn't go with him; they continued with Duke Robert to Calabria.'

'I seem to remember that Odo died suddenly in Palermo. Is that right?'

Pope Urban nodded. 'He was taken with a sudden illness after dinner one evening, and within a week, he was dead.'

Chatillon shook his head. 'So undoubtedly poisoned then, and Flambard has his way—another obstacle removed that could have prevented King William from keeping Normandy. I would not be surprised if Robert suffered a fatal accident, or deadly injury, on this crusade. Probably an arrow or spear from behind,' added Chatillon resignedly.

Urban steepled his fingers and looked at his nephew. Once, he had been almost constantly by his side as his Papal Legate and envoy, but he had not used his services at all since the attack. He now felt it was time to bring Piers back into play. He needed him, and he missed his razor-sharp mind when it came to the politics of Europe and, honestly, his blade when removing obstacles.

'I do believe that King William Rufus and his advisor, Flambard, are becoming more of a force to be reckoned with than we expected, Piers. Perhaps it is time for us to rein them in somewhat. I invited Flambard and Archbishop Anselm to Rome in the early spring and would like you to attend. I need you back at my side. The search will continue for Isabella no matter where you are in Europe.'

Piers said nothing, and Urban could see the mulish expression around his mouth. He may have reached Piers in one way, but he knew he would need to work over the next few weeks at building the change and extracting him from the chateau. He seemed to be gaining comfort from its walls as the last place he had seen Isabella, and for a man such as Piers De Chatillon, that was unhealthy.

Piers bade him goodnight and left his uncle in a thoughtful mood in front of the fire's dying embers. Urban put another few logs on and poured himself another goblet of wine as he thought about the best way to handle this. There was no doubt that Piers needed more voices in his ear, he thought of summoning Gervais de la Ferte from Paris, but Urban knew that as Seneschal of France, Gervais was a busy man, and the time he could give would be limited.

Just then, there was a noise behind him, and he turned to see Ahmed returning.

'Come and sit, old friend, have some wine. I am in somewhat of a quandary here as to how to shake my nephew out of this inertia, this self-indulgent grief for someone who may still be alive.'

Ahmed accepted the wine and stared at the fire. 'This is why I summoned you; we've tried everything, but he has retreated behind walls and locked doors in his mind, where he replays, and questions, everything repeatedly. What if he hadn't gone on the crusade? What if he had killed Pierre? Would Annecy and Cecily still be alive? He swims in a sea of guilt and sometimes breaks out into uncontrollable rages.'

'Yet this man, my nephew, spent years searching for young Conn De Malvais, finding him in the most hidden and inaccessible place, defeated a swarm of warrior monks against all odds and brought him home.'

Ahmed put his head to one side and looked at Urban. 'Perhaps that is just what we need!'

Urban looked puzzled at first as Ahmed continued.

'Piers didn't do that on his own—he had two of the most formidable Horse Warriors in Europe at his side, the Malvais brothers. Two men whom Piers respects more than anyone else I know, saving you, of course,' he smiled.

Urban drained his goblet and slapped Ahmed affectionately on the shoulder. 'Ahmed, you're a mind reader for I have already sent a message to Brittany. If anyone can shake him out of this, then Morvan De Malvais can.'

Ahmed smiled; his plan was coming together. With the right kind of help, Piers could find Isabella and bring her home.

31

Chapter Thirty

Domfront - December 1097

Henry Beauclerc had bided his time. He had taught himself patience. He had watched in increasing frustration as his brother, William Rufus, had established himself in Normandy, issuing new laws and raising taxes. However, he was pleased to note that William Rufus had stayed away from him and his lands in Domfront. He knew that if he did not act soon, he would never be able to dislodge his brother from the Dukedom of Normandy. If, or when, his eldest brother Duke Robert returned, he also would have no chance of regaining his dukedom without paying back the immense sum agreed in the Vifgage arrangement. It was an impossible sum, a lifetime of money, and unless he came back loaded with gold and plunder from the Crusade, he would never do it.

For Henry, there was only one solution—King William Rufus must die, and he firmly believed he had the right person to do it.

He had learned with interest that Chatillon's home had been

attacked, his children and his wife kidnapped. He knew now that the boys had been rescued almost immediately, for he would expect nothing less of Piers De Chatillon, one of the most feared men in Europe. However, his adversaries had been clever, and Isabella De Chatillon had still not been found. If all went to plan, this could give him the leverage he needed to persuade Chatillon to assassinate his brother.

To that end, he had gained a man in Chatillon's household who was on his payroll, not a new man whom they would be suspicious of, given recent events. This man had been a groom there for several years, but now he needed money for a sick mother in Paris who needed a physician. The man, when approached, had still been loyal to the family and refused to do anything to hurt them, but he was willing to pass over information on how the search for Isabella was progressing.

Henry was now aware that a certain Sheikh Ishmael had taken her and that Chatillon's men had searched Tripoli from end to end and found two blonde German girls, but no sign of Isabella. He had heard of Sheikh Ishmael and made it his business to find everything he could about this man and the cause of the blood feud between him and Chatillon.

The most important information that Henry gleaned from other contacts was that the Sheikh had a double life, and was, in fact, the respectable Yusuf Ibn Hud, the brother of Abu J'far, the head of the Hud Dynasty in Zaragoza. From his time in Leon, Henry knew that this was the same family that had made peace with King Alphonse of Leon and Castile in return for his help against the Almoravids. The Hud dynasty now paid tribute to King Alphonse to keep that peace, and they were his allies.

The Christian king would be horrified to learn that his ally's brother, Yusuf, had kidnapped the Papal Envoy's wife.

Another thing that Henry had learnt during his prolonged exile with his cousin in Leon and Castile, was that Alphonse needed money. He was borrowing from the Jews, but he needed ever more to buy weapons and mercenaries to pursue his war against the Almoravids. If his plan succeeded and both his brothers were dead or missing, Henry could promise a considerable amount of gold to his cousin King Alphonse in return for information. This information would give him exactly the leverage he needed with Chatillon to persuade him to kill his brother William Rufus.

Henry called for his Steward. He decided to go south to Leon and visit his cousin. He had heard that King Alphonse had suffered an ignominious defeat at Consuegra, so would want revenge against the Almoravids and would be willing to listen to him.

If anyone could bring the Ibn Hud dynasty to heel, then King Alphonse could, and with a little pressure, they could find Chatillon's wife if she were still alive, which he secretly doubted.

Isabella was very much alive. She had been there for a year and had never set foot outside the tower. Occasionally if she had particularly pleased him, he would bring the ladder from below and take her up to the top of the tower, especially if it was hot. At first, she was pleased and excited, but she found he always used her roughly up there on the roof as if to make her pay for the privilege. She would have scratches and grazes from the coarse stone for days as he enjoyed taking her in the open air. She tried to be as calm and compliant as possible when she was with him, but that often infuriated him more, and he would sometimes beat her with a cane to get a response from her until she dropped to her knees and begged for mercy.

She counted the days until he would go to sea again, for he was often away for weeks at a time. However, during these times, without him here to protect her, Zaynab and the other women from the seraglio would sometimes visit to humiliate or beat her. They resented the time he gave to her when he should have been with them, and so they punished her.

Isabella had stayed strong. She had no idea why Chatillon had not found her yet in all this time, but she did not doubt he would come, and so she still scratched the passing of every day on the bed, telling herself it would be the next day, or the next week, that she would be free.

However, this week, she stopped counting and marking the days. She lay curled up in a ball on the bed, eyes tightly closed, tears trickling down her cheeks, for she now knew she was carrying the Sheikh's child. She had worked out that she must be three or four months, but she had ignored it when her courses did not come thinking it was the anxiety and unhappiness that had caused it. Now her breasts were sore, and as with Annecy, she was nauseous on a morning.

So instead, Isabella prayed that Chatillon would not find her now, for she could imagine the disgust, hatred and revulsion he would feel when he came in to find her big with the Sheikh's child. She had no doubt he would reject both her and the child. She felt a wave of hopelessness and sadness, for she knew, she could now never leave here or see Piers and her family again.

32

Maps

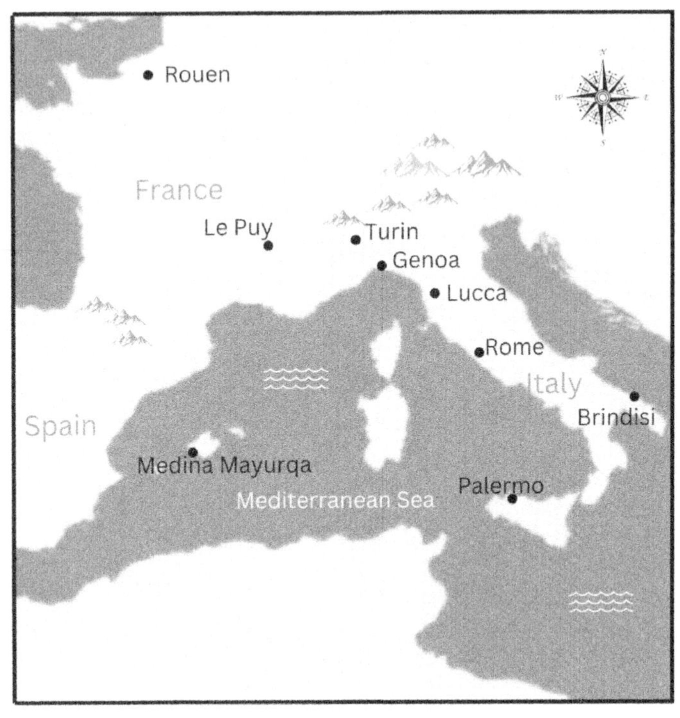
Rouen
France
Le Puy
Turin
Genoa
Lucca
Rome
Italy
Brindisi
Spain
Medina Mayurqa
Mediterranean Sea
Palermo

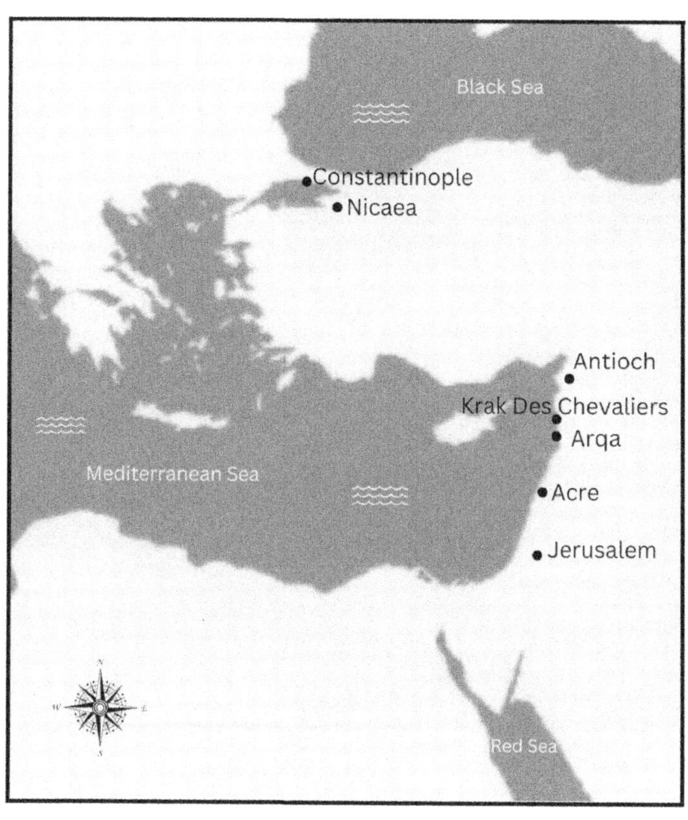
Black Sea
Constantinople
Nicaea
Antioch
Krak Des Chevaliers
Arqa
Mediterranean Sea
Acre
Jerusalem
Red Sea

France
Bay of Biscay
Leon
Aragon
Empire of Leon
Huesca
Battle of Alcoraz 1096
Zaragoza
Tarragona
Battle of Consuegra 1097
Valencia
Medina
Mayurqa
ALMORAVID EMPIRE
Mediterranean Sea
Atlantic Ocean

33

Glossary

Armiger – Formerly an armour bearer of a knight but later a privileged position as the chief warrior who commanded all of a lord's men.
Bailey - A ward or courtyard in a castle, some outer baileys could be huge, encompassing grazing land, stables, blacksmiths and huts.
Basilica – An early Christian church or cathedral designated by the Pope and given the highest permanent designation. Once given, the title cannot be removed.
Braies - A type of trouser often used as an undergarment, often to mid-calf and made of light or heavier linen.
Castellan – An appointed official or governor of a castle.
Chasuble – The outermost vestment worn by clergy.
Chatelaine – The lady in charge of a large establishment, holder of all the keys.
Chausses – Attached by laces to the waist of the braies, these were tighter-fitting coverings for the legs.
Citole or Vielle – An early stringed instrument similar to fiddles.

Cog – A ship – Clinker-built trading ships with a single mast and a square-rigged sail. They had wide flat bottoms allowing them to load and unload in shallow harbours.

Dais – A raised platform in a hall for a throne or tables, often for nobles.

Donjon – An early name for the innermost keep of a castle.

Doublet – A close-fitting jacket or jerkin often made from leather, with or without sleeves. Laced at the front and worn under or over, a chain mail hauberk.

Emir – A monarch or aristocrat in the Arab world.

Fealty – Sworn loyalty to a lord or patron.

'Give No Quarter' – To give no mercy or clemency for the vanquished.

Gambeson – A padded or defensive jacket often worn under chain mail.

Gunwale – The top edge or rail of a ship's hull, previously known as the bulwark.

Holy See – The jurisdiction of the Bishop of Rome – the Pope.

Keep/Donjon – A fortified tower, initially made of wood, then replaced by stone, built on a mound within a medieval castle.

Largesse - Money or gifts throw freely to the crowd.

Lateran Palace – The main papal residence in Rome.

League – A league is equivalent to approx. 3 miles in modern terms.

Leman – An illicit lover or mistress.

Manacles – One or two metal bands joined by a chain on wrists or ankles.

Maghreb - The North Africa Minor of the ancients, including Moorish Spain.

Mozarab – A name given to Christians living under Muslim rule that adopted the Arab language and culture but did not convert to Islam.

Pallet Bed/Palliasse – A bed made of straw or hay. Close to the ground, generally covered by a linen sheet and also known as a palliasse.

Pell – A stout wooden post for sword practice.

Pell Yard – A large yard in which warriors trained using a variety of weapons.

Pottage – A staple of the medieval diet, a thick soup made from boiling grains, vegetables, and meat or fish, if available.

Prie-dieu - A kneeling bench designed for use by a person at prayer.

Reconquista - a campaign in medieval Spain to take back territory from the Moors.

Refectory – A dining room in a monastery.

Saracen – Members of Arab tribes who professed the religion of Islam in the middle ages.

Sayyid – Arabic word for a lord or noble person.

Seneschal – A senior position or Principal Administrator of the royal household in France.

Sennight – The space of seven nights and days.

Simony – The practice of selling church roles or sacred things, considered an offence against Canon law by the Holy See of the Catholic Church.

Solar – The solar was a room in many medieval castles on a top story with windows to gain sunlight and warmth. They were usually the private quarters or chambers of the family. A room of comfort and status.

Stews – Low-grade houses of ill repute, often dangerous establishments.

Synod – A council in the catholic church usually convened to discuss church law or an issue, such as the call for a crusade.

Thuribles – A metal censor suspended on chains in which incense is burned.

Trencher - Slice of thick stale bread on which stew would be poured.

Tonsured – The shaving of some part of the head for religious purposes.

Vavasseur –Manservant, majordomo, a right hand man.

Vedette - An outrider or scout used by cavalry.

Vellum - Finest scraped and treated calfskin, used for writing messages.

Vielle - European bowed stringed instrument used in the medieval period, similar to a modern violin.

Vifgage – A living pledge to repay a debt in return for providing security on a loan in the form of land or buildings. (Duke Robert pledged Normandy)

34

Character list

Fictional characters are in *italics*, and real characters are in **bold.**

Chatillon Estate at Chatillon sous Bagneux

Piers De Chatillon.

Isabella De Embriaco – now his wife.

Gironde & Gabriel – their twin sons.

Annecy – their daughter.

Odo de Chatillon – Piers' uncle and Pope Urban.

Edvard of Silesia – Chatillon's Vavasseur and friend.

Finian Ui Neil – Irish lord & mercenary.

Dion - Finian's wife.

Ahmed – Physician, apothecary and expert poisoner.

Lazzo –Finian's captain.

Maria – his wife.

Cecily- a maidservant.

Madame Chambord – Housekeeper & cook.

Jean – The Steward.

Cormac & Fergus –their sons.

Padraig MacDomnall – Finian's long-lost cousin.
Pierre)
Rollo) – Padraig's men.
Jean)
Philippe)
Abdo – Apothecary in Paris.
Old Louis – the gatekeep.

Rouen
Robert Curthose, Duke of Normandy.
Stephen De Blois.
Duke Alan of Brittany.
Count Robert II of Flanders.
Odo, Bishop of Bayeaux, Earl of Kent, Robert's uncle.
Archbishop William Bonne-Ame.
Henry Beauclerc –youngest son of William the Conqueror.
Jacob the Jew & his wife, Miriam.

Le Puy
Bishop Adhemar – Papal Legate.
Sir Walter Tirel – English knight.
John Fitz-Gilbert – English knight.

London
King William Rufus.
Ranulf Flambard - King William's Chancellor.

Genoa
Marietta De Monsi – Chatillon's ward.
Signori Guglielmo Embriaco - Leader of the Genoa

Republic.

<u>Beaune</u>

Eudes - Duke of Burgundy.

<u>Huesca & Consuegra</u>

King Alphonse of Leon & Castile.

King Peter of Aragon.

Count Garcia Ordonez.

Rodrigo Diaz de Vivar - El Cid.

Diego Rodreguez - Only son of El Cid.

Emir Yusuf Ibn Tashfin - Leader of Moorish forces.

Conn Fitz Malvais - Son of Morvan De Malvais.

Georgio of Milan – Friend and warrior comrade of Conn.

<u>Zaragoza & Medina Mayurqa</u>

Yusuf Ibn Hud - Sheikh Ishmael, Saracen pirate.

Malik Ibn Hud - The murdered son of Sheikh Ishmael.

Abu Ibn J'far – Head of the Ibn Hud dynasty in Zaragoza.

<u>Morlaix</u>

Luc De Malvais – Breton lord & Horse Warrior.

Merewyn – his wife.

Lusian – his eldest son.

Chantelle – his daughter.

Garrett – his youngest son.

Morvan De Malvais – brother of Luc, father of Conn.

Ette De Malvais – his wife.

Gervais – his son.

Marie – his daughter.

35

Read More

The Papal Assassin's Wrath

It is 1098, and Piers De Chatillon, assassin, master swordsman, and powerful French Lord, has had his life and family destroyed by the Barbary pirate Sheikh Ismael. Seeking revenge in a blood feud for the death of his son, the Sheikh arranged an attack on Chatillon's chateau while Piers was away in Italy with the First Crusade.

On his return, Piers found that the Sheikh's men had kidnapped his twin sons for the slave markets, while his small daughter and granddaughter had been brutally murdered. His wife Isabella had also been taken and is now either dead or a prisoner of the Sheikh. Chatillon managed to rescue his boys, but he despairs at the loss of his beautiful wife, Isabella, spending a full year scouring the Mediterranean for her to no avail.

While Chatillon searches for Isabella, Duke Robert of Normandy has bravely led part of the first crusade to the Holy

Land to retake Jerusalem, leaving his country in the hands of his brother, King William Rufus. Meanwhile, their younger brother Henry Beauclerc believing that Robert will never survive the crusades, plots to kill William Rufus to seize all their lands. He believes that he has finally found the leverage to force Piers De Chatillon to undertake the killing of the King.

Unaware of this, Chatillon refuses to believe the reports that Isabella was burnt at the stake in Tunis, so he keeps searching for her but sinks further into despair when he cannot find her. When all appears lost, help appears in the shape of his friend and Horse Warrior, Morvan De Malvais, who arrives with his sons to help him and to persuade Piers to use his anger to take the war to the Sheikh.

They begin a campaign to burn the Sheikh's ships and bases across the Mediterranean. However, Chatillon fears that if Isabella is alive, then Ishmael may kill her in retaliation. In addition, if he rescues her and kills the Sheikh, how does he stop this blood feud from continuing with Ishmael's many sons?

You can read the first chapter of The Papal Assassin's Wrath on the next page...

The Papal Assassin's Wrath will be published in June 2023

36

The Papal Assassin's Wrath

Chapter One

March 1098 – Marseilles

Chatillon sat on his own at an isolated corner table, unusual in the crowded, bustling establishment, for this was one of the more notorious and dangerous inns on the dockside in Marseilles. The rooms were low, dark and smoke-filled, used by boat captains, their mates and crew alongside the gutter life of Marseilles. They seemed to rub along together, this mixed clientele, but every now and then, a knife would flash, and a victim would drop to the floor, either wounded or dead. The innkeeper's thugs quickly threw the injured man unceremoniously onto the cobbled quayside outside or into the dock to be taken out by the morning tide if he was dead.

No one came near Piers De Chatillon. His reputation was well known on the dockside of Marseilles, and the bodies of any who had tried to rob him numbered in double figures. The tale was still told to any newcomers in the inn of the four Sardinian pirates who, seeing his rich clothing, tried to take his purse in there one night. The first man lost the hand that was reaching for the Papal Envoy's belt, while the other three decided to rush and overpower him. All three lost their lives in the blink of an eye.

Chatillon was not a regular at the inn, but he came enough when travelling to meet his informers and garner information from the seafarers. He was generous with his silver, and although widely feared, he was respected and left alone.

He waved for more wine, although part of him knew he had already consumed enough. The innkeeper appeared with a jug of his best. He kept a small stock of this, for he knew that Chatillon and his guests would not touch the cheap donkey piss he served to his usual regulars.

'It is unusual to see you on your own, my Lord. Is Edvard not with you on this trip?' the man ventured but received only a malevolent stare in response. The innkeeper had a lived-in face that would frighten small children. Scarred, swollen, and weather-beaten from years at sea. However, Piers knew the man was a survivor; he had bought and turned this run-down hovel into a thriving business dealing stolen and smuggled goods in its dark back rooms. Therefore, Chatillon relented, sighed and shook his head at the man. The innkeeper left him to it, for he had heard the rumours that the ruthless Sheikh Ishmael had kidnapped Chatillon's young wife, they said. Perhaps that was why the Papal Envoy was so morose, as the innkeeper had not seen him like this before. Usually, he was alert and confident, eyes everywhere, constantly asking questions and gathering information. Instead, he seemed to be drowning his sorrows. The innkeeper shrugged, it was none of his business, and every man had the right to do that occasionally.

Piers sat cloaked in misery. He had met with an informer several hours before—a man he trusted, a merchant with ships travelling to all parts of the Mediterranean, a man whose information was always of good account and accurate. Piers could hardly bring himself to revisit what this man had told him. He did not want to believe what he had heard, for he still needed hope for himself and his twin sons. Isabella had been taken in December 1096, and for the last fifteen months, he and his men had scoured the ports of the Mediterranean and North Africa. They had searched every known base and port Sheikh Ishmael and his pirates used but to no avail. His enemy had been clever, for they had wasted time finding and rescuing other blonde captives planted by the Sheikh who turned out to be German or of Viking stock. His uncle, Pope Urban, had told him to desist and to accept that Isabella was dead, but Piers could not do that. He felt in his heart that Isabella was still alive and waiting in some dark hole for him to rescue her.

However, tonight that had changed. His Venetian merchant had told him that a tall blonde woman had been executed in public in the square in Tunis last month. The onlookers told his men she was beautiful with long, dark blonde hair. They said that she had fought like a wildcat all the way to the stake until it took five men to hold her.

This was different, for the Sheikh had been there with some of his wives and Captain Al Cazar. They had sat under an awning, in the shade, to watch as the woman was tied to the stake and burnt alive. She had shouted curses in French until she began to scream.

The merchant had apologised for being the bearer of such news, but he was convinced that it was true, as the word in the crowd was that she was the wife of an old enemy. The Sheikh had used her for a year but had grown tired of her. Chatillon had gone cold to the core as he had listened and felt numb with the horror of it. He had offered the merchant money, but the man had refused.

Now Piers sat there, filled with despair, repeatedly playing the scene in his mind as he realised that his uncle might be right and Isabella, his beautiful, intelligent wife, was gone. Piers dropped his head into his hands and, closing his eyes, fought against the emotions that threatened to overwhelm him. For the first time, he felt total and utter despair.

He had not parted on good terms with his uncle, Pope Urban. However, he had fulfilled his obligation to him and recently went to Rome to be by his side as his Papal Envoy during a difficult time. Still unable to contain his anger any longer, he confronted Urban about Cecily. She was the granddaughter he never knew he had—the granddaughter kept secret from him by his Uncle and who was murdered by one of Sheikh Ishmael's men. When challenged, his uncle had stalled at first until he finally admitted...

'I should have told you about your daughter Marie, Piers, but you were very young, and I thought it was for the best to pay them off.'

'A beautiful black-haired daughter that I never knew existed, that I never met before she died in childbirth at the tender age of seventeen, giving birth to a daughter. Then you, my housekeeper, Steward, and parish priest, all knew and worked to hide them from me. To make things worse, you allowed her daughter, my granddaughter Cecily to be employed as a servant in my house when she was fourteen. God's blood Uncle, what were you thinking? Cecily, my young granddaughter, a scullery maid for years.'

'I swear I did not know about that, Piers, and when I discovered it, I resolved to tell you who she was, but then the rallying call for crusaders at Clermont had far-reaching effects that I never envisaged. Tens of thousands of crusaders answered the call, and I became so embroiled in the planning that every thought of Cecily went out of my head.'

They had stood in silence and stared at each other, each wrapped in regret, and anger on Piers' part.

'You know what you have done, Uncle? You have given me another layer of guilt, another burden. It is my fault that I did not see what was afoot in my home—the betrayal. I should have killed Pierre when I first discovered that he had threatened my little Annecy, but I let him live for some reason I cannot explain. He then went on to kill my daughter and granddaughter before kidnapping my boys. I will blame myself for that until my dying breath.'

'I am sorry, Piers; you know you are more like a son to me, and I would never wish to hurt you. I may be the Pope, but I am not infallible, and I beg you to forgive me for my mistakes.'

Piers had turned away and, walking to the window, stared out over the Lateran Square towards the Basilica of St John.

'I am going home, Uncle. I need to be with my boys. Both have suffered greatly through this ordeal. I will take a ship to Marseilles tomorrow.' Without another word or mention of forgiveness, he'd left his uncle standing there, staring after him in dismay.

Now, after several jugs of wine, he knew he would forgive him, but he doubted if the pain of Cecily's brutal death would ever go.

He decided it was time to make for his bed, and he threw several coins on the table as he stood, looking forward to the walk to clear his head. He swung his heavy woollen cloak over his shoulders and fastened it. He realised he was unsteady on his feet, so he threw the right-hand folds back so that his sword was clearly visible to any guttersnipe who wanted to take a chance. He always stayed at an inn in the northern streets of the city, a far more respectable and salubrious establishment but quite a walk uphill from the docks.

As he emerged from the small battered door of the inn, he saw that a sea fret, typical for this time of year, had descended on the port, and now he was faced with a wet mist that seemed to envelop the streets.

He set off at a pace in the gloom. At first, it was a slight incline out of the lower port area, but he had to put out an occasional hand to steady himself on the walls. The ground underfoot, awash with the usual layers of stinking refuse, was also slippery in the wet mist and fine rain. He found he had to concentrate on keeping his footing, especially as the hill became steeper.

As usual, he glanced over his shoulder constantly, but the sea fret had reduced visibility, so buildings ahead seemed to loom out of the gloom at him. The fog also muffled all sounds; the streets of Marseilles were not quiet at night. Shouts, laughter, and people banging on doors could be heard, but it was as if a great distance away.

Chatillon, after so much wine, found it all disorientating. He knew he had not much further to go, as his inn was near the top of the hill that towered over the town. There was an old fort on its summit, originally Roman. It had been added to and fortified because of the pirates and was now manned as a lookout. Eerily, as the mist was heavier near the ground, he could see the torch or brazier of the sentries above, although it seemed to be floating disembodied in the sky. He walked further up a steeper slope and then stopped for a second, leaning on the wall to get his breath, and that was when he heard them.

'I tell you that was him coming out of the inn, and he was the right height and shape. He must be just ahead of us.'

A younger voice answered. 'I don't know how you could possibly be right, for we can see nothing in this mist.'

Chatillon moved quickly and increased his pace. A dog suddenly appeared and nearly tripped him. He swore as he realised how stupid he had been to get this drunk alone in Marseilles. A large lime-washed wooden merchant's house suddenly loomed on his left, and he knew he was in the wealthier area just before the Eagle Inn. Higher up, the mist was clearing and flattening himself against the wall, he could see three shapes emerging below him. Outnumbered, he drew his sword with an unmistakable rasping sound as it came from its scabbard.

They heard the noise, and one shouted, 'That is him ahead, the dark shape on the left.'

Chatillon ducked into a dark alley with a narrow set of steps down the hill's western side that only one man could come down at a time. It would have worked perfectly if he had not lost his footing on the wet steps and clattered down the steep second half, dropping his sword in the process and hurting his ankle. He retrieved his sword and propped himself against the wall at the entrance as they came after him.

He suddenly found that he did not want to die here in the backstreets of Marseilles. His twin boys needed him, and they could not lose both parents. He cursed himself for being a reckless idiot and, pushing himself away from the wall, drew his dagger in his left hand and positioned himself to attack the man he could hear running down the steps.

He heard a shout. 'Be careful. He will be armed and ready!'

To his surprise, the first man laughed as he jumped out but dropped straight into a crouch, avoiding the swung blade that would have removed his head. It was as if he knew exactly the move the Papal Envoy would make. He leapt up and grabbed Chatillon's left wrist with his right hand to immobilise the dagger he knew would be there while he brought the hilt of his sword down hard on the Papal Envoy's right shoulder to numb the arm. In seconds, the man's dagger was held hard against his throat, and Piers, dropping the sword from his numb fingers, knew with certainty that he would die as the two other men, swords drawn, appeared beside his attacker.

37

Author note

The end of the eleventh century was an interesting but disturbing period as the religious fervour for a crusade to free Jerusalem spread across Europe, promulgated by Pope Urban II and his bishops. There was no doubt that it was madness to recruit, attract and then try to manage and manoeuvre such numbers across Europe and the stark environment of the Middle East. If you combine all the strands from the different regions heading for Constantinople, conservative estimates put the figures close to eighty thousand people. These came from all walks of life, from poor pilgrims to rich lords and merchants who left their homes and livelihoods to participate in the first crusade of 1096. Only a fraction of these ever reached the Holy Land or Jerusalem.

Critics describe the first crusade and the events leading up to its departure as no more than 'sanctioned violence' by the Pope and the Church. This violence was seen especially to fall on the innocent and hapless large Jewish communities in Rouen and Germany. Thousands of men, women and children were slaughtered, the attackers encouraged by some bishops and local lords.

To finance the crusade, Duke Robert indeed signed away his country to his brother, William Rufus, who did personally bring sixty-seven barrels of gold across the English Channel to pay him. Bishop Odo, always at Robert's side after his failed invasion of England, decided to leave the crusade and visit a friend in Sicily, where he died suddenly with no prior signs of ill health. He is buried in the cathedral in Palermo. When the crusade reached the southeast coast of Italy, Hugh the Great, of France did indeed lose his whole fleet when trying to cross in the winter. To make things worse, he was rescued from drowning, but that boat also sank. Fortunately, he was washed up on the shore with some of his men and taken to Durazzo on the Albanian coast, but he had lost everything. Duke Robert was sensible and waited for spring, but no sooner had his first ship left the shore in March 1097 than, for some reason, it began to break up and sink. Robert and his lords watched helplessly as almost a hundred men drowned with their horses and weapons.

Young Diego Rodriguez was betrayed by Count Garcia Ordonez and was slaughtered with all of his father's men at the battle of Consuegra. They say that his father, El Cid, never recovered from his son's death, and he died two years later. El Cid's wife, Jimena, tried to hold the city of Valencia, but in 1102 it was taken by the forces of the Emir. El Cid and his wife had managed to hold it for eight years under constant attacks even though it was completely surrounded by Berber territory. King Alphonse spent the rest of his reign fighting the Almoravid invasion, holding them at bay and protecting Toledo, which never fell to the Emir.

Muslim raiders conquered Mallorca in the early tenth century and controlled it for hundreds of years. The island became part of the Emirate of Cordoba. They expanded the large port town of Palma and renamed it Medina Mayurqa. The island was to remain in Moorish hands until the thirteenth century. It was always a regular base for the pirates from the Barbary Coast as it was ideal for attacking the shipping and trading vessels on the Mediterranean.

If you are in Mallorca, an excursion to Castell Alaro, where Isabella was held, is worth it for its spectacular views. It was originally an early Moorish fortress, and it was so impregnable that one Moorish commander managed to hold out for two years after the Christian re-conquest of the island. Unfortunately, Isabella will be there for some time; she may even die there, but that will be resolved in Book 4 of the Papal Assassin series, 'The Papal Assassin's Wrath', to be published in the early summer of 2023.

S. J. Martin
February 2023

About the Author

I have had an abiding love of history from an early age. This interest not only influenced my academic choices at university but also my life choices and careers. I spent several years with my trowel in the world of archaeology before finding my forte as a storyteller in the guise of a history teacher. I wanted to encourage young people to find that same interest in history that had enlivened my life.

I always wanted to write historical fiction. The opportunity came when I left education; I then gleefully re-entered the world of engaging with the fascinating historical research into the background of some of my favourite historical periods. There are so many stories still waiting to be told, and my first series of books on 'The Breton Horse Warriors' proved to be one of them. The Breton lords, such as my fictional Luc De Malvais, played a significant role in the Battle of Hastings and helped to give William the Conqueror a decisive win. They were one of the most exciting troops of cavalry and swordmasters in Western Europe.

I hope you enjoy reading my books as much as I have enjoyed writing them.

You can connect with me on:

https://moonstormbooks.com/sjmartin

https://twitter.com/SJMarti40719548

https://www.facebook.com/people/SJ-Martin-Author/100064591194374

Subscribe to my newsletter:

https://moonstormbooks.com/sjmartin

Also by S.J. Martin

The Breton Horse Warriors

The Breton Horse Warriors series follows the adventures of our hero Luc De Malvais and his brother Morvan. It begins in Saxon England, during the Norman Conquest and travels to war-torn Brittany and then Normandy. Luc De Malvais is a Breton lord, a master swordsman and leader of the famous horse warriors. He faces threatening rebellion, revenge and warfare as he fights to defeat the enemies of King William. However, his duty and loyalty to his king come at a price, as his marriage and family are torn apart. He now has to do everything he can to save his family name, the love of his life and his banished brother...but at what price?

Ravensworth - Rebellion. Revenge. Romance.
Rebellion - Deceit. Desire. Defeat.
Betrayal - Beguiled. Betrayed. Banished.
Banished - Subterfuge. Seduction. Sacrifice.
Vengeance - Passion. Perfidy. Pursuit

Printed in Great Britain
by Amazon

62090919R00211